D0860597

and the
shadows
took him

Also by Daniel Chacón

Chicano Chicanery: Short Stories

and the shadows took him

A NOVEL

Daniel Chacón

ATRIA BOOKS

New York   London   Toronto   Sydney

ATRIA BOOKS
1230 Avenue of the Americas
New York, NY 10020

Copyright © 2004 by Daniel Chacón

ISBN: 0-7434-6638-1

First Atria Books hardcover edition April 2004

10 9 8 7 6 5 4 3 2 1

ATRIA BOOKS is a trademark of Simon & Schuster, Inc.

Manufactured in the United States of America

For information regarding special discounts for bulk purchases, please contact Simon & Schuster Special Sales at 1-800-456-6798 or business@simonandschuster.com.

for my father, Richard Chacón,
for your guidance, wisdom, and love

acknowledgments

I would like to thank those who read prior versions of this novel, especially the four hundred–plus page draft, when it was called *What Manner of Love Is This?* The novel didn't know where it was going and had changed titles three times (*Joey Molina!* and *Father of a Thousand Heads* were the other two). Joey was all over the place, like a cow newly freed. How my friends got through these long early drafts, I don't know, but I figure it must have been love for me or for literature or both. I thank Rich Yañez, Francis Cruz, Carolina Villarroel, Ted O'Connell, Thea Kuticka, Lex Williford, and Veronica "la comandante" Guajardo. Thanks to Lucy Fischer West for not only reading the first draft, but for doing it in *one* day and returning it to me with a smile, and pen marks and gentle questions all over the pages. Thank you Malaika Adero and Victoria Sanders, *shadow*'s editor and agent, respectively, for believing in the novel before it was finished. I'd also like to thank my students in the graduate fiction writing classes at University of Texas, El Paso. I was writing this book and running the workshop at the same time and found little means of separating the experiences.

Also, thanks to Dennis Breen and Michelle Otero.

¡Y gracias a Jamón, Pancho y todos los Rudos de Motown, Califaztlán!

part one

Their father never took them to restaurants, because he thought it a waste of money when they could open up a can of beans, sprinkle on Tabasco sauce, stuff their bellies, and it would all shit out the same way anyway. When the kids cried and whined to go to McDonald's for cheeseburgers, he stood over them and growled like a bear that they only wanted to go there because it was so expensive. They wanted life to be like *The Brady Bunch,* but they were poor Mexicans, not rich movie stars, and they better eat whatever the hell he put on the table, whatever it was, even if it was food they hated.

Like steak.

For them, steak was a cheap strip of meat that their mom fried in lard until it was hard and charred and tasted like burnt wood.

And if the kids didn't want to eat the meat—if they pushed it around their plate with a rolled-up tortilla, as if that strip of steak were the very thing in life that they found distasteful—they saw the shadow of their father's hand rise up the white wall of the kitchen. "Don't make me do it," he'd say. On his fist's fingers, his hitting fist, were tattooed letters that spelled "L.O.V.E."

The kids didn't know that a steak could be thick and juicy and explode with flavor, because they had never been to a steak house. On the rare occasions that they went to the drive-in movies, the father pulled the car into a grocery store parking lot, and while they waited in the hot backseat, he went inside for a big bag of salted pigskins and two six-packs of warm generic sodas. Then he drove across town by the factories and the stinky lumberyards and bought them a bag of burgers at Munchies. The burgers were ten cents. They held the warm bags on their laps until they got back across town to the drive-in movies and ate in the car during the first feature. Munchies burgers tasted like liver meat, so they balanced burgers on their knees and smothered them in ketchup and mustard. Billy, the older son, said he had heard that they were so cheap because they used old horsemeat instead of beef, but Joey, the youngest, liked them anyway.

Joey liked food.

On days that the mother went for groceries, he was so distracted while she was gone, imagining the good things she would bring home, that he couldn't concentrate on playing with his best friend Ricky Jones or doing his homework or whatever. Once while his mother was gone buying groceries, he was supposed to be helping his father fix the Ford. The father lay on his back, under the car, his torso and legs visible, with the smell of grease rising from the heat of the asphalt. He cursed the car.

"Give me a three-quarter wrench," the father yelled to Joey, who watched for his mom's car to turn the corner and handed him a crescent wrench instead.

"You worthless piece of shit, go get your brother!"

While the father, William Molina, and his older son, Billy, fixed the car, Joey sat on the curb in front of the house and waited for her

'63 Chevrolet to turn the corner, slow and heavy, the music beating from down the block, Rachel's head bopping up and down, black sunglasses and strawberry-blond hair. He reverently stood up before she pulled in the driveway, as if greeting an important relative he was in awe of but had never seen.

It was the boys' job to unload the bags. Billy carried two or three bags at a time, grasping them in his muscular arms like a dockworker, but Joey only carried one, hugging it to his chest, the itchy brown paper against his forearms. He placed the bag on the counter or the table, but before going back to get another one, he looked inside the bag for something good, a bag of chips, cheesy crackers, or a box of sugary cereal.

After the mom and Vero, the oldest child and only daughter, put the groceries away, he took out bologna and American cheese and tortillas and mustard and made himself a couple of burritos—he used three slices of bologna per tortilla—and tore open a bag of corn chips. Afterward, even though his stomach felt bloated, he opened the refrigerator door and looked at all the food and tried to decide what he would have for breakfast the next morning. He liked fried eggs and wieners, which he cut in half. He liked fried bologna, which puffed up in the sizzling lard like a Chinese hat and filled the kitchen with that wonderful fried, salty smell. He'd warm up three fat flour tortillas.

One evening William Molina came home, stood above Joey, and told him to get his ass off the couch and turn off the TV. Joey, who was enjoying a rerun sitcom about a 1960s middle-class family, asked, "Why?" The father said that he was taking them all out to dinner, and he wanted Joey to tell everyone to get ready.

"No way!" Joey said.

* * *

Billy was lifting weights when Joey ran into their bedroom with the news. He was doing curls with barbells and wearing no shirt—his fourteen-year-old muscles glistening with sweat. "You mean, like at a restaurant?" His long black hair was in a ponytail, and every time he lifted the barbells toward his chest, the ponytail seemed to want to crawl up his back.

"Yeah, a restaurant," Joey said. "So hurry. Get ready."

Joey pulled off his shoe while still standing, hopping and losing balance, exaggerating the comic movements a bit, and after he got one off, he did the other. "Hurry, before Dad changes his mind!"

"You're a liar. Dad ain't taking us to no restaurant."

Vero, the oldest at fifteen, sometimes let her boyfriend, Paul, a Chicano in a low rider, come by the house when the parents weren't home. They would stand at the curb outside and listen to music under the shade of the fruitless mulberry tree that covered the yard. If Joey came anywhere near them, Vero told him to go away, although he didn't know why she didn't want him there. She and Paul never hugged or kissed in front of the house; they leaned against the car as if it were the coolest thing in the world that teenagers could do. She was an urban Chicana, dressing in baggy pants and oversized T-shirts with *raza* images like the mustached Lowrider man or a brown fist proclaiming "Chicano Power." She would listen to acid rock or oldies in her bedroom with the door locked. She never let Joey see inside her room, as if she didn't want him to look too closely at her. For Joey, her room was a place of mystery and imagination. Whenever he was near her door, he would imagine noises, mysterious sounds—a lion's roar? A shovel scraping on cement? Noises that he didn't know he was imagining. When she came out or went into the room, he would peek in, but she'd push him away and slam the door. Glimpses inside were all he ever got, a poster of Jimi Hendrix, a candle, a turntable with a record spinning.

When he knocked on her door and told her in a singsong voice to get ready because Dad was taking them to dinner at a restaurant, she didn't respond, just turned up the music.

Oh oh no no
don't want you to go

He knocked louder and said, "Vero, guess what?"
"Get out of here," she said.

Please, please.

"Dad's taking us out to eat," he yelled, and then he put his ear against the door. "To a restaurant. Get ready." She turned the music down.
"Really?" she said.
"Yeah, really!" Joey said.
The door opened, revealing her round, dark face. *"Our* dad?"

Rachel sat in a chair before her beauty, leaning into a makeup mirror with lights all around the frame, painting on purple eye shadow. "I guess you know," he said.
"I know," she said.
"I wonder where he'll take us," he said.
"Someplace nice, let's hope," she said.
"I'm kind of scared," he said.
"Why?"

"What if I don't like what I order?"

She looked in the mirror at him and sighed and slowly shook her head. "Oh, Joey," she said. He thought that she was sighing about him, at what he had said, and he felt guilty, but then she said, "I don't know what to do with your father." Her Mexican accent came out strong. She was the only one in the family with an accent, the only one who had been to Mexico, except for when Vero went to Tijuana with her cousin Norma and some friends. Rachel was also the only one in the family with blond hair and blue eyes. Everyone else had dark skin, Vero, Billy, Joey. William looked like the son of an Aztec, black hair slicked back, tattoos up and down his arms, one on his chest of a spider, the legs of which reached out from his tank top undershirt, and tattoos on the knuckles of both hands, LOVE on one hand, HATE on the other, a tattoo that had been popular among Chicano boys when he was a teenager. Rachel was a white Mexican from Jalisco, the seventh daughter in a family of blue-eyed *hueros.* Joey was embarrassed when neighborhood kids watched her walk across the lawn or step out of her car in a skirt. Every time she came out in the front yard in shorts and bent over to move the sprinkler, someone was watching. Her shape was what men and boys liked, buxom, wide hips, long legs. One time, a kid at school who watched her drive up to the curb and drop Joey off said, "Wow, your mom looks like Marilyn Monroe."

Now she looked in the vanity mirror and pouted her lips as she put on lipstick. This time she said it in Spanish. *"Ay, Joey, ¿Qué voy hacer con tu papá?"*

"What's the matter?" he asked.

She turned around. "I don't know if I should kiss him, or kick him really good in the *cojones.*"

* * *

William was having second thoughts. Rachel was ready to go, wearing red and black. Joey was standing by the front door, but William was still in his tank top undershirt, sitting on the couch and looking suspiciously out the window as if the world outside were waiting to push him to the ground and beat him. The principle of eating out, the entire concept of paying extra for someone to serve you food, always bothered him. He used to say that when he was a boy he had to share an apple with three brothers, how his mom cut it into slices as they eagerly awaited, their hands cupped for the offering. Since he was the youngest, he got the smallest slice, with seeds and stem, tastes so bitter he had to spit them out.

Now Rachel buys fruit and they don't eat it before it goes bad and she has to throw it out. What kind of lesson would he be teaching them by taking them to a sit-down dinner? Even as they gathered, Billy sitting on the edge of the couch, Vero standing in the doorframe of the hallway as if life were just a fact, the father seemed like he hadn't fully resolved that he would follow through. He stood up and said, "Maybe we should go get some Chinese take-out, and we could eat at home."

"No way, Dad," Joey said. "That's not fair."

"I knew it wasn't true," said Billy.

Even Vero was disappointed. "Figures," she mumbled, and headed back to her room, until Rachel told her to wait.

"William, don't do this to us."

"Do what? I'm not depriving you of anything. You never had it, how could you be deprived of it? Huh, *vieja*, think about it."

"Don't try to reason your way out of this."

"You said," Joey whined. "You're depriving us of our desire to go, the desire you created for us."

"Good point, Joey," said his mom.

William sat on his love seat and put his head in his hands. Everyone watched him, the thinker thinking. He rubbed his chin. "All right," he said. "Let's go eat."

"All right!" Joey said.

"Let's go!" Billy said.

"And no Munchies," Joey said.

"No Munchies," Rachel agreed. "A real restaurant."

As they sat in the car, the motor running, Joey looked at the house. It was one of those rare times when it was empty, when the entire family would be gone at the same time, and there was something sad about it. The father looked at the house too, and he commented about how drab the brown paint looked. He wondered aloud, If he were to paint the house some bright color, would it have a subtle psychological effect on them and make them happier? Vero said that was ridiculous, and William said that there were psychological effects on them that they weren't even aware of, and color was one of them. "Why do you think actors wait in the green room before going onstage? Because green is a calming color. It's called the subconscious, and it's something we don't even know it's there, but it's always with us."

"You mean like an angel?" asked Joey.

"No, stupid, not like an angel—not anything like an angel. I'm talking scientific stuff that's been proved."

"No kidding, Dad," Vero said, "I know what the subconscious is, but I'm just saying. A different color won't make us any happier."

"I want a happy color for the house," he said. "It could make a difference."

"You'd have to change more than the color," she said.

William looked at her in the rearview mirror. Then he studied the face of Joey and then Billy. He looked at his wife, and she smiled at him. He winked at her. "How about yellow. Who wants to live in a yellow house?"

He parked the Maverick in front of the windows of the Thrifty Café, located between a pool hall and a vacuum-parts store in a strip mall. In the windows handwritten signs announced "Chicken Fried Steak and Eggs," "Discount Turkey Dinner," "Early Bird Special." After he stopped the engine, no one said anything or got out of the car. He raised his butt from the car seat and reached for his wallet. He counted the bills to himself, then looked up at the ceiling and closed his eyes as he calculated the numbers. He sighed loudly and put the wallet back in his pocket while Rachel watched.

Billy had his head sticking out the back window. "I never heard of this place," he said. "Why are we going here?"

"Where the hell do you want to go?" William said, "the Four Seasons?"

"What's that?"

"You want the most expensive restaurant? Would that make you happy, Prince William?"

"I'm just asking."

"Let's go to Happy Steak," said Rachel.

"No way," Joey said. "I don't want no yucky steak."

"It's good, Joey. Come on, William."

"Oh, sure, and after Happy Steak, why don't we go buy a luxury car? Anything else, Princess?"

"I'm sure it's better than . . ."—she looked sadly at the restaurant—". . . than the Thrifty Café."

"Are we going to sit in the car forever?" said Vero.

"What wrong with sitting in the car together?" Joey said, scrunched in the middle between his brother and sister. "This is neat." He rested his head on Vero's shoulder, but she jerked it off.

"It's hot in here," said Billy.

Joey felt the urge to hug Vero.

But he knew she'd slap him.

"How come we don't hug in this family?" he asked, putting his hand on her shoulder. She flicked it off with her finger.

"Why do you want to hug?" asked Billy.

"To show our love for each other," he said.

"Little shit, you think spending my money on feeding and clothing you ain't enough love?"

"No, I'm just saying. Some families hug."

"You mean *The Brady Bunch?*" said William.

"You better not try to hug me," said Vero.

"Me neither," said Billy.

"I'm just saying."

"I'll hug you, Joey," Rachel said, but she didn't. "Come on, William, what are we going to do?"

"I'm thinking."

"The kids are hungry."

"I'm not a kid," said Vero.

"Then don't act like one," she said.

"The kids ain't going to starve," William said.

"The kids *are not* going to starve," Joey corrected, and his dad turned around, raised his fist, and clenched his teeth. "Boy, you better shut the hell up."

"Sorry."

"What's your reason for choosing this restaurant, William? Why here?"

"I heard things about it. Good things."

"From whom?"

"Someone at work."

"What did they say, that it was cheap?"

"Mom, open the door," said Vero, as if it were an emergency.

"What's wrong?"

"Just open it, please."

"All right." She opened it, and Vero slipped between the seats and stepped outside and stood in the parking lot. She put her hands in her baggy pants pockets.

"What are you doing?" Rachel asked.

"Getting some air," she said.

"Little brat," the father said. "You too good to sit in the car like the rest of us? I should leave you here."

"Please do," she said, not loud enough for him to hear, but Joey heard because he had his head out the window, hoping for a breeze.

"How about a good-bye kiss?" he said to his sister, puckering his lips.

She looked at him, a short cold stare, and then she looked away. "When you guys decide, let me know." She walked to the storefront windows and looked into the pool hall, which was empty except for two guys drinking beer, and they both looked at her. Between them, the reflection of her face appeared like a ghost in the glass, round cheeks, sad eyes. She wrapped her arms around herself and walked past the vacuum repair shop, her vague reflection sliding across the storefront window, where old vacuums shone like torture instruments. She looked away and walked to the next door, a Laundromat, looked inside, sighed, shook her head as if she had decided something important, and walked to the next door, a liquor store. She read the newspaper through the glass case.

"Can I get out too?" Joey asked.

"You sit the hell down," William said.

13

"William, let's decide, please. I'm getting hungry and hot."

"Okay, we'll eat here," he said, and Rachel said, *"Ay, dios,"* and moved to get out, but William stayed seated.

"What is it now, William?"

"I was thinking . . ."

"What were you thinking, William?"

"Maybe Sambos," he said. "Maybe we should try Sambos."

"Yeah, Sambos!" Joey yelled. "I want to go to Sambos!"

Rachel smiled at her man.

"We want Sambos!" yelled Billy.

They often looked longingly at the sign aglow at night, a cartoon of a ferocious Bengali tiger, SAMBOS, and inside the restaurant was lit up like a stage, walled by picture windows, people sitting at the timeless booths, drinking sudsy sodas from sparkling fountain glasses.

"Sambos!" Joey yelled.

"That would be nice, *viejo,"* said Rachel.

"They got good deals there," he said to himself.

"Let's go," said Billy.

"All right," he said. "The boys want Sambos: Sambos it is!"

He started the car, but Rachel said, "Don't forget your daughter."

He rolled down the window and said, "Hey, girl. Want a ride?"

"Don't take rides from strangers," Billy yelled.

"I'm not strange," the father teased.

She rolled her eyes.

"We're going to Sambos," Billy yelled.

She looked at her feet as if sending a message for them to start walking. Then she wrapped her arms around herself and slowly walked back to the car. Three *cholas* came out of the liquor store, hard-core barrio girls wearing dark eye makeup and baggy pants, and they stopped walking and stared at Vero. They looked liked they wanted to beat her up.

"Let's go," William said, honking the horn at Vero.

"Don't, Dad," Joey said.

When Vero reached the door, Rachel opened it and stepped out of the car.

She was dressed in a snug red blouse and black polyester pants, black cat-eye sunglasses, and her blond hair was up in a bouffant. She looked like an incognito movie star. The *cholas,* pointing at her, started laughing, and even though Joey didn't know why they laughed, he didn't like it.

"Let's go, Dad," Joey said.

"We're going, you little shit," William said. "Have some patience."

Inside was narrow like a river, and there was only one occupied booth in the back, a bald man and a teenage girl. She had a gift in front of her, a box wrapped in silver paper and a bright red bow, which she looked at as if afraid to see what it might contain. The waitress, who walked across the shiny floors with a handful of menus, wore a light blue waitress's dress with a white apron, her hair in a bun like a TV mother from the past. Her name tag read ALICE.

"Good evening, folks. Can I start you off with something to drink?"

The boys yelled for Cokes.

"How much are they?" William asked.

The waitress sighed. "Fifty cents," she said.

"All right," he said, but after she left the table, he shook his head in disbelief. "You guys better suck slow on those things. You're only getting one."

On the menu Joey found the hamburger section.

"This is why I hate restaurants," William said as he read, shaking his head. Then he looked at the boys. "Don't go ordering something just because it's the most expensive thing on the menu."

"William, let them enjoy themselves," Rachel said.

"I just don't want them to think they're the royal family."

Vero slammed down her menu.

"What's wrong with you?" he asked.

"I don't want nothing if that's how you're going to be," she said.

"Good," he said. "Save me some money."

She stood up, put on her dark *chola* sunglasses, and held out her hands. "Can I have the keys? I'll wait in the car."

"Sit down, Veronica," Rachel said. "You can order whatever you want."

"Are you paying for it?"

"If I have to, yes," she said.

"Horseshit."

"Can I have a cheeseburger and fries?" Billy said.

"Me too," Joey said.

William looked up cheeseburger and fries on the menu and said, "Why do you want cheese? You could have brought some from the house."

"William."

"All right. Have what you want. We're here to have fun, right? To celebrate. " He looked up at Vero. "Sit down. Order whatever you want."

Joey put down the slick menu and was so excited that he rubbed his hands together and licked his lips. He looked around the place, at the lights, the curves of the booths, a round clock over the metal counter, beyond which the cook in a tall white hat stood over a sizzling grill. Vero reluctantly sat back down, but she left on her sunglasses and frowned until Rachel whispered to her and she took them off.

The waitress came back with old-fashioned soda fountain glasses, and she placed the sparkling drinks in front of them. I could stay here forever, Joey thought.

Alice flipped open her order book and said to Joey, "What'll it be, sweetheart?"

That thrill that came right before you do something brave or crazy like jumping into a cold canal or going to talk with Sherry Garcia came over him like strong wind, but when he tried to speak, no words came out, and the thrill disintegrated into doubt. Was he ordering the right thing? It was a decision he'd have to live with. The waitress held her pen point to the pad, but he was thinking that maybe he should try something other than a cheeseburger, because he might never come back to a restaurant, ever again. He read descriptions that seemed so good: "A generous stack of ham smothered in two kinds of cheese and stacked with strips of crispy hickory bacon." Or "Prime Rib Sandwich: A fat slab of roasted prime rib of beef." And he hoped it wasn't just the language that made them sound good and that the words actually meant what they evoked.

"Well?" Alice said.

"I'm not ready yet," he said.

"Let's start with you, then," she said to Vero.

"Me either," she said.

Alice flipped closed the order book. "I'll give you more time."

Joey, happy for more time, sucked cold cola through a straw.

"I can't decide either," said his mom. "I really can't decide. What are you thinking?" she asked Vero.

"I was thinking of the club sandwich," she said.

She leaned over Vero's menu, touching her shoulder with a hand, and said, "Where is it?" Vero pointed to the club.

"Oh, that does sound good. What about you, *viejo?*"

"I don't know. I can't find the *chile verde con arroz y tortillas.*"

Vero laughed.

William, surprised and pleased that she laughed, continued. *"Ni el menudo ni pozole."*

"This ain't no Mexican restaurant," said Billy.

"It ain't?" he said, feigning surprise. "I thought this was Sambós."

"It's Sambos," Billy said.

"You guys of course know that *ain't* does not exist as a word," Joey said.

"Oh, shut up," said Vero.

"I want a cheeseburger," said Billy.

"Maybe I'll have," said Rachel, looking intently at the menu, "the chef's salad. Or maybe the soup and sandwich."

Alice came to the table with her pad already flipped open. "Okay, folks. What'll it be?"

Vero put down her menu and said, as if she were speaking at a formal occasion, "I'll have the club sandwich, please."

Then the waitress looked at Rachel, who said, "Oh my!" hand over her mouth as if she were making the most important decision of her life. "I guess I'll have"—and she closed her eyes— "would you recommend the fish and chips?"

"It's great," Alice said like she didn't really care.

"All right, I'll take that. But instead of the fries, can I have mashed potatoes?"

"Sure, sweetie, whatever you want." She wrote it in her pad.

"Then it wouldn't be fish and chips, *mensa,*" the dad said. "It'd be fish and mush." He laughed and looked at Vero to see if she was laughing, but she wasn't, so he frowned and read the menu.

"What about you kids?" asked Alice.

"I want a cheeseburger and fries!" Billy said.

"How do you want it cooked?" Alice asked.

"Huh? What do you mean?" Billy asked.

Rachel answered for him. "Well done."

Then she looked at Joey, but he was thinking that maybe he should try something different and new because where he was now he would be forever, he would never forget this day, he would live it over and over again.

"Can you ask me last?" he asked

"What do you want?" she asked William.

"Let me have the Salisbury steak with mashed potatoes."

"Soup or salad?"

"Uh, I don't know. Does it cost more?"

Alice rolled her eyes when she said, "It's included with all the dinners."

"I want the soup!" said Billy.

"Not the burgers, just the dinners," said Alice.

Billy deflated. "Oh."

"This *is* dinner," he whispered to Joey.

"What kind of soup is it?" asked William.

Alice lowered her pad as if it were too heavy to hold, and her shoulders slumped. "Vegetable beef or cream of broccoli."

"Try the vegetable beef, *viejo,*" Rachel said. "You'll like that."

"All right," he said. And then, as if making a proclamation: "The vegetable beef."

"You got it." She wrote it down. "Well, sugar," she said to Joey. "You're the last one." She pressed her red ballpoint pen to her pad.

He felt everyone's eyes on him and that thrill like wind, like going over a small hill in a fast car, his stomach falling, and he blurted out, *"Primeribsandwich."*

"Good choice," said Alice.

"What?" the dad said, opening up the menu. "What the hell?"

"I want to try something new."

"That's two dollars more than a hamburger," he said.

"William!"

"You better eat every bit of it," he said.

"How do you want your prime rib cooked?" Alice asked, and he looked at his mom because he didn't understand the question.

"Well done," she said.

The family kept looking at Joey after the waitress left. "You're stupid," Billy said.

"No, he's not. It's good to try new things," Rachel said.

"I think it's pretty cool of you," Vero said.

"I already know what a cheeseburger tastes like," he said.

"You don't even know what prime rib is," Billy said.

Which was true, but he pictured TV ribs like Fred gets on the credits of *The Flintstones,* a slab of meat so big that his car tips over when the carhop sets it on the tray. With his hands clasped on the table, he waited.

"Well," William said. He looked at Rachel, who with a gleam in her eye looked around at the kids, and when she looked back at William, she nodded. He cleared his throat. "Go ahead," he said to her. "You tell them."

"Kids, do you know why your father's taking us out to dinner?"

All night, on nights when he didn't work with his clay, William Molina sat at the kitchen table drawing plans on how to be more efficient on the assembly line at work, a company that made vending machines. Sometimes the managers used his ideas, and every Christmas he got a bigger bonus than any of the other laborers. He knew they paid him less than he was worth, a worker's pay, so he started applying for other jobs that paid more and had a better chance of advancement—and he made sure his bosses found out about it. One day as he was pounding a hammer on metal, the managers approached him and brought him into the glass-cased office that looked out on the assembly line. They shook his hand and told him to sit down. He still had his hammer, which, after he sat, he set on his lap. It was round on both sides, dark metal, and along the wooden handle it had his name written in felt pen, with an exclamation point at the end, MOLINA!

Some of his black and Chicano friends working on the assembly line looked in at him sitting in the office talking to the top three bosses. They felt sorry for him, because they thought he was in trouble. But the bosses offered him something cold to drink and William wasn't sure if they meant like a beer or a cocktail, so to be safe, he said he'd take a Shirley Temple.

"How about a Coke?" said a boss, and William said a cola would be fine. As a rule, he didn't want to use the word *Coke* to indicate anything other than that particular product, because he didn't want to be a sheep like all the other sheep.

The main boss himself, who wore black-framed glasses and had his hands clasped as if in prayer, went to the half-sized refrigerator to get the can, Pepsi, telling William that they were very pleased with his ideas and how efficiently he had done his work over the years. He admitted that William had come up with so many labor-saving ideas that they wondered if his talent wasn't being wasted on the assembly line.

They offered him a new job, dispatcher, a managerial position, on a new pay scale. He would be a great role model, they said, for the other workers, especially the Spanish speakers. "You *do* speak Spanish?" one boss asked.

"*Simón qué* yes!" William said.

They told him how they wanted to be able to promote more deserving individuals like him, and as he listened, he tried to act causal, as if it were something he had expected. He crossed one leg over the other, forgetting the hammer, which began to slip, heavy-head first, between his legs. Quickly, he clasped his thighs together so the hammer wouldn't fall, and he lifted it and held it in one hand while the other held the cold can of cola. Then he thought he probably looked silly holding a hammer, as if he were about to fix something, so he set it on his lap again.

They said that he would be the first Hispanic manager in the company, ever, a fact he certainly couldn't find insignificant. And then they told him how much he would be making. The hammer fell between his thighs and thumped the floor.

Before he left the office, a photographer from the company newsletter came in and took a picture of all of them standing together, arms around each other, all of them with big smiles, William in the middle, as if he were one of the boys. That picture would be framed by his wife and hung on the wall.

The bosses in the photo were all pale men in shirtsleeves and ties, and William was as dark as wet tree bark. He wore a blue work shirt with his name stitched on it, the sleeves rolled up, showing the bottom half of a tattoo witch diving into flames.

A hammer lay at his feet.

William walked back out on the assembly line, and the blacks and Chicanos surrounded him to ask what was going on.

"Why did they take your picture?" one guy asked.

"Did they catch you stealing?" another asked.

Now William sat back in the Sambos booth like a man with power, and Rachel looked at him and smiled. "Your father has gotten a raise. A good raise. A significant raise. We'll be over the median income for Fresno."

"What does median mean?" Billy asked.

"It means we'll make more money than half the families in Fresno," Joey said. "It means that we're no longer poor Mexicans."

"Wow," said Billy. "Can I get a new bike?"

"What we need is furniture," said Rachel. "That old ratty stuff is embarrassing."

"Hey, let's not count the eggs before they fall from the chicken's ass," William said.

"We can at least order dessert, right?" Joey said. "I want an ice cream soda."

"We're still poor," he said. "This don't start for another month. So don't start acting like you're all big shots."

"No one's going to be like that," said Vero. "It's not like you're going to share the money anyway."

"What does a dispatcher do?" Billy asked.

"Basically I'll point at things and say, 'What should we send first, dis batch or dis batch?'"

Joey looked in their eyes, from face to face, and he thought he saw a gleam of ambition he had never seen before, all but Vero, who looked bored, bitter, like she hated her father. The boy felt for his sister and wanted to say something for her, not to protect her, but to be on her side.

"You know, there's things more important than money," he said.

"Man, shut up," said Billy.

"I'm just saying. You guys act like this is the best news in the world. There's other things, you know."

William shook his head as if he couldn't believe what Joey had said.

"Joey, this is a giant step up," said Rachel. "It's good for all of us."

"Big deal."

William turned to Rachel and said, "You better shut him up, or I'm going to hit him right here."

"*Cállate,* Joey," she said.

Billy socked him hard on the arm.

"Hey! Ow! Mom?"

"You deserved it," Billy said.

"Billy, stop that," she said.

"What a selfish little brat," William said. "I ought to leave you on the side of the road."

"Oh, would you stop with that?" said Vero.

24

"With what?"

"I-ought-to-leave-you stuff. You say that, but you never do it."

"Is that what you want?" he said.

"Yeah. You bet," she said.

"Okay, okay, just stop it," said Rachel.

"Look!" Billy said, pointing toward the kitchen.

They looked up and saw Alice walking toward their table, her arms—extended like an angel's—full of plates piled high with golden delights.

She said aloud what each item was as she set it before them, "Club sandwich with fries, Salisbury steak with mashed potatoes."

Vero's club sandwich looked and smelled better than any sandwich any of the kids had ever seen, double decker, cut into four pieces, sliced turkey hanging out the sides. Billy's cheeseburger looked even better. It was huge, with the fries piled high. When Alice had unloaded all the plates, Joey's space was still empty. "Where's mine?" he asked.

"I can only carry so much at once," Alice said.

"Why do you have to embarrass us?" William said between clenched teeth.

Billy started right away with gobbling down the burger and stuffing his mouth with fries.

"Wait," said Rachel. "Let's wait for Joey's food, and then we'll say grace."

They all watched Alice walking over with his plate. She set it before him like a platter of gold, a huge sandwich with a large slab of meat and a heap of French fries. It smelled better and looked better than any cheeseburger, ever.

"Wow!" Rachel said, awed by the sandwich.

"You better remember this day, boy," William said.

Joey looked up at his family with a great big smile.

"Let's say grace," Rachel said.

They placed their hands on the table and said in unison, in mumbles,

"God is great
God is good
God, thank you for this food."

And then they attacked. William shoveled heaps of mashed potatoes and Salisbury steak into his mouth. Rachel lifted a piece of deep-fried fish, flaky white and steamy, and she squeezed lemon on it and dipped it into the tartar sauce and sucked on it. Even Vero shoved food in her mouth as if she had never eaten before. But Joey waited.

Confused about how to start, he stared at his plate. Two tiny dishes, one with brown juice and the other with what he guessed was mayonnaise, lay on his plate.

Alice came by to ask if everything was all right.

"Tabasco sauce," William said.

"What's this?" Joey asked, about the brown liquid.

"That's au jus," Alice said.

"Ah jew?" he repeated.

"Yup. It's for dipping your sandwich. Just like a French dip."

"A French what?" he asked.

"It's for dipping." Then she left.

He took the bread off his sandwich and poured the white stuff on it, the entire dish, and spread it around with a spoon. Then he put the bread back on, lifted the sandwich—it was bigger than his hands—and took a big first, happy bite.

"Yuck!" he exclaimed, spitting out wet pieces of food, getting Vero's T-shirt.

"You idiot!" she said.

"What is this?" He cried. Tears rolled from his eyes. "This is terrible!"

"What's wrong, Joey?" Rachel asked.

"There's something wrong with it."

"Not good enough for you?" William asked.

"No! There's something wrong with it. It tastes bad."

Rachel took a bite, squinted her eyes and shook her head, then drank a lot of water. "There *is* something wrong with it," she said, pointing to the sandwich as if it were a murder weapon. Billy tried next, and he almost gagged, spitting the wet food into his napkin. "I'm glad I didn't order that," he said. He took a drink of his soda and happily returned to his burger. "Mmmm," he said, "this is delicious!"

With the tip of her finger, she touched the white stuff and placed a dab on her tongue, squinted her eyes. "Oh, God," she said. "That's horseradish."

"What's that?" Joey asked.

"They put it on prime rib."

"Who does? And why?"

She scraped the horseradish from the bread and meat, but the taste was still too strong, so Joey couldn't eat it. She gave him a piece of fish, and Vero gave him a quarter section of her club sandwich, but nobody wanted to eat the prime rib.

"You better eat the damn thing," William said.

"It really is horrible, William."

"Bullshit, somebody likes it—a lot of people like it—otherwise, why would they put it on the plate? He's just spoiled." He pointed his fork at Joey. "Eat the damn thing."

"I wouldn't eat it," said Billy.

"You don't have to eat it, Joey," said Rachel.

"I hate it," Joey said.

William slapped the table. "You're paying for it then? You think you can buy the most expensive thing on the menu and just decide that it's not what you want after all? Horseshit. You eat it, or I'll shove it down your throat."

Vero dropped a French fry on her plate, as if giving up on eating. "Why do you always have to ruin everything?" she said.

"What the hell are you talking about?" he asked.

"Nobody likes you," she said.

"You think I give a shit if anyone likes me? Especially you. You ain't shit for me to worry about whether or not you like me." Suddenly his anger kicked up a notch and he almost yelled, "Who the hell are you that I should care if you like me?"

"It's not just me, it's everyone. No one likes you. No one."

"I don't fucking care. I won't stop doing the right thing in this family just because it's unpopular."

"The 'right thing'? Oh, God. That's it, I'm leaving," she said, standing up. "I'll walk home."

"Vero, it's too far."

"I'll call Norma," she said.

"You sit the hell down," William said.

"Make me," she said, looking right at him. Then she turned around and walked away.

"Make you? Get your ass over here." But she was headed for the door. She was embarrassed, because the cook, some muscular Chicano guy leaning over the metal counter, was watching, and so was the waitress. The bald guy and the blond teenage girl weren't even paying attention. The girl stared at her unopened gift in the silver box, and the bald man watched her.

Vero pushed open the door and disappeared into the night.

Joey wondered if there were a phone nearby and where she would have to wait for Norma to arrive. His instinct was to run after her and walk with her, maybe talk her into coming back, but he looked at his dad, who grasped his fork like a weapon and tapped the end of it on the tabletop as he stared at the door from which she had left. "That's it," he said, tapping the fork, "That's it." His eyes were so full of rage that Joey didn't dare get up or say anything. He looked at the meat sadly hanging from the sides of his sandwich.

"What is *it?*" asked Rachel. "What is *it?*"

"We'll see how she likes it on her own. She's not getting shit from me."

Rachel threw a piece of fish at William. She yelled in Spanish that if he could let his own daughter walk at night alone in the city and if he could be such a horrible father and ruin the one night out they have had as a family since who knows when, then he's not worthy to have anyone care for him. No one. And if he doesn't go after Vero and beg her to come back, he could be middle class on his own. She'd take the kids and leave and would never come back. He could get a new family, one that could put up with his bullshit. "But not for long, William. Once they figure out what a horrible person you can be, they'll leave too."

He stayed silent for a while, then finally he dropped his fork and said, "Oh, horseshit," and he slid out of the booth and stood up. "I'll be back."

After he left, Rachel looked at the boys triumphantly, as if she had just won an arm-wrestling match against a bigger opponent.

They stared at her in awe. She looked sadly at the sandwich and then at Joey. Suddenly an evil look came over her face, and then a sinister smile, her eyes sparkling.

Joey perked up. "What?" he asked.

"Now that he's gone," she said, and then she leaned over the table and practically whispered to them, "After we get Joey a cheeseburger, let's order dessert."

In the barrio called Pinedale, Rachel's family was a rarity: they were well off. Ernesto Bledsoe Navarro, her father, built a brick house across an unpaved road from a field of grapevines. He surrounded the house with an eight-foot-high chain-link fence, to keep out people like William Molina, who lived two blocks away in a tiny house that would be condemned shortly after the birth of Joey. The Navarros were the only wealthy family in the barrio, and people began to refer to their home as La Hacienda. The girls went to school with Chicanos and other Mexican immigrants, but Ernesto forbade them to mingle with anyone, especially the *pochos,* unless they were from a good family, and since there were few people in the barrio whom he considered from a "good family," the Navarro children had no friends but each other.

School kids thought that Rachel and her sisters were stuck-up girls, pretty blonds with blue eyes who spoke perfect Spanish and kept to themselves. Many of the *vatos,* the urban Chicanos with tattoos who formed small street gangs, tried to talk with them in Chicano Spanglish, but the girls ignored them. The *vatos* sometimes walked by La Hacienda at night, drinking beer, smoking *yesca,* and

they sat across the street in the grape fields and watched the house beyond the tall fence. In the second-story windows with white lace curtains, yellow light glowed, and they guessed that was the girls' room.
They imagined the girls lying on a big brass bed or brushing each
other's hair. The only boy who had gotten near the house was the
newspaper boy, who went to their door to collect every month, and
sometimes the *vatos* surrounded him as if they were going to kick his
ass, but all they wanted to know was what it was like. He told them
how he had gotten a glimpse past the mother and saw into the house,
bright with expensive furniture and mirrors, and he saw one of the
blond girls sitting at the piano, playing a sad song.

The *vatos* knew they didn't have a chance to ever meet the girls in
a social situation, because it was known that the Navarros, especially
the brothers, hated *cholos*. But William Molina, whom the homeboys
called El Cuete, didn't give a shit.

One day Rachel was walking home from school with two of her
sisters when William rode up on his bicycle, weaving around them,
black jacket, greased-back hair, black eyes staring right at her. He
looked like a Chicano James Dean, somewhat unshaven, a cigarette
behind his ear, movie-star handsome. He rode around her in circles,
watching her, ignoring the sisters. "What's your name?"

"Rachel."

"Ah, Rachel," he said, as if he had known it all along.

"What?"

"Rachel."

She got dizzy watching him weave around like a figure eight.

"I guess that name fits you."

"Why?"

"Rachel," he said, "Like in the Bible."

"You dirty greaser, stay away from her!" Her brothers saw the *cholo* talking to their sister, saw the tattoo ink on his arms, and they ran toward him, but he saw them coming and stopped his bike right next to Rachel. "Let me buy you a soda," he said, as if he had all the time in the world, as if her brothers weren't on their way to kill him.

"Stay away from her," said Rachel's sister.

"Maybe," said Rachel. She looked at her brothers running toward them. "You better go."

What he did next, she retold the kids with the same precision of detail every time she told it, so they believed it to be true, like a story from the Bible.

William rode off—*swoosh*—not away from her brothers, but right at them. They spread out like a football team trying to tackle the *cholo,* but he rode his bike right between them and gave each of them a slap on the head. He turned his bike around with a skid, faced them. His feet up on the pedals, he balanced the bike without touching the ground. "Come on, dummies," he said. The brothers turned around and ran toward him again, and he said in a slow Chicano drawl, "Dummies." He shot off toward Rachel, circled her once, and said, "I'll see you, Rachel," and he rode off.

She told her brothers and sisters that she had joined a school club, but it was only so she could meet him after school until he had to go to work. They spent afternoons walking and talking or he watched her as she studied, her books spread out on a picnic table. "All that stuff they teach you about history is bullshit," he said. "You know that, don't you? White history written by white people."

"Am I white?" she said.

"Yeah," he said, "but you're not a gringa."

Once they walked the aisles of Sanchez Market pretending to be married and to be buying food. In the fruit section, he picked up a cantaloupe and held it like a football and ran backward and said, "Go long! Go long!" She said, "No, William!" but he threw it up in the air and she had no choice but to catch it. She laughed until the greengrocer appeared, a severe man with a thin mustache, who walked right up to him and told him, *"Pa' fuera!"* but William told him that all he was doing was checking the ripeness of cantaloupes, the Mexican way. He told the man to try it and threw the melon to him. The grocer caught it and said, "All right you kids, get lost." He laughed and patted William on the back.

One day after school he didn't show up. So Rachel started the walk home alone, sad because he was not there and angry at herself for growing so fond of him. She walked home, holding her books, staring at the cracked sidewalk, hearing Spanish words coming from the windows of houses close to the sidewalk, smelling fresh roasted chilies, flour tortillas, and salty pork. She walked through tiny children playing half naked on the sidewalk, their dark skin glistening like leather.

Suddenly a car's shadow slid along her side and overtook her.

She was afraid to look, but from the corner of her eyes she could see her reflection in the shiny black paint, like in a funhouse mirror, her body stretched and headless. She slowly turned.

The new black Mercury was long and sleek.

"Hey, baby," she heard, William, his arm hanging causally over the red knobby steering wheel, wearing dark sunglasses. He smiled that smile.

"Want a ride?"

"Oh, William," she exclaimed, her hand over her mouth.

They drove around town and out onto the vineyards, where they stopped and listened to the radio. Miles away they could see the Navarro hacienda sticking out of the purple grape fields.

They became boyfriend and girlfriend. Her sisters knew and her mom knew, but it was kept secret from her father. She thought William was articulate and smart. She believed that there was something hidden about him, something good and unique. He was so handsome. Girls stared at him wherever they went, especially now that he had a brand-new car. It felt good to be with someone who looked like him, but she wasn't sure if they had a future. She knew that her father wanted her to marry an American, a white guy. He had planned to send all his daughters to the university so they could meet their future husbands there, lawyers, doctors. Rachel's private plan was not to even have a boyfriend in college, not until she graduated. She planned on getting a good enough education to have a career wherein she supported herself. She fantasized about living alone, a single girl, in her own apartment, having her own car. So even if she fell in love with William, she would not under any circumstances consider marrying him. Ever.

But one day, they sat in the Dari Freeze drinking sweet sodas. She got up to go to the bathroom. After she returned and sat down, she saw that he had been drawing on a napkin, a picture of an old man sitting on a wooden chair, a cane between his legs. Everything was so detailed, down to the creases in the baggy pants and the shadows the flaps of those creases made on his legs, an image she would keep for years. "William!" she said.

"What?"

She pointed at his drawing.

"What? This? It's just shadow and light," he said.

She never forgot what he said about it, shadow and light. She thought a lot about those words and began to think that someone who would reduce the impact of an image to the construction of it understood art on a level that went beyond talent. He had acumen. Subsequent pieces he created on her urging, and the few paintings he did, convinced her that he was a potential genius, a diamond in the rough. His tough Chicano upbringing would never allow him to reach his potential. It was her job to fix him. And as naive as it would seem to her later on, the seventeen-year-old girl then believed that her job on this earth was to help this beautiful artist. This great man was a great child who could never do it alone. He was too immature to handle his own talent, like a too-beautiful child cannot handle his or her beauty. Left to his own, William would start drawing pictures of naked girls or kitschy images of dragons and monsters or low-rider cars. She knew also that William wouldn't have even understood the level to which she was referring, that he didn't know the meaning of art, so she knew it would be better to work on him slowly, to ease him into it by encouraging him.

It was her plan to nurture him, to make him. How naive and stupid, she would one day tell Joey.

One day she skipped school, and they drove to San Francisco to look at the paintings in the museums. When William stopped before one and stared at the image as if it were whispering something to him, she backed up and let him soak in the feeling before she slowly came up to his side. The painting was called *Lazarus and the Rich Man,* the image of a desperate beggar in the dirt—dogs licking his wounds—begging at the outdoor table of a rich man. "You could do that, William," she said.

From memory, and for her, he painted it himself, and it wasn't a bad effort. The body parts were a little out of proportion, but she knew it was art, because the lines, the shadow and light, created an image that seemed to be saying something to her, or had said something, or was about to say something.

When he asked her to marry him she said, "Of course I will, William," but she gave him a condition. He had to finish high school and go to college to get a degree in something, anything, but especially art. He said yes, yes, and before the big day, he passed the GED test to graduate high school, without even studying for it, and he enrolled in art classes at Fresno City College. It wasn't until years after the marriage that Ernesto Bledsoe Navarro would come to accept him in the family, at least enough to allow him to come over on holidays with Rachel and the kids. William mostly went into the backyard with the other husbands and drank beer, but unlike them, he got drunk and loud and argued like he used to argue in the barrio, saying things like, "You're stupid if you think . . ."

After the first year of college, he flunked out because the transistor radio factory had closed. He took a job as a maintenance man at a vending machine company, and his working hours conflicted with class. Over a ten-year period he went off and on to college, but he never graduated, because life always got in the way. Somewhere between housewife and receptionist for a lawyer's office, Rachel quit thinking of her role in his life, and began to understand the reality of her own life. A cleaning woman on weekends. Someone to have sex with. Someone to bear the brunt of his mistakes. She needed something more, so she herself went to night school at the community college, just to take classes, literature in English and Spanish. She started studying music again and played every night on a piano that had belonged to her grandmother.

William came home from work, read the paper, ate, slept, watched TV, but then some voice that only he could hear would call him, and he would spend all night in the garage sculpting his heads from clay. Sometimes, when he was working on a new series of heads, he barely spoke to anyone. He came to bed late at night, even after her piano stopped. She didn't care—or bother to think—that his art was the work of a genius. In fact, she thought it juvenile and uninspired. She hated the mess in the garage, hated stepping over his art supplies as she lugged loads of laundry to the washer. The fact that they couldn't use the garage for anything else but his heads made her hate the garage. She hated going in there at night with all those eyes staring at her. She hated that he spent hundreds of dollars on large plastic bags of clay that he piled against the walls and that he bought the best kiln he could find and he had carving tools spread out all over his worktable. Just when she was getting to think that she could leave him, he started changing, putting energy into his real job, he quit drinking, and now, with the raise, her children would be among the privileged. They could do so much with the new money.

Billy wanted a bike. Joey wanted a cow. Vero wanted nothing. She never participated in the conversations about what they would do with the middle-class money. William raised the idea of converting the garage into a studio for his art. Rachel mentioned a new car or maybe a family vacation to some place they'd never been. "Disney World!" yelled Joey. William said, "Disney World, my ass." He said that a new studio would add value to the house, and that it would be a while before they could buy a new house. He liked his neighborhood, because there wasn't a lot of crime and it had friendly neighbors and now they would be the most well off family on the block. He could fix up the house really nice, starting with the studio, which could be used by future families as a den or an extra bedroom.

Rachel wanted new furniture. William said there was nothing wrong with what they had: the couch fit his body, the contours according to the years of his weight, the table was scratched enough so they didn't have to worry about ruining it, and the console TV was almost new. Joey insisted that a cow would be a good investment because of the milk. Billy said he wanted a ten-speed bike, and he would ride it to school. William told them that they were all crazy wanting so much so new, that there was a certain comfort in old things. One night at dinner, Rachel raised her arm, bent it, and slapped her elbow, which was a Mexican gesture that meant he was cheap.

"What did the little bird say when he flew over the Molina house?" Joey said.

Everyone looked at him, as if thinking, "Here he goes again."

"Cheap! Cheap," he said.

William told his son to shut the hell up.

One day William said to Joey, "Let's go. We're going to Kmart."

"What for?" he asked.

"We're going to get something. Something for all of us."

But Joey was going to play with Ricky Jones, the kid across the street, so he said that he didn't want to go.

"I ain't asking you," he said.

"Will you buy me an Icee?" he asked.

"Maybe."

"Let's go!"

Kmart smelled of submarine sandwiches and popcorn, and the lights blared so bright that Joey couldn't look up at the ceiling without squinting. The PA system announced in that timeless voice that at the blue light spinning from a pole were special bargains—as much as half off!—and people threw down boxes or left their places in the long cashier lines and raced down the main aisles, some of them slowed down by their shopping carts.

William ran to the light, too, slipping like a matador through the slower shoppers, while Joey fast-walked to keep up. Shoppers raced past him, ladies clutching new clothes as they ran, children dragged along by the hands. One family rolled through the crowd like a roller-derby team, the lady in front carrying an aluminum baseball bat, like she was going to a fight that she knew she would win. And then he saw a man, a Chicano man, dressed in slacks and a white T-shirt and a necktie, as if he worked in an office. He wasn't running toward the light but he was walking there pretty quickly, like an important man whose time was valuable. He had a pair of expensive sunglasses on his head, cocked up, and he was clean-shaven and handsome. He carried a bag of popcorn, and some kernels fell as he walked by, and Joey caught one, stopped, popped it into his mouth, and watched the man disappear. It was the first time he had seen a Chicano professional. Someday, he thought, that's what I'll be like.

Joey couldn't find him but didn't care. The store was his labyrinth, and he went down one path and then another, guided only by his imagination, as if he were taking the path to some secret place, someplace wonderful, someplace magical, or like a time machine, where at the end of each aisle he could end up in another era. The bright colors on the shelves made him feel as if he were a native flowing his canoe through a flower-lined river. He turned on one aisle of pots and pans and silver kitchen utensils, like a metal hallway of some twisted future, and then on another aisle, he zigzagged through the people, onto another aisle, where he bumped against his father.

A woman and her two kids blocked the aisle, so his dad couldn't pass.

She held two packages of men's underwear, boxers and briefs. The little blond girls on either side of her, looking up at William, shriveled like sunflowers against her legs.

"Uh, you're in my way," William said, indicating the cart, but the mother didn't hear as she read the packages of underwear. She hummed softly a song that Joey recognized but couldn't remember.

"Hey, lady. Uh, or, uh, miss," William said, but not loud enough for the mother to hear.

The little baby girls looked at Joey. They pushed the fabric of the tennis skirt farther up their mother's thighs. She set down the briefs and examined the boxers, and with the other hand free, she unconsciously reached behind her and pushed the cart back and forth as if it were a cradle, and William slipped by and went running to the blue light. He turned a corner and was gone. Joey stood and listened to the woman hum, determined to recall the tune. One of the girls stuck her tongue out at him, so he sniveled and wiped tears as if his feelings were hurt, and the little girls giggled. The mother hummed the overture to *Carmen*. Joey recognized it because it was a tune his mom sometimes played at night on the piano when she thought everyone was sleeping, and she had told him that it was the story of a matador who falls in love with a prostitute, but he hadn't known what a prostitute was, so it had little meaning then; but now, as the blond lady picked underwear for her lover, he knew what a prostitute was, and like an epiphany, he realized what the opera was about. He got chills thinking of such manner of love. For a second, he had to fight back tears.

He wandered the store humming *Carmen*, comforted by the tall shelves that rose around him like stadium crowds, and he raised his arms like a famous matador and said, "Gracias, gracias." A lady in a red hat pushed a squeaky shopping cart right at him, and he pretended it was a metal bull. The lady laughed, and he suddenly felt silly.

Besides, it wasn't logical that he would be bullfighting in Kmart. He had to make up a logical story to go with his fantasy, because what was the point of dreaming about doing something that could never happen?

He found his dad looking at the cans of exterior house paint. What if he fantasized about pushing his dad into the shelf? He could watch paint cans fall all over him.

The speakers announced, "Attention Kmart shoppers," so William looked up to listen, but the blue light was on ladies' clothes, so he looked back at the cans.

"Now that's a color," he said. He pointed to a can of "Hot Pink."

Joey thought of a logical fantasy: He was the owner of Kmart, and his dad was the manager. A stupid manager. A worthless manager who never got things right. Whenever Joey came to inspect the store, he couldn't believe how dumb the manager was and could hardly contain his anger. "Red paint next to green paint?" he imagined yelling. He imagined lifting a can of red paint and smashing it on the floor, watching it splatter on his dad's frightened face. "This is unacceptable!"

William stepped away from the shelf to see how hot pink stood out among the other colors, his fake leather sandals squeaking with each step. His hairy thighs and calves were thick, but his ankles were skinny and hairless. He opened his arms as if he were about to hug the can. "See, Joey," he said. "That's unique."

Joey swept paint cans off the shelves, colors colliding on the floor like an abstract painting. "You worthless piece of shit, don't you have any brains?"

"Hey, idiot," William said. "Get your ass over here."

"What is it, dad?" Joey said.

"You see that hot pink? Now that's unique." With his hands on his hips and the tattoo spider reaching from the chest of his tank top undershirt, he sighed contentedly, and said to himself, *"Orale.* That shit is unique."

Joey stood next to him and put his hands on his hips, too. "What's that mean?" he asked, looking at their shadows side by side.

"Unique? Better than everyone else," he said.

"Yeah," he said. "The best."

A lady racing through the aisles came at them and had to swerve her cart around because she was going too fast to stop. "Excuse me," she said as she passed.

"Tomorrow we'll get up early and paint before it gets too hot," William said, two fingers on his chin, rubbing it in thought. "Bright and early."

"But tomorrow's Saturday," Joey said.

"No shit, Sam Spade."

"What about cartoons?"

He glared at Joey like he might hit him. His black hair was cut short and slicked back around his ears, and Joey could smell the Mexican hair stuff he used on weekends. "How old are you? Twenty-one?" he asked. The green-tinted five-o'clock shadow on his face made him look like a gangster.

"I'm twelve," Joey said, as he backed up.

"Hmmm. . . . Boys your age still like cartoons?"

"Well, I do. But I'm . . ."

"What?"

"Unique."

He chuckled. "You're okay," he said. Then he actually tousled his hair, just like a father on TV.

"So can I watch them? Maybe join you guys later?"

He grabbed a fistful of Joey's hair and pulled back. "Boy, why did you have to go ruin the moment?"

The boy listened to his parents loudly fighting, recognized the rhythms of their song, and wondered how it would crescendo, in the up-tempo four beats a second that meant that things would explode, a dish thrown against the wall, a table overturned, or if there would be a slow soft ending, about a beat a second, which meant they were simply irritated with each other. When the arguing got fast, the boy got scared about what would happen next. One time Rachel was so angry that her words pushed her to the kitchen counter, where a rack of drying dishes stood next to the sink. She swept them off the surface onto the floor, the shattering and crashing filling the house. For hours afterward the kitchen floor with its chipped white glass and shards of dishes looked like a bomb had gone off in a Sheetrock building.

Their fighting, however, never went to violence against each other. She never lashed out at him, and he never dared to hit her, knew what it would cost him and was not willing to pay the price. Still, for her it was enough that in his most confused rage he sometimes spoke physical threats, his tattooed fingers, LOVE, HATE, clutching the air as if he might find a weapon there, things like, "I oughtta beat you," or "I should slap you down," comments that raised the volume of her own rage, to where she felt like hitting him. Instead, she picked up something, anything, and threw it, let the crashing noise express what she couldn't, dare not, and he, laughing at her impotency, would show her a thing or two and would grab something to throw against a wall. One time, into the television, he hurled a black work boot so hard that the glass busted, and they couldn't watch TV for weeks until he got a new one. Those nights Joey and Rachel spent reading books in different rooms, and Billy would sit at the dining room table drawing on his sketchpad, and behind her door Vero would write poetry or letters (Joey could hear the sweeping of her pen under the music she played). The house was voiceless, and every time the father came in from the garage where he spent evenings with his clay and he passed through the living room, he looked at the TV and felt like a fool, as if it were an object that showed his own stupidity, broadcast to the family his own foolishness. He promised Joey that as soon as he could, he'd get another set. Joey missed TV the most. He would read for an hour, go into the living room, and stand before the TV, seeing beyond the jagged glass inside the box at the sad cold innards, and then he'd go back to his book. He read biographies he checked out from the library, Frederick Douglass, Annie Oakley, and he enjoyed imagining the movie of their lives, but still, he was happy when his father told him to get his butt up and go with him to pick out another TV, and things returned to normal. At night, Billy, Vero, and Joey sat on the carpet and watched the screen, their legs touching or an arm brushing against a head of hair or a foot, the only physical contact between them, one intimate yet incidental enough that it didn't draw attention to itself as affection, so that none of them had to acknowledge to themselves that it was intimacy. They were not a physically affectionate family, not even Rachel, whose rare hugs to her children were awkward and stiff, and as if to try and make them seem as if they were normal maternal hugs, she would pat their backs a few times, tap tap tap, and then disengage.

Two couches crammed the living room, a long one and a love seat on which the father always sat or lay. Over the years, it shaped to his body, and even when he wasn't around, the children rarely sat on it. It had William's thick smell of sweat and shaving cream. Whenever Joey sat in his father's love seat, he held his nose as he sank down so far into the innards of the couch that he felt as if he were being swallowed. He hated the smell, and even if he got comfortable with his position, the way his body twisted, eventually he would feel the shadow of his father's body overtake him, and William, wanting to sit down, would slap him across the head—lightly, to get his attention—and say, "Get the hell out, boy."

The beatings Joey received were not so much beatings as physical warnings, a slap across the head, a boot to the butt, because with Joey William contained his anger. He only spanked Billy, and hard, too, with a belt, with a switch from a tree, and once, when it was the nearest thing available during the height of his rage, with an extension cord, which left red marks on Billy's back and chest. A beating like that, even for Billy, was rare, but it happened, and it was one of the things Rachel told her husband that she would not tolerate. He could act like an asshole all he wanted, but he better not beat the children. She swore she would leave him, but every time he beat on Billy, he would later apologize to her, and explain his philosophy on raising children, which he summarized by saying, "Don't spare the rod." She would tell him he didn't know the meaning of the word *philosophy* or hadn't enough integrity to practice one, he was arbitrary and inconsistent with his punishments. Some days he was in a good mood, and nothing the kids could do would bother him, but other days, when he felt bad, anything could cause him to yell or throw something or lash out at Joey or Billy. Vero he didn't hit, not even once. He didn't even threaten her with violence. She knew it, and she wasn't afraid of him. She argued with him, not just in moments of anger, but about anything and at any time. William could say he was a Democrat, and Vero might say that there was no difference between the parties, and then father and daughter would be at each other, arguments so intense about politics or religion that it could only be an expression of their love for each other. No one could care that much about a debate subject.

Rachel and Vero spent time together in a way Vero spent with no one else in the Molina family, but when she became a teenager and a *chola,* she quit wanting to be seen with her mother in public, so the time they spent together they spent at home. Vero was irritated by the way her mother was, how she dressed so femininely, wore perfume, tried to look beautiful and be ladylike, and Rachel was bothered by her daughter's Chicanisma, by the *chola* lifestyle, the low riders, the baggy pants. She hated the word *Chicano,* preferring Mexican, or American, or Mexican-American. But at home Rachel and Vero had each other, they were all they had, and when they fought, the entire house was silent. If the fight lasted several days, things shut down, and William and the boys were careful not to be noticed.

They were sometimes serious fights, tears, screams, names so hurtful none of them could ever forget, but they never threw things or hit each other, and after a day or two they would make up and be so close together that the spirit of normality would come back into the house and the boys could talk without whispering and William could be himself again.

Since Vero wouldn't go out of the house with Rachel, like she had before she was a teenager, Rachel went out alone, but sometimes she took Joey. Once when Joey was nine, she was in line at the grocery store and a well-dressed man with a European accent kept giving Joey dimes for the mechanical horse in front of the store so he could ride and ride until his mom came outside. Her cart, full of grocery bags, was heavy, and pushing it forward, she said, "Let's go, Joey." The man introduced himself as Guillermo from Spain and offered to push her cart for her, and he was gallant and handsome, but she said, *"Gracias, pero mi hijo puede hacerlo."*

They pushed the cart together, as the man watched Rachel's flower-print skirt swish from side to side. They both packed the grocery bags in the trunk, and being that he was smaller, Joey put the bags he loaded at the edge of the trunk, so the mother had to bend over, lean over, and place the bags farther in the trunk, her skirt rising up her thighs, but knowing she was being watched, she carried the bags one at a time with one hand, holding down her skirt with the other.

When they got inside the car, she didn't start the engine, she looked out the windshield as if she were at the drive-in watching a good movie. "Wow," she said, and she bit her lip.

"What?" Joey said.

She looked at him with mischief in her eyes. "I just thought of something wicked," she said.

Joey was very interested. "How wicked?" he said.

"Let's you and I, on the way home, stop for an ice cream. How does that sound?"

Joey twinkled his fingers like a witch. "Fiendish," he said.

Suddenly her face turned serious. "Okay, Joey, but you have to promise not to tell anyone. Not your sister or brother, and especially don't tell your father, okay? They'll get jealous."

"I promise."

"It's our secret," she said, and they drove to a Dari Freeze and got two cones, Joey's dipped in chocolate coating, and they licked and sucked them down as they waited in the city traffic.

But often she went out by herself, usually in the daytime, dressed pretty and smelling nice, her blue eyes glistening, so pretty that whoever was around watched her get into her car. When she started taking literature classes at the community college, she was radiant on the nights she went to school, and the extra duty of reading and writing papers was for her a pleasure, and because she took classes in both English and Spanish, she was more articulate in either language than her husband. One of her English professors, a frumpy man with curly black hair and black-framed glasses, fell for her and tried to get her to meet with him outside of class, but she was savvy enough to know that he would fall for her, that he was falling for her, so she kept him at a distance. She made friends with some of the lawyers in the office where she worked as a receptionist, and sometimes she accepted their invitations to lunch or happy hour, if there were more than just the two of them, a bunch of people from the office, so they wouldn't get a wrong impression about her availability. No matter how much they flattered and flirted, she knew lawyers were liars, and what they ultimately wanted from her was a good time, not a wife in her mid-thirties with three children.

William knew that if he were to lose Rachel, he would have a hard time of it. He knew he could find someone else—women often paid attention to him—but he knew too that Rachel, despite the three kids, was young and beautiful and intelligent and articulate and that she would live a more dynamic life without him than the one she had with him. He wanted more than anything else not to lose her, to hang on to his wife. Sometimes he loved her so much that it hurt.

But when they fought, even though he sometimes—not all the

time—wanted to give in and say, "Yes, dear," he came to this conclusion: If he didn't act her equal, he would lose her. She wouldn't respect him. She would leave for another man. Sometimes when they fought, when in her anger she turned her head and he saw the curve of her neck, or coming in close he smelled the floral shampoo in her hair, he felt the urge to tell her that he loved her, but he fought anyway. She needed to know he was no wimp. She needed to respect him. But often, if he wasn't in a rage, to him their fights were . . . well, they were cute, as if they were stars in a romantic comedy musical, and this was one of their numbers.

Now the boy, who recognized the rhythm of nonserious fights, carefully listened to their argument as he lay in bed, and he couldn't understand this one, so he didn't know what to think about it.

"William, have some sense. It looks like Pepto-Bismol."

"Bullshit. It'll be the best-looking house on the block."

"Do you think it's serious?" he whispered to Billy, who lay on the bed underneath the window. Moonlight spilled in through the part in the curtain and outlined his body under a white sheet. His hands were crossed on his chest like the dead. The sheet glowed in the moonlight. "Billy? Are you awake?"

"Yeah."

"Do you think it's serious?"

"We'll be the freaks of the neighborhood," Rachel said.

"People'll be jealous," William said.

"I don't know. Might be," Billy said. Then he said, as if he had been containing it for some time, "Dad's an asshole. I hate him."

"It's an expression of our heritage," William said.

"What does that mean?" she said.

"In Mexico pink houses are everywhere."

"You've never even been to Mexico, Chicano boy. I was born there, and I didn't live in a fuchsia house."

"Don't cuss at me," he said.

Rachel laughed.

"What?" said William.

A pause, and Joey waited for the next note, which turned out to be his father. "No really, what?" and Rachel laughed, and then William laughed.

"If you have this need to express your heritage," said Rachel, "stick with your clay. Do a bust of Zapata."

"Billy? Are you still awake?"

"Shut up, I'm sleeping."

"You watch, it'll look great," he said. "Just give it a chance."

"Are you giving me a choice?"

Joey agreed with his father in this case: he wanted a hot pink house. It would be unique.

Footsteps passed their room and entered the bedroom at the end of the hall, where the bed groaned and shoes fell one by one. Then springs creaked, and he let out a long sigh.

Except for some neighborhood dogs barking, everything was quiet now.

"Billy? Do you really hate Dad?"

Suddenly they heard Rachel's piano, "Moonlight Sonata." Slow. Peaceful. But when she got to a difficult change of chords, her fingers, like always at the exact spot in that song, stumbled, and she slammed the keyboard in anger.

In that way the boys fell asleep.

The day they painted their house, Billy was in a bad mood, but Joey felt good. Joey wanted to express that feeling to his brother, not so much to share it with him as to irritate him, to rub it in Billy's nose that he felt fine, but not enough rubbing to where he would hit him. Irritating them was the only weapon Joey had against other family members, the only way he could make them feel something, the way they made him feel bad when they picked on him. He was good at balancing it, giving out the right amount of personality that would irritate them enough but not bring them to violence. Billy rarely hit Joey, but when he did, it badly hurt, so he was careful not to get too much on their nerves that hot morning in the blasting sun. Billy was in charge of painting the sides of the house with a roller dipped in hot pink, which he did angrily, as if he hated what he was doing, hated the color, while William painted the roof trim black, and Joey did whatever they told him to do.

"Hey, queerboy," said Billy, "pour some paint in my pan."

He picked up a gallon-sized can, the thin wire handle digging into his fingers, and took it to Billy. On his knees, he tried to fit the flat edge of a screwdriver into the slat around the top of the can, but the screwdriver slipped. He swept the hair from his eyes and tried again, pretending to be an expert safecracker under pressure to get it open.

"What are you doing?" Billy asked, his long, black hair in a ponytail hanging to the middle of his back. He looked Native American, wide brown eyes, and he wore a black T-shirt tight around his muscles.

"You said you wanted more paint. Pink paint coming up, kind gentle sir."

"There's an open can right there, idiot," Billy said.

"Oh, *that* one. Who's the genius that decided not to tell me that?"

"Get out of here," he said, "before I paint *you* pink."

"Then I'd be unique," Joey said. "More unique than you."

By the collar, Billy lifted Joey from the ground and brought his face close to his own. "Not today, Joey, I'm warning you," and then he let the collar go and Joey fell to the ground.

"Sheesh," he said, wiping the dirt from his pants. "Tough crowd."

"I'm warning you."

Joey stood beneath the shade of the fruitless mulberry tree, watching his dad on the roof, hunched over, painting the trim.

The house suddenly seemed to sigh when the swamp cooler turned on, so he wanted to go inside and stand underneath it.

"Get me another can of paint," William said.

Joey picked up a can of black paint and held a rung of the old wooden ladder. The rusted nails that held the rungs stuck halfway out of the metal hinges, and Joey took a step up. He took a second and third step up, handed the can to William, then quickly grabbed the ladder with both hands and held on.

The small neighborhood was surrounded by fig orchards and cow pastures, isolated from the rest of the city. At the end of the street, he could see cows lying around in the grass.

"Can I get down?" he asked.

His dad slammed down the can. "Boy, are you stupid? It's not open! How the hell am I supposed to get the paint out?"

"Well, you didn't say open it, did you?"

"Open it, you little idiot."

"All right, all right. But next time maybe you should be more specific."

"Don't make me come down there," said William.

Joey stepped down the ladder, set the can on the lawn, slowly walked to get the screwdriver—sweat gathering under his thick, long hair—and found it on the driveway. Overhead a bird squealed.

He tried to wiggle the screwdriver into the lid, but his hand slipped, and the sharp point stabbed his palm.

"Ow!" he yelled.

"Hurry up!" William yelled.

"But—"

"Don't make me go down there."

He wedged and wiggled the driver, but it slipped again and poked his palm again. "It's stuck," he said. "There's something wrong with the can. We should take it back."

"You worthless piece of shit, go get your brother!"

William always yelled for Joey to get his brother whenever he was at the point of losing his patience. In a way, it had become a way for Joey to get out of being around his dad when he was in a bad mood and a way to get out of work when his dad needed help fixing the car or repairing something around the house. Joey would act incompetent, like he didn't know how to follow instructions, bringing him the wrong tools, saying the wrong things, until William, angry, would yell, "Go get your brother." Billy would have to help him instead, and Joey was free to play with his best friend Ricky Jones.

Now he looked up on the roof at his father's angry eyes, and he knew he was pushing him a little too far. He tried desperately to open the little black paint can, but Billy walked over like a warrior, opened the can with the screwdriver—one flick of the wrist—and slapped Joey on the head. "You act like you're five years old, you baby."

As he held the open can, he cautiously climbed the ladder and gave the paint to his dad, then got down on the ground and stood, waiting for his next order.

From inside, the cooler whined and pushed on the windows. It was hot and dry, the sun was burning his long black hair and the side of his face.

"I got to go to the bathroom," he said.

William, face like stone, said nothing.

"Can I go?"

"Tell your sister to get her ass out here. She thinks she's too good to work."

"Okay," he said.

He walked down the hallway to where the swamp cooler blew from the ceiling, and he stood underneath it, the cold, wet air lifting his hair. "Ahhh!"

Then he knocked on Vero's door. He could hear rock music.

O, tower
Who you gonna kill?
Who you gonna thrill?

He knocked again.

"What?" she said.

"Dad says to get your you-know-what outside to help us paint."

There was no answer.

The music got louder.

He knocked still.

"Get out of here!"

"But Dad says."

"I don't care what he says."

"Okay, but you're in trouble."

"I'm shaking in my boots."

He didn't have to do number one or two, but he figured it was a good way to get out of work, so he closed the door and sat on the toilet, feeling happy. "Well," he said, looking around the bathroom. "What now?" The cooler didn't blow in the bathroom, so he started sweating and he pretended to be in prison for murder, a man so tough that they had to throw him into the sweatbox to teach him a lesson, but he would endure it. After two days, the guards would open the door and their mouths would drop open at what they saw. Joey Molina would stand up, smile, and say, "Beautiful day, isn't it?" not even a bead of sweat on his brow.

But it was hot, and sweat ran down his face.

He wrapped toilet paper around his fingers and wiped his forehead.

"Joey, get the hell out here," his dad yelled from the roof, his voice coming through the window.

"I'm going number two," Joey yelled.

Near the bathtub was a fist-sized hole in the wall.

Once he had been taking a bath, playing with plastic army men who were getting shot and falling into the tub, and he hid a few men inside the hole in the wall. When he reached in the hole to pull one out, a black spider crawled on his fingers. He splashed his hand into water, and the spider swam toward him with muscular legs. He screamed, and the family barged into the bathroom and saw him standing naked in the corner of the tub, pointing at the drowning spider with one hand and protecting his genitals with the other. They laughed, he cried. Rachel brought him a towel, wrapped him up, and led him from the tub, saying, "It's all right, Joey." But she giggled, too. "Sorry," she said, wiping tears of laughter from her eyes.

He flushed and stood up in front of the medicine-cabinet mirror, running the tap water so it sounded as if he were washing his hands, because if he were going to fake going number two, he had better fake washing up afterward, or else his dad would call him *cochino* and maybe slap the shit out of him.

He looked at himself in the mirror: black hair to his shoulders, unstyled like on a 1970s rock star, brown eyes wide like on a cow, fat eyes. One time Rachel had called him Fat Eyes. "Such fat eyes," she said.

He didn't like the word *fat*.

Now he smiled at himself. "You don't have fat eyes, Joey Molina."

He looked past himself into the other bathroom reflected in the mirror.

How strange that beyond that other door, that is, the one reflected in the mirror, was another hallway, another living room, another mom and dad. Once he left his reflection, that other Joey would still exist, doing exactly what he did, saying exactly what he said.

But what if it wasn't only the image that was reversed in the world of the mirror but it was everything backward—not just letters or furniture facing in the opposite direction—but everything reversed, including personality?

"Wow," he said, thinking of the possibilities. In that other world, he could be the opposite of who he really was. He'd be strong.

He said to his reflection, "You are Big Man On Campus," and he winked at himself.

If he could get that Joey from the mirror to trade places with him at school for a day.

Maybe the next day, he'd show up at school, and Sherry Garcia would come up to him and say, "Hi, Joey! What do you want to do after school?"

"What do you mean, Sherry?"

"Well, don't you think a boyfriend and girlfriend should do

something together?" she would say, grabbing his hands. "Yesterday was so great."

"Get out here, Joey," William yelled. And then he stomped on the roof with his work boots. "I'm going to kick your ass, boy."

"Coming," he yelled. "I was going caca."

He looked at himself again, and he thought he saw a sparkle in his eye, one that was evil, and a smirk on his face, evil, as if his reflection was up to something that would get the real Joey in trouble. He feared the boy in the mirror, because it wasn't him, but someone like him, but with power, someone with the sole intent of ruining things for him, of destroying his life.

"Worthless piece of shit, get out here!"

"Coming."

Ricky Jones joined Joey on the lawn while they painted. "What the heck kind of color is that?" he asked. His wide cheeks were so out of proportion with the rest of his face that he looked like the kid on the cover of *Mad* magazine, a constant smile even when frowning.

"Pretty cool, isn't it?" Joey said.

"That's muffed up," he said, his blue eyes sparkling with amazement.

"Are you kidding?" he said. "This'll be the best house on the block. Maybe in all of Fresno."

"It'll be the dumbest."

"You just don't understand," Joey said.

"Am I your best friend?" Ricky said, putting his hands on his shoulder like a pal.

"Forever."

He shook his head, as if he had bad news: "Take my word for it, Joey: that's a funny-looking color."

"You know what the real problem is?" Joey said. "You have a limited mind."

"There you go talking like that again," Ricky said, slapping his own forehead with his palm.

"Talking like what?"

"Big words and stuff."

"'Limited mind' is not a big word."

"You mean that I'm stupid. That's what you're saying."

"No, I'm not. It's just that, well, you think this is such a bad color because no one else has it. That means you can only like what everyone else likes. This color here is unique. That's what it is."

"You what?"

"Unique."

"What does that mean?"

"Better than everyone else. See, there's a lot of people in this world. Just think about how many people there are in Fresno alone. It's growing big."

"So?" He extended his arms in a *why?* position.

"So, how do you stay ahead of everyone else? How do you make your mark on this world?"

"Who wants to make a mark? I want to make money."

"You don't want to go through life being a poor sucker, do you? No, you want to . . . You want to be better than everyone else."

Ricky looked across the street at his own house: driveway spotted with oil stains, and off to one side was parked an old Ford Falcon with primer spots. Suddenly his face turned sad. "I'm going to be rich when I grow up. That's all I know."

"Not if you don't stand out," Joey said. "Not if you don't start now." He pointed at his house. "See, this is my future. My life's going to be unique." He looked across the street at Ricky's house and sadly shook his head.

"What?" Ricky said.

"Nothing."

"I wonder if my mom would paint our house," Ricky said. "I'm going to ask her." He was about to run off, but Joey told him to wait, because the twins from next door, Raul and Felipe, were walking over. They were a few years younger than Joey and Ricky, and their mother dressed them exactly alike, baby blue short pants, short-sleeved button-down shirts, their hair combed and slicked back with hair gunk, and their faces red from being scrubbed so much with soap and water. They stood side by side.

"*¡Ay caramba!*" Felipe said.

"*¡Ay dios mío!*" Raul said.

"Pretty impressive, isn't it?" Joey said.

"*Es muy feo,*" Felipe said.

"Yeah, real ugly," Raul said.

"Man, you guys don't know nothing." Ricky laughed, patting Joey on the back as if the joke were between them.

"What don't we know?" Raul asked, stepping in closer as if to be let in on a secret.

"Nothing. Forget it," Joey said. "You're too young to understand."

"If you weren't so ignorant," Ricky said, "you would know that that there color is eunuch."

"Unique," Joey corrected. "It's unique"

"You *qué?*" the twins asked.

Ricky Jones looked up to the heavens, rolled his eyes, and lifted his hands back and forth as if he were pleading with God. Then he sighed. "Maybe you better explain it to them," he told Joey.

"I don't think they'll be able to understand."

"We'll understand," said Raul.

"Well, I'll try," he said. "It's like this."

They stood erect, but their heads inched a little closer, faces crunched in concentration, poised to understand.

"Let's see. How can I put this?" he said. "See, the categories of property are steadily increased by sanctions as such that the procedure of unique is quite good actually."

"You said it!" said Ricky.

"Do you follow me so far?" he asked.

Raul nodded his head. "I think so."

"It's quite, how shall I say . . ." He rubbed his chin, as if that action would provide him with words. "Masterful. It's quite elementary, my dear, uh, neighbors."

"I don't understand," said Felipe.

"Of course you don't," said Ricky, "because you're stupid."

"Now, now, my dear gentleman," Joey said to Ricky. "No need to graduate the mellow. Please be a gentleman."

"You're talking funny," said Felipe.

"That's unique," he said, indicating the house. "You guys are never going to amount to anything if you can't see that.

"Look down the street," he said. "What do you see?"

The street dead-ended at the cow pasture.

"Cows," said Raul.

"Look down that end," he said. "What do you see?"

At the other end they saw a field of weeds, and beyond that an orchard of fig trees, and even farther away brown foothills and then purple mountains so far away that they faded in and out of view.

"Figs," Raul said.

"And mountains," Felipe said.

61

"Exactly," he said. "You don't see houses, do you? Even though the street is full of them. You see *past* the houses. Well, not anymore. If anyone looks down the street now, the first thing they're going to notice is this house. The Molina house. We'll stand out. If you want to do something with your life, you have to stand out. It's the, uh, the perspective litigate."

"I'm going to paint mine black with yellow polka dots," said Ricky.

"We'll paint ours red, white, and green, the colors of the Mexican flag," said Raul.

Then Mr. Muñoz, the father of Raul and Felipe, came by. He had just arrived home from his butcher's job, still wearing the white shirt and pants splattered with blood, and he stopped to look at the house.

"William? *¡Ea!* William?" He was a skinny man with a mustache and a thick Mexican accent.

"*¿Cómo 'stas, 'mano?*" William said from the roof.

"*Bien, bien.*" Then he said, as if he were talking to someone who had committed a crime, "What, uh, what are you doing to our neighborhood?"

William stood up on the roof as if proud. "You like it?"

The mailman, walking by with his sack, looked at the house and started to laugh. It was over one hundred degrees, dry, and he fanned the sweat on his forehead with a handful of letters. He placed the letters in the Molina mailbox, but he didn't walk off; he looked at the house, at the kids on the lawn, and he laughed some more.

Suddenly the door to the house opened.

Rachel walked through the door and stepped down the two porch steps.

Everyone watched her walk across the lawn. Her hair soaked up the sun, even though it was in a ponytail that hung down one shoulder, and her blue eyes pierced like a Catholic picture of Christ. She wore a tank top and short pants.

"Hi, Raul," she said.

"What you think of this color?" Mr. Muñoz asked.

"I tried to talk him out of it," she said.

The mailman opened the box, pulled out the letters, and handed them to Rachel.

"Thank you," she said.

"My pleasure," he said.

She looked at the house, her shoulders sadly slumping. "Oh, William," she said. "He says houses are like this in Mexico."

"This isn't Mexico," Mr. Muñoz said.

She turned to the mailman as if for sympathy.

"Well," he said, "at least it's unique."

"See?" Joey said to the kids.

Rachel walked into the house, the mailman and Mr. Muñoz left, and the front door opened again. "William, I think you better see this," she said.

Joey watched his father enter the house, saw the doors seal shut. He wondered what she had to show him. Somehow he knew it was something big. *William, I think you better see this.* Somehow, he feared it might have to do with him, as if evil Joey in the mirror had done something bad at school, and it was a letter from the principal. Whatever it was, he figured it was big. He walked into the house, the cooler blowing on his face and arms. His dad sat at the table reading a typewritten letter while his mom looked over his shoulder. "What do you think of your old man now?" he said.

"I think he's great," she said.

He folded the letter, and she hugged him.

"What is it?" Joey asked.

"Go help your brother," he said.

"Why can't you tell me?"

"Get out of here, you little shit." He came after him as if he would hit him.

"William! Leave him alone," she said.

"Go outside," he said.

Joey wanted a black-and-white cow, and he didn't care what anyone said about it, he would train it like a dog. His cow, whom he would call Herman, would know the commands "sit," "stay," "roll over," and he would walk with him through the city streets. When Joey asked one night at dinner if he could have a cow, please, he would train him and take care of him, his father shook his head in pity and said, "Boy, you're as dumb as a cow."

Billy snickered.

"What do you mean?" Joey said.

"You can't train a cow," William said. "They're too dumb."

"Yeah, like you," said Billy.

"You can if you start when they're real young," Joey said.

To practice for that big day, he would go out into the backyard and try to teach Droopy, his dog, to sit, but Droopy just stared at Joey with fat eyes and a look of wonder, so in anger he told Droopy to go away because he was a worthless mutt. One day Joey found a picture of a cartoon cow on a milk carton, so he drank all the thick milk, until his stomach stretched and his mouth felt coated. He cut out the image with scissors and hung it above his bed. He called the cow Herman, because that would be his cow's name when he got one.

"God, you're an idiot," Billy said to him when he saw the picture.

"So I like cows," Joey said. "What's the big deal?"

"Herman's a male name, idiot."

"I want a boy cow," Joey said.

"There's no such thing as a boy cow, dumb fuck. Cows are female. Bulls and steers are males."

"Not all of them, " Joey said.

"Man, you're such a stupid idiot. Are you sure you're my brother?"

And it bothered him to think of cows as only female, because he didn't like the name Hermina, nor did he think that a bull or a steer would be cute, not like a cow. He loved the way they slowly chewed grass, how their big eyes looked so round, so he decided that gender made no difference, his cow would be Herman, and he/she would be cute and trained. Joey would impress his friends by having the only pet cow in the neighborhood, maybe ever, and he could yell "Sit" or "Run" or "Come," and Herman would obey with tail wagging. On days at school that left him fatigued, he could ride home on Herman's back, and from the backs of their mother's cars, kids would stare enviously at him riding along a rural road on the back of Herman.

Every morning when he walked to school with Ricky Jones, they went through the cow pastures for a shortcut, where hundreds of them were scattered around the pasture. Joey looked every day for the one he liked best, the one he hoped someday would be his Herman, a fat black-and-white cow with eyes wide apart.

This morning he looked around for her, finally seeing her lying in the tall grass under the shade of a small tree, chewing grass, two smaller white cows on either side of her. She looked so peaceful as she caught

Joey's eyes. He said to himself but to her, hoping she could read his mind, "Hi, Herman. How are you, fella?"

"Don't wait for me after school," Ricky said.

Herman said, "Hi, Joey, want a ride to school?"

"No, thanks, I'll walk today. Maybe tomorrow."

"Did you hear me, Joey? I'm not walking home with you."

"How come?" Joey asked.

"Can't tell you. Just don't wait for me, that's all."

Joey looked at Ricky and could tell that he was trying to be mysterious, that he wanted Joey to ask him why he would be staying after school, but Joey didn't feel like asking him. "What do you think about that cow?" he said, pointing at Herman.

"Come on, we're going to be late," Ricky said, walking on. "Today, you walk home alone."

"Yeah, I heard you," he said, sounding uninterested. "Fine with me. Maybe I'll walk home with Sherry Garcia."

"You wish. Besides, why would you walk home with my girlfriend?"

"You wish."

"You want to know why I can't walk with you?"

"Not really."

"You don't?"

"All right, why?"

He stopped, turned around, put his hands on his hips, and said, "I'm trying out for the school play." His face smugly waited for Joey's reaction. "Audition's today."

"That's sissy stuff," Joey said. He looked back at Herman and waved good-bye.

"Are you kidding? It's the manliest thing you can do. First of all, it's fun." He handed Joey his books and climbed the wood-framed barbed-wire fence that separated one cow pasture from another. "Second thing is, if you get a good part, life is real good."

"What do you mean?" Joey asked, handing him their books, and he climbed over. The grass was wet and the earth soft, and the air smelled of dew and manure and fresh sunshine. They walked to the end of the pasture and into a tunnel of fig trees, and it felt like they were in a dark forest, the thick hairy leaves blocking the sunshine, and when they came out the other side, they faced the back of an old white house on the highway. A dog tied to a tree in the yard barked at them.

"Girls love actors," Ricky said. "Why do you think movie stars have so many girlfriends? And you get all those girls yelling your name. And if you're really good, they stand up for you."

"Wow," Joey said, picturing Sherry Garcia standing up for him. "Maybe I should be in the play."

Ricky laughed, bending over, pounding his thighs with his fists. Then he stood up and pointed. "You? I don't think so."

"Why not?"

"You have to be a good actor to get a part. I mean, really good."

"How do you know I'm not good?"

"I just know, okay. I'm an actor. Take my word for it. I'm a method actor.

"What's that?'

"It's the best acting there is, because you really know your character. You really believe it. Marlon Brando's a method actor."

"Never heard of him," Joey said. "Maybe I'll try anyway. What time are they?"

"Just forget about it. The answer is no."

"Why?"

"Because this is serious, Joey. You're just going to act all goofy and make me lose my concentration."

"Are you saying you don't want me there?"

"I don't want you there."

"Fine."

"Good."

Joey finished the spelling test quickly because they were all easy words, words like *cemetery* and *profound,* so he sat bored while the rest of the class hunched over their desks trying to remember the order of letters. Ricky concentrated hard, his lips moving as he thought about the questions. Joey tore a piece of paper from the corner of his workbook, wadded it up, and threw it at Ricky's head, and right as he released it, Mr. Pumpkinhead, the teacher, looked up. They called him Mr. Pumpkinhead because he had red hair and freckles, and Joey thought he looked like Danny Partridge, a redheaded bratty teenager from a TV sitcom he watched.

Pumpkinhead stood in front of Joey, his newspaper rolled up in his hands, but he looked like a forty-year-old kid, and Joey wanted to laugh. Joey pictured his father beating the crap out of Mr. Pumpkinhead.

"Why did you throw that?" he said.

"Throw what?" Joey said, as if he were offended by the accusation.

"You have detention."

"What for?" he asked, but the teacher walked away.

So when school was over at three, Joey stayed. At a little before four, Pumpkinhead pointed his head toward the door and said, "Get."

The school was empty and quiet, other than a janitor's cart outside of a classroom and the sound of desks scraping the floors. Joey looked in and saw Joe the janitor standing among the small student desks, like he was a king ruling over his silent and empty kingdom.

"Hey, Joe," he said, and Joe looked up, a short beefy Armenian man with dark hair and a face like a bulldog. A lollipop was clamped in his teeth like a cigar, and his eyes were crossed, pointing opposite directions, so Joey could never be sure where he was looking, forward or backward.

"Hey, Joey," the man said.

"What you doing, Joe?" Joey said.

"You know what I'm doing," he said. He pushed aside another desk and swept. "The question is what you're doing." One of his eyes looked at Joey, and the other seemed to be looking backward at the chalkboard.

Nothing was written on it, just smeared white chalk after an eraser.

"Had to stay after school," Joey said.

"That's what I'm doing," Joe said, "staying after school. What did you do?"

"I messed up," Joey said.

"Me too," he said. "Messed up so bad I have to stay after school for the rest of my life."

Joey knew little of Joe's life, just that he was from Fresno but had no family, and he knew his eyes had been like that since birth. As he watched the man's thick hairy arms sweep the floor, he wondered what his home looked like, picturing a small apartment with an eating table and a single chair and a radio on a shelf. After the janitor was done sweeping, the boy helped him move the desks back into their places, big Joe on one side of the room and the boy on the other, pushing the desks to the middle. One desk that old Joe pushed hit the desk that Joey was about to push, so Joey, in retaliation, made sure that his next one hit Joe's.

Then it was desk wars.

Joey shoved a desk and watched it slide across the room and hit the one old Joe was getting ready to slide his way. "Score!" Joey yelled, and he held his arms up in victory but had to quickly put them down and get out of the way of a desk coming right at him. "You're dead," Joey said.

After they played awhile, Joey helped him empty the trashcans from the other classrooms, and big Joe let him push the cart down the hall for him. It started to get heavy and it was late, so the boy told him that he had to leave.

"Wait," the janitor said, reaching his thick arms to his back pocket and pulling out a fat wallet. He opened it—and Joey could see the fatness was a bunch of papers, as if it were his desk drawer—and the janitor thumbed through the papers looking for something specific. Then he pulled out a folded letter and between the folds found a dollar bill, and he handed it to Joey.

"That's okay," Joey said. "I like helping you."

"Take it," he said, and the desire to have the dollar was greater than his reluctance to take it, so he said thanks, and the janitor patted him on the shoulder and said, "You're a good man, Joey."

Joey pictured the things he could buy with a dollar, a cherry Slurpee, candy, chips—a cheeseburger and fries at McDonald's—and he said to himself, but out loud, "Beautiful."

"Want to see something beautiful?" the janitor said. "I'll show you beauty."

"Let's see," Joey said.

The janitor took the lollipop out of his mouth, no more candy at the end of the white stick, just wet shredded cardboard, and he threw it in the trash. The janitor's eyes were sad, and Joey wondered if the lollipop was his last one. He pulled from the wallet a worn photo and showed it to Joey, a little girl, about ten years old, dressed in purple pajamas, smiling, arms crossed, and leaning against a chest of drawers. The janitor's eyes pointed in different directions, so Joey wasn't sure where he was looking, backward at the photo, at the past, or forward to the door, the future. "She was ten years old," he said.

On his way through the empty school he heard children's voices coming from the cafeteria. He peeked inside. A bunch of kids were lined up on the stage.

"Okay, now I want you to be a cow," said a lady holding a clipboard. And all the kids looked at each other to see who would start. Finally, one of them said, "Mooooo." Then they started making cow sounds and moving their mouths as if chewing cud.

But Ricky Jones was different.

He walked around the stage saying, "Moo. Moo. Moo moo moo," as if he were a human who said moo instead of words.

Sherry Garcia, a skinny girl with straight black hair and black eyes, stood on the stage.

Joey walked into the gym.

She moved her head up and down like an ice-cream scoop as she said moo.

The drama teacher turned around and saw him.

"Are you going to try out?" she said.

He stood still, dumb as a cow.

"Go up onstage," she said. The teacher had short black hair and held the clipboard pressed against her flat stomach. He got up onstage, the wooden floor light and shiny, and you could see the reflections of the kids in the surface. Joey wanted to get down and touch the smooth, wooden planks. He imagined the wood cool to the touch. He stood at the end of the line while the other kids mooed. He moved next to Ricky, who acknowledged him with a nod of his head and a "moo" greeting. And then Ricky angrily asked, "Moo moo moo?"

He shrugged his shoulders and said, "Moo," and Ricky started in with more moo lecture.

Joey raised his hand. "Excuse me, ma'am?"

"I'm Mrs. Roberts."

"What are we supposed to be doing?"

"You're a cow."

"A Methodist cow?"

"What do you mean?"

"Are we supposed to act like a real cow or like a person who just says moo?"

"A real cow," she said.

So he was a cow. Like Herman.

His eyes widened, and his face fell, dumb-looking, and he frumped along the stage. He stopped in front of some kid and said, "Muu," in three syllables.

Then he clopped away, stopped, looked down at the brilliant floor; he wanted grass. "Muu."

He kneeled, touched the cool wooden floor, saw his face in the reflection.

"What are you doing?" asked Mrs. Roberts. "What's your name?"

"Joey Molina," he said.

"Joey Molina, why are you kneeling on the stage?"

"Eating some grass," he said.

"Oh," she said.

He bent down and started to bite, saw his big teeth in the reflection, but he didn't swallow the grass, because there was something wrong with the taste, some sour smell like spoiled milk. He walked down the stage, over to Mrs. Roberts, imagining that she was the lady who owned the cows, and he pushed his face inches from hers, tilted

73

his head, and wondered what she had done to his grass. He said, "Muu."

Why do his cow friends keep disappearing? he wondered.

She laughed. "You have cow eyes," she said.

Next she wanted the kids to act like a dog, and all the kids stood on-stage barking. Joey looked around and thought of Droopy, who only barked when he wanted something and who would run out of the backyard anytime someone opened the gate. Joey had to keep him back with his feet, because if Droopy got out, he ran wild all over the neighborhood and wouldn't come back for days, hungry, sometimes bloody, and they would put him in the backyard again. Dogs were wild. So Joey closed his eyes and gave himself up to the dog, so that when he opened his eyes again, he was a dog. He ran up and down the stage, smelling the butts of other kids, and if he didn't like how they smelled, he growled. He didn't bark, because you have to save your barks. After smelling a few other dogs, he just hung out on his street corner. His tongue out, breathing hard, he was a happy dog. After he lifted his leg to pee, he ran off the stage across the cafeteria and lay on his back and wiggled his legs, bathing in the sunlight that came through the windows.

The teacher pointed her clipboard at him and said, "Now that's a dog!"

The other kids, getting it now, started running around the cafeteria, too, yelping, lifting their legs, smelling each other. One kid pretended to take a dump. Joey weaved through the kids and came up behind Sherry Garcia. "Bow wow," he said. She turned around and said, "Joey!"

She crawled toward him and sniffed at his neck, pulled away, and puckered up her face as if she didn't like the odor. He tilted his head and whimpered as she ran away, so he ran after her. A dog chasing another dog. The gym was loud with yelps and barks, and he saw the blur of her leg as she ran behind some other kids, so he ran in that direction, but then he had to stop chasing her, because some boy jumped in his path and growled and bared his teeth at him. They faced each other and growled and circled each other.

Rage.

Spilled through his eyes.

He wanted to put his teeth into that other dog, and pull him apart chunk by chunk, but the boy, with one last growl, strutted away, as if he were the victor.

But the boy had backed down.

Everybody could see that.

Except for Ricky.

He stayed onstage by himself, walking back and forth, having a deep conversation with an imaginary dog friend. "Uh, bark bark ruff ruff. Ruff? Ruff ruff ruff? Ah, ruff! Bark," his dog no different than his cow.

The teacher said, "Okay. That's good."

The boy who had challenged him stood up and held out his hand to help Joey up, who accepted and said thanks.

Inside he was trembling with rage.

The next thing they were supposed to do was pick up a script, read a monologue to themselves, and then one by one go on stage and read it. For the boys the part was a mean king.

As Joey read it to himself, he heard the king's voice say each line, brusque, commanding, yet with a slight whine that came out on short words. He heard it clearly as if it were not only in his head, but something audible.

The first boy read,

"I rule this place.
Do you understand?"

After a few minutes, Mrs. Roberts thanked him and called the next boy.

This boy yelled,

"I rule this place
Do you understand?"

And he put his hands on his hips.

Mrs. Roberts thanked him and wrote on her clipboard.

Ricky was next. He walked upstage and read it slowly, as if he were having a serious conversation with someone, just like his cow and dog.

"Uh, thanks," she said.

"Would you like to see more?" he said.

"Perhaps later," she said.

She called Joey.

But he didn't get up from his chair. The kids thought that maybe he had chickened out, because this was the only time in the audition when you're up there alone, but then they saw that something was happening to him as he sat there. They all watched. He sat smugly, vainly, with his legs apart, his arms resting across the chairs next to him. He slowly looked from face to face, and then he laughed sinisterly. He looked at his fingernails, then back up at the kids.

"I RULE THIS PLACE!!!"

Kids jumped.

Joey stood up and grabbed Ricky by the collar and pulled him up from his chair, and whispered, "*Do you understand?*"

Ricky nodded, and Joey pushed him back on the seat and walked up the steps to center stage, where he stood facing his subjects, fists on his hips.

"I get whatever I want."

On *want* that little whine came out because he said it with almost two syllables, and Mrs. Roberts nodded her head and wrote on her clipboard. Kids watched with open mouths, Sherry even. She sat down, crossed her legs, and bent her body forward to get a better look.

Joey felt chills on his arms as he lifted them to the heavens and said his lines without reading the script, because he remembered what came next.

"Where is my queen?
I want her."

He pictured the photo of the little girl in Joe's wallet.

"I want her."

And he wept.

Real tears. Then he exaggerated some sobs, so the king would appear funny, someone people laugh at.

"Incredible," Mrs. Roberts said.

Kids nodded their heads to each other, and after Joey was done, they applauded. He walked offstage and, feeling the pats on his back, went into the echo of the boy's bathroom, into an empty stall. He closed the door. Tears fell into his palms. He couldn't stop, but he didn't know why he was crying, for something that just happened, or something that would happen in the future?

Mrs. Roberts told him that she wanted him in the lead role. Other kids came up to him and congratulated him. "You were good," one boy said, shaking his hand heartily.

"Thanks," he said. He caught a glimpse of Sherry leaving the cafeteria, red schoolbag over her shoulder.

Most of the walk home, Ricky was silent, and occasionally he looked up at Joey and shook his head.

"What?" Joey said.

"It's not fair that you're good at everything."

"What do you mean?" he asked.

"All I'm good at is acting, but you got the lead role."

"I was just lucky," he said. What else was he good at? he wondered.

"You watch: Monday at school, kids will treat you way different. You'll be a star."

"I wonder if Sherry Garcia will like me," he said.

"Like you? She'll marry you."

He stopped and sat on a rock. "Something happened," he said.

"What?"

"I don't know." Joey didn't want to say it, as if that would make it less real, but somehow he knew that something had been decided about his life, his future. Maybe he didn't have the words to say it, but he felt that the earth, the universe, God, all worked together to lead him on the right path. His mother had said to listen to the universe, because all things are connected, and today there was something to listen to, something about acting. He had walked in the gym when he did only because he had to stay after school—and they were doing cows. Cows.

His favorite animal. And then Sherry Garcia was there. Would he have stayed had she not been there? And the king's voice came to him as he was reading, a voice outside of himself, and as he said those last lines he thought of Joe the janitor—he *was* Joe the janitor.

He looked up at Ricky. "I'm going to be an actor," he said, feeling the truth of that statement in his stomach.

"That's stupid," Ricky said, as if he didn't want to hear any more. "Come on, let's go. This is stupid."

W hy the smirk?" Rachel asked Joey as she slapped pork chops into beaten eggs, then flip-flopped them into a pile of bread crumbs.

"Just happy," he said. He would tell the family at dinner.

She wiped her hands on a dishrag and with the back of her hand brushed away a bead of sweat on her forehead. The sun came in from the kitchen window above the sink, filling her hair with light and bringing out the brightness of her eyes, blue like water. "I'm ecstatic," she said. "You know what that means?"

"No," he said.

She wrote on a piece of paper.

ECSTATIC.

"What do you think it means?" she asked.

He looked at it closely, scrunched up his face in thought. "Does it have to do with electricity, like when you walk across a carpet?"

"No," she said, "That's *static*. Guess again. Ecstatic."

Billy walked like a zombie through the kitchen, right between his mother and brother, and headed for the sink to fill a glass of water. The sun in the window caused him to squint his eyes. Around his shoulders, reaching to the ground, he held a white sheet. It looked like a cloak, like he was a tired martyr, his face sleepy, his eyes large and sad.

"Look at this word, Billy," Rachel said. "It's a new one."

"No thanks," he said, yawning, and he walked out of the kitchen with his glass.

Rachel and Joey looked at each other and smiled. Whenever she learned a new word at the lawyer's office where she was a receptionist, she would come home eager to share it, but Joey was the only one who listened. He had his favorites, which he used whenever they seemed to fit the moment and often when they didn't, sometimes making up meanings and fitting them into any conversation. But some words he respected so much that he was only satisfied to use them correctly, words like *trite* and *triumvirate.*" He liked how they made him another person, like he was smart and different from all the others. With such language he could think of himself as rich, driving a new car, living in a big house, being able to walk the aisles of any store and buy anything he wanted. People who used such words, he was sure, were like that, like the lawyers for whom his mother worked. Rachel wrote down the new words, and he kept the pieces of paper as if they were dollars, words like *peripatetic, anathema,* and *superfluous.* He liked to thumb through them, smell the paper, wave them in front of his friends. Now he looked closely at the new word.

Ecstatic.

"Does it mean that things never change?"

"No."

"Is it something about the future?"

"I guess it could be."

"Then it's something to fear?"

"Not even."

"I give up," he said.

"It means 'very happy,'" she said. "Right now I'm ecstatic."

"So, does that mean if you're *very* ecstatic, you're *very very* happy?"

"I guess it would."

"That's what I am," he said. "Very ecstatic. Very very ecstatic."

"You look it," she said. "Why?"

"I'll tell you later."

Soon his father would be home from work and they would eat and he would tell the family the good news. He sat in front of the TV waiting, smelling the pork frying in lard. He watched old sitcoms that were made before he was born, *I Love Lucy, Leave It to Beaver.*

William was in a good mood when he got home, throwing his metal lunch box underhanded onto the couch. He wore work pants and a blue work shirt with his name patched on the chest. His black hair was flat, pressed against his skull from the hard hat he had worn all day.

"Joey, Joey, Joey," he said quickly as he slipped off his shirt, exposing his chest and the tattoo spider between his breasts. He had long black hairs growing around his nipples and some on his chest, not a lot, just a few long strands as thick as spider legs. Rachel ran from the kitchen, wiping her hands.

"Hey, baby," he said, opening his arms. She ran into them like a schoolgirl. He kissed her on the forehead, then the cheek, then the neck, and she giggled and said, "William, stop it."

William lay on the couch reading the newspaper, which, by the time Rachel announced dinner, ended up spread across his chest while he snored. Joey was the first one at the table, sitting straight up with good posture, hands clasped. "I'm ecstatic," he said, "that we're finally going to eat." The house smelled of salty pork and potatoes fried in lard.

She called for Billy and Vero. Joey sat and waited, but no one came. William snored. Rachel put a plate of tortillas at the head of the table where he would sit. Then she sat down at her seat and pulled sections of paper towels from the roll.

She called, "William, Billy, Veronica."

William got up, lovingly touched Rachel's cheek with his thumb, as if she were a head he had sculpted from clay, and he sat at his chair and began to eat.

"Billy! Vero!" she called again.

Joey feared that his father, who ate fast, would be done and gone from the table before the rest of the family came.

"Go get your brother and sister," she said.

He walked into their bedroom, where Billy was curled up in a sheet listening to a hand-held radio, singing along with it.

"Mom says come eat. Now!"

"I'm coming," he said.

Then Joey went to Vero's room and knocked on the door and listened. "Vero?"

"What?"

"It's time to eat."

"I'm not hungry," she said.

"Vero?"

"Go away."

"I think you should be here. Some news might make you feel good."

"Mom told me already."

"What? That's . . . How could she do that?"

"Just go away."

She didn't come, but Billy did, reluctantly. Before he sat, he stood over the table, wrapped up in his sheet, white, which glowed. Without unwrapping himself, he slithered into his seat.

"Where's your sister?" Rachel asked.

Billy shrugged.

"She doesn't want to come," Joey said.

He gobbled his food, loving the taste of fried potatoes, how the lard coated the roof of his mouth. Billy picked at his food, bored.

Rachel disappeared to talk to Vero, and then she came back and said, "She's not feeling well."

"Horseshit," William said. "She thinks she's too good to eat with us."

Joey was ready to make his announcement. He wiped his mouth and formed the first word on his tongue.

But before he could say anything, Rachel said, "We have some news for you kids." She looked at her husband and smiled like a schoolgirl. Then she looked at Joey and said, "I think it'll make you kids ecstatic. William, would you like to tell the children?"

"You do it," he said, his mouth full of food.

Billy perked up. "Tell us what?"

"I have an announcement, too," Joey said, but no one heard him.

"Okay, I'll tell," she said.

"Tell us what?"

"Kids, your father has been applying for better jobs. Jobs that pay more money and have more of a chance to advance. But he was only doing it to scare his bosses. Well, he got an interview for one he applied for. It's a good job. More money than his raise at work."

"Can I get a stereo?" asked Billy.

"He doesn't necessarily have the job, but we're pretty sure they'll make an offer."

"Your old man could be a big shot," said William. "It's a supervisor position."

"But," she said, "if he gets it, we'll have to move."

"Out of Fresno?" asked Billy.

"Out of state," she said.

"Leave California?" Joey asked, horrified.

"It's in Oregon."

"You mean by Washington? That's the state above Washington, right?" asked Billy, excited. "The capital is Salem."

"Very good," she said, "but it's before Washington. The name of the town is Medford."

"Where the hell is Medford?" Joey asked, saying "Medford" as if it were something nauseous.

"Don't talk that way," his dad said, pointing a rolled-up tortilla.

"He goes on the interview Monday. They're going to pay for our gas and our meals. They're going to get one of the wives to show me around town while they show your father the factory. They're even going to put us in a fancy hotel. Imagine that."

"Will it have room service?" asked Billy.

"Yes, and the company will pay for everything," she said.

"Even a hamburger?" asked Billy. "And a milkshake?"

"She said anything, stupid," the dad said.

"Wow!" said Billy.

"It would be so nice to get out of California," Rachel said. "The crime is just getting out of hand, the gangs, the drugs. Oregon's not like that. I hear it's very beautiful there."

Nothing was decided, she said, but the part they would like, she was sure, was that on Monday and Tuesday they wouldn't have to go to school. They would spend those two days at Grandmother Molina's. Vero would stay with their cousin Norma.

"But I *have* to go to school on Monday," Joey said. "Tomorrow's Saturday, then Sunday. That's four days of no school!"

"Since when did you start liking school?" his dad asked. "You're the dumbest kid in class."

"I was cast in the play," he said. "That's what I wanted to tell you. The school play. I got the lead role. I'm going to be in the play."

"Not if we move, you're not," she said.

"Plays are for sissies," Billy said.

"But . . ."

"Shut up. Before I get up and kick your ass," William said.

"Can I help?" asked Billy. "We can make this a family project."

"Selfish little shit," William mumbled.

Rachel said to tell Mrs. Roberts to find another actor, because his dad might be getting a job in Oregon, but when he got to rehearsal, the other kids in the play surrounded him, and he never had so much attention in his life. They asked him if everything was all right and where he had been for two days. He had to believe, to cross his fingers, that his father wouldn't get the job.

They sat in a circle, and Mrs. Roberts told them to say something about themselves, so one by one the kids spoke. When it was Ricky Jones's turn, he stood up and put his hands in his pockets, rising up and down on the balls of his feet as if that would help him think. "Okay, let's see. What can I tell you fine folks about me? I'm Ricky Jones. My full name is Richard Howard Jones the Third. I'm playing a soldier. I don't have any lines in this play, which is real bunk because I'm a really good actor and I should've gotten a bigger part only I didn't and it's too bad because I should have. I'm what's known in the business as a method actor. Guys like me and Brando."

Sherry Garcia was next, so she stood up and looked at the ceiling.

"Hi, there! Hello! I'm Sherry Garcia." She looked at Joey. "I'm playing the queen."

Joey smiled, nodded his head, and thought, "My wife."

"I live with my mom. We're from L.A., but we moved here because it's too expensive there and there's lots of gangs where we lived. It's all right here, I guess, but it's kind of boring. My mom's a waitress." She paused and looked down as if trying to think of something else, and then a sad expression came across her face and she continued speaking. "She has a boyfriend who I think is a real creep. Anyways, we're here in Fresno. That's all."

Joey intended to speak humbly because he didn't want people to think that the lead role had gone to his head, and he didn't want God to take it all away from him for being proud. He had never spoken in front of a group, other than family and friends, half of the time with no one even listening. He stood up.

"I'm Joey Molina. And I'm glad to be here."

He stopped. An immense sadness came over him. The other kids blurred in the background, and he was alone. He didn't know how long he was silent, but Mrs. Roberts said, "Tell us something about yourself, Joey."

"Well, I'm Joey Molina. Born and raised in Fresno. I, uh, have a brother and a sister. A mom and a dad. A dog named Droopy.

"I want a pet cow," he added.

Everyone laughed.

"Cows are cute."

They laughed, but he didn't feel like laughing. "Herman," he said.

"Tell us what you want to be when you grow up," Mrs. Roberts asked.

"I don't know," he said.

"Well," she said, "maybe you'll be a famous actor. Then we can all say we knew you."

He looked around at all the kids. Ricky looked upset. "Maybe," he said.

He didn't sit down, even though the tone of Mrs. Roberts's voice was clearly giving closure to his introduction, but he stayed standing. "I think I might hate my father," he said.

And he sat down to complete silence.

Rachel stood over the kitchen counter, which was sprinkled with flour, flattening the dough with a rolling pin as Billy and Joey sat at the table, floating in the scent of sugar and cinnamon and sweet baking bread. They had licked the bowl in which she had made the filling and now were eagerly waiting.

"Why do they call them empanadas?" Joey asked. "Why don't they just call them turnovers?"

"What do you think it means in Spanish, you idiot?" Billy said. He was sketching in his drawing pad, his pencil moving slowly and making a swishing sound.

"Really, Mom? Is that what it means?" Joey said. "*Empanada* means 'turnover'?"

"Not really," she said, sounding suddenly like a professor. "The origins of the words are actually quite different."

"Origins?" he asked.

"Where it comes from," she said.

"Origins," he repeated.

"I'll tell you what *empanada* actually means," she said, moving her slender body back and forth with the rolling of the dough. Her hair was tied in a ponytail that hung over a shoulder, and her eyes looked not at what she was doing, but off, distant. "What it really means, *empanada,* is 'pig stuffed with blood and guts.'"

"That's sick," he said.

"She's lying," Billy said.

Suddenly, as if an idea had come to him, Billy flipped to a blank piece of paper and quickly began sketching a new image.

"I wouldn't lie to you kids," she said, looking at them with sincere blue eyes. "That's why they're shaped like the bodies of pigs."

"They are not," Joey said.

"You're thinking of pig cookies. Grandma gives us those," Billy said.

"No, look closely next time. Like pigs. It's a meal that dates back all the way to the Aztecs."

"Who are they?" Joey asked.

"Your Mexican ancestors. Your Indian side. And they believed that if you ate the guts of a pig, you would turn out to have magic powers. It would sprinkle from your fingertips."

"What would?" he said.

"Magic dust," she said.

"She's lying. I can tell," Billy said.

"Would I ever lie to you?" she said, placing a palm over her chest. "I'm your mother. We're not allowed to lie." She resumed her rolling, and there was an imprint of a white hand on her apron.

"Well, I don't care what they were to the Ascots, I like them," he said. "And I'm going to eat a bunch of them."

"Yeah! Hah!" Billy said, as if an even better idea came to him, and he sketched more furiously.

"When I took my motherly oath from the government, it was agreed that I would never lie."

"Your what?" Joey asked.

"Oh, come on, don't tell me you didn't know. Whenever you have a kid, you have to take a test. Like a driver's license test, only with questions about raising children. A long series of tests given by the government."

"I never heard of that."

"Joey, how much harder is it to raise children than to drive a car? Do you think they'll let just anyone do it? That wouldn't be very smart. Can you imagine someone with no experience trying to raise a kid? They could screw up a kid for life.

"Anyway, if you pass the exams, you take an oath saying that you will never ever lie to your children. It's against the law. I could go to jail."

"Call the police," said Billy.

"How come I never heard of this?" he said.

"Because you're an idiot, fat boy."

"Don't call me that."

"Shut up, fat boy."

"Mom, Billy's calling me fat boy."

"Then you better lose some weight," she said.

Billy laughed loud. "See? You're a fatty."

"You better not eat too many empanadas," Rachel said.

"I'm not fat," he said. He felt his stomach. Squeezed the flab. Maybe he was fat, he thought. Not like Billy, whose stomach was hard.

"Look at this. This is you when you're twenty-six," Billy said. He slid the pad in front of Joey and showed him a drawing of a fat-stomached man who had Joey's face. His hair was the same length, but his cheeks were chubby and his face was pimply, and he had a double chin. He was wearing a sleeveless shirt and had a tattoo that read "Fat Boy." Running away from him on all sides were a bunch of frightened pigs, their eyes and mouths wide open in fear. He had two pigs in his hands, squirming to get out, and one in his mouth. Under the drawing was written:

Joey "Fat Boy" Molina at 26 years old
Eating empanadas

"You're stupid," Joey said. But the image disturbed him.

"That's your future. A big failure. A big piece of worthless flesh, like the Blob, eating and eating but with no other purpose in life."

Just then a buzzer went off. Billy put down his pencil and looked.

"There's the first batch," Rachel said, putting on an oven mitt and opening the door. She pulled out a large pan with the piping-hot turnovers, heat rising into the air. The smell pulled them from their chairs.

"Go get your father," she said. "He gets the first one."

William was on the couch snoring, shirtless, the evening paper over his belly, which rose and fell with his breath.

"Give me one," said Joey. "I know what to do."

She placed a hot empanada on a paper towel and handed it to Joey.

"Fat boy's going to eat it," Billy said.

"Watch this," Joey said, giggling mischievously. He tiptoed toward his sleeping father.

"Watch this," he said, and they looked at him, saw him kneeling down next to the couch. He giggled and said sweetly, "Dad?" in two syllables. "Guess what I have?"

William didn't move, just snored, *putt-putt* like a car in need of a tune-up. Joey placed the turnover right beneath his nose so that the sweet smell of cinnamon and bread would entice him awake.

They could almost see the scent rise up to his nostrils, which twitched.

His eyes popped open.

In a quick movement he sat up and punched Joey above the eye, the impact knocking him to the carpet, the turnover flying from his hands and into the air, straight up like a pop ball, slowly falling, past William's face, with an angry squint, his eyes looking down on Joey, so intense it was as if tiny spots of red light were in each pupil. The empanada fell and slapped on the shoulder of the boy. William jumped onto his knees and slapped the boy over and over. The boy covered his face and body with his arms.

"Who the fuck you think you are?" he yelled, his teeth clenched in anger.

"Don't, Dad!" Billy said through tears. "Leave him alone!"

"William, stop!" Rachel yelled. "Stop, William, stop!"

By the time Vero came out of her room, William had stood up, panting. Vero saw Joey on the floor. Rachel rushed to him, kneeled beside him and cooed to him. His face, red with slaps and wet with tears, stung like an open sore.

Vero began to cry.

"You shouldn't do that," William mumbled.

"You're the one who shouldn't have done that," Vero said.

He turned around. "You shut your mouth."

"Go to hell!" she screamed through her tears. She went back to her room.

He looked down on Rachel, who had Joey in her arms. "He's all right. He's faking," he said.

"He's not faking," she said.

"I didn't hit him that hard."

"We saw it, William. You should apologize. You're in the wrong."

93

"Bullshit," he said. "This whole family is full of shit," he said, walking out the door, into the garage, where he would stay most of the night sculpting heads from clay.

She rocked Joey, who continued to cry, although now the screams were whines. She repeated to herself, her voice a murmur, "Let him go alone."

While they lay in bed, Joey wondered if his mom would really stay in Fresno if his dad got the job in Oregon. He looked across the room at his brother, barely able to make out the shape of his body under the white sheet. "Billy, do you think Mom meant it?"

"I don't know."

"Do you think she would though?"

"Go to sleep."

Then someone knocked on their door. "What?" Billy asked.

William opened it, stuck his head in, saw them in their beds.

"Want to see my new head? It's Nixon. Looks just like him."

They didn't say anything.

"Look, I just wanted to say that I'm sorry," he said. "I shouldn't have done that."

"That's all right, Dad," said Joey, in a monotone, as if he were still mad at his father.

"All right," William said. He looked at something on the wall. "All right." And he closed the door.

Joey silently cried. He loved his father, because he had admitted he was wrong, and Joey knew his father was wrong because after it happened everyone was nice to him. Billy had spoken softly to him, and when Joey walked down the hallway, Vero opened her door and asked him how he was, and she left her door open as she stood there. Joey got a good look inside, at the Chicano Power poster, the strong brown fist, and the black-and-red UFW eagle. He saw a candle on a small table and some incense in a ceramic holder in the shape of a woman's hands.

And Billy was nice, too, and Joey felt a sense of privilege, as if having been a victim of injustice, he could win the hearts and the favor of others. He had said, as Rachel touched his shoulder, "I just wanted him to have an empanada." He cried and said through squeals, "I wanted one too."

Rachel told Billy, "Go get Joey an empanada," and he did it quickly, the brown warm turnover offered to him on a paper towel. "Here you go, Joey, eat it."

So Joey knew that his father was in the wrong, and he knew that his father knew it too, and he cried now for him. He must feel pretty bad, Joey thought, and he wished his father would feel better, wished that he had been more enthusiastic to accept his apology. He wept with regret.

Rachel's piano began "Moonlight Sonata," and Joey, calmed by the music, almost fell asleep, until she got to the difficult chord change, and in frustration, banged the keys. Joey jerked in his bed.

During recess and lunchtime Joey and Ricky walked to the far end of the field to a baseball backdrop, where they played like they were scientists who had created a time-machine spaceship. Joey was the pilot and the serious one, while Ricky was the comedy relief, the fool, a part he didn't play well because he tried too hard to be funny. They set off for adventures in time, the past, the future, anywhere but back to the present, which they found boring. Occasionally Felipe and Raul would come out and say hi to them, but after a few minutes of watching them sit around doing nothing—because they were too embarrassed to let them know what they had been playing—the twins would join a soccer game at the other end of the field.

Before the play, Joey had been able to walk down the hallways during lunch or recess, and all the faces of the kids would be blurs to him, extras in the movie that was his life, but now, all of a sudden, he was known. Kids he had never met said, "Hi, Joey," as he passed them in the halls, or they came up to him and started talking as if they wanted to hang out with him. This new popularity brought Ricky popularity also, at least on Joey's coattails, and Ricky loved having people listen to his jokes. One lunchtime, as Ricky and

Joey were out in the field playing their time-travel game, they saw a group of about seven kids walking toward them, Sherry and her friends. When they got to them, Sherry said, "Hey, Joey and Joey's friend!"

"Richard Howard Jones the Third," said Ricky.

"Yeah, right. What you guys doing?" she asked.

"Hanging out," Joey said. "What about you guys?"

"Same thing," she said.

So they hung out together, and after that day they ate lunch together and became a kind of group, sitting together in the same spot in the cafeteria and then walking together out to the far ends of the school field. When Joey said something that made everyone laugh, Sherry said, "Oh, Joey!" and punched him on the arm.

One day while they sat in the cafeteria, Sherry bent over and whispered into Joey's ear, "Tami likes you. She thinks you're cute."

He looked across at Tami, a pretty blond.

"You don't like her, do you?" asked Sherry.

"I like someone else," he said.

She slapped Joey on the arm, and it stung. "Lucky girl," she said. "Whoever she is."

When their group would walk together, they walked side by side, their shoulders touching, hands brushing together. Tami, sensing their growing relationship, acted loud and flamboyant, and at one point she lifted her dress and said, "Oops," and giggled. Sherri rolled her eyes, and they had a private laugh.

Ricky tried too hard to entertain everyone, especially when Joey said something that made people laugh or nod their heads in agreement, which made him feel he had to say something right away that would exceed Joey's comment in cleverness. He got on people's nerves, and sometimes, when he got up to go to the bathroom or to get his lunch, one of the kids would say to Joey, "Why do you hang around with that dork?"

"He's my friend," Joey said. "I like him."

One night the family, all but Vero, was gathered around the TV watching a game show, and during a commercial Rachel lowered the volume. Billy, wrapped in his sheet, lay sideways on the floor, and Joey lay with his head pillowed on his brother's legs. William sat on the love seat, legs crossed, arm stretched across the back. Rachel joined him, leaned into his arms.

"He got the job," she said. "We're going to Oregon."

"I'll be working in a lumber plant, supervising a crew of maintenance engineers. I'll be management."

"Your father and I love the town," she said. "It's much smaller than Fresno, and it's so pretty, so nice. Surrounded by hills. Oregon is so beautiful. Everyone rides bikes. They even have lanes just for bicycles."

"Can we get new bicycles?" Billy asked, sitting up.

"What's wrong with your old one? Not good enough for you?" the dad said.

"What old one?" said Billy. "We don't got no bikes."

"We don't have *any*," Joey corrected.

Billy looked at him as if he had just backed up his story. "See? That's what I'm saying." Then he looked at his mother. "Can we get bikes?"

"Maybe somewhere down the line," Rachel said. "But my point is that you're going to love this place. We'll buy a house, right, William? Maybe something with brick. Something with two bathrooms."

"Two bathrooms?" Billy said, getting excited.

"You can shit in stereo," the dad said.

"And the schools seem very good," Rachel said. "Mrs. White, the woman who showed me around, told me they're much better than the schools in California. She's from California, too."

"How many high schools does the town have?" Billy asked.

"I think there's two," said Rachel.

"Two?" Joey said. "That's a hick town. Who wants to live there?"

"Is it near the ocean?" said Billy.

"A couple of hours away," she said.

"But Fresno is growing," Joey said. "It's not a good time to leave. I mean, this city is the future of California, California the future of the world."

Vero came from her room and leaned against the doorframe with her arms crossed. Her features were round like an Indian's. She had long, straight black hair and big brown eyes.

"He got the job," Billy told her.

"Duh," she said.

One time when the family was watching a cowboy movie, Joey had asked his dad during commercials whatever happened to the Indians, how come they didn't see them in Fresno. He shook his head and laughed. "Boy, you are the stupidest kid in the world."

"What?"

"I agree with that one," said Billy.

"Why am I stupid?" Joey asked.

"Where the hell are the Indians? Is that your question? Where have they gone? You ignorant Mexican. Look at your sister!"

She sat at the kitchen table, a scoop of beans spread before her, plucking out rocks and bad beans and tossing the good ones into a tin bowl, the flare of her nose rising and falling.

"What do you think she is?"

And for the first time he realized she was an Indian.

"Can't you picture her walking around half naked?" his dad said.

"Gross," said Billy.

"Look at your brother," William said. "Look at your own damn self in the mirror. You're going to see an Indian staring back at you. That's what became of the Indians. We watch TV now, too dumb to even know who we are."

"We're Indian?"

"Man, you *are* stupid," Billy said. "What do you think Mexicans are?"

"Mexicans," Joey said.

"We're Indian and Spanish," Billy said. "Everyone knows that."

"Some of us more Indian and some of us more Spanish," said the dad. "Some of us not Spanish and all Indian. Your grandfather, your mother's father, he's a Creole. That means he ain't got a drop of Indian blood in him. But he's one hundred percent Mexican."

The next day, still stunned by the realization, Joey sat at the step of his front porch and watched the neighborhood, the heat so blasting that it seemed to moisten the tar on the street; the branches of trees shone, and the leaves seemed wilted. Across the street Ricky came out of his house, walked to the edge of the lawn, and yelled, "Let's play in my backyard."

Joey took off his shoes and socks, put them on the porch, and walked across the lawn. His tender white feet, pricked by the blades of grass, began to turn pink. He reached the curb, and looking up at Ricky, he walked across the asphalt.

"Where are your shoes, Joey? Are you crazy?"

They burned.

* * *

Now William turned around to get a look at Vero. She leaned on the doorframe, her arms crossed.

"There's lots of cute guys in Medford," he said. "They even have some low riders."

She almost smiled.

"There's Chicano power in Medford," he said.

"Are there really Chicanos there?" Vero said.

"There's a small Mexican community," Rachel said.

"There's pear orchards," said William. "You think *gabachos* are going to do that work? They have to import their Mexicans."

"It's not the same," Vero said. "I'm not into cowboy hats and *banda* music."

"I don't think we should go," Joey said.

"Shut up," Billy said.

As they continued talking, Joey watched them as if he were not a part of it, but a camera going from face to face. He walked to his room, and with the lights out, lay on his bed and listened to the murmur of their excited voices.

After a while, Billy came in humming a song, and he flicked on the light. He didn't even seem to notice Joey as he rummaged through the top drawer of the dresser, pulling out T-shirts and tossing them back in as he sang,

"I'm leaving this place for good
Never gonna come back again."

He pulled out a shirt, smelled the underarms, and threw it on the dresser top. He turned around and noticed Joey on the bed.

"What are you doing, lamo?"

"I don't want to move to Oregon," he said.

"Dad's taking us to a restaurant." He paused, waiting for Joey's reaction. "To eat," he added.

"A restaurant?" Joey said, sitting up on the bed. "Again?"

"Yeah, pretty cool. He's in a great mood."

"Are you sure he didn't say Munchies?"

"No, a restaurant. You better hurry up, fat boy." He pulled another shirt out of the drawer, and something flew from the fabric and landed on the floor. Joey jumped and picked it up, a small canister, SHOALS. "What the heck is this? Chewing tobacco?"

"Give it to me before I kill you," Billy said, holding out his hand and raising the other one in a fist.

"It's not yours, is it?" Joey asked.

"Of course not, fat boy. I'm holding it for someone." He put it back in the drawer, underneath some shirts.

Joey wanted to hate his father and to let it be seen in his mood. He wanted to sulk. If anyone in the family said anything to him, he grunted wordless answers. But as they drove through the city, no one talked to him or noticed how he sat in the backseat with his arms crossed and a big frown on his face. Vero and Billy, also in the backseat, leaned over the front seat and listened to William talk about Oregon and the new job. "They got pine trees everywhere," he said, "I kid you not. You look out your front door, and all you see are pine trees and mountains and rivers with fish so big all you got to do is stand on the bank drinking beer and they'll jump up at you and you grab 'em with your bare hands."

"Oh, William," said Rachel. "You're exaggerating."

"Portland's a pretty big city," Vero said. "Norma's ex-boyfriend moved there with his family."

"Well, we won't really be too near Portland," said Rachel.

Joey blocked everyone out and looked out the window at the city blurring by, as if it were blurring away from his vision and hope forever, as if they were already on their way to Oregon. He had to figure out a way to stay, to be in the play, whatever it took. Perhaps I could convince them to stay, he thought, as he looked from his brother to his sister to his dad and his mom. Rachel looked back at him, and their eyes caught. He quickly turned his head, frowning, sad.

"What's wrong, Joey?' she said.

He whispered, "Nothing," very softly, as if he didn't want to talk about it because he was too hurt. He hoped she would press him, that she would be so concerned about him that she wouldn't join the other conversation until she knew that he was all right, and in the meantime, while she tried to get it out of him, the family, one by one, would hear him, feel for him. By the time they were all sitting down for dinner, they would have listened to his story, reasons why they shouldn't leave the present for the future. If they went to Oregon, something bad would happen.

Ask me again what's wrong, he thought, but she looked away and joined the other conversation.

She didn't care that Joey was suffering, and this made him suffer more. He sighed loudly and recrossed his arms, as if to get a tighter hold, but when no one noticed, he started kicking the bottom of the seat in front of him, his mother's cushion. He knew what he had to do next, say something that would get their attention but that wouldn't make them mad, but rather would immediately get them all to sympathize, something like, "I don't feel good," and he could hold his stomach and pretend like he might throw up, but then William did something that changed it all.

He pulled the Maverick into McDonald's.

"Wow," Joey said. "McDonald's!"

Billy's eyes were wide with disbelief. "Are we . . . eating here?"

"You bet," said William, pulling into a space and opening the door to the car. "And you could get anything you want."

"Wow," said Joey. He looked at Billy, and they high-fived each other.

They all got out of the car and walked toward the entrance of glass and into the restaurant, and as the kids ran past them, Rachel grabbed her husband by the arm and smiled at him. He winked and said, "Look what I got." From his shirt pocket he pulled out a few slices of individually wrapped American cheese.

She socked him on the arm and laughed.

Joey gobbled his two cheeseburgers and fries faster than anyone else, even before his mom had finished half her fish sandwich. All he had left was a yellow empty burger wrapper spread before him and a sad spot of ketchup where he had dipped his fries. He looked around at the food of the others, hoping they would give him some of theirs, but no one noticed him because William was talking about Oregon and what it meant to be with the kind of income he'd be getting. The family listened to him with their eyes glowing. Joey had to find a way to get more food, so when Billy wasn't looking, he slowly slid his hand over to his burgers and fries, and he touched the fries with his fingers—now pretending to be listening to his dad. He pulled a single fry toward him, but Billy smashed his hand against the table and said, "Hands off, fat boy."

"Mom," Joey said. "I'm still hungry. Can I have another cheeseburger?"

The father, a fry in his hand, pointed it at Joey. "You better shut up, boy."

"I'm still hungry."

"Make a Spam burrito when you get home," he said, and then he started talking again about Oregon.

Joey watched his family and felt bitter and empty. He had to do something to stop this move. When his father had hit him the other day, Rachel said that she would leave him. Joey believed that if his father blew it enough, she would stay in Fresno, and then he could be in the play.

Suddenly the answer to his problem came to him.

He would find a way to split up his family.

He would find some way to get his mom to leave his father. He hated him anyway. Sometimes.

As he watched his father talk and eat, chewing with his mouth open and drinking big sucks through his straw, he hated him, the very sight of him. He'd figure out a way to get rid him.

He left the house in the morning and crossed the street and knocked on Ricky's bedroom window. Ricky peeked his sleepy, disheveled head out the window.

"Man, do you know how early it is?" he said.

"I'm leaving," Joey said, and he explained it all to him, how his parents told him he couldn't be in the play because they wanted to go to Oregon, but that he felt with a certainty he had never known before that this play was his opportunity, that things would be different, he didn't know how, but he felt it. "So I'm running away," he said. "I'm going to be in the play because I'm staying in Fresno, but not with my family."

He didn't tell Ricky that he would stay away only long enough for his dad to get mad and beat him, so his mom would leave him and let him go to Oregon by himself. He'd be a victim.

"Just go with your family, Joey." Ricky said. "It's only an elementary-school play. Big deal. I'll do your part."

Joey walked to the apartment building where Sherry lived and knocked on her door. She answered wearing jean cutoffs and a white tank top, her hair in a ponytail. She leaned against the doorframe, her skinny hip sticking out and her arms crossed. "Joey Molina," she said.

He told her about Oregon and what he was going to do, speaking quickly like a child who didn't want to forget anything, how he was going to run away because he didn't think it was fair that he had to go now that he had finally found something in his life that mattered to him. "I think you better come in," she said.

The apartment was cluttered with new furniture, wooden stuff with brass-colored trim and leather chairs and couches, the kind of things his mother would dream of owning. In the small dining room was a giant hutch that reached to the ceiling, dainty dishes displayed behind the glass, and a wooden table with elegantly carved chairs with red velvet backs. The apartment was so small that it felt like storage space, like you would have to walk sideways to reach the kitchen. She led him to an oversized couch, and they sat. It was the most comfortable couch he had ever sat in. He held on to the cushions with both hands and tested the softness by moving up and down. Sherry did the same, and they were bouncing next to each other. Then he looked around the house. "You got nice stuff," he said.

"My mom likes nice things," she said.

Over the TV was a painting of a matador twisting his torso around a muscular bull, red cape flaring over the bull's horn. "My grandma has that one," Joey said.

"I love bullfights. Have you ever been to one?" she asked. Joey shook his head. "We saw one in Tijuana," she said. "It was so cool. You ever been to TJ?"

Joey said no, but that his sister had, and she brought him back a Hell's Angel.

"A what?"

He described the ceramic skull with the spiked Nazi motorcycle helmet, and with coin slot on top because it was really a piggy bank. And he remembered how his dad looked at it when she put it on the table, how he shook his head and said, "That ain't art. It's kitsch. I could do a better head than that."

And he did, too, a series of skulls with motorcycle helmets, his Hell's Angels series, faces so scary that they looked like they were indeed from hell, worms boring from their skulls, eyes popped out, knife scars running across their cheeks, but you couldn't put coins in their heads because they weren't kitsch, they were art.

They watched cartoons on the giant color console TV, and during commercials they talked. "How will you live?" Sherry asked.

"I'll figure something out," he said, and she nodded. During the next commercial she said, "I don't know, Joey." And she punched him lightly on the arm.

He looked at where she hit him and then looked at her. "Ow," he said.

"Ow?" she said, scooting in close to him. The cushions gave in under her weight and pushed him a little closer to her. They were face to face. "Are you being realistic?" she asked.

He looked into her black eyes. She seemed so much older than twelve. She seemed like an adult, and he wanted to kiss her. He backed up a little and said like a man, "I can handle myself."

She grabbed his wrists and bent them. "Oh, yeah, prove it."

Joey could feel it, she was stronger than he was. Her grip was tight, and her thin arms had muscles pulsating under the skin, so rather than fight her, he pretended to give in and said, "You win."

She came in close, bending his wrists back farther, her face so close to his that he could smell her toothpaste, and he felt himself flush with excitement. "Are you sure you can handle yourself?" she said. Her nose touched his. "Come on," she said, bending his wrists until they hurt. "Fight."

"I don't fight girls," he said, slipping from her grasp and shaking off the pain, but then she grabbed his hands, entwined her fingers into his, and again he could feel the strength. But she just held his hands. He wondered what her life had been like in L.A., what kind of neighborhood she grew up in. Was she forced at an early age to be tough? He wondered if she could conceive of the fact that Joey at twelve years old had never been in a fight. He didn't know how to fight. He didn't live in a nice neighborhood, per se, they were poor people—although they wouldn't be for long—but it was a small neighborhood, and everyone knew each other and no one fought, not like neighborhoods on other sides of town. He liked all his neighbors and they liked him.

"Come on," she said, pulling his hand back and forth. "Let's see what you're made of, Molina."

"Can you fight?" he said, trying to ease his hands away, but she pulled on them.

"You better believe it," she said. "How about you?"

"I'm a lover, not a fighter," he said.

"A lover," she said, like she was impressed, her ponytail swinging and falling over her face. She had to swing her head to get it out.

"But I can take care of myself," he said.

"Prove it," she said. He could feel her warm breath on his face.

Suddenly, from another room, they heard a woman moan, and Sherry let go of Joey and said, "Oh, God, here it comes." She sat with her back against the couch and crossed her arms.

"What?" Joey asked.

"Their morning sex," she said. She lifted the remote control off the coffee table and raised the volume.

Joey had never seen a remote control, and he wanted to hold it, but he was more interested in what was going on down the hall. The moans got louder, and the woman said, "Oh, yes."

Sherry turned off the TV and stood up. "Come on," she said.

Joey, disappointed that she led him outdoors, followed her down the cement steps and around the apartments. They sat on the warm hood of a car, but he kept looking at the apartment window.

"I wish you could stay with me," she said. "That'd be fun."

"Yeah," he said.

"We could wrestle. Do you like to wrestle?"

He would like to wrestle with her, he thought, but he'd lose, and that intimidated him. He watched her as she leaned against the car, her hands on the hood behind her back. She looked around as if she owned the neighborhood. Suddenly he felt that he wasn't good enough for her, wasn't strong enough, man enough. Maybe, like his brother said, he was too fat, although his mom said he was skinny. Still, he thought, Sherry was pretty, and it would be nice cuddling up to her every night before sleep and waking up for their morning wrestle.

"You know, Joey," she said, "the play's not that important. I mean, you have a family."

"Yeah, and I hate them all," he said.

"Don't even say that," she said.

"You don't know them," he said.

"I know family's family. All that furniture, this cheap car—I can't tell you how many times they've come by in big white trucks and took it away. And you know what, it don't mean nothing. But my mom, now, that's my mom. Tell me you don't love your mom."

"I love her," he said.

"Well, you love your dad and your brother and sister too. You just don't know it yet. Shit, when my brother Nacho was killed, I learned damn well how much I loved him."

"How was he killed?" he asked.

"Hey, that's L.A.," she said.

A young black man walked by carrying a soda and a bag from 7-Eleven. He wore shorts and no T-shirt, a comb sticking from his Afro. He pointed at Sherry, with the bag hand, and said, "What's happening, homegirl?"

"Hey, Roger," she said. "You hung over again?"

He laughed.

Joey looked at her, at those shiny black eyes that knew so much. Yes, she was too good for him. She would never want a boyfriend like him.

"Come on," she said, and they walked out of the complex and down the street from her house. They crossed through a large parking lot full of cars and into the grocery store. She led him to the bins of candy that sold by the pound, and she took one for her and one for Joey. They walked down the aisles looking at the stuff as they popped the candy into their mouths. When they passed by the milk cartoons, Sherry said, "Don't forget to get milk for Junior," and Joey said, "Of course, dear, how could I forget our little one?" Pretending to be married, they went into a furniture store and picked out couches for their house, a TV, a table, and a bed. They went to Kmart and picked out sheets and towels and small kitchen appliances, and they ran after the blue lights spinning on the poles like cop sirens. They stopped to watch a circle of ladies wearing scarves on their heads surrounding a table full of T-shirts and shorts, grabbing what they could before the blue light went out. He loved the way they held up the clothes, light shining on their arms, their faces serious as they examined the fabric, like ladies in a religious painting. When he looked at Sherry, he could see by her fascinated eyes that she too thought there was something beautiful about those women.

They crossed the wide avenue to look for a new car, and they called each other "dear" and "honey," and at one point they looked at a new Oldsmobile Cutlass Supreme, which Sherry said in a cool Chicano drawl was *bien firme.* Then she said to Joey, "Kiss me, dear," and he did, right on the lips, a loud smack, and he liked it.

As they were walking through the empty schoolyard, Sherry said that it was getting late and she had better get home. She stopped and sat on the lawn, and Joey sat next to her. "I got to teach you how to kiss," she said.

"What do you mean by that?" he said.

She licked her lips to wet them, and then she leaned over and kissed him, but when he tried to move away after the smack because he thought it was over, she held his lips to hers and moved them around. They slid back and forth over his lips. Then she looked at him, in his eyes. "Now that's a kiss." He wanted to try it again, so he went in for another one and they kissed and kissed until a car passed and honked and someone yelled an obscenity. "They're jealous," she said.

She stood up. She grabbed his hand and helped him up. "I hope everything works out all right," she said.

"It will," he said. "I'm still your king."

"Oh, you are, are you?"

"The future's a good thing."

"Oh, the future," she said, as if the word had been pursuing her. "I don't even want to think about that."

"It'll be good."

"Let's promise something, okay? No matter what happens, Joey. Let's keep in touch, okay? Even if it's when we're old. Last night I had a dream about you. I think you're going to make it."

"What do you mean?"

"You're going to be famous. I can feel it."

Although falling apart, downtown Fresno still had some of the 1930s elegance. The fountains in the plaza spurted out clean fresh water, and the carved brownstone buildings still housed the city's most expensive department stores, but the surrounding buildings were crumbling and graffiti stained, and an elegant hotel where the VIPs used to stay in decades past was now a rooming house for indigent men, who walked in and out with bottles tucked under their arms or who stared out their windows smoking. Still, downtown was the place to shop. The stores in this outdoor mall were always busy, families walking in and out of the revolving glass doors.

Joey loved the smells of downtown street vendors, tacos, hot dogs, cotton candy, snow cones, and there was the salty scent of popcorn coming from the sliding glass doors of Woolworth's.

There were Mexican stores too, right off the main walkway, and secondhand stores and *panaderías.* He walked through the army surplus store and through some secondhand stores. In the book section of the Salvation Army, he found a book called *Best American Plays of 1966,* and since it was only ten cents, he bought it. Back in the plaza, as mariachi music blared from a record store across the way, he read a play called *The Indian Wants the Bronx.*

He was amazed that such a play could exist, because somehow he had thought that plays were written for and performed by kids, but there was a complex world of theater out there that he knew nothing about. All he knew was he wanted to be in *Indian.* He could see himself as one of the hoods who harasses the poor Hindu man. He could play a hood, a tough Chicano, although in the play the character that he wanted to play, that was originally played onstage by Al Pacino, was a Puerto Rican. Close enough, he thought.

Chicano teenagers walked around the plaza, and although they looked tough, they didn't bother anyone except for other teenagers who dressed like they dressed, baggy pants, flannel shirts buttoned to the top, headbands. He watched the way one muscular boy walked, one hand in a pocket, a cool stride like he was in no hurry and afraid of nothing, not even time, not the future. Joey could play the part of a tough city kid, tattoos and baggy pants. Cool Chicano stride. He wanted to practice the walk, but he wanted more not to be noticed, at least not here, not now, so he read the next play in the anthology.

After dark in downtown Fresno, the families and the old men who had been sitting with their canes watching the children play all went home, and it was just the gang members who were left. A group of them were standing underneath the dark awning of an unlit building. They looked over at Joey. They were about to walk over to him when another group of kids on bicycles swarmed though the plaza like wasps. They yelled, "East Side *rifa.*" One of the boys on a bike threw a bottle against a wall, and it shattered and echoed through the tunnel of buildings.

He ran from the mall and went to get the last city bus home.

* * *

He threw a pebble at Ricky's window, who parted his curtain and then pulled up his window. "What do you want?"

Joey asked if he could stay with him, and Ricky shook his head and said, "Not going to happen." And then he shut the window.

So he walked down his street, under the shadows of trees, and he went into the field near their house and sat on the bank of a ditch, where it was so dark that the only light was the half moon and its twin reflection in the ditch water. Distant dogs barked, and some creature rustled the bushes that lined the ditch. He should go home. It had been long enough. His father would be enraged. Besides, even if his plan didn't work, and his father didn't try to beat him and he had to move to Oregon, it couldn't be that bad. After all, if there were other plays out there like *The Indian Wants the Bronx,* then there were other theaters, and maybe someday, if his acting ability wasn't a fluke, there would be other opportunities. He knew he wanted to be an actor, but he also knew that he couldn't make it on his own; but what if, he hoped, a talent scout for Hollywood happened to be watching the king play and he could be discovered? This could be the turning point in his life, the big thing that would happen to him, that he was impatient to have happen to him, that would make his life wonderful. Maybe Oregon would be a bad move for his future. Maybe his only hope was that when he got home that night, his father would beat him and his mother would divorce. Otherwise, he had to go with his family. He had to give up his dream. Now something screeched above his head, and he looked up at the black branches of a giant eucalyptus tree visible in the moonlight, moving slightly—and he heard it again, like the cry of an alley cat, only deeper, slower. He felt like he was being watched.

At the front door, he heard his parents arguing.

"If he does it again, I'll give him the belt," William said.

"No, William, he has to be punished," she said. "This is one thing I will not tolerate."

He opened the door and walked in.

His mom was pacing back and forth full of anger, while his dad, resting comfortably on the couch, watched TV.

"He's a stupid kid," said his dad.

"No," she said. She sat on the piano bench. "I don't accept that."

"I'm not making excuses for him. It's just that—"

"I'm home," he said, dramatically, and then, in an Oscar-worthy performance, he held out his skinny arms as if to declare, Beat me! and said, I'm sorry for what I did.

"Get out of here," his dad said. He was too angry to speak to Joey. He would have to wait for his punishment. He walked into the dark hallway and went toward his bedroom, crying like a baby and muttering, "I'm sorry, I'm sorry." He heard some noise coming from the bathroom. It sounded like a bad impression of a roaring lion.

Roarrraorraoraoorachke!!!

"What the heck?" he said, looking around for someone to have said it to. Suddenly a feeling of irony came over him, comedy, exaggeration. A picture of the pope hung on the wall, too dark to make out much more than the shape of his pope hat and his shoulders, but he became Joey's audience.

"What was that?" he asked the pontiff.

And then it sounded again.

Roarrraorraoraoorachke!!!

"Hey," he said, knocking on the bathroom door. "What's going on?"

Vero's door swooshed open, the light spilling out and putting a round spot on Joey, like he was onstage alone. He stuck out his arms and said, "Ta-da!" She stood on her threshold with her arms crossed, but her round face was sad, her eyes concerned, as she looked at the bathroom door.

Roarrraorraoraoorachke!!!!!!

"What the heck," he said. "Did you just hear that? Or am I going crazy."

They heard moaning, like a sick child, and then "Oh, God . . ."

Roarrraorraoraoorachke!!!

"What is this, candid camera?" he asked.

"Joey," she said, shaking her head. "Not now."

"What's the matter?" he asked.

Roarrraorraoraoorachke!!!

"Is he okay?" He pounded on the door. "Billy, are you all right?" The door slowly opened. Billy, on his knees, looked up at them. He had vomit on his mouth, and his red eyes were watery. He held out a hand and grabbed at the air, like a beggar reaching for a handout. "I'm sorry," he cried.

William's huge, dark figure appeared as a shadow at the end of the hallway, and it came closer and got bigger and bigger until his face shined in the light.

"Are you okay, kiddo?" he asked Billy.

"What's going on?" Joey said.

"I'm sorry, Dad," Billy cried.

Joey hadn't noticed, but his mom was right behind his dad. She stepped into the light that spilled from Vero's room. Her blue eyes were darkened, and her red face scowled in anger. "There's no god-damn excuse!" she yelled at Billy.

He had never seen her so enraged, nor had he ever felt the in-stinct to hide behind his father to protect him from her, but that's what he did. Vero stepped back into her room, closing the door, so all you could see were her bangs of straight black hair and one eye.

Roarrraorraoraooorachke!!!

He held the toilet bowl with both hands and heaved his head inside of it. Then he looked up, pained, saying, "I'm sorry, Mom."

"God damn you!" she screamed. "No child of mine will come home plastered! *¡Sin vergüenza!*" She stepped around William and hit Billy with an open hand, but his father grabbed her and pulled her back. "You little bastard," she screamed to Billy, and went off to her room crying.

That night, as Billy moaned in his bed, occasionally bending over the side to vomit in a bucket, someone knocked on the door, and Joey said, "Come in."

The father peeked inside. "How's he doing?" he asked.

"Okay, I think," Joey said.

The father looked at Billy, and then he turned to Joey, nodded his head once, and said, "So what did it feel like, running away?"

"I'm sorry, Dad," he cried.

"Every kid does it once in his life," his father said. "No big deal."

"How did you know I was running away?"

"Your little friend from across the street came over this morning and told us."

"You're not mad?"

"Not this time. Once. Just like that." He indicated Billy moaning in his bed. "Once."

He winked at Joey and closed the door.

Rachel's piano played, not "Moonlight Sonata," but Mazurka no. 32 by Chopin. The hall door was shut, and she must have placed a pillow to cover the crack at the bottom, because the muffled notes sounded far away, slow and sad like a child standing alone on an empty street in the city—but then it takes off faster and happier, as if that child was now at a carnival with a clown who led him by the hand into the place of fantasy, rides, game booths, balloon vendors, a familiar place, a trite fun place. The happy faces of the barkers and ticket takers are family and friends. Sherry—oh, so pretty in tights and sequins—is the magician's assistant. *Ta-da!* She smiles, turns on her high heels. His father is a roustabout, taking tickets at the roller coaster, a giant metal insect, clanking over his shoulders into the dark sky.

The boy loves the smell of corn dogs and *churros,* loves the beeping lights and clattering rides and children screaming with delight. And the clown is running ahead of him toward the fun house, to the rhythm of Rachel's piano, as if each of his rubber-shoed steps were a note, up and down, side to side, up the stairs of the fun house entrance, across the metal-plated floors, into the maze of mirrors, motioning for Joey to follow. *Come on! Hurry! Don't miss out.*

The song slows down again.

Sadness.

He slowly enters the hall of mirrors. He is surrounded by himself, beside himself with fear.

But suddenly the piano keys pound along faster and faster, like children scattering across a schoolyard under fire, and it goes faster and the clown appears among the mirrors. Joey can't see his face.

She pounds on the keys, chord to chord, note to note, true god from true god, begotten not made, each finger pounding the keys, notes shooting into the night like trembling stars. From the distance a dog barks.

The fun house lights dim, dark purple light, and the footprints on the floor glow fluorescent green, the notes angry, the clown angry, the notes harsh, discordant. Joey doesn't want to follow the clown, but it's too late, he keeps following, as if pulled against his will into the future. The clown is evil, dark, with hunched shoulders, and he turns around. Joey can't see his face in the darkness, but the white hands reach out to him. The boy runs the other way, trying to find his way out of the mirrors, all the other Joeys surrounding him. The notes keep going, so Joey keeps running, into walls, into himself, into hallways that lead deeper into the dark. He reaches a dead end. He turns around. The clown walks toward him.

And Joey sees it.

The clown is Joey, like the picture Billy drew, Joey at twenty-six eating empanadas. He's unshaven and dirty, and his cheeks are fat. He says with a booming voice that sounds like the devil: "I'm your future, you son of a bitch!"

One day Rachel and Joey were standing on the lawn looking up on the roof at William and Billy fixing the cooler. Suddenly William hit Billy across the head with an open hand for not being fast enough in handing him the tools that he needed, and Joey watched how angry Rachel got at him. "Your children are not punching bags," she yelled. For the rest of the day Rachel wouldn't talk to William, and when he came inside the house after fixing the cooler, she grabbed her purse, put on her sunglasses, and headed toward the car. "Where are you going, Mom?" Joey asked, but she said that she'd be right back, and when William asked her, she said, "None of your damn business." All day that day William was nice to Joey, and Joey took advantage of it. He asked for some money and got a dollar. All day he thought about how he could get William to hit him, too, not hard, but in front of Rachel so she would get mad. If Joey shriveled up on the floor and bawled his eyes out, maybe she would think it was a bad hit and she would get extra mad and would divorce him.

Ah, divorce!

How nice a word, what a beautiful sound, especially that sliding *s* at the end. Yes. Divorce. So sweet.

The opportunity came one evening right before dinnertime. William was sitting on the couch, reading the paper. Rachel was setting the table. She had a clear view of the couch and would see everything. Joey looked on the carpet, where the father had a large plastic glass of iced tea, and Joey walked up to the couch—his dad unable to see because he was behind the paper—and tipped over the glass with his feet. The ice and the tea spilled all over the carpet. "Oops," Joey said.

William lowered the paper, looked at Joey, and then he bent forward and looked off the edge of the couch and saw the spilled tea. He looked back at Joey, who shrugged his shoulders, smiled, widened his eyes, and said, "Accidents happen."

William laughed. Then he went back to reading his paper.

Hit me you, fool, Joey thought. Hit me.

Father of a thousand heads.

Nothing could keep him away from the garage, from his bag of clay, from the clumps he plopped on the workbench and looked at carefully, skeptically, as if deciding who the blob would become. Even as all the other stuff was packed in boxes ready for the move to Oregon, the clothes, the dishes, and even as they were eating sandwiches off plastic plates, William of a thousand heads wouldn't let his sons pack the garage. That would be last, not because he was out there every night, but because he didn't want to miss the opportunity if he felt the inspiration to go out there. He was an artist who relied on inspiration, or what he mistook for inspiration but often turned out to be desire or anger. If he needed to work, he worked, if he didn't, he didn't. He could go months without creating, but then he'd be out in the garage every night and weekends for just as long, so that things around the house went unfixed. As a matter of principle, Rachel fixed nothing. If William wanted to clean, to cook, to buy groceries, then she would get the toolbox and fix things. Otherwise, he was responsible for everything broken.

During his more "inspired" artistic moments, she had a long list of tasks waiting for the muse to finally leave him. She suspected that sometimes, when the list was especially long, he stayed in his studio just to get out of doing work around the house. As she carried a basket of laundry to the garage, she'd catch him pacing back and forth or reading the newspaper, and she'd sense no presence of the muse or any other creative spirit, just blackness, boredom. She'd say, "If you're not doing anything, there's the list," and he'd immediately get back to uninspired creation.

Sometimes he sculpted political figures. For those whom he admired, like César Chávez, he did flattering likenesses, but for the ones he didn't like, like Nixon, he exaggerated their qualities and made them comical. Sometimes he did a series, as he called them. Once he did comical heads of the most visible figures of the Watergate trials, making them all look like the crooks he knew they were, and he entered the series in a county art contest and won first prize. The picture of his heads came out in the Sunday arts section of the newspaper. At least once a year, he did the heads of each of the family, sometimes more often. He created a happiness-to-sadness family series, where he wanted to catch all of their different moods. His favorite subject was Vero. When she was a little girl, all he had to do was order her out in the garage to sit on the stool, but when she became a teenager, he had to find ways to convince her that a photo wasn't good enough, that he needed her to sit for him. The job took hours, but usually he didn't have a hard time convincing her to pose. As much as she argued with him and said things about him behind his back—like how she wished that he would just disappear—she spent hours in the garage with him. During these times they talked. She told him about the Chicano movement, what she was doing with MEChA, and he told her stories of growing up Chicano, how when he was a *cholo,* the cops would chase him, pin him to the street, and pull out scissors and cut off his ducktail. Occasionally, you could hear them laughing, alone, in the garage.

* * *

Joey was the worst subject. He squirmed on the stool, whining to be let go. He complained that he didn't want any more stupid heads. William told him to shut up or he'd smack him, and Joey cried.

The boy's first head was made when Joey was two years old, and the latest, the father did when he was twelve. He hated being in the garage. He hated looking at himself. Finally, the weekend before they were supposed to get the moving van to pack up for Oregon, he hated that his father gave him the job of wrapping all the heads in newspaper and packing them in boxes.

He packed heads for hours before he even got to his head at six years old, the halfway point. He lifted his six-year-old self and put him on the workbench, where he had a stack of newspapers, and he looked at himself. He looked so scared. What did he fear that day his father made him from clay?

William had been in a bad mood, so if Joey so much as squirmed on the stool, he yelled and raised his hand. Six years old, so afraid. Now, at twelve, having been given the job of packing his father's heads in boxes, he wished he could assure his six-year-old self that the future was fine. He remembered that right after his dad was done sculpting his head, he'd get an ice cream. "Let's go get you an ice cream, boy," William had said. And that afternoon as they walked through Thrifty Drug Store to get the cone, Joey saw a kite, and he pointed to it as if to ask if he could have it. "Hell, no," the father said. "I have something better for you."

He took him home and built a kite from newspaper and balsa wood. He said they were better than store-bought kites, which is what all the other kids had. After the kite was complete, they entered the field down the street. They ran alongside the ditch, the scent of fresh sage and ditch water in the air, sunflowers blooming along the banks like children. Joey screamed with joy when the kite got so high in the sky that some kids down the street pointed at it, their mouths open and their hands covering their eyes from the sun. Then it made a quick nosedive and got caught in the branches of a eucalyptus tree. The boy watched his father climb up, his strong arms pulling him from branch to branch, and then William said, "Look out below," and dropped the kite, which flopped to the ground like deadweight. The other Molinas were gone that day, Billy playing with friends, Vero and Rachel doing shopping, so it was just the boy and his father. William jumped from the tree and then looked sadly at the kite. He patted Joey's head. As they picked up the broken pieces, they laughed, and the father said, "Let's go to Kmart, boy. Get you a kite." They drove there in his pickup, bouncing along happy as puppies, and Joey followed him into the crowded store and picked out a plastic kite with crossbones and a skull. After he put it together, the father proudly held it up, his head side by side with the skull.

Now the overhead garage door was open, and inside the house the family was packing. He was so fragile at six years old, his little round cheeks drooping around thin, sad lips. His eyes so scared. The twelve-year-old Joey packing heads before the move to Oregon lied to six-year-old Joey.

"The future's great, Joey," he said, but he couldn't help but picture Joey "Fat Boy" Molina, twenty-six years old, eating empanadas, the fat face, the big stomach, a tattoo that said "Fat Boy." He pictured the older Joey sitting in the garage watching him, twelve-year-old Joey, talk to the head of six-year-old Joey. There were three Joeys in the garage that day.

Fat Boy laughed at the other Joeys. "You're going to hate life, boy," he said.

Joey sometimes wished that time wouldn't move so slowly, because now he wasn't happy, yet he didn't want the future to come either, because he'd have to go to Oregon.

Everyone in the play relied on him. He hadn't realized before how much time it took to rehearse, to get things so they looked right, and for him to just leave would set them back, all their work wasted. Time was going too fast.

The following week at school was supposed to be his last. He had tried so many ways to get a beating, so many ways to get Rachel to leave his father, but nothing worked. He had asked Sherry for one of her mother's bras, and he hid it in his father's car and tried to get Rachel to find it, but she never went to William's car, and Joey couldn't figure out how to get her there. He tried talking back to his father, but he had been in such a good mood lately that all he did was laugh and pat Joey on the head. As the day to move to Oregon got closer, Rachel only seemed more in love with her husband.

The garage smelled of motor oil and wet laundry, and the sound of the washing machine churning out the very last loads competed with the whirring of the dryer. Joey stared at his six-year-old head. "Joey," he said, as if to get his attention. "Don't worry." He gently touched his cheeks, ran his fingertips across his forehead down the bridge of his nose, outlining his lips. "We'll think of something."

"Joey," said Fat Boy, "worry."

"Don't listen to him," he said. The six-year-old had a crew cut, his ears showing. "You look sad."

"Your whole life is sad," said Fat Boy Molina. "Do you want to know what's going to happen in Oregon?"

"You shut up," he said.

Billy stood under the overhead garage door. "You're a freak, man. Talking to yourself."

"I'm practicing my lines in the play," Joey said.

"What for? We're moving."

"Habit, I guess."

Billy walked into the mouth of the garage to the seven boxes of the father's heads stacked up next to each other. "Our dad's weird."

Joey said nothing because he still felt the presence of the older version of himself, a vision he didn't like, snickering at him in the dark corner of the garage. Joey took one last look at Joey at six, into his wide eyes.

He lifted his head and placed it in a box.

"Hey, I'm going to take off for a while," said Billy. "Just a little while. If Dad asks for me, just say you don't know where I am."

"Well, I won't know where you'll be unless you tell me."

"I'll be back, freak boy," he chuckled.

He ran away.

Older Joey laughed. "Freak boy," he said.

Cousin Norma pulled in front of the house in her mom's beat-up Gremlin, and both Joeys watched her get out, walk up the driveway toward the house, but instead of going to the door, she came to the garage. "Vero's inside," he said.

She wore a halter top and tight jeans. "Hey, Joey! Getting ready to leave us?"

"I guess so," he said.

She had tiny brown eyes and an aquiline nose, which she twitched, as if she smelled something but hadn't yet determined if it was fragrance or stench. Whatever it was, it pulled her closer to the garage.

"I almost forgot she looked so sexy," said older Joey.

"Are you playing in here?" she said, saying "playing" as if she were teasing him. She stepped into the shadow of the overhead door.

"I'm boxing heads," he said.

She looked at the remaining busts on the shelves, even two of her, one when she was a kid and one more recent. She stepped into the garage and walked over to her heads.

She touched the nose of her younger self. "Kind of creepy," she said, turning toward her head at sixteen, sculpted a year earlier. She stared at her head, as if trying to find the answer to a question about herself. Then she shuddered. "Creepy."

"I like that one of you," Joey said.

"I don't know," she said. "Sometimes I wish I were pretty."

"I think you look okay."

"Yeah? Really?"

He continued boxing. "Did you see the one of Vero?" he said. It was still unwrapped on the workbench, a haunting image of her that was very recent, not even a week out of the kiln. Her eyes were open wide, her pupils black holes in the clay. "That one scares me," he said. He knew it was among his father's favorites, and it was the first one of Vero as a *chola,* an urban Chicana, tough-looking, mean.

Norma had her key ring dangling on her finger, and she seemed to unconsciously jiggle the keys, like tiny bells. She looked around the garage.

"Where's Vero?" she said.

"Hey, you want to hear a story?" Joey said. She turned around and looked at him, kind of surprised. "A story?" she said.

"Yeah. You know, a story."

She walked over, sat on a box, opened her legs, and rested her hands on her knees. "Okay, tell me a story."

"It takes place a long time ago," he said. "Back in the days when there were dragons and knights and princesses."

She scooted a little closer. "Oh, I love stories about dragons and handsome knights." She bent over and put her elbows on her knees.

"No ordinary dragons, or ordinary knights. Special ones."

"Special?" she said.

"And a princess, the most beautiful princess." He stood right in front of her. "So beautiful that just to look at her caused pain."

"Pain?" she said, so intrigued by the word that she leaned closer. That's when the flap of her top opened enough, and it was right there in front of him, nipple and all.

"Oh, yes, pain. Because . . ." The rafters in the garage ceiling were dusty and full of cobwebs. "You know, to know that such beauty will never belong to you can be painful."

"Oh," said Norma, "tell me more."

Older Joey in the corner of the garage was making moaning noises and saying, "Oh, yeah."

"What are you doing?" Joey asked his older self. "That's disgusting."

"Let's see them little nipples," Fat Boy said.

"Stop it," Joey said.

"What is your problem?" Norma said.

Suddenly William came out of the house, clearly in a bad mood, dressed in a white tank top undershirt and shorts. Norma said, "Hi, tío," but he said nothing to her.

"Where the hell's your brother?"

"I don't know," Joey said. Then Rachel came out behind his father, and he could see that she was upset with William, so he grabbed the opportunity by taking a head off the shelf. Vero's head. He pretended to be trying to carry it to the box, but he let it drop from his fingers. Vero's head shattered all around his feet. "Oops," he said. "Accidents happen."

The father froze for a moment. He came right at Joey and started hitting. Joey fell to the ground, and Rachel grabbed her husband and told him to stop, but he was so angry that red dots of light seemed to come out of his eyes. He yelled, "You fucking idiot!" and he slapped Joey over and over. He pulled back Joey's arms, which were covering his face, and slapped him again and again.

Rachel yelled, Norma cried, and then Vero came out of the house. "You asshole!" she cried, loud enough so that everything stopped.

"Let's go," she said to Norma. "I'm leaving this place. I hate you."

"Shut the fuck up," he yelled, walking toward her.

"William, don't talk to your daughter like that."

"Bullshit," William said, getting closer.

"Mom, I'm sorry," said Vero in tears. "I can't live with him anymore."

"Go ahead and leave," he said. "Get lost."

"Honey, no, we're a family," Rachel said.

"My God, Mom, look what he did to his own son. I can't take it anymore."

Joey felt like standing up and saying, "No, actually, I'm all right. I did it on purpose, but Mom was supposed to leave Dad, not you."

"You're not my father. Come on, Norma," she said. "I'm going with you."

William stood with his fists and teeth clenched, as angry as the spider tattooed on his chest, and for a second he seemed to feel all those eyes on him and he twitched a little and blinked, but anger rescued him and he yelled, "I ought to beat the shit out of you. But I never did. Never. That's why you turned out the way you did. You think life owes you luxury. You think every day should be a happy picnic in the fucking park. That ain't life, that's TV. You'll see."

"Honey, please," Rachel said to Vero.

"Let her go," he said. "But you remember one thing, Princess Grace. You will never be a part of this family again."

"Oh, big deal," she said.

She looked at her mom. "I'm sorry."

"Tell me, in your stupid mind, what I did that's so bad," William said. "Tell me right now what I did to you that's so goddamn bad that you can't live with me. Huh?"

"It's just you," she said. "You. *You.* That's what's so bad. I can't stand you. I can't be in the same room with you. The sound of your voice makes me sick."

"Get the fuck out of here!" he said.

"What do you think I'm doing?"

"Don't you ever come to us for nothing."

"Come to you? For what? A dose of asshole?"

He stepped up to her as if he would hit her, but he had never hit her. He was so angry he had to hit something, someone.

He looked at Joey.

The hard part was telling the drama teacher that he had to move. He could tell she was angry, and so were most of the people in the play, including Sherry Garcia, who said to him, "You knew this would happen." The last two days of school he spent alone, because even Ricky hung out with the rest of the actors during recess and lunch, calling Joey names to the others and saying how a real actor would never betray his fellow cast members. Joey walked into the field by himself to the backstop that used to be their time machine. He sat against it and closed his eyes and brought himself to the past, how he would have quit the play when he had had a chance, so someone else could have done the part and he would still have friends. But when he opened his eyes again, the future was there. Droopy and Rachel and Billy were in one car, and he was with his father in the moving van. In the rearview mirror he saw the past, the downtown Fresno skyline. Then fields and farms, then the Sacramento skyline. They bounced in their seats, and William talked of how great it was going to be in Oregon. "You'll like it," he said.

"I'm going to miss my friends," Joey said.

"Kid like you," he said, "will have no trouble making friends."

"What do you mean, a kid like me?"

"Smart. Good-looking. Just like your old man."

Joey laughed, and William hit him on the shoulder with an open palm. "You'll be okay."

By the time they reached the mountains, the truck puttering up the curving hills, it was dark, and all they could see was what was in the headlights, a length of road and the black trunks of the tall trees. The road signs flashed yellow in their eyes, Deer Crossing, Falling Rocks.

"There's deer out here!" Joey exclaimed.

His dad looked at him, smiled, and slowly shook his head. "That excites you?"

"I've never seen one before," he said.

"Deers are some of the stupidest animals there are."

"Deers? You mean *deer?"*

"I mean deers are stupid, as stupid as cows. Sometimes they run out in the middle of the road and stand there. Their eyes just stare at the oncoming car, but they don't move."

Joey sat up straight in the seat to get a better look through the windshield, and he said, "Cows aren't stupid."

"I'm talking about deers, and yes, cows are stupid."

Not his cow, not Herman, she would be smart, he thought. He'd train her to fetch the morning paper and to scratch at the door when she wanted in.

The tattoo on the father's arm glared green in the lights from the dashboard as he tapped a tune on the steering wheel. It was an image of an evil angel riding a lightning bolt over a full red moon.

"Cows are even dumber than deers," he said. "But you know what's even dumber? Sheep. They're the dumbest. Can't even count to ten."

"No animal can count to ten," Joey said, as if informing his fa-

133

ther, who quit tapping his tune and looked at his son. "No shit, Sam Spade. It was a joke."

"What about dogs? Are they smart?"

"Not your dog. Stupidest dog in the world. You call him, he just looks at you."

"No one ever trained him," he said.

"Too late now. Once you become a dummy, there's no turning back. You, for example: You'll be a dummy the rest of your life."

"He's a good dog though."

"Sometimes I feel like taking a shovel and beating him to death."

"That's mean."

"You can get a new dog. Start all over again. Train him right this time."

"Dad?" he said.

He looked at his son. "What is it . . . ?"

"Dad!"

"What?"

"Stop!" but it was too late, the truck smashed into it, and the impact slammed Joey against the seat. He held his arms straight out so as not to slam his head against the windshield.

"What the hell," William said when the truck bounced over the body.

"You ran him over," he said. "Stop."

"Who?" he said as he pulled the truck to the side of the highway. "Who was he?"

They got out, but it was moonless black and they could see nothing behind the truck other than the black outline of trees that lined the highway. William said over and over, "What would someone be doing out here?" Then from the rise of the road came headlights, which lit up the road. In the glare, William could see a body lay on the asphalt. "It's a deer," he said, relieved to know it. "A fucking deer."

The car slowed down, then pulled over, leaving the lights on. The doors opened and Billy and Rachel ran out.

Hands over her mouth, Rachel stepped into the glare of the headlights where the deer lay. "Oh, my God."

"It's a deer," William said, walking closer to the body.

Except for Joey, they all stood around the deer. Their shadows stretched by headlights were taller than the pine trees on the side of the road.

"Oh, my God," said Rachel, looking at the deer as if it had been a loved one.

"What are we going to do?" Billy said.

"What do you mean?" William asked.

"You can't just leave her here, William," Rachel said.

"What am I supposed to do, take it to a hospital?"

"Let's take him to a vet," Billy said, leaning closer, his shadow stretching across the road.

"Who's going to pay for it?" he said. "The deer's insurance?"

"We have to do something," said Rachel. "Poor thing."

"That's a lot of blood," Billy said.

"There's nothing we can do," William said. "Come on, let's go." He wasn't looking at the deer but at the road ahead, as if trying to figure out where they needed to go. "We still got a long way," he said.

"We can't leave her in the middle of the road," Rachel said.

"This stuff happens all the time," he said. "It's a normal occurrence out here. The highway patrol'll come by and move it off the road. They might even take home some of the meat."

"Deer meat?" said Billy. "That's gross."

"It's a delicacy," said the father. "Gourmet restaurants serve deer meat all the time. Why do you think so many people hunt for deers? It's the meat. If we had everything arranged at the new house, we might even take some ourselves. We could make deer burgers," he said.

"Really?" said Billy.

"With fries and a milkshake," he said. "Come on, let's go." He started walking back to the truck.

Droopy was in the backseat of the Maverick, barking and slobbering on the windows, because he wanted out. That's when Joey walked closer to the deer. The deer's big black eyes were blinking, as if he were giving up his spirit, and his furry head was soaked with blood. Joey started crying so loud that his moans seemed to echo down the road and into the blackness. His mom came up to him and put a hand on his shoulder and said, "It's okay," but it wasn't okay. He bawled like a baby. She squeezed his shoulder, as if she might have wanted to hug him but didn't know how.

"It's okay, Joey."

Those black eyes against the pavement suddenly looked up, right at him. They were soft, as if he forgave him, but when Billy started crying too, that set Joey off more because he couldn't stand the weight of seeing his older brother cry. Billy said, "He's in pain. He's in pain," and the father threw his hands up in the air and said, "Damn it, shit. What is wrong with this family? It's fucking roadkill."

"We got to help him," Joey cried.

"Help it do what?" the father said. "It's dead."

"No, he's not," Joey said. "His eyes are blinking."

"It'll be dead," he said.

"She's suffering, the poor thing," Rachel said.

"You guys aren't kids," he said. "You're not babies. Take my word for it, this isn't normal, the way you guys are acting."

"William, I would have done anything to avoid hitting the poor thing. You act like you don't even care."

"Let's get him to a vet," Billy said.

"Get in the car, now," William said. "Joey, get your ass in the truck."

But Joey collapsed onto his knees and got closer to the deer, who looked at him. He gently put his hand on his head. Then Rachel and Billy kneeled around him too.

"It's okay, beautiful," she said to it. Then she said, angrily, "She's still alive, William."

"Let's find a vet," said Billy.

"Okay, here's what we'll do," she said. "I'll drive up the highway until we find a phone. They should have a phone book. Okay." She stood up. "I'm going to call a vet. I don't care how much it costs. Joey, you come with me. Billy, you take care of her while we're gone. Joey and I will get some help." Joey listened to his mother's voice, but in the background he heard the faint squeal of a metal door sliding open, and in the blur of his peripheral vision, he saw the father take a shovel from the back of the moving van.

What they saw first was his shadow.

Poured over them like a dark spirit.

They saw the shovel dull in the headlights. William grasped the handle, his face puckered as he raised it over his head. They scattered out of the way as he pulled back to get more momentum. "No," Joey screamed. Droopy barked from the backseat of the car. They all cried out against the father, but his cheeks were puffed up and his eyes squinted with effort. Suddenly, blue and red lights flashed across his chest and face. The siren whooped and the police radio crackled. The father froze in the cop's searchlight, his eyes lit up like a deer's.

* * *

Joey rode with Rachel the rest of the way. They stopped at a motel in Mount Shasta, and the entire family shared a room with two big beds, Joey and Billy in one and the parents in the other. Joey liked sleeping in the dark and hearing the syncopated waves of everyone's breath. The next morning he rode with Rachel again. When they got near a town, she looked for radio stations but found only country and western. "No Mexican stations out here," she said, but she found a rock station and they sang aloud together, until that station cracked into static.

After an extended silence, she said, "I promise you your father will never hit you like that again. Like that day in the garage. I can promise you that."

"What did you do to him?" Joey asked, hoping for a detailed story where his mom was the hero and his dad the villain humiliated at the end, maybe a scene heavy with poetic justice, where the dad, holding his bloody belly, falls to his knees, and then to the floor, and suffers—blood coming out of his mouth—an elongated painful death. But all Rachel told him was that before she agreed to go to Oregon without Vero, she had made sure that William understood what he had done to Joey. That was why he apologized to him and was nice to him ever since.

"Just don't be afraid of him, because it'll never happen again."

Maybe Joey's fantasy was a bit too violent, he thought, and he began to feel a little guilty about having created it.

"Why don't you ever leave Dad? I mean, you say you will all the time."

"Don't worry about that," she said. "This family has got potential. You kids are dripping with potential."

"Do you think Vero will join us?"

"God, she better not," said Rachel.

"You don't want her around anymore?"

She looked at Joey, confused at his comment. "Joey, she's free from your father. Free. She's mature enough and responsible enough to be better off without him. Your sister is a very sane woman. She'll do what's best for herself. Besides, I can't imagine Vero being so *bien Chicana* in a town like Medford. She'd run away."

"Why? What's wrong with Medford?"

"Nothing's wrong with it, per se, it's just that she wouldn't like it."

"Why?"

"It's kind of . . . Oh, I don't know the word for it. Culturally isolated."

"What does that mean?" Joey asked, getting worried. "Where are you guys taking us?"

"To your future," she said.

He looked nervously through the windshield, as if any moment the Valley of Hell might appear over the rolling mountains. "You didn't say anything about a future."

Medford could be seen from the freeway, surrounded by bald hills with tree stumps sticking out of them like roots on a shaved head. The logging factories shot smoke into the air, and because the town was surrounded by these hills, the smoke couldn't rise over them. The yellow air was thick.

They got off the freeway and drove into town, through downtown, storefront windows, people walking up and down, kids riding bikes. Joey told Rachel that it looked small, and Rachel said that even though it was smaller than Fresno, there'd be plenty to do. They turned onto a narrow street that looked run-down: cars parked on lawns, fences leaning over. Most of the houses had trees in front of them, some of them of the same variety, and Rachel said that they were apple trees. "They're everywhere in this town," she said. "We'll have free apples for the rest of our lives."

"Are we going to be here the rest of our lives?" Joey asked.

In front of some houses, beer cans were piled around the lawns, and at the edge of the street, a factory hissed yellow smoke. That was where William would be working, she told Joey. They pulled onto a court, with seven houses in the circle, a dead end.

The house at the end was their rental, blue and small, but cute, with a flower garden around it, two apple trees on either side of the door, and a window on top of the house that made it look like it was a two-story, which excited Joey until his mom told him it was the attic.

Some kids hanging out in the yard next door watched them jump out of the car. The girl was Joey's age, and she sat on the top step of her porch, while two boys about seven years old sat around her like dogs. She looked a little unkempt, her face smeared with dirt and her pants soiled as if she had been sliding into bases. Her hair was uncombed, and she was barefoot. She was watching Joey, saying stuff to the other kids, which made them look more closely at him. Her wild hair hid most of her face, but Joey could tell she was kind of pretty, her nose upturned and her eyes bright blue. William and Billy pulled up in the moving van and got out of the car, and they all went inside with their hands empty, just to get a look at the new house. He watched the girl, and she watched him walk up the walkway and the steps to the house. Maybe Oregon wouldn't be so bad.

Inside it was cold, and the emptiness made their voices echo off the walls. The carpet was a purplish shag, the color of vomit, Joey thought. The place smelled of oil and dust. "This is it?" Joey said. Out the curtainless window, he saw the two boys getting all excited, making faces and walking funny to make the girl laugh. "Oh, Ronny!" she said, laughing. She pulled her hair back and exposed her face as she looked in the window at Joey.

She was cute.

William showed them around the house, which bedrooms would be theirs, showed them the tiny backyard with the tall grass and skinny trees, the attached garage where he would set up his studio. "Let's start unloading," he said.

The kids watched Joey as he unloaded, and he had this sense they would be his first Medford friends. He didn't look back, just carried boxes and things heavier than he was used to carrying, because he didn't want to look weak; and although Billy must have looked much more impressive than Joey looked, with his muscles and tight T-shirt, carrying two boxes at a time, one stacked on the other, they looked at Joey. She looked at Joey. Finally, standing in the middle of the lawn, he looked right at them. They giggled, and one boy said to him, "Speekee Eengleesh?"

"Huh?" he said, not registering what he had meant.

"No, I don't think he does," said the girl. "Try telling him *Hola.*"

"*Hola.* No speekee Eengleesh?" the little boy repeated. They all laughed.

"Only speekee Mexican?" said the boy.

"Ah, the natives possess language!" Joey said.

"What?" the girl said.

"Not as primitive as I imagined," he said, carrying another box into the house.

Although school was in session, William said the boys could stay out for a couple of weeks to help around the house, so after their chores were completed for the day, usually before noon, they went exploring Medford. They walked all day, and sometimes, if Rachel slipped them a little change, they bought ice cream and doughnuts on Main Street. They felt like explorers, uncertain of what they would encounter and at times a little afraid that they might walk into a bad neighborhood where gang members would ask them, "*¿De donde son?*" and maybe beat them up for being in their turf, but they soon learned that Medford had no bad neighborhoods and no gangs. What they saw when they walked down a tree-lined street with dogs barking and dirty white kids playing barefooted and half naked was another tree-lined street, or a school or a park. There were rich neighborhoods too, or at least they seemed rich to the boys, houses with two-car garages and big lawns, some of them with two stories and big picture windows in the front. Joey noticed that there were no kids playing in these neighborhoods, and he wondered why only poor kids seemed to play outside. He figured that rich homes had so many fun things inside them, snacks, big-screen TVs, pool tables, pinball machines, so many distractions, that the kids never wanted to go outside.

One afternoon as they were walking past a grove of pear trees, a pickup truck zipped by, and some teenagers yelled, "Go back to Mexico!"

"Did you hear that?" Joey asked.

"No, what did they say?"

"They told us to go back to Mexico."

"No they didn't," Billy said.

At the middle school where Joey would be going, they walked by during lunchtime. All the kids were spread out on the field and the blacktop, playing, their voices fading in and out like sprits. The boys watched from behind a church, through a chain-link fence. The yells and laughter rose and fell. Hanging out together in the far reaches of the field were some Chicanos, two of them, with a black guy and an Asian boy. One of the Chicanos wore a blue bandanna around his head, shining in the sun, almost covering his eyes. He had long hair like Billy, only his was wavy. These brown boys stood out among all the white kids, a contrast Joey had never before seen or noticed.

"See any pretty girls?" Billy asked.

Joey looked around and saw some girls sitting in the grass in a circle, talking and laughing. Suddenly one of them stood up, a redhead, and she started walking toward the school buildings. She had a sexy walk and he could hardly believe she was in junior high. Her red hair was wavy and long, and she wore a green blouse. "That one," he said, pointing to her.

"Yeah," said Billy. "She's really pretty."

"She's fine," he said.

"Maybe you could make her your girlfriend," he said.

"I wish," Joey said.

"Don't wish. *Do.* Besides, didn't you know that girls always go for the new guy in town?"

Because Vero wasn't with them, the boys got their own bedrooms, which Joey didn't like because at night he was lonely and his imagination too active. One night, he went to Billy's bedroom. Billy was sitting on his bed listening to "Sweet Home Alabama" by Lynyrd Skynyrd, and he chewed tobacco, not bothering to hide it from Joey, every now and then spitting in a plastic cup. He sat shirtless but with a sheet wrapped around his shoulders, his hair in a ponytail, and he was drawing a landscape with pine trees and sunset and clouds.

"You're getting good," Joey said.

"Thanks," Billy said. He held it up so Joey could get a better look. "In the background I'm going to put Mount Shasta."

Through the open window, they could hear the moaning of the lumber factory.

"I miss Fresno," Billy said. "But this could be good. Being in a new place and all. We'll make friends."

"What if nobody likes me?" Joey said.

"You'll make friends."

They were silent. Then Billy started humming a song that Joey vaguely recognized. "What song is that?" he asked.

Billy sang.

"I'm the new boy in town.
Won't you be my friend."

And Joey joined in.

"New boy. New boy.
Look at the new boy."

Billy stopped, and then Joey stopped, and Billy said, "No, keep going," as he reached over and turned off the radio.

"Why?" Joey asked.

"You sing it better than I do."

Joey sang.

"New boy. New boy.
It's hard to be the new boy."

Suddenly Rachel's piano sang out, the notes resonating. She was playing a song he didn't know, and so passionately that he could imagine her fingers blurring they went so fast. He pictured a sad woman in white standing on a cliff at night, about ready to jump, the ocean roaring below, waves crashing against rocks. Then suddenly it crescendoed, and it was so beautiful that he felt chills all over his body and a tear came to his eye. He lay on the floor, his head pillowed on some of Billy's clothes.

Billy hummed and drew on his pad, slow and intense.

"Moonlight Sonata" started, but when she messed up at the same spot, she pounded the keys and started again. Peace, frustration, peace, frustration. And in that way he fell asleep on the floor of Billy's room.

Rachel played more often and with more intensity in Medford now that she found herself staying home all day. William didn't want her to find a job right away, but with everything adjusted and the house settled, she had nothing to do during the day but be a housewife, a role she didn't play well. In the mornings she made flour tortillas, because she couldn't find them at the grocery store and they were used to having them with every meal. She had to call her mother on the phone to find out how to make them, and at first they were misshapen and fat and too salty or raw in the middle, but eventually they became rounder and more consistently tasty. Almost as fast as she pulled them off the *comal,* the boys would spread the end of the margarine stick right on them and watch it melt into yellow liquid, then they rolled up the tortillas and ate. She cleaned windows and dusted furniture and shelves. She did crossword puzzles and read novels, but mostly, and most vigorously, she played piano. She played pieces she had always wanted to play but never had the time to learn. One day the boys walked down the sidewalk into their court, after spending the day exploring more of Medford, and as they got closer to the house, they could hear the piano. A woman sat on the porch of the house next door, her eyes closed, her body moved by the music, and sitting next to her was her daughter, the girl Joey's age, seemingly bored. The mother looked up as the boys stepped on their lawn. "She plays real pretty," the lady said. "That your mama?"

"Yes, ma'am," Billy said.

"Real pretty," the lady said.

When they entered the living room, the drapes were drawn, and Rachel was hunched over the keyboard, her hair flying all over and a face so focused that they didn't dare say anything to her. When she was done playing, the last notes were suspended in the air like the chimes of a church bell. She stood up and walked around the house with bitter energy, saying over and over, *"Sí, sí. Dios mío! Claro que sí!"* She looked surprised to see them. "Home already?" she said.

One night William came home from the lumber factory with a bunch of red roses for Rachel. She opened the card and read what he had written, "For the most beautiful woman in the world." She laughed and hugged him and said that she loved him. "Yeah? Then maybe you could cook up something special tonight?"

She pushed him away and grabbed the roses, and as she arranged them in a vase and set them in the middle of the table, she said, "Why would I bother cooking something nice? It'll all shit out the same way anyway. You might as well take me to dinner."

They went out for dinner, and as they sat around the table, the boys gobbling their food, Rachel and William were flirting with each other as if they were on a date.

Then he said, "I have a surprise for you."

"Oh, William, another one?"

The boys looked back and forth at their parents. Rachel bit her bottom lip in anticipation.

He handed her an envelope. She opened it and read.

"What is it?" said Joey.

"What is it?" said Billy.

She put her hand over her mouth. "But, William," she said. "We can't."

"Sure we can."

She stared at the card, her eyes lighting up. "It sounds so nice, it really does, but honey, we can't."

"Why can't we?" he said. "They don't give invitations to any dummy," he said. "I was invited by the vice president himself. They like my work."

Joey could picture his dad at work, whistling, joking around. Work seemed to make him a good person.

"But it's black tie. You don't even have a suit. And what would I wear?"

He told her that she could buy a new dress, anything she wanted, and he would rent a tuxedo, and they would have a great time. *"Viejo,"* she said affectionately, slipping the card back into the envelope, "this is nice."

"You're going to be the best-looking wife there," he said.

After the first day of English class a kid came up to Joey, pushed his black-framed glasses up his nose, and said, "Pleased to meet you." He extended his hand for a shake. "You're the new kid," he said.

"I'm Joey," he said, aware and amused that their conversation sounded trite, like an after-school movie about a new kid in town. He liked imagining himself as the star of the movie. Maybe it would be a love story, and that redhead he had seen earlier would be the female lead. So he played the part, even tried to act like a rebel movie star. "What are the kids like here?" he asked as he rubbed his chin.

The boy had curly red hair and freckles, and he dressed like he was five years younger than Joey—high-water pants, a button-down short-sleeved shirt—and he was skinny and tall. He was a small-town stereotype, and Joey pictured him in denim overalls and bare feet, carrying his fishing pole to the lake.

"It's your first day," said the boy, "so I thought you might want to have someone to play with."

Joey noted the word *play*. Where he was from, they would have said, "Let's go mess around." Nobody would have said "Let's go play," unless it was referring to sports. Joey felt so much more mature. He *was* the rebel in this after-school movie special.

The kid said his name was George, and Joey laughed. It had to be George. What else?

During lunchtime they walked around the school, and George pointed out things as if he were a tour guide. He seemed to have no spontaneity, no jokes or sense of irony. He brought Joey through a hallway and told him to be careful, that they were walking through Loogey Lane, and Joey looked up and saw dried spit and *mocos* clinging to the ceiling. He said, "Well, that's a monument this school must be proud of," and George said, quite seriously, "No, it isn't. It's ugly."

"Golly! You're not proud of spit?" Joey asked as if surprised.

"Not at all," he said, "but some boys are like that."

"Oh, are they?" he said. "Well, jeepers!" George was unaware that Joey was making fun of him.

And once, when they were watching some girls playing tetherball, Joey said, "Ain't they grand!" and George seemed to want to tell him that *ain't* wasn't a word.

Then Joey saw her walking onto the field with some of her friends, the redheaded girl. "Who's that?' he said.

"Karla Horton," he said.

"I do believe she's the prettiest girl in school." As he watched her walk, he lost all sense of irony. "She's beautiful."

Suddenly she and her friends looked back at him, and he could hear one of the girls say, "He's cute," and Karla just looked. She had green eyes. Then she turned away.

George said that she had a high school boyfriend and would never go out with someone her own age. "And her dad is rich. He practically owns the town."

He saw the two Chicanos hanging out against the side of a brick building with the black guy and the Asian, and he asked George who they were. George warned him to stay away from them. "Why?" Joey said.

"Because they're bad," he said, meaning *baaad*. "They could kick anyone's butt. That guy," he said, pointing to the one with long hair and the blue bandanna, who was playfully (but probably painfully) punching another guy on the arm, "that's Johnny de la Rosa. He's pretty tough." The other guy he pointed out, a short-haired kid with big ears and glasses, squatting Chicano style against the wall, was a good fighter too, George said, and mean. "Don't even mess with him," he said. "That's Gilbert Sanchez. The black guy is Walter. I'm not sure about the Chinese guy. But I think he knows kung fu."

One day, as they were walking home, Joey invited George to come home with him. As they walked onto the court, they could vaguely hear the piano coming from the little blue house in the middle of the court, and they could see the lady next door sitting on her porch with her hand over her mouth, looking worried. When they got closer, they could hear the piano was eerie, like wails. There didn't seem to be any melody, just cries, sounds, things that are broken. "I hope she's all right," said the lady.

"What the heck is that?" George said.

"That's Mom," Joey said.

They entered the dim living room, which smelled of wax and pine-scented cleaner. Rachel was hunched over the piano, pounding keys like a madwoman, the sounds rising around them like pillars. Everywhere they turned, a new pillar rose in their path so they couldn't move, were trapped. George watched with amazement or fear, and Joey wasn't sure if he should be proud of his mom or embarrassed. Suddenly the pillars were sucked into the ground, and the song she played took form, like music after a mass, something by Bach written for organ. Her fingers moved fast, and her back waved up and down, and George watched with his mouth wide open. Joey decided he was proud of her because the music was so beautiful. Then she stopped. She wiped sweat from her head and was breathing hard. She turned around and looked at them. Her eyes were glossy.

"Well, seems like I have an audience," she said.

"Hi, Mom," Joey said. "This is my new friend from school."

"A new friend?" she said. "How sweet. A *new* friend from your *new* school. What's his name? George?"

They laughed at her joke, and Joey said that George *was* his name, and they laughed more.

"I suppose I should serve cookies and milk," she said. "Maybe he'll stay for dinner." And they laughed.

"Oh, I *do* hope so, Mummy," Joey said, clasping his hands.

George, however, wasn't laughing. He looked worried. "Come on," Joey said, leading him to his bedroom. He followed, but as he walked, he looked back at Rachel, and when they reached the room, he said, "How did she know my name?"

"She was joking," he said, "making fun of a trite situation."

"What does *trite* mean?" George asked. But then he looked around the room, as if he could read Joey by what he had inside it. Above the unmade bed hung a poster of Jimi Hendrix, his hair floating around as if he were underwater. After their house in Fresno had been emptied and swept, Joey had gone into Vero's room, which was still full of all her stuff. She had told Joey that he could have the Jimi Hendrix, so he untacked it from the cold wall, the room smelling like cinnamon incense, and he rolled it up.

George looked around Joey's room, at clothes strewn about, and on a chest of drawers was an old pair of Rock 'em Sock 'em Robots.

Joey had kept them because they were from so long ago, and it made him laugh to see little Joey excitedly playing with them. Tied around the neck of the red robot was a bow tie that he had found in the field near their house in Fresno. Stacked next to the toy were some second-hand books that he had bought at the Salvation Army. He had read all of them, Best Play collections from 1965 and 1971, *The Plays of Eugene O'Neill*, a collection of Arthur Miller plays, and a hardback copy of Antonin Artaud's *Theater and Its Double*, which he had tried to read but couldn't understand.

George sat on the bed.

The piano began again. It sounded like carnival music, only darker, slower. Joey felt a pleasant buzz under his skin.

"What about the milk and cookies?" George asked.

"That was a joke, too," Joey said.

"I don't get it," George said.

The music changed. On one hand the tune was fast and high-pitched, like the voice of a demon, while the other hand played the low part of the keyboard, bassy, slow, as if the two sides of the piano were having a conversation.

"I have to go," George said.

On the way out, George looked at Rachel, still hunched over the piano, and he wouldn't take his eyes off her until he reached the door and ran off.

Joey went up behind her, put his hand on her shoulder, and squeezed, felt her soft flesh, her hard shoulder bones, and then he moved his fingers in tiny circles as if massaging her. She stiffened up with tension at his touch. She said, "What is it?"

"Remember that hug you said you'd give me? I want it now."

She didn't turn around. "What hug?" She hit a couple of keys, and it sounded like a voice shrilly asking, *What hug?*

"Don't you remember?" he said.

"Oh, Joey, you're such a card," she said, and then she hit the piano, which said, *Oh, Joey, you're such a card.*

"Play 'Moonlight Sonata,'" he said.

"I'll mess up," she said.

"So, play it, please."

"I haven't got it yet. I don't know why. It's not the hardest piece to play. But I just mess up."

"I know, but play it. When you mess up, that's my favorite part."

One day Mr. Williams told the class that they were going to read *The Odd Couple,* a comedy by Neil Simon, aloud. He asked for volunteers to read the parts, and although Joey wanted to read one, he kept silent, because he wasn't sure he could act. Maybe what had happened in Fresno was beginner's luck. Besides, he didn't want to take away from that rebel tough-guy image he was sure people started to see in him since he was from California, which for them conjured images of L.A. and San Francisco. By virtue of that alone he was more sophisticated than these small-town Oregonians. Perhaps six hours to the north, in Portland, he'd be no big deal, but here at the frontier of the Pacific Northwest, he was something new. So as Mr. Williams distributed the parts and as they ran thin, he felt himself emptying out. "Okay, let's start reading."

So they began to read, and Joey read along in his head, and he could hear the voices of the characters. He knew how he would read the lines if he were doing it. The kids read slowly, as if the words were individually stamped on separate pages, sans emotion or voice inflection, except for one kid. Randy Abbot. He read the part of Oscar and was clearly having fun with the role, but he was more amused with himself than the character. Clearly he thought he was doing a good job, but he was overacting, doing slapstick comedy, trying to make the kids in the class laugh. He was irritating Joey.

At one point Mr. Williams, himself irritated by the kid, said to him, "Randy, would you like to rest for a while?"

Randy said, "No, this is fun." When the bell rang and the kids headed for the door, George fell in behind Joey.

Joey had never noticed how many Mexicans there were in Fresno until he moved to Oregon. In Fresno, he never noticed because it was so normal walking into a Mexican store, speaking Spanish on the playground, driving through neighborhoods where none of the billboards were in English, but Oregon was so white that he couldn't help but notice. Billy claimed not to notice anything different, shook his head when Joey mentioned it to him.

He said it to his dad, who said, "We're in Gringolandia." He told his mom, and she said that it might be good in the long run, because that way they really get to know the life of America and would be less confused about who they were. "But I'm not confused," he said. "I know who I am."

She was sitting in front of a mirror, putting her hair in curlers. She had been trying new hairstyles, getting ready for their big night out, an underlying happiness and feeling of hope coming out in the way she hummed a tune. But still, there was something complicated about her happiness that couldn't be expressed by her body or face, but only by the glare in her eyes, something private, only slightly recognizable, as if deep into her eyes she lived a life completely outside of her actions, the lifting of a curler to her blond hair, the twitching of her nose, the smile at Joey in the mirror as they talked about Medford. Joey could see himself in the mirror, too, in one corner, small-sized, across the dim room, and his mother sitting right before the glass, life-sized, under the lights, her eyes like crystal.

"Okay, then," she said. "Who are you?"

"I'm Joey Molina," he said.

She laughed and looked at him lovingly. "And who is Joey Molina?" she said.

His own answer surprised him. "An actor."

"Well, that's not really what I mean," she said. "Are you an American or a Mexican?"

"Both," he said.

"It's hard to explain," she said. "But some people get confused about their identity. Especially if they sense racism."

"Racism?"

"But you're too handsome," she said. "Who could hate you?"

The kids at school weren't racist, as far as he could tell. They treated him like the new kid, not the new Mexican kid. One day George handed him a note on the playground and said it was from a girl, to whom he pointed, playing tetherball, a skinny blond girl.

The note read, "I like you. Do you like me?" and there were yes and no boxes for him to check. The first two weeks of school he received four such notes, and this popularity surprised him.

He didn't feel a sense of otherness, that being a Chicano was a burden, but still, he noticed the demographic differences.

One cold morning he couldn't find any clean shirts, so Rachel told him to wear one of his dad's flannel shirts, and because it was cold that day, he buttoned it all the way to the top. People at school looked at him differently and looked away quickly when he looked back. He didn't understand why. What had changed? Then George saw him, and his eyes—magnified by the thick glasses—went wide as he looked Joey up and down. "Wow," he said.

"What?" Joey said.

"You look like a Mexican," he said.

"I am a Mexican," Joey said.

"I thought you were Italian."

Joey went into the boy's room and looked in the mirror. The flannel, buttoned up to the neck, did make him look like a Chicano, kind of tough, like a *cholo*. He posed, put a hand in his pants pocket, and extended the other. *"Orale,"* he said.

Later that day he was standing in the hall with George, going through his locker, when George tapped him on the shoulder and said, "Don't look now."

Three of them were walking toward him with a cool stride, the two Chicanos and the black guy. They were led by the Chicano with long hair and bandanna. He looked older than the rest of them, with a goatee and teenager mustache, but they all walked inner-city cool. The other Chicano looked a little geeky, metal-framed glasses and short hair, but his pants were baggy and he wore a crisp white T-shirt. He was muscular, his chest pumped up, and his arms were defined, his biceps huge. The closer he got, the less of a geek he seemed. That one stared at Joey hard, scrutinized him. That was Gilbert Sanchez.

They stopped in front of Joey, and other kids scattered but looked back, wondering if there was going to be a fight.

The leader in the blue bandanna, Johnny de la Rosa, nodded his head coolly. *"¿De dónde eres?"* he said.

"Soy de Fresno," Joey said.

"Orale, Califas," said Johnny as he extended his hand for the Chicano shake, which Joey knew, gave, and something took hold of him. He was playing the part of a *cholo*. He suddenly felt like he had been a *cholo* all his life, like he was tough, someone not to mess with, one of the kids who hangs out in downtown Fresno.

"Hi, Gilbert, how's it going?" said George. He waved.

"Go get me a soda," Joey said. "I'm thirsty."

"Excuse me?" George said.

"You heard me. A cola. And hurry up about it."

George scratched his nose. "Uh, okay. Uh, I guess I'll go." He started, but then he turned around. "Is that all you want, Joey, just a Coke?"

"Yeah, yeah," he said. They watched George hurry off. "Why do you think I keep the little *gabacho* around?" Joey said.

"We thought maybe he was your friend," said Gilbert.

Joey took Gilbert's hand for the shake and could feel his strength. With little effort, he could squeeze Joey's hand and break his bones, and Joey was about to lose his coolness, but he remembered the role he was playing.

The black guy had a comb sticking out of his Afro, and he wore dark sunglasses. He was cool. "This is Walter," said Johnny.

"I'm from Oakland," said Walter, as if proud.

"*Q-vo,*" Joey said.

"Fresno's a pretty cool place, man," said Johnny. "Lots of gangs there."

"Oh, yeah, we're pretty tough over there."

"Why did you come here?" he asked.

"My dad's work. But I tell you, man, I miss Fresno. So many white people here."

They laughed.

"And I miss my gang," he said, just meaning his friends, Sherry and cast of the play, but it occurred to him that they would think that he had meant that he was in a gang. He remembered what he looked like in his dad's flannel. He could act any part he wanted to act, especially in a new town, a new state. He could re-create himself.

"You were in a gang?" asked Walter.

"Oh, yeah," Joey said. "Everyone is over there, man. It's not like this place."

They nodded agreement.

"Man, over there, you're stupid if you don't carry a knife."

"Oakland's like that too," said Walter.

"Shit, how would you know?" said Gilbert. "You haven't lived there since you were five."

"What was the name of your gang?" Gilbert asked, like he was skeptical.

"Uh, Los Aztecs."

"Hey, that's cool," Johnny said.

"Los Funky Aztecs," Joey said.

"Yeah!" Johnny said.

"My cousin Pelón lives in Fresno," said Gilbert. "I never heard of that gang."

"It's pretty new," Joey said. "We had to start our own because the other ones were just a bunch of *maricones.*"

"That's cool," said Johnny.

"What's that mean?" Walter said, and he tried to say the word.

"Sissies," Joey said.

"Really?" he said, as if excited to learn it. "I'm going to remember that word."

"We were thinking about starting a gang here," said Johnny. "But there's only a few of us."

"That's all it takes, *ese,*" Joey said. "We started off with two Funky Aztecs, man, but by the time I left there were about eighty of us."

"You should join us, man," said Walter.

"Although there ain't too many of us in this whole town," Johnny said.

"Yeah, yeah," Joey said. "This is Gringolandia."

They laughed. When George brought back his soda, Joey patted him on the back and said, "You're a good kid for a *gabacho,*" and they laughed again. He opened the can and took a swig. "Damn, this shit tastes good," he said. He looked at George. "I like your *cola.*"

He had said the last word with a Mexican accent, because he thought it would sound cool, not realizing that it had changed the meaning.

"You like his *cola?*" asked Gilbert.

Then it occurred to him that *cola* was "butt." They started looking disgusted with him.

"The *other* gangs were *maricones?*" said Gilbert. "Are you sure it was the other gangs?"

They laughed at him.

"Well, I mean . . ."

"Maybe we should leave these two alone," said Gilbert.

"Shit, man, you guys don't know fucking shit," Joey said, even though he didn't know what he would say next.

"What don't we know?" said Johnny.

Gilbert stepped in closer.

"In Fresno, man, in *Califas,* when you say you like someone's *cola,* man, it means that they better not mess with you, uh, because you want to kick their ass. You want their *cola.* To kick it."

"Oh, I get it," said Walter.

"Yeah, all the *vatos* in Fresno say it," he said.

"That's cool," said Johnny.

"Man," he said, shaking his head in pity. "You guys have been in Gringolandia for way too long. You don't know shit. You better take some Chicano lessons, man."

"Maybe you can help us," Walter said. "We're thinking about starting a gang."

"We don't need no help," Gilbert said.

"Yeah, man, maybe you could give us pointers and shit. It's been a long time," Johnny said, and he offered Joey his hand for the Chicano shake.

She had bought a new dress, had her hair done, and all day long hummed to the Mexican records she played on the turntable, and she had rented a black tuxedo for William. She looked so beautiful and he so handsome that the boys followed them to the car and opened the doors for them and felt proud when the neighbors peered from their windows. The boys stood on the curb and waved as their parents drove away. They spent the evening impatiently watching TV, waiting like excited parents for their teenagers to come home from the prom so they could ask them for details, how was the place decorated, did you dance, did people watch you walk in? Joey pictured Rachel and William entering the hall, walking across the floor like a royal couple as all the people watched, the husbands with their mouths hanging open to see Rachel's beauty, the way the light blue dress swerved with her curves, the way the light seemed to caress her cheek and neck, the way the souls of her ancestors shined in her eyes.

"Who are they?" people would ask each other, and someone would say, "The Molinas."

"The Molinas? You mean the new Mexicans in town?"

Before midnight, they heard the car pull up.

A door slammed.

Rachel came in by herself. They could hear the car skid off into the night. Without looking at the boys, who were sitting on the couch in the blue glare of *Movies Till Dawn,* she walked to her bedroom and said, "Your father deserves to have his balls cut off."

The next day William still wasn't home, and she still said nothing other than an occasional "He's not a good man." The boys talked about what might have happened that night. All they knew was that their father had been drunk, very drunk, because when he came home Sunday afternoon, he brought with him two cans of soup (the Medford stores having no *menudo)* and a bag of Fritos, and all morning he drank beer with tomato juice, and he was extra nice to the boys. Joey asked him for five dollars, and his father looked at him and said, "Shit, boy," but he gave it to him.

Rachel talked a lot on the phone with Vero that weekend, but whenever one of the boys entered the room, she changed the subject to the weather in Fresno compared to Oregon, or she put her hand over the phone and said, "Honey, I'm on the phone now," and waited for the boys to leave.

The third day of reading the play, Randy Abbot still wanted to read the part of Oscar, but no one volunteered to read for Felix. "Come on! Who'll do it?" And like a good teacher, Mr. Williams could see in Joey's eyes that he wanted to do it but wouldn't volunteer.

"Joey, will you read it?"

Inside he was excited, although he tried not to appear that way. He sighed. "Oh, all right," he said, as if reluctant. It may not have been that he identified so strongly with Felix, who was neat, a bit prissy, but he understood him. When he read, the lines seemed to disappear, and he spoke in Felix's voice. The funny lines got laughs from the kids, not because of the way Joey delivered them, but because they were good lines. Randy Abbot, however, seeing that ·Joey was getting laughs, thought that by exaggerating his voice and gestures, more kids would laugh for him, but it had the opposite effect. Randy was a big kid for his age, thick and tall, and he had wavy brown hair, almost shoulder length, and wire-framed glasses. His most striking feature, however, was his big nose, flat like a boxer's, and seemingly pockmarked, rough. His teeth were crooked, and his brown eyes were as wide as quarters. For some reason, Joey liked him.

In desperation to be funny, Randy Abbot started adding his own comments, like, "That was funny" or "This is hilarious."

Mr. Williams interrupted the reading. He said he wanted to show the class something about acting. "It's an exercise," he said. He asked Randy to leave the room, to which the boy stood up and said, trying to make people laugh, "Oh, no, you're kicking me out! I didn't know she was your daughter!"

"No, no," said Mr. Williams. "We're going to do this acting exercise. See this?" He held up a book with a yellow cover. He said that he was going to hide it somewhere in the classroom, and it was Randy's job to find it, as everyone watched. "Cool," said the boy, and he went outside. The teacher put the book in his desk drawer, and after a moment, he said, "Okay!"

The boy came in.

He held out his arms as if expecting applause from the kids. Then he started. "Hmmmm, where did I leave that book?" He slapped his forehead and said, "Hmmm, I wonder where it could be." He pointed at his head on "wonder." Then he walked across the room with exaggerated steps, as if making fun of a cat burglar walking through a dark house at night. "Where could it be?" He put his hands on his cheeks and opened his mouth in a circle. "I really really must find it!"

"Thank you," Mr. Williams said, but the boy didn't want to quit. "But my oh my! I must find that book of mine!"

Mr. Williams pulled it out of his desk.

"Oh, yes! Yes! Yes! There it is!" Randy held it up and pretended to be happy, and just in case his facial expression didn't get the point across, he said. "I'm so so happy. The end."

"Joey, outside," said Mr. Williams.

Joey stood up and went outside, and when Mr. Williams called him in, he looked for the book. It wasn't in his desk, so he looked on the bookshelves. He found it under the desk of one of the students. He walked to Mr. Williams and gave it to him.

"Class," he said. "That's acting."

"I would have found it," said Randy. "You didn't give me enough time."

"That's not what I mean. Acting is believing what you're doing is real, to be into your character so much that you become that person. It's not trying to be funny or trying to be dramatic. A real actor doesn't fake emotion. He evokes it."

After class Mr. Williams stopped Joey before he left. "You're good at this, Joey. Have you ever thought of trying out for the school play?"

Joey told him about the king he was going to play at his old school and how he liked acting and hoped someday to do it again.

"Well, you've come to the right place."

"What do you mean?"

"You don't know?" he said. "You really don't know where you are?"

"Where am I?"

"Joey," he said. "You're practically in Ashland."

"Yeah. So?"

"Joey, people come from all over for our Shakespeare Festival. On the West Coast, after L.A., there's no better place for theater people than Ashland, Oregon."

Outside the gang waited for him, including the Asian guy. Johnny said, "We got to talk with you, Joey." When he got closer, Joey could see that something was wrong with Walter. He had a black eye and he looked beaten up, and even though Joey didn't know him that well, seeing his hair messed up and his face bruised, he felt as if he were a cousin, and he felt sad and angry. "What happened?" he said.

"Some white boys jumped him," said Gilbert.

"They called me nigger, so I flipped them off."

"This is it," said Johnny. "It's time. We need to start the gang."

"Last week, I was jumped," said the Asian. "Three guys beat the shit out of me when I was walking home. They called me chink and told me to go back to China. Stupid bastards, I'm Filipino."

"These hillbillies need to know that if they fuck with one of us, they fuck with all of us," said Gilbert.

Walter looked at Joey, swollen eyes, fat lip. "You said you would help us, man."

"We need you in the *clica*," said Johnny.

"Let's get out of here," Joey said. "Make some plans."

George had been waiting for him too, like he always did after class, but now he looked too nervous to approach the people of color. Joey looked in his eyes and shook his head, saying good-bye, but when he walked with the boys out into the field, George followed a few steps behind. "First thing we need is a name," said Joey.

"A name?" Walter asked.

"Yeah, something cool, something that nobody in their right mind would mess with."

"Like what?" asked Walter.

"How about Los Bad Boys?" asked Johnny.

"How about 'no,'" said Joey. "I said something cool, something different, something like the Dark Shadows."

"That's cool," said Kurt.

"Or the Killer Aztecs," Joey said.

"I like that one," said Gilbert.

"How about the Pathetic Losers?"

Joey turned around and saw that beyond George stood Joey "Fat Boy" Molina, twenty-six years old. "How about the Worthless Pieces of Flesh?" He laughed.

"Go away!" said Joey.

"Ooo, you're so tough! I'm so scared," said Fat Boy Joey.

George thought that Joey was looking at him, and now all the boys were looking at George as if he were an intruder.

"What are you guys looking at?" George asked.

"Why don't you get lost?" said Gilbert. "No white boys allowed."

"Yeah, get out of here," said Joey. "Get lost."

"How about the Idiots? How's that for your gang, you loser? The Idiots. The Big Fat Idiots."

"Get out of here!"

"I'll kick your ass if you don't go," said Gilbert.

George walked backward, until he was far enough away, and then he turned around and ran away, running all the way back to the school buildings.

part two

He was an utter failure at gangs, and since the leadership fell to him, the whole gang was a failed experiment. By the time they were in high school, the guys quit throwing the hand signals that he had created and they quit yelling out the secret *grito* he wrote to identify each other on the dark streets at night. He didn't understand what went wrong, because in junior high all the little white kids were afraid of them and thought that they were tough like gangsters in the movies, and they got out of their way when they walked the halls together. Joey called them the Killer Aztecs, KA, which he said could also stand for Kick Ass, but they never got in a fight because most of the members would get their asses kicked by their parents if they got in trouble.

He tried to teach them everything he knew about gangs—mostly from the movies or things he remembered seeing in Fresno. He told them about being jumped in, but he didn't want to get jumped in himself or to beat up someone else for that matter, so he told them that it meant that each member of the gang had to pay the gang treasury five dollars. He said they usually used the money to buy drugs or weapons, but maybe they could go out for pizza instead, and they all agreed that was a good idea. They complained, though, that their dads didn't make as much as Joey's dad, so it wasn't fair they had to pay so much. Joey pointed his finger in their faces and said, "What's a matter with you small-town hicks? Street life is hard! You better do what you have to to get the money—rob or steal if you have to."

The actual collection came up to twelve dollars and seventeen cents, but everyone had pretty good excuses for not bringing the entire amount, so Joey let it slide and bought bags of chips and cookies, and they ate in Johnny de la Rosa's backyard, gobbling up the goodies like starving Mexicans. They liked hanging out in Johnny's backyard because he had a shack back there, since the house was too full with his family, where he and his uncle Clemente slept, and it became like their clubhouse, KA headquarters, a one-room shack with a bathroom and two beds and a couch and Santana posters on the walls. Clemente was older, but he didn't care what the boys were up to and sometimes he gave them beer or taught them fighting techniques. Usually he was at work when the boys gathered and made plans.

One time, as they sat around in the shack, Joey told them that to prove their loyalty to the gang, they needed to kill someone. The boys looked nervous, and Joey said, "Let's go." They walked around town looking for a victim, the sun falling over the treeless hills, the gang members in single file, Joey first, George the white guy, Kurt the Filipino, Walter the brother, and Johnny and Gilbert the Chicanos, all trying to look tough and serious. Joey had a bulldog look on his face, his fists clenched, repeating over and over, "Let's kill someone." They climbed the spiraling cement staircase that led to the pedestrian freeway overpass, walked across, aboveground, like they were walking into heaven, the sun shining orange in the background. Joey took off his T-shirt and wrapped it like a turban around his head, and the other boys did the same, so from the freeway you could see a line of marching boys.

A kid who they thought looked especially killable—a little boy delivering the newspaper—said hello to them as he passed on his bike. Joey turned to Kurt the Filipino kid and said, "All right, you go first."

Kurt said he could never kill no one.

Joey warned him about using double negatives. "It's kill *any* one."

And then he pretended to get angry, because Kurt was a coward. He held Kurt by the collar and yelled, "Do you want to be with us or not?"

Kurt nodded.

Joey pointed down the street, to the kid throwing the newspaper across a vast front lawn, and he said, "Take him out."

Kurt started crying, and Joey pretended to be disappointed, and he threw up his arms and said, "All right, damn it! We won't kill someone, not this time, but let's go egg a teacher's house."

But this innocent fantasy of living *la vida loca* was when they were twelve, thirteen, at a space in time when the image of being in a street gang had more meaning for them than the experience, more than the *real* "crazy life," the rivalry of colors, the young brown fingers twisting into deformed hand signs. Joey, the gang leader, wrote their script, directed the movie in which the others were unaware they were performing. Despite the gritty drama he had intended for them, the narrative often played like a farce, but because he had convinced them that they were tough and mean—not so hard for boys of color in Medford—none of them could see their lack of verisimilitude. It wasn't just the boys who believed themselves tough, other kids believed, some old people too—and so many extras acting in their movie—who watched the Killer Aztecs walk into Mann's department store as if they owned the place or saw them stride coolly across the blacktop at school, spitting on the asphalt, kids moving out of their way. Most of Medford believed. According to whose reality were they *not* tough California minorities? This question sometimes kept Joey thinking. Had Joey fooled a lot of people, or were the boys really in a gang? But sometimes he didn't think of this at all, he just lived day to day, playing the role: Chicano gang leader. A rebel.

The homeboys in the barrios of Fresno poured bottles of beer into the earth or watched the yellow liquid spread over the concrete in honor of their dead homies, but in Medford, the Killer Aztecs had no dead homies. The town barely knew of death, as if they had buried that immortal theme beneath the action of their lives. The occasional black hearse sliding through the tree-lined streets of town had an ominous feeling, like watching a silent film, and as the shadows of the funeral procession slid past, the townspeople subtly swallowed or looked up into the sky or onto the ground or they scratched a nose, to pause without pausing, to acknowledge death without acknowledging. Joey wanted a reason to use the "spilling beer for the dead homie" ritual.

When Kurt's cat died, Joey was glad. He told the gang they had to spill their 7-Eleven Big Gulps on the ground, out of respect for their homie Kurt, whose cat died. The kids were so impressed by the street gang ritual that Joey tried to introduce it as much as he could. He looked so hard for death that he sometimes saw ghosts standing on the sidewalks or sitting alone at a table in a restaurant, but then he'd shake his head and the table would be empty again. Reality returned.

He continued looking about the town for death, but never found it. Instead, he turned it into an abstraction: "Spill your soda into the earth for the death of cowardice," he told them, and they spilled. "Pour it into the earth for the death of love, like a chant," and they poured, "For the death of ennui." "Of what?" And he explained what it meant and Walter shook his head in approval and said, "That's a cool word."

Walter liked words.

Eventually Gilbert and George got tired of the same story. Impatient for rising action, they took trips to Portland, where there were real gangs, and they came back to Medford with stories more exciting than the ones Joey had created. They told of drive-bys, broken bones, busted jaws, Latin Time Bombs, just a little story about a Glock nine clip. Joey told them that he didn't think the KA boys were ready for that yet, but now that they knew, they better get used to the idea. Death would be involved. That was when he ordered them to kill a kid, but none of the KA boys wanted to do it.

But they all agreed to throw at least one egg at a teacher's house.

Later George, the white boy, said something to Joey, quite seriously, with a gleam in his eye that Joey would never forget. "I would have done it. You should have given me the order. I'd a done it."

"I know you would have," Joey said, patting him on the shoulder.

In high school, the gang was virtually dead, even though the former members were still friends. Some of them were pretty serious about school, especially Kurt, who wanted to be a doctor, and Walter, who wanted to go to college and major in English—and figured the only way to be able to afford to go was to play sports. Johnny de la Rosa had the same girlfriend since the eighth grade. He spent most of his time with her. It was clear that after graduation he would work for a living, get married, have kids. Gilbert and George never got too serious about school, but they liked to fight, they liked the life, even after KA no longer existed.

When Joey was a junior, sixteen years old, something happened that made him want to put KA together again.

William needed some stuff for his hair, which he kept slicked back and combed. He made Joey go to Mann's department store with him because he didn't want to go alone. When they parked the truck in front of the store and got out, Joey saw his old English teacher, Mr. Williams, from junior high. He asked Joey how he was doing. Joey said fine, and he asked Joey if he was still acting, and Joey said no and then introduced his father, who reached out his hand to shake with Mr. Williams. The teacher noticed his LOVE fingers.

"Your son's very talented," Mr. Williams said.

"Thank you," William said, and then he said to Joey, "I'll see you inside," and Joey said, "Sure, Dad."

The teacher and Joey were silent as they watched William go through the glass doors, as if they were waiting for him to be out of sight so they could talk about him, and Joey felt slightly ashamed at what they might say.

"So that's your father," said the teacher.

"That's him," said Joey.

The teacher watched the doors of the store long after the father had gone in, the still, glass doors in the metal frame. He said, sentimentally, and with a rhythm in his voice as if it were the title of a song, "Going downtown with your dad."

Joey suddenly wanted to be with his dad, wanted to walk down the aisles of the store with him. He suddenly liked his father.

Going downtown with your dad.

He found him on the aisle looking at the various brands of hair gook, hair spray, brushes, and combs.

"Hey, Dad."

"Hey, kiddo," William said.

William was dressed in casual white pants and a pullover shirt and a pair of loafers. If it hadn't been for the tattoos on his arms and knuckles, he might have looked like a father on TV dressed that way. William picked up a jar of hair stuff and read the label and said, "I wonder if this is like Tres Flores."

"I doubt it," said Joey.

"What this town needs is a Mexican store," said William.

"Yeah, so both families could shop there," said Joey.

"I bet this is like Tres Flores. Go ask the salesguy," William said, handing Joey the jar, but he didn't take it.

"I'm sure they've never even heard of Tres Flores," said Joey.

"Bullshit, it's famous all over the world."

"You're delusional."

"What did you call me, boy?"

"Delusional. You have a bad case of the inability to deal with reality."

"What did your teacher mean that you're talented? You're as dumb as they come," the dad said. "If you don't want to ask, I'll ask." He started to walk toward two salesboys leaning against a counter, talking socially. Joey recognized one of the kids from school, Perry Doyle, popular, football team, rich family.

"Dad, don't ask them," Joey said.

"Why not?" He stopped, turned around, and looked at Joey.

"They've never heard of Tres Flores."

"No harm in asking."

"Just don't."

"Why?" He smiled and winked at Joey. "Embarrassed to be a Mexican?"

"What? Where the hell did you get that idea from, genius?" Joey said.

"Don't say 'hell.' I'll kick your ass."

"You say it all the time."

"It's too late for me. You can still learn."

"I'm waiting in the car."

"Joey's a Mexican! Joey's a Mexican!"

"Would you stop it, Dad? That has nothing to do with it. I just don't think they ever heard of—"

"Beaner!" he said, pointing at his son. "Hey, let's go ask them where they keep the tortillas and tomatillos. We'll make chile verde and invite your girlfriend. What's her name? Heidi?"

"Amy."

The two salesboys stopped talking and looked toward Joey and William. "Come on, Dad, let's go."

"From now on, I'm going to talk to you in Spanish," William said.

"Yeah, like you could speak it," Joey said.

"*Yo hablo español,*" said William. "*Yo hablo muy bien, como Mexicano.*"

"Don't make me laugh."

"*Soy orgulloso de ser Mexicano,*" said William.

"*Estar,*" Joey corrected. "It's *estar,* not *ser.*"

"*Piensas que tu eres mejor que yo, ese?*" he said, as if he were a hoodlum ready to fight. "Just because you take Spanish classes at school, taught by some *gabacha?*"

"Please, Dad, your Spanish is horrible. Mom's the only one in the family who speaks it decently."

"I could even sing in Spanish," said William, and he started to, but Perry Doyle and the other salesboy appeared behind William.

Perry said, "If you're going to buy that, then buy it. Quit playing around." Then they walked off, as if they expected William would be intimidated by them.

"I ought to kick that little white boy's ass," William said.

Joey thought he understood his father's rage, because he felt it too. He knew that those white boys were so arrogant that they thought they had authority over his dad, only because he was Mexican, dark brown, because he had tattoos and greased-back hair like a 1950s rebel. They weren't used to giving respect to people like him. Joey felt like chasing after them and punching them, throwing them into a shelf of jars and bottles exploding on the floor, holding their heads by the hair and smearing their faces in the goo of mayonnaise and pickles and broken glass.

But it was only a fantasy.

Despite the years of posturing as a tough guy, he still didn't know how to fight, he didn't know how to punch or twist an arm. He had been acting in his comedy for so long, for so many years, so convincingly, that nobody in junior high had wanted to fight him. He had never had to fight. But in high school the gang had lost its reputation, and no one feared him anymore. Perry Doyle had gone to a different junior high, and he had no idea who Joey used to be.

So enraged, embittered, he watched William go back to looking for what he needed on the bright and colorful shelves of America, ignoring the insults, the truth, and he suddenly hated his father. "I'll wait outside," he said.

His father watched him walk away. "Joey?" he called out quietly, concerned.

Now, as Joey waited outside the store while his father continued to buy things, Joey wanted to teach those boys a thing or two, but he was aware that someone like Perry Doyle probably knew how to fight. Joey hated pain. He feared it.

Still, he had to do something.

Across the parking lot he saw Mr. Williams get in his car and wave. Then the teacher slowly drove by, rolled down his window, pointed his finger at him, and said, "Joey?"

"Yeah," he said, hands in pockets, leaning against the wall.

"Act. Please act."

Joey told his friends, the former KA boys, about what Perry Doyle said to his father, exaggerating the detail, saying that Perry said bad things about spics and—he looked at Walter—and niggers—and Kurt—and Flips—and white trailer trash, too, he told George. George, who had been waiting years for the chance to fight, bunched his hands into fists, and his face got redder. "Let's kill those honkies," he said.

"They actually knew I was Filipino?" asked Kurt. "I'm impressed."

"Actually, they said Chinks," Joey said, "but I knew what they meant."

"Those assholes!" Kurt said.

Joey got them excited about the gang again, but only for a while, as everyone started to go back to their own lives, so to encourage them more, he figured they needed a victory, something that would make them proud to be KA. He needed to make them want KA, but he couldn't have planned what happened next.

One day after school, Kurt challenged Joey to one-on-one basketball on the courts, and Joey agreed to play, but he wanted a game of Horse instead. He didn't tell Kurt that he couldn't dribble a ball, that he would rather play charades than basketball, or write skits and perform them than play football. No one knew the real him, the kid always chosen last for sports teams. I'm a wimp, he thought to himself as they walked, Kurt bouncing the orange ball on the blacktop, eager to get to the court, like a Christian joyfully walking to church, on fire to praise God. I'm a loser, Joey thought, watching the ball bounce and slap against Kurt's brown hand.

Before anyone even scored the first letter, they saw Perry Doyle and his friends come up to an adjacent court, and they started shooting baskets and zipping across the asphalt like imps. Joey said in a low voice—but loud enough for them to hear—"White trash!"

Perry held the ball, and they all walked over to Joey and Kurt. They all had scowls on their faces, as if they hated who they saw, and a few of them had their fists clenched. Perry Doyle, leading at the front, looked with his hard blue eyes right at Joey, as he held the ball with both hands like it was a head and he was going to squeeze the brains out of it. They surrounded them, a white wall of boys. Joey thought that maybe he had made a mistake, maybe he shouldn't have said anything. These boys were tall and svelte, except for one fat muscular kid with a neck the width of a tree. The fat kid looked familiar, but Joey wasn't sure why.

But he knew those guys could kill them, that he and little short Kurt would have no one to help them. They could leave them on the sidewalk, bleeding and broken.

Joey looked up at all the red young faces and pretended they were actors in his movie. He pointed his finger right at Perry Doyle and said in a mean and intimidating voice, "Do you know what you're doing?"

"What do you mean?" Perry asked.

Joey put his hands on his hips and looked at all the faces of the boys, and he shook his head, as if he felt sorry for them. "You don't know, do you?"

"What?" Perry asked.

Joey turned to Kurt. "I don't think they know what they're doing."

Kurt was too frightened to say anything.

"I suggest," Joey said, "that you little boys go home now. Before you find out what Chicano Power really means."

The boys were silent as they looked at Joey, as if trying to figure out what to think of him, and then finally the fat boy blurted out, "Fuck you, greaser."

"What did you call me?" Joey yelled, sticking his finger in the fat boy's face. *"What did you fucking say!?"*

"You heard me, beaner," the boy said.

Perry Doyle added, "Yeah, that's right. You heard."

He was losing ground, losing his audience, losing the suspension of their disbelief, so he had to think of something to bring them back into his illusion. He felt the sudden urge to get down on his knees and cry and beg for mercy, but he didn't entertain that thought for very long, deciding instead to do something crazy, a final bluff. The white boys were closing the circle more and more. He could hear their breaths and could see inside their noses and could smell their cologne and sweat, and he knew now that he was going to feel pain like he had never felt before—if he didn't find a way out.

He put a hand in his right pants pocket, and inside he made a fist. "Hey, fat boy," he said to the fat boy. "You know what I got in my pocket?"

All the boys looked at Joey's pants pocket, at the bulge within it.

"Do you stupid fucks want to know what I have in this pocket? You guys just don't get it. I ain't from around here. I'm from the streets, man. This place over here, you guys over here, you're a joke."

The boys looked at each other, and Joey didn't like the expressions on their faces, as if they were not scared by him but amused.

Then one said, "Why don't you go back to California?"

"Go back to Mexico," another said.

"And China," another said to Kurt.

"I'm Filipino," Kurt whispered.

"Are you listening to me?" Joey said. "I'm from the streets, and I don't play your little small-town games, got it?"

"You went to my junior high," said the fat kid. "You ain't shit."

Joey turned to Kurt. "I guess we'll have to teach these boys a lesson." Kurt was petrified. Suddenly a smack exploded on Kurt's face, and he grabbed his red cheek and held the pain. The fat boy withdrew his hand and then looked at Joey. "What did you say?" he said to Joey.

Joey knew he was next, and he started to feel tears come from his eyes, and he was going to squeal, Please help me God, when they heard a whistle. The white boys spread out and turned around, exposing the PE teacher, who said, "You boys break it up now."

The boys looked back at Joey. Kurt held his sore, red cheek and looked at the fat boy with rage and hate in his eyes, and his anger made him look tough. He knew that before Kurt's brother went off to the army, he had taught him to box, and Joey could see that now Kurt was so angry he could surely fight. Joey pointed at the fat boy. "You're lucky, man. Somebody saved your life today."

"You ain't crap," said the boy. "I'll pulverize you and your nigger and greaser friends, all by myself."

Kurt told the gang about what had happened and he kept looking to Joey to add more to the story, but Joey was quiet. He didn't want to have to think about facing that fat boy again. He could just picture

183

his bull neck, his yellow teeth, and then it occurred to him that he, the fat boy, didn't seem to fit in with the rest of the group, who were good-looking, obviously rich boys. The fat boy seemed to come from poor whites, otherwise would his teeth have been so crooked and yellow?

Kurt told the gang that they should arrange to meet those boys after school. "I'm ready to fight," he said, and all the gang agreed, except for Joey, who said, "They're just scared, man. Besides, they wouldn't even show up."

"Joey was cool, man," said Kurt. "You should have seen how he handled those guys."

The gang agreed to challenge the boys in a gang fight, and they sent Johnny de la Rosa to arrange the details. Gilbert and George seemed pleased, as if they had been waiting a long time for something like this, and only Joey seemed to be the one who didn't want to fight. He heard a voice within him saying, "Now, just wait a minute fellas! Let's be reasonable!"

But he didn't say anything. He knew he'd have to fight.

For nights he lay awake when he should have been sleeping, thinking of a gang fight. Each narrative that he imagined ended with his blood soaking into the earth. He saw a sparsely attended funeral, and he realized that he had done nothing with his life, that if he were to die, who would remember him? His family for sure, but it wouldn't be long before they forgot about him or got used to him not being around, and his existence in their lives would be reduced to what used to belong to him, dusty boxes of books and clothes. Outside of that, no one would remember him. Perhaps every now and then Sherry Garcia might say, "I wonder what ever happened to that boy who was going to be king?"

After he died, he wanted his face on the news, for the nation to mourn: Joey Molina, the great actor, who has won so many acting awards, has tragically died today, at the age of ninety-three.

Then the camera would jump to an image of weeping fans outside of Joey's California estate.

But not now. He had done nothing. He was, quite frankly, worthless. He was a piece of flesh. No soul. No spirit. He had to change his life, but now he might not be able to. A fight with boys—athletes and a fat monster—could get him killed, and he would lose the real fight of his life: success or failure. Would he make something of himself, or would he be worthless like the picture his brother had drawn, worthless like he had always been?

Suddenly he saw the fat white boy's face, and it shrunk and got younger—like a quick reverse of time.

Randy Abbot.

That's who he was, Randy Abbot. The boy in his seventh grade class who always wanted to read the plays but was a terrible actor. He remembered how Randy had read the parts, as if he thought he was doing so well. What was Randy doing hanging out with the rich? He was poor white trash. Must be sports. Today they were teammates, friends, but as the future became the past, the other boys would go to college and marry pretty blonds and buy large homes, while Randy would fix cars or mend fences and live in a trailer park with his girlfriend and her three kids of different fathers. After a while, as more future becomes more past, Perry Doyle and the others would even quit waving at Randy, or saying hello when they saw him around town.

Two nights in a row he had a nightmare about the fight, that they would cut his face and poke out one of his eyes, and he would be scarred for life and his acting days would be over before they even got started. One night he got up and went to the kitchen, opened the refrigerator but saw nothing he wanted to eat, so he went into the living room, clicked on a dim table lamp, and looked through the record albums his mother had in a rack next to the stereo. Most of them were old uncool singers like Bing Crosby or Dean Martin, so he chose the opera *Carmen,* put it on, plugged in the earphones, lowered it very softly, and lay on the floor. The record, very old, had little scratches in it and the music kept skipping, so that the smoothness of the violins was interrupted, but still he loved the emotion, loved the voices. In this way he fell asleep.

They got used to the house, so William bought it. As years passed and raises kept pushing them up the economic ladder, he never wanted to move to a nicer neighborhood. Instead, he added a large, wood-paneled family room. This useless room was mostly empty, because at most times everyone in the house was in a separate room, Rachel playing the piano, William sculpting heads in the garage, Joey reading in his bedroom. Billy was hardly ever home, because he spent most of his time with his girlfriend's family, probably in *their* family room, watching TV and telling each other about their days. The Molina house at the end of the court was the nicest, saddest house in the neighborhood, new windows, new roof, and two apple trees in front that kept the yard in shade all day. During the spring there were always bags of apples in the kitchen ready to eat, but no one but Rachel ate them, so the bag got soggy and brown on the bottom and sometimes scented the entire house with syrupy apple, and by the end of the apple season you couldn't walk across the front yard without feeling the rotten apples squish under your shoes. Rachel cleaned inside the house, and William and the boys were responsible for everything else. Saturday, the day of KA's first fight, William had plenty of work for them to do in the yard. They had to pick up rotten apples, mow the lawn, and then clear out some spider-infested boards that had been stacked on the side of the house for a couple of years. They were going to haul them to the dump in Billy's truck. Then they had to move the refrigerator from the kitchen to the side of the house where the boards had been, because the new one was supposed to arrive from Mann's department store that day. Joey knew another pile of junk would start, and over the years it would get full of black widows, but William wanted to keep the refrigerator because he thought he might be able to one day fix and sell it.

"You're not going to do shit with it," Joey mumbled under his breath as the three of them struggled to carry the big white coffin across the backyard.

It began to slip from Joey's hands, and he said, "I'm going to drop it."

William yelled, "Put it down!" They set the heavy box on the lawn, rubbed their sore hands, and took a breath. "Boy, you're worthless."

"It was heavier than I thought," he said.

But William must have been grumpy about something beforehand, because he looked enraged with Joey, as if he wanted to hit him, and he stepped closer. "Heavier than you thought? What did you think, idiot? What is fucking wrong with you? How could you be that stupid? It's a fucking refrigerator. Of course it's going to be heavy, you stupid piece of shit. How could you be so stupid? I mean, *how?*"

He paused, as if waiting for Joey to answer. "How can anyone be as stupid as you? I don't understand that. I mean, I'm baffled. The rest of us may not be geniuses, but we're not as stupid as you. So where did you get it from?"

Joey wished his father would get it over with and hit him. At

187

least he'd be able to cry, to hold himself where it hurt, to point at the injury, but now all he could do was wait for it to pass, so, head down—he didn't want to see the man's eyes—he listened.

"Heavier than you thought? You stupid idiot. What did you think? That it was made of marshmallows? Of course it's heavy! Did you know sky was blue? Is sky bluer than you thought? Did you know that shit stinks? God, you're stupid."

He lifted a hand, as if he wanted to hit his son, but then he put it down and walked back to the refrigerator. "Come on, let's move it. Oh, by the way, stupid: It's heavy."

They lifted the refrigerator again, and Joey was so mad that the weight seemed like nothing. After they set it down, William looked at him and shook his head at his son, as if he were about to say something. Joey, looking down, saw his handprints on the white refrigerator, and across from his, he saw his dad's handprints. Billy's hands must have been clean, because he didn't leave any on the big white box, just the two, father and son, enemies, hands now almost the same size.

"Boy, you better go to college."

"Why?"

"You're not only stupid, you're lazy."

"If I'm lazy, why would I want to go to college?"

"You think you could do work like this all your life?" and then he said, as if it were the dumbest thought ever, "Heavier than I thought."

He walked away, and Joey said, "Just fucking die."

"What did you say?" he said, turning around.

"Nothing," Joey said. But he had wished his father were dead, and although he didn't really want it, the idea appealed to him, and he suddenly pictured his father's corpse stuffed in the refrigerator, ankles sticking out, but the image was so stark that it almost scared him. He pictured the handprints in blood.

Still, how much more peace would there be in the house without the old man? How much happier would his mom be? Maybe Vero would live with them again, or at least visit them. They could fix up the family room, open the shutters, let the room flood with sunlight, maybe put a few plants around, a geranium hanging from the ceiling, a sun-filled rhododendron shining on a shelf. Even though it had wall-to-wall carpet, he imagined the room with wooden floors so shiny you could see your reflection walking across the room.

Whenever the family went to Fresno, Vero was so excited to see Rachel and even the boys, but she barely looked at William and spoke to him as if he were a cop, answering his questions in short sentences until he left. The four of them, Vero, Billy, Rachel, and Joey, waited to hear his fading footsteps, his car starting, to hear him drive off to visit an old friend or a brother, and when they were sure he was gone, they acted like a family. They sat around a kitchen table or on lawn chairs in Grandma's backyard and talked and laughed. After the shared laughter of some comment had died down, they looked into each other's radiant faces, and they felt how nice it would be to be a family.

Billy hated his father.

That afternoon, while he and Joey were still working in the yard, they saw their dad in the kitchen window drinking a glass of water, taking a big breath, and drinking some more. With hatred pushing from his eyes like iron bars, Billy said, "There's got to be a way to get rid of that asshole."

"What do you mean, get rid of him?" Joey asked.

"I don't know," he said. "There's got to be something."

The narrow street was lined with pear orchards. All the boys were listening to the music, Johnny, the driver, moving his head up and down, mouthing the song's lyrics, as the warm fragrance of pears blew on their faces. Between the shuffling rows of tree trunks, wooden crates of yellow-green fruit appeared like through a projector, an occasional brown body bending over to lift one. In the backseat, Walter's face grimaced as if he hated the wind, and Kurt sat still as a statue. The '69 Impala low rider drove slowly across a concrete bridge, bouncing on the tiny tires. Joey sat on the passenger's side, leaning into the open window, his hair blowing out. He pretended to be ready to fight, but he felt timid and weak, as if one punch would be too much pain to bear.

Not Johnny.

Johnny was ready to rumble.

He beat a tap on the door to the song on the stereo.

Baby!
Since we're now together . . .

The orchards gave way to abandoned labor camps of Mexican workers in decades past, wooden shacks next to the hill, where the spirits of dead workers still floated around like in a ghost town. Joey saw the blurs of tired men looking out boarded windows, sitting on the front steps.

Johnny turned his car into a clearing right in front of the shacks, his back bumper low to the ground, the underside scraping in the gravel and dirt. They got out of the car. Joey thought of the Mexican laborers who used to work in the pear orchards and live in these camps. Nowadays during picking season they lived in town, Mexican men without women or children, sharing run-down apartments or small houses on poor streets, leaving town as soon as the work was done. But years ago, townspeople didn't welcome them and made sure they knew it, NO MEXICANS signs, no service in restaurants and stores, and they were confined to these shacks. How many had stepped out of cars and trucks and buses and seen the shacks leaning against the hills the way Joey was seeing them now? He could imagine one of them taking off his cowboy hat, someone fresh from Michoacán or Jalisco, looking around, saying, "Another season."

"Another what?" Walter asked.

"Mexican workers used to live in these shacks," Joey said.

Then another low rider drove into the dirt with Gilbert and George. At seventeen years old, Gilbert was thick, muscular, his huge legs stepping out of the car. He stood at the edge of the lot and looked around, dark *cholo* sunglasses hiding his eyes. From the passenger's seat of his car, a tall freckled-face boy appeared, George. He had a shaved head and the face of a bitter boy. The tattoo on his neck in Old English font read "El Gato." His transformation from a geeky kid to a hard-core hoodlum wasn't so much an evolution as a revolution, as if one night one side of him won over the weaker side, killed it forever, probably violently, with a knife to the throat. One day he had come to school crazier than all of them. He had been thrown into juvenile hall twice, for robbery and assault. He came back with tattoos and talking like an ex-con, and he and Gilbert became best friends.

"Where are the white boys?" Gilbert asked

"Why you asking me?" Johnny said. His hair was long, down the middle of his back and in a ponytail. He wore a bandanna. "I look like their travel agents?"

"I told you they'd be too scared to come," Joey said. "We win by default."

Suddenly a bang rang out, and they all turned around.

Kurt was picking rocks off the ground and throwing them high into the air, trying to hit one of the shacks. The wooden cabins sadly leaned over from weakness and age, and Joey imagined he heard voices in Spanish. Kurt was tiny, with the body of a Thai boxer. His mother raised him and his brother, now off in the army, by herself. A nurse's assistant at a rest home, she worked long hours. Joey had often been to Kurt's house, but he had never seen her. Kurt was always alone, sitting in the only bright room, the kitchen, two windows on either side, sitting on a stool at the counter playing solitaire.

Now Kurt gathered more rocks, examining them for size and weight, and then he threw one. The rock banged the side of a cabin. "Watch me get one in the window," he said.

"They're probably not even going to show up," Joey said. "They looked pretty scared."

"I'm ready to kick some ass," said George.

Walter picked up a rock and hurled it high into the sky, and it fell and smacked a shack. George bent down, his flannel shirt waving and creasing, and picked up a few rocks.

"Shit, I can hit it," said Johnny, and he bent down for some rocks.

But then they saw the rumble of trucks, dust rising around the tires, like cowboys in covered wagons. The truck in the lead was a red four-wheel drive, and it belonged to Perry Doyle. Some of the boys in back were carrying baseball bats. Gilbert reached in his car and pulled out two crowbars, giving one to George, who slapped his palm with the metal while smiling.

Joey might have to fight. He was so scared that he couldn't look at one spot but kept looking around, as if desperate to find someone to stop this before it happened, and he imagined he saw Mexican workers eerily standing in front of their cabins, calling to him, *Come join us on the other side.*

The white boys jumped out of their trucks, and when they saw

George and Gilbert holding crowbars, they threw their baseball bats in the backs of their trucks, so Gilbert and George threw their bars on the car seats. They slowly walked toward each other. Perry Doyle walked in front.

Two triangles of boys, the points, Gilbert and Perry, facing each other, George and Johnny on either side of Gilbert, and in the third row Kurt and Joey and Walter. The faces of all the boys were serious, trying to look mean and tough, except for Joey's, fear filling him so intensely he wasn't sure he'd be able to de-root himself from the earth. He was a tree.

"What do you know. The *maricones* showed," Gilbert said.

"Speak English, spic," said Perry.

"They sure do look like *maricones* to me," said Walter.

"Fuck you, nigger."

"Fuck you, white trash."

Gilbert got impatient and punched Perry, who fell to the ground, got up again, and rushed. Everybody rushed, and they were fighting. Limbs and faces blurred in the dusty tumble of bodies.

Except for Joey's body and one other. An idea had come to him, and he had sought out Randy Abbot, who looked around at the fight as if wondering which boy to beat on. Joey went up to him and said, "I want to box you, Abbot."

"I'll kick your ass," he said, charging like a bull, but Joey, like a matador, twisted out of the way and said, "No, I mean box. Box. Like men. If you think you can handle a few rounds with me."

"Box, huh?"

"Let's do it," Joey said, dancing around like a boxer, but keeping far enough away that Randy couldn't reach out and whack him.

"Randy Abbot," he said, as if facing an archenemy.

"I'm going to make you cry, Molina."

"After I'm through with you, your mama'll be crying."

They danced around, punching the air. The people around them were fighting.

Gilbert grabbed one guy by the ears and pulled his face to his knee. Someone jumped Gilbert from the side, crashing his head into his ribs.

Johnny had some guy in a one-arm chokehold, and he punched him repeatedly on the head, using his fist like a hammer.

Randy and Joey danced.

"I'm going to make you bleed, Molina," Randy said.

Joey put down his arms as if he didn't want to fight anymore. "This is silly," he said. He stood still.

Randy lowered his arms.

"What is?"

"You," Joey said, and he let out a punch that came close to Randy but didn't connect, and Randy got back in position, and once again they were dancing around each other.

"Are you still acting?" Joey asked.

"What do you mean?"

"Don't you remember? You read Oscar in *The Odd Couple*. Seventh grade. Man, you were good. I remember thinking, man, this guy's got talent."

"Oh, yeah! I remember that."

"You still acting?"

"Well, I never did no plays or nothing. I'm on the football team."

"That's a shame. Not everyone has the gift."

"It was fun, I remember."

And they danced some more.

Punches and kicks sounded like the slapping of raw steak. George laughed like a crazy man as he walked around hitting with elbows, fists, feet, going for quantity and laughing the whole time. He grabbed one guy by the shoulders and rammed his head into the side of the car, and then when the guy fell, George laughed as he stuffed the guy's mouth with gravel.

"Come on, Molina," Randy said. "Let's fight."

"What the hell do you think we're doing?" Joey said.

"Yeah, good point," he said in low comedy mutter, and Joey couldn't help it, a laugh slipped out.

Joey thought of the cartoon about the sheepdog and the wolf. The wolf seeks to kill the little lambs, and the sheepdog does his duty and beats the wolf, but wolf and dog have no hard feelings for each other and perhaps even feel affection toward one another, but it's their job.

Joey liked Randy.

"Check this out," Randy said. He made fast karate chops and squinted his eyes and yelled Chinese noises like Bruce Lee. Joey laughed because Randy looked so goofy, with those yellow teeth and the scrunched-up face. He didn't see the blur behind Randy, which was Gilbert coming from behind. Joey didn't have enough time to warn him, although he would realize later that he wouldn't have warned him anyway, so all he could do was watch and pretend to like what he saw. Gilbert kicked Randy in the backbone so hard that he fell forward. He kicked him over and over in the head and chest until Randy looked dead. He looked up at Joey and smiled, indicated the body, and said, "Go ahead. Free shot."

"He looks like he's had plenty," Joey said.

Gilbert stood arms akimbo, looking at the body. "Yeah, he does," he said. "But what the fuck." He kicked Randy a couple of more times in the head.

Suddenly a horn honked. A pickup truck came racing toward them. All the fighters stopped to see who it was coming so fast.

"It's your brother, Joey," said Kurt.

Joey walked out of the circle of boys toward the truck. He had told Billy about the fight, but didn't understand why he would show up. He hated Joey's friends and his *cholo* lifestyle, and in fact identified with cowboys, so if he were to join the fight, it wouldn't be with Joey's wannabe gangbanger friends. He braked to a stop, and the truck skidded a few feet on the loose dirt, and he got out. Billy's hair was short now, a crew cut, and he wore Wrangler jeans and cowboy boots.

"What do you want?" Joey said.

"Get in the truck. Now," he said.

"What are you talking about?"

"Joey, now!" he said, snapping his fingers like a foreman, spitting a glob of tobacco in the gravel.

"What do you want?" Joey asked.

Everyone had stopped fighting and was listening to the Molina brothers.

"It's Dad," he said.

"Is something wrong?"

"Something happened at work," he said. His voice cracked. "Let's go."

"I'll be back," Joey said. He ran around the truck and got into the passenger side. Billy skidded a U-turn, and they bounced to the street and took the turn so fast that the truck fishtailed on the asphalt. Joey could see that the fighters were dispersing, that Randy was sitting up.

"What's going on, Billy?"

"I don't know. Mom told me to get you. It's something about Dad."

"Is he all right?"

"I don't know." He looked worried. He tapped the steering wheel with a fist. "I don't know."

There were accidents at work, incidents, arms and hands shredded by machines, logs rolling over people's legs, and one time there was even a death that William had witnessed, but Joey had never worried that anything would happen to his father. Sometimes he wished it would.

Billy told him that he had walked into the house, and their mom yelled for him to find his brother, something about their dad. He tried to ask, but she said, "Go get him."

Joey pictured a stack of logs rolling over and crushing his legs, maybe his whole body, crushing his head.

They skidded to a stop in front of their house and jumped out. The neighbors could tell something was wrong, and they gathered on their porch. The twelve-year-old boy that Joey liked, a kid named Ronny, walked toward the brothers. "What's the matter, Joey?" he asked.

Joey shook his head.

He was out of breath when he walked into the house. Rachel sat at the table with the phone in her hand. "He's here," she said into the receiver. Then she handed the phone to Joey. Billy watched.

"Joey?" William's voice said.

"Dad? What's wrong?"

"No, no, nothing really." He paused. "Hey, you know that old refrigerator we moved today?"

"Yeah, Dad, what about it?"

"Well . . ." His voice trailed off, unsure how to continue. Through the slightly parted curtains, Joey could see Ronny riding around in circles on his bike, looking at the Molina house, concerned. Three Molinas, framed by the window, blond Rachel sitting at the table, Billy standing next to her, both of them watching Joey hold the white phone to his ear.

"Well, you know not to get inside of it and close the door, right?" asked William.

"What do you mean, Dad?"

"You would suffocate. I've heard of kids doing that before."

"Dad, I'm sixteen."

"Yeah, well, just making sure. I was working, and all of the sudden I pictured the refrigerator. I pictured you fighting to get out of it. Scared the hell out of me."

"I'll be all right," Joey said.

"Oh, okay," he said. "Just, you know, don't get inside of it."

"Okay, Dad."

"Tomorrow I'll tie some cord around it so it can't be opened. You know, just to make me feel better. Well, I guess I better get back to work."

"Okay, Dad. We'll see you."

"Joey?"

"Yeah?"

"Uh, bye."

He hung up after he heard the click at the other end.

"Well?" Billy asked.

"He just wanted to make sure I didn't play in the refrigerator."

"All that for nothing," Billy said.

"He just wanted to make sure I was all right," Joey said to his mom. Rachel smiled at him and squeezed his arm, as if it should have meant some sort of reassurance, although Joey wasn't sure of what.

"Son of a bitch," Billy said. "Waste my time like that. You can walk back to your little gang fight."

"What gang fight?" Rachel said, grasping his forearm like an angry mother.

Theater and acting create illusion, and in order for it to work, there must be a suspension of disbelief on the part of the audience. The better the acting, the more willing the audience is to suspend that disbelief, to believe what they know not to be true.

But not everyone cooperates. Skeptical audience members look for the actors to make mistakes, to forget lines, to drop a prop, like a cigar, and not be sure how to pick it up without breaking character. They'll watch that cigar for the rest of the play, wondering how they will get it offstage. These skeptical ones count the number of times a character onstage dials a phone number, making sure it's seven numbers, because if the actor dials five or six, the skeptical person can say to the person next to him or her, "Ah-hah! This is so fake." Fundamental to this exchange, that is, the skeptical one bending over to whisper into the ear of his or her companion, is the telling of his disbelief to someone else. The skeptical person cannot keep it to himself, but must tell someone. "Did you see that? He only dialed five times." It's as if they feel a need to expose as false what they know to be false.

Joey, convincing as a tough guy after years of playing the role, suspended his own disbelief and sometimes forgot he was playing a role. One particularly convincing night as the crew sat outside in Johnny's backyard on lawn chairs—a stereo sitting in the window of the shack playing Mexican *rancheras,* which Clemente liked to listen to all the time—Joey closed his eyes and felt it.

This was his real world. He had been in a real gang fight, therefore he was in a real gang.

Johnny's uncle Clemente had bought beer for the boys, and they were drinking, Johnny, Clemente, Kurt, Walter, and Joey. Johnny's long hair was loose, and he wasn't wearing a shirt, his brown skin shining under the lights that came from the moon. He stood with a beer in his hand. "Damn, we got those punks good," he said, and he set down his beer and got into a fighting position. "We was kicking ass," and he punched the air, his arms extending, muscles flexing, and he made sounds every time he pretended to connect, *bam, wham, pow.*

"It was cool," said Walter. "We were triumphant!" He said the last word as if the word itself were triumphant, and he looked at Joey and smiled big. "Didn't we triumph, Molina?" he said.

"*Claro que* yes!" Joey said.

"*Que* hell yes!" said Walter.

"Did you use that shit I taught you?" asked Clemente. He was squatted Chicano-style against the wall, beer dangling from his fingers. The light from the moon cast a green hue on his cheek. The music flowed from over his shoulders.

La luna es verde
Y mi amor se fue

"We didn't need no knives," Johnny said, his hands behind his head, gathering his thick hair into a ponytail, stars and planets shining around his head.

Kurt was throwing horseshoes on the far end of the lawn. "They were losers," he said over the clanking of metal on metal.

Everything was perfect. Life was beautiful. They were like mythical gods.

"Anybody want to play?" said Kurt, releasing another horseshoe, like a black bat flying in the starry sky. The full moon shone.

"I'll play," said Walter.

Joey was comfortable in this role, but the skeptical one was not there.

Gilbert Sanchez, a tough audience member, from the beginning seemed not to believe Joey. He questioned him about his gangbanger past, so much so that Joey had to keep his lies written down in a notebook, *The Book of Lies* he called it, so he would know how to answer a particular question. Gilbert's skepticism turned into dislike, as if he not only didn't believe him but would have loved to expose him as a phony, to break for everyone the illusion, the suspension of disbelief. And because Gilbert and George were best friends, George, too, began to doubt Joey. "What's the last fight you got in?" Gilbert had asked him one day, and George crossed his thick arms, waiting for an answer.

Joey thought of *The Book of Lies,* the fight he had gotten into with some Ashland white boys in the parking lot of the school. One of the boys had a red cap, which Joey stuffed in his mouth after the guy was down.

Gilbert must have had his own book of lies, because he asked detailed questions about old narratives. "Red? I thought it was blue?"

And Joey would stumble but remember the story. "No, man, it was red."

* * *

Tonight everyone talked about the fight, and Joey felt comfortable because Gilbert and George weren't around.

"You guys won that fight because of me," Clemente said, and he stood up from his squat. "I'm making you guys martial arts experts." He wore black work boots and a white tank top undershirt. He had a belly, but his arms were cut, defined, and on one of them he had a tattoo of a dagger stuck in a heart. He was thirty years old. Joey couldn't help but stare at his pocked face, and he couldn't help but feel the sadness coming from his eyes.

"Joey got that big guy good," said Walter. "He looked dead when you left him. Fucker was on the ground bleeding. And he's a big fucker, too."

"Right on," said Clemente.

"Yeah, that was pretty good, Joey," said Kurt.

"His name is Randy Abbot," said Joey.

"KA kicks ass," someone yelled. Then Gilbert and George walked into the yard from the side of the house. George went to the beer case, grabbed two, handed one to Gilbert, who drained it down his throat, squeezed the can, and looked around at the others. "What are you guys talking about?"

"How Joey kicked that Abbot's ass."

"Really," said Gilbert. "Joey Molina?"

Randy Abbot suffered a minor concussion and remembered little about how he ended up so broken, and it quickly spread around the high school that it was because Joey Molina had kicked his ass. Kids started to fear him again, like when he was in junior high. They watched him walk by, got out of his way, and he enjoyed the power he had. One day two boys were sitting on a bench in the quad, and Joey snapped his fingers at them and said, "I want to sit."

They said, "Sure thing, Joey," and they got up and left.

Luckily (maybe providentially?), Gilbert had hit so many guys during that fight that he hadn't known it was really him who had done the damage to Abbot, so he seemed for the first time pleased with Joey. "Good way to go," he said.

That was how it got in the new gang rhetoric that Joey was one of the best fighters, Gilbert, George, and Joey. Don't mess with Joey Molina.

One afternoon, Joey and Kurt were walking home from school. Kurt looked anxious, twitching, scratching where it didn't itch. "Come on, Molina, let's go play some pool or some video games or something."

On the way to the pool hall, they passed the gas station minimart. Joey looked inside and saw his brother standing in line at the counter, so he told Kurt he'd be right back and he went inside. Billy nodded hello as Joey walked in, and the people in line watched him walk in, the *cholo,* the hard-core Chicano gangbanger. He stopped next to his brother, "Hey, bro."

"Hey," Billy said. "What's going on?"

"Nothing." He looked around the minimart, and then down on the breath mints and gum display. "Where's your girlfriend?"

"She's working," Billy said.

They reached the head of the line, and the cashier, some cowgirl, said, "Howdy, Billy," and Billy said, "Hey, Margie."

And then she looked at Joey's face and then at Billy's face. "Wow," she said to Billy. "I didn't know Joey Molina was your brother."

"You know my brother?" Billy asked.

"I know *of* him," she said.

Medford was a small town.

* * *

Billy offered Kurt and Joey a ride in his truck, but Joey said no thanks, that they were going to mess around awhile, and before Billy walked off, Joey held out an unopened package of gum. "Want one?" Joey smiled a mischievous smile.

"You stole that?"

"Why not?" Joey said.

"Don't you have any money?"

"That's not the point."

Billy grabbed him by the arm and dragged him near his pickup truck. "What is wrong with you?"

"It's just twenty-five cents. No big deal."

"You're not stealing bread." He let him go, got in the truck, shook his head in disbelief, and pulled out of the parking lot.

Joey watched his brother's truck enter the freeway on-ramp. He walked back into the store, secretly slipped the gum back in its place, and walked out again. "My brother's so stupid," he said as they walked along the sidewalk. "I hate him."

"Let's go play pool," said Kurt. "Come on, let's play. I got a dollar."

"I got five," Joey said. "It's on me."

One night the brothers were in the kitchen together. Billy stood at the counter spreading gobs of mayonnaise on white bread. "Hand me the weenies, lamo," he said.

"Get them yourself, you loser," Joey said, his head inside the refrigerator, looking through the lunch meats and cheeses. Billy came up behind him and grabbed his arm and forced it behind his back in a ready-to-break position, pushing his head farther into the cold. "I want the weenies, lamo. Now."

"Ow, ow! Let me go!" His nose brushed against the cold cartoon of milk. He grabbed the package of hot dogs and handed it to his brother.

"Little baby," Billy said, and let go. "Some big bad Chicano you are," he said. "I should tell all your friends what a baby you really are."

"*Chale con eso,*" Joey said, grabbing a plastic bag of tortillas. He set them on the counter, grabbed a tortilla from the bag, and turned on the gas stovetop. He flip-flopped it on the flame until it was warm, and then he placed a cold weenie on a fork and held that over the flame. Billy put a weenie on a fork and held his over the same flame, and they began to smell salty and burnt. Joey placed his weenie in the tortilla and spread on some mustard.

He shut off the stove, pulled a paper towel from the roll, and held the burrito in his hand. Billy cut his hot dog in half and lay it in the bed of mayonnaise.

"Check this out," Joey said. "I'm all Chicano and shit, and you're all like a white boy now. A coconut and shit. I'm eating tortillas, and you're eating white bread, but ultimately we share the same meat, the weenies. What we have inside is the same."

"Shut up," said Billy.

As they sat on the couch with their food waiting for *Movies Till Dawn* to start the first feature, Billy told Joey, "I think Mom's going back to school full-time."

For a while she had worked as a receptionist for a doctor's office, but the wages in Medford were so ridiculously low compared to California that as a matter of principle, she quit and spent more time on the house and her piano. "She bought a bag full of books," Billy said.

He would have said more, but Rachel came out of her room, hoping to play the piano. She saw Joey and Billy sitting side by side, so close that their shoulders almost touched, and she started laughing.

Billy, a white sheet on his lap, held his sandwich with a paper towel, close to his mouth. "What?" he said.

"You guys are so cute!" she said.

Billy rolled his eyes.

"Hey, Mom, I was telling Billy what a perfect metaphor we have with our sandwich and burrito. We're different on the outside—you know? I'm cool, he's a dork—but on the inside, we have the same meat. Wouldn't you say that's a pretty good metaphor?"

"What kind of meat?" she asked, sitting on the arm of the couch.

Joey, suddenly realizing, blushed. "Well . . . hot dogs."

A laugh squeaked out of her, and she covered her mouth. "There's your metaphor," she said.

"Would you guys shut up?" said Billy, putting his sandwich on the coffee table. "I'm trying to watch a movie." He lay on the couch, his head on Joey's thigh, and he pulled the white sheet over his body. Joey touched his brother's hair. "You should grow this out, white boy."

"I like it short, greaser."

Rachel touched his head too, her fingers brushing against Joey's fingers, and he brushed his against hers, felt their warmth. He was happy.

"Are you thinking of going back to school?" Joey asked.

"I already registered," she said.

"What are you going to major in?"

"Spanish," she said.

"But you already speak Spanish," said Billy.

Joey and Rachel looked at each other and smiled.

"I was thinking of going to college," Joey said.

"I'll kill you if you don't go to college," Rachel said.

* * *

206

The first movie was a western. Joey kept rooting for the Indians even though he knew they would be slaughtered, and Billy rooted for the cowboys, and during commercials Rachel played piano.

But then on one commercial, she slammed on the keys and turned around toward the boys, and they both knew she was going to say something, so they were quiet, watching her. They could hear a car pull into the court. It got louder and louder until they were sure it was William pulling into the driveway, coming home from the swing shift. "Don't tell your father about the school," she said.

"Why?" asked Joey.

"It's none of his business."

She stood up and went to her room.

William spent a lot of time in the garage, sometimes working so late at night that he put a cot in there and sometimes fell asleep. Joey hardly saw his father except when he told him to bring him something, iced water, coffee, or something to eat. He made Joey make him sandwiches or heat up cans of soup and wrap hot tortillas in aluminum foil. Joey brought the stuff to his father out in the garage, which was dim, except for a lamp shining on the latest head. The radio played pop hits converted into elevator music without lyrics. William sat on a stool, bent forward, looking at his head.

He was making a new Rachel, her eyes slanted, almost shut, and her lips slightly open, a slight grin, and a tiny tip of tongue. On the workbench were an open case of watercolors, a pencil-thin paintbrush, and a Folgers can of water. He lifted the brush, wet the tip.

"Your water, King Ubu," Joey said.

"Who?" he said, putting down the brush and taking off his work shirt, underneath of which he had a white tank top undershirt. His tattoos, the spider on his chest and the witch on his arm, seemed black in the pale light, as if they were iron brands burned into his skin.

"Ubu Roi. A character from a French play."

"He better be the good guy," William said, picking up the paintbrush.

"He's a great character. He always says, 'By my green candle!'"

"What for?" He dipped the brush in the red and swished it back and forth to moisten the color.

"Instead of saying, 'For goodness sake' or 'Heavens to Betsy,' he says, 'By my green candle.'"

The glass of iced water was so cold that he shifted it from hand to hand as he watched his father stare at Rachel's face. Joey thought he would use the red for her lips or her tongue, but he brought the brush to her eyes and began to spot them with red. Then he pulled back and looked at the head. "Hmmm," he said.

"This is horrible music," Joey said. "Why do you listen to this crap?"

"I like it. It allows me to think. My mind can wander."

"It sucks."

He held out his arms. The paintbrush had a tiny drop of red clinging to the end of it, ready to fall. "Right now, with this music, I can imagine myself"—and he closed his eyes—"driving down Blackstone Avenue. Oh! There's Kmart. I'm walking through the parking lot. Now I'm inside! Ah, the aroma of fresh popped popcorn and submarine sandwiches!"

"I get the point," Joey said.

"Besides, with this music I have no memory. I don't think of things that were happening when the song came out, how I messed up or felt pain or anger. I don't know the songs. They remind me of nothing."

He pointed his brush at Joey, the red drop falling from the tip. "The stuff you listen to doesn't help you think. It does the thinking for you."

"I'm not influenced by the music I listen to. I just like the style."

"Horseshit. Anyone listens to a song that says 'I want a Coke I want a Coke I want a Coke' over and over is going to find themselves thinking, You know, I want a Coke. You might think it's your decision, but it's the song."

"That's stupid," he said.

"It's unconscious is what it is," he said. "You don't know you're being brainwashed, but you are."

"Gosh, Dad, I didn't realize you were such an intellectual."

"And since so many songs are about romantic love, everybody thinks that if they just find that one true love, then life will be happy. But what happens is they get married and find out that the paychecks don't cover the expenses, so they fight, or the girl at the party is sexy and the wife gets jealous and they fight—or whatever. People fight and then they think, Maybe this person wasn't the right one. They think they 'fell out of love,' so they get divorced and look for someone else. They continue to hope and search for that one true love that they believe life owes them because of those stupid songs. But this is the truth, Joey: Love is a choice, not a feeling, a choice. This music," he said, pointing to the radio, "doesn't tell you what to think. It's just music."

"And it's ugly. You could listen to classical."

"Who needs your opinion?"

"You do, Dad. You'd die without me."

"Go get me some iced water," he said.

Joey looked down at the cup that he held, and he saw his reflection in the water. "Without me trembling in the reflection of your water, you'd die of thirst."

"Just get me some damn water."

"Sure, whatever you say, Ubu." He set the water on the work-table and walked to the door and turned around to close it. Under the glare of the yellow light, William stared at Rachel's frozen face, her red eyes. "By my green candle!" he said.

Joey had a regular Saturday-night thing, that's why he couldn't hang out with the boys on Main Street, where they parked their cars and stood around watching people go by, listening to music, Al Green, Is-ley Brothers, Slave, and he couldn't stay and party in Johnny's back-yard either, not on Saturday night, because of his regular thing. His secret and wild nightlife. They tried to get from him what he did, but he would only imply, never lie, saying things like "Music, laughing, partying." Which was the truth, but the truth was that his mom didn't allow him out after eleven o'clock, even if it was a weekend and he was sixteen, so he had to be home, and since she required Billy to be home by midnight, both of them watched *Movies Till Dawn,* Joey's regular Saturday-night thing.

Most of the films were old black-and-white gangster movies and horrors and westerns, and they especially loved the comedies with Peter Sellers as the French inspector. They sat or lay on the same couch, and often Rachel joined them, and during commercials she and Joey talked about the characters and themes. While watching a Pink Panther movie, Rachel said she couldn't believe how much the boys giggled at the bumbling detective, and she said, "That's not even funny."

Joey told her not to be so haughty, that the inspector was in the same tradition as the Three Stooges and Laurel and Hardy, visual, yes, slapstick, sure, but pure comedy, a modern commedia dell'arte, and she said the others he mentioned weren't funny either. He asked her did she find Cantinflas funny, and she said yes and he said, "Case closed."

Whenever Rachel and Joey argued about a movie, Billy would curl up tighter in his white sheet, until finally he yelled, "Be quiet, I can't hear!" and Joey and Rachel would giggle like kids. One night Billy and Joey were both disappointed that a musical starring Bing Crosby was the next movie, but Rachel said, "Finally, something good." Joey was ready to go to bed, but Billy stayed seated, his head on Joey's lap, and Rachel sat on the piano bench facing the TV, so Joey moaned as he watched Bing fall in love with Dorothy Lamour, who was probably as old as his grandma by then. Then the violins started, and he knew Bing would sing, so he got up to find something to eat. "This is stupid," he said. He stuck his head in the refrigerator. The tune from the TV caught him tapping his feet, and then the voice started.

Joey pulled his head from the refrigerator.

It sounded familiar.

Smooth.

He closed the refrigerator door and walked back, sat on the couch, and listened. Bing danced around Dorothy, wooing her, his voice so smooth. When Bing stood before a picture window that looked onto a cityscape at night, he hit a long note and his voice sort of wavered, and Joey felt goose bumps on his arms. "This is stupid," he said.

"His voice is so beautiful," said Rachel.

"Beauty's definitely in the ear of the hearer," he said, watching Bing and Dorothy spin and spin.

After Billy went to bed, Joey stayed with Rachel, and every time Bing sang he felt himself liking it more. When he did a duet with the woman, Joey laughed out loud, not because it was funny, but because he somehow had to express what he felt even though he wasn't sure what he was feeling. He didn't want the movie to end, and when it did end, he hoped for another musical and was disappointed that it was a detective movie.

As he lay in bed that night, he kept thinking about it, and he knew he had to hear more. Knowing everyone was asleep, he tiptoed down the hallway back into the living room, clicked on the lamp, and went through his mom's albums, all of which she had bought at secondhand stores. He thumbed through the piano pieces, Chopin, Beethoven, a few operas, *Carmen, Death in Venice,* and some symphonies by composers whose names he couldn't pronounce. She also had Herb Alpert and the Tijuana Brass, Tito Puente, Javier Solís, and the latest Santana. There was Dean Martin, Frank Sinatra, Woody Herman, but no Bing. He put Dean Martin on the turntable and plugged in the earphones. The big band blared with horns and violins, a sweet song that made him want to swing, snap his fingers.

And then something happened.

You left me alone at the edge of the city
thinking that you would return
Why must you be
so cruel to me?

He loved the voice. When he closed his eyes, he pictured himself singing the song, dancing around his girlfriend, Amy, his friends watching, clapping. He played it over and over, and once he got the words down, he started to sing along. He sat up and snapped his fingers, moved his upper body.

Why must you be
so very very
cruel to me?

He must have been moving too much.

In the middle of the chorus he felt a pain on his arm. He looked up and saw that his dad had just kicked him, teeth clenched like he would do it again, which he did. Billy was behind the dad. Joey took off the earphones and noticed that the music was still on, still blaring. He noticed that it was almost shaking the windows of the house. "Turn it off," his dad yelled. The earphones had come unplugged, but he hadn't noticed, because his head had been between the speakers, because the music had brought him outside of time.

Billy bent down and turned off the stereo. "You're stupid," he said.

"What the hell's the matter with you?" William said as he kicked Joey again.

"I'm sorry," he said, curling up for protection.

"You know what fucking time it is?" he yelled.

"I thought the earphones were on."

"I should kick your ass good."

"Can I help?" asked Billy.

Sure, he was being hit and yelled at and he should have felt horrible, but he didn't; and in fact, inside he was happy and singing,

Why must you be
so very very
cruel to meeeeee??

He just wanted to sing.

* * *

At home, happy when no one was around, he played all his mother's crooner albums and the ones he had started buying at the secondhand store. He loved the voices, learned the songs, and started singing when the house was empty. Dean Martin and Frank Sinatra were his favorites.

In his bedroom he had books of plays he had picked up over the years at secondhand stores stacked on every possible space, on the chest of drawers, on an old bookshelf, against the walls, and he started stacking records, too. He had read all the books, and now he listened to all the records. These things were his treasures.

One afternoon he sat in a park on a picnic table with his legs wide and his girlfriend, Amy, in between them, his arms around her. She was a skinny blond with an upturned nose and hair so thin it felt like milk. He played with her hair, put his nose on her neck, and took a whiff. In the early part of the day, she smelled of vanilla soap, like now, and it was one of the things he liked about her, but she smoked a lot, and late in the day her hair and clothes smelled bad. She was seventeen, a year older than Joey, and her mom let her smoke. In fact, they shared packs of cigarettes.

Amy was smoking now, the wisps rising over her head and around Joey's eyes.

"My mom wants you to teach me and my brothers to fight," she said.

"What for? I thought she was a hippie."

"She said she'll make you some marijuana brownies."

Beyond the pine trees that lined the edge of the park, trucks and cars zoomed by on the freeway. "Let's walk," he said, and they walked across the park, across the street and under the freeway overpass and into the railroad tracks and brick buildings on the back roads of downtown, the backs of stores and restaurants, garbage Dumpsters, empty crates.

"Your mom is weird," he said, waiting for a black car to pass before they crossed. She blew out her smoke and it went into his face and he fanned the smoke from his eyes.

Sometimes, Amy and he and her mom and Amy's two younger brothers sat around in their dim apartment, smoking weed and watching TV. The first time he had been with Amy in a sexual way, it had been at their apartment in Amy's bedroom while the family sat in the living room watching TV. After they were done and they went out of the room, her mom said, "So how was it?"

They entered Main Street, passing storefront windows.

"I admit my mom's a little weird," Amy said. "But what about yours?"

"True. She's kind of different."

"Joey, she plays piano like she's possessed."

They stopped before the window of a dress shop and could see themselves standing side by side in the reflection, Amy, short, with blond wavy hair, Joey, tall, thin, with black hair and eyes.

"My mom thinks we're going to get married."

"And what do you think?"

"It's our destiny," she said. "Don't you feel that?"

"Who knows?"

They walked across a parking lot between two brick buildings.

"Does the idea repel you?"

"No, of course not."

"Well, can you picture it?" Amy asked.

"Seriously, I try not to picture the future. It scares me."

"Why? You got a great future."

"What makes you think so?"

"I just do. You're going to be someone important."

"But not your husband."

"Hmph," she said. She flicked her cigarette butt across the hood of a car and wrapped her arms around herself, leaned against a car, and pouted. "I'm not going to kiss you anymore, ever again."

"Come on, honey," he said. "Please." He put his arms around her and tried to kiss her neck.

"No, no, no," she said.

Without thinking he started singing.

"You left me holding the baby
and a bag of fresh fruit
Honey, honey how cruel . . ."

As he sang he walked with her, swayed hand in hand. They reached the entrance of Mann's department store, where people walked in and out, and when he hit the last high note, a couple of smiling ladies walking into the store applauded and nodded. Joey turned red and stopped.

"What the heck was that?" Amy said.

"Sorry. I was just playing around," he said.

"Joey!"

"I was joking."

"No, Joey, that was nice. Sing some more. Please."

"If you kiss me," he said, and she did, a long one, and when it was over she looked in his eyes. "Sing to me."

He took her hand, led her along the sidewalk, and sang.

"The way your fingers curl around
a glass of champagne . . ."

Ever since the big fight, the KA boys were popular at school. Kids wanted to join them. There weren't any more minorities in the school, so the boys who wanted to belong were white. One lunchtime the KAs were hanging out in front of the high school by Johnny's car, which he had parked on the curb. Music blasted, all the doors open.

Fight!
Fight the 'pressor!

Amy, smoking a cigarette, leaned against the car with some other white girls. The guys stood around in a circle on the grass, Johnny, Walter, Kurt, and Joey and some white guys.

"Shit, man, if those guys used their bats," said Walter, "I was ready, man."

The boys were nodding their heads, enraptured, impressed.

"What would you have used?" asked one of the white kids.

Walter held up his fist. "This," he said. "This is all I need."

"Damn," said the boy, in awe, looking at Walter's knuckles.

It was a sunny day, green, the trees blowing in a breeze, the scent of pears in the air. Gilbert and George came up. "What are you guys doing here?" Gilbert said to the white boys.

"They were telling us about the fight," said one of them.

"The fight. The fight. The fight," said Gilbert, looking up into the sky. "I'm tired of talking about the fight. It wasn't shit."

Kurt held a miniature Nerf football, twirling it around. "Anyone want to play?"

Gilbert looked around, surveying the schoolyard. "The white boys said they're going to get Joey," he said.

"Who told you that?" Joey asked.

"Heard that Perry Doyle was saying that they put an SOS out on Joey Molina," Gilbert said.

"SOS?" asked one of the white boys.

"Smash on Sight," Gilbert said, looking at Joey. "They said they're going to get you for what you did to that Abbot boy. He had to get stitches."

"Who told you this?" Joey asked.

"Are you scared?" asked George.

"No, I'm just wondering why me. We were all in the fight."

"Yeah, I heard something too," said one of the white guys. "They say they're going to get Molina."

"Joey ain't scared," said Walter. "Right, Molina?"

"What, me worried?" He pulled at his collar in a farcical gesture, picturing himself as Alfred E. Neuman on the cover of *Mad* magazine, but nobody noticed the farce, only his words, and they nodded in approval.

His assigned desk in honors English was the middle row behind a tall girl who smelled of strawberry shampoo. She hunched over her desk, writing. When she sat up, her hair moved a few inches from his nose, strawberry shampoo, a kind of dorky girl with glasses, and gangly, a bony body. She dressed with no sense of fashion. Today she wore faded red pants and an off-white T-shirt with a teddy bear on the front. Her name was Leah.

The teacher, Mr. McNally, with the big belly and black hair parted in the middle and long, curling mustache like the cartoon of an Italian chef, droned on and on as he handed back their assignments. "This assignment made the difference for many of you. Will you pass English? Will you graduate? Do you want to go to a good college?" He placed a paper on Leah's desk, and, hunched over, she turned it over. Her shoulders rose and fell.

"If you flunked this you need to do it again. Believe me, you don't want a C on your record." He stood before Joey now, looking at his paper. "Molina, despite your efforts otherwise, you're probably going to graduate." The teacher put the paper facedown.

Joey turned it over.

A+.

The A was normal, the plus wasn't. It was an essay on Arthur Miller's *A Bridge Too Far,* which he had read before on his own, so the paper came easy to him.

The class dragged on that day. The teacher tried to get a discussion going about the reading, which Joey hadn't done. So he stared at the clock and at then at Leah. He moved his upper body closer to her. He touched her back with an open palm. She turned around and whispered, "Well?"

"The same," he said, deciding not to tell her about the plus.

"Me too," she said, which meant she got a B, something that made her angry, frustrated, since she worked so hard on her papers. "He's harder on you," Joey said.

"But why?" she said,

"I don't think he likes girls."

She smiled at this, exposing her silvery braces. She really was a geek. But she had gray eyes, pale gray, a color that he had never noticed on anyone else. He liked the smell of strawberry shampoo.

"Seriously," he said. "You notice how we never read any woman authors?"

"I hadn't noticed, but you're right. Maybe he's a misogynist!"

He didn't know what that meant, but rather than ask her, he decided he'd look it up later that day.

"You should have gotten an A," Joey said.

"Thanks," she said, smiling a dorky metal-mouth smile.

"Tell us, Molina," the teacher said, walking up to his desk. "What is it that makes this character so alienated?"

He crossed his arms and waited for Joey's answer.

He didn't say anything, and Leah finally said, as if she were impatient with the teacher, "Duh. Everyone's so hypocritical and biased." She looked right at the teacher.

"Yeah," Joey said, "bunch of fascists."

Mr. McNally looked at Joey. "Fascists, huh? Very good, Joey," he said, walking away, and Joey looked at Leah and shrugged his shoulders. She pointed at herself as if to ask, Wasn't it my answer?

She laughed when Joey whispered, "Fascist number one," and pointed at McNally.

"Misogynist number one," she said.

"That may very well be how he viewed them," said the teacher. "Hypocritical."

At the bell everyone stood up and headed for the door. "See you," said Leah.

"See you," Joey said.

Stories quickly spread around school that Perry and Randy—and in some narratives the entire Medford High football team—were after Joey, promising to give him a "lasting memory," which they implied and everyone understood to be scars. Joey, although nervous when he walked around town alone or with Amy, tried to pretend that it didn't bother him, scoffed at it when someone brought it up. School kids seemed to respond to Joey in one of two ways—they stayed away from him, or they seemed to admire him. In fact, now that he was a wanted man, he was more popular than ever. Even teachers liked Joey Molina, sometimes joking around with him in front of the class. One day as Joey and the KAs hung out in front of the school, Johnny's car parked at the curb, some girls were walking in their direction. It was Karla Horton, the one with red hair and green eyes whom Joey had admired since junior high. She was pretty, dated college guys or athletes or both. She and her friends walked right by them. They were the prettiest girls in school, and rich. Joey couldn't help but look at her.

"Shit, if I could get a girl like that," said Johnny.

"She's fine," Joey said, and right when he said it, Karla looked over at him and their eyes caught. She almost smiled before she turned away, mouthing something to her friends. He looked at Amy, who was leaning against Johnny's car with her girlfriends, and as if she knew he was watching her, she looked over at him and smiled, puckered her lips, and threw him a kiss.

In the hallway between classes both Randy Abbot and Perry Doyle walked toward him, and when kids noticed, they stuck around to watch. When the boys reached Joey, they stopped, face to face with him. "You going to die, greaser," said Perry. Abbot just stood there, stone-faced, not even looking at Joey, as if, perhaps, embarrassed.

"You better hope you never catch up to me," Joey said, and just then Mr. McNally, belly first, walked out of the classroom. He looked from boy to boy. "Molina, I need to speak to you."

"What do you want?" he said in his best rebel delivery.

"It won't take long," he said, and after the two boys walked off, he led Joey inside the empty classroom and indicated a chair where Joey should sit. He sat across from him, not at his desk, but on a chair, and leaned over. "Joey, do you know where the Blue Lion is? It's a Chinese restaurant on Main Street?"

A student came in and walked to his desk to pick up the backpack he had left there. "Sorry," he said, as if he had disturbed something private. McNally watched for the student to leave before he bent over again.

"They got great food there. Have you ever tried it?"

"No," he said.

"Well, take my word for it. It's good. Do you like Chinese food?"

"What's this about?" he said.

"Joey, I want to invite you to lunch at the Blue Lion. Saturday afternoon. What do you say?"

"Why would you want to do that?"

"There's someone I want you to meet. Actually, someone wants to meet you."

On the walk downtown, Joey couldn't help but look over his shoulders or at any shadow that seemed to pass on the street, expecting to see a pickup truck, a red four-wheel drive full of white boys. He entered the downtown restaurant and found a white lady on the phone near the register, writing down an order. She eyed him suspiciously as he looked around the dim restaurant. In the corner of a booth in the back, Mr. McNally was sipping some soda and looking at his watch as if he were waiting for a date. Something didn't feel right, and he was about to turn around and leave despite the fact that he was enticed by the smell of the food, but then McNally saw him and smiled, lifted his arms as if to say, At last! He stood up. Joey slowly walked over. "What's up?" he said.

"Joey. It's so good to see you. Sit down. You want a Coke or something?" He raised his hand for the waitress, the old lady on the phone. "Mabel," he said, "bring Joey something to drink, will you?"

She walked halfway over and stopped to look at him. "What'll it be?"

"Coke, please," he said.

"One Coke."

She left, and Mr. McNally stared at him as if proud. "Joey Molina!" he said.

"What?"

"I'm glad you came."

"So what's this about?"

223

"Do you have any idea what the work of the other kids is like compared to yours? Sometimes I read your papers and I think, This boy is made to go to college. I'm not flattering you, Joey." He put his elbows on the table and rested his face in the palms of his hands. "Tell me about your parents."

"They work."

Across the restaurant was a single young mother, skinny and wrinkled, feeding her chubby-faced blond baby boy who sat in a high chair. "That's a good baby," she cooed, feeding him another spoonful of baby food. Then she rolled noodles around her fork and took a mouthful.

The waitress came back with the Coke and asked if they were ready to order. McNally said they were waiting for others. "Okay, hon. Do you want some appetizers?"

"Joey, you want some appetizers?"

He did, of course, but he said, "Whatever."

"Give us the sampler plate," the teacher said, and from then on all Joey could think of was what it would contain. Despite his coolness or attempt to look cool, he was pretty excited. He sipped cold sugar through the straw. "I like this place."

"Have you thought about college?"

"Oh, so that's why I'm here," he asked, "to talk about college. I've heard this before, you know."

"You must have had pretty caring teachers."

"Why do you say that?"

"If your teachers have tried to encourage you to go to college, they must see something in you that they care about. A spark. Potential. Nobody *has* to encourage you. But when a teacher sees a kid like you with potential oozing out of your pores, it excites us. Do your parents encourage you?"

"Yeah. Sort of. My mother said she'd kill me if I didn't go, and my father told me I was too lazy *not* to go."

"Well, you're lucky to have parents that value education. I know with a lot of immigrant families the parents don't understand the value of college."

"I'm not an immigrant, pilgrim."

"Well, anyway, mine didn't, and my teachers didn't see anything in me that caused them to go out of their way to encourage me. Fortunately I made it through college, but not law school. I failed before I even started.

"Joey, I'd hate for this to happen to you. Maybe those teachers who've encouraged you feel the same way. You know, I've been teaching for almost fifteen years, and you're, well, you're unique."

"You think so?"

"I do."

The waitress came by with a platter stacked with egg rolls, chicken wings, and fried pork. Joey was beside himself with joy. Mr. McNally told him to start, and he gobbled the stuff so fast, his cheeks full, that the teacher smiled. Between bites he drank Coke, and without asking him, the teacher ordered him another one.

"I think of you, Joey, and I think, This kid could do whatever he wants with his life."

Mouth full, he said, "So that is why you invited me? You want to convince me to go to college?"

"No," he said, "that's not why. That's why." He pointed to the door.

A thin man in his twenties walked into the restaurant and looked around as his eyes adjusted to the dimness. He saw McNally, waved, and walked over. But who he was with made Joey almost choke on his barbecue pork. She was beautiful, a Latina, with dark straight hair so shiny black it shone like a record album. She had an aquiline nose and big black eyes. She was his age, but he had never seen her before. In fact, the only Chicana girls in town were sisters of Johnny and Gilbert, traditional girls, Catholics who were no fun to be around. This girl he would have noticed. Joey stood up with Mr. McNally and wiped his hands and mouth with the paper napkin.

The man looked vaguely familiar and had a book tucked under his arm. He walked right up to Joey and held out his hand. "Joey Molina," he said. "It's good to finally meet you."

"Uh, yeah. Hi."

"I'm Mark Bollen, call me Mark, and this," he said, indicating the girl, "is Carmen Fernandez."

"Hi," she said. Joey nodded.

"Greg," he said to the English teacher.

"Good to see you, Mark. Sit down."

"Joey," said the stranger. "Do you know who I am?"

"You're a cop?" he said.

He laughed, looked at McNally, and laughed some more. "Excellent, excellent. Rich." He laughed more. "No, I'm not a cop."

"He's not a cop," said McNally.

"I'm the drama teacher at your school," said the stranger.

The girl smiled.

"What do you want?" he asked.

"Joey, do you remember Mr. Williams from your junior high?"

"Yeah."

"He told me about you."

The waitress took their drink orders. Bollen ordered an iced tea, and so did Carmen.

"Let's order," said McNally, handing out the red menus. Carmen took hers and held it like a book. She looked up, and Joey, shyly, quickly looked away. They were silent as they read. Bollen was the first to put his menu down, then McNally, but Carmen and Joey still read.

"I have a proposition for you," said Bollen. "We're doing a production of *West Side Story*. Do you know the play?"

He nodded.

"Well, we have it cast, and they're good people, Joey, but there's one problem. We're having trouble finding Hispanics to play the Sharks, just a bunch of blue-eyed white boys who don't fit, if you know what I mean. Now we can dye their hair and put a little makeup on them, and they'll get by, but Joey, if we only had someone to play the part of Bernardo—if we only had a Hispanic. Do you know the role of Bernardo?"

"It's been a while since I saw the movie," he said.

"He's the leader of the Sharks, you know, the Puerto Rican gang. He needs to be tough and handsome, but he also needs to be a good actor. Mr. Williams is my former teacher. He told me about you. He told me to look out for you when you got to high school, but for the past two years I hadn't heard anything about you. I saw you a few times and didn't know who you were."

The waitress came by with the drinks and to take their order, asking Joey first, but he wasn't sure what to get, so he asked if she could take his order last. Carmen was next, but she hadn't decided either, so she asked to be second to the last.

When it was his turn to order, he closed his eyes and blurted out, "Sweet and sour pork."

"I used to see you around school hanging out with your friends," Bollen said. "I like watching you guys. That may be why I got the idea to do *West Side Story*. But I noticed you the most, Joey. I do that with people sometimes. Look at their faces and see what kind of actor they could be, what kind of characters I could see them doing."

"What about her?" Joey said. "Who could she be?" He pointed

to the single mother with the baby. She was sucking a fork of noodles.

"Blanche DuBois," Bollen said.

"That woman's poor white," Joey said. "If anything Blanche is falling into poor white, but she certainly wouldn't look it. I see her in one of those movies of the week about triumphant women putting up with abuse from her alcoholic husband and an insensitive bureaucracy. Something called *Shattered Dreams.*"

"Yeah, okay," Bollen said.

"It'd be a tragic story," Joey said.

"Yes, but with a happy ending," Bollen said.

"She triumphs at the end," Joey said.

"She kicks out the man." It was Carmen. "She realizes she doesn't need a man to survive or feel self-worth."

"When I decided to do *West Side Story,* I thought no one who auditioned would make a good Bernardo. That's when I remembered the Hispanic actor Mr. Williams told me about. I didn't connect that it was you. But I got your name and, well, Greg here told me you were in his class. I think you'd be a good Bernardo."

"I don't want to be in any plays," he said. "That was something from a long time ago."

"But this part, Joey, it's a great part. He's a gang leader. He's tough. He's handsome. Just looking at you, I can tell you look the part. Doesn't he, Greg?"

Mr. McNally nodded his head. "Yup," he said.

"What do you think, Carmen?"

"He definitely looks the part."

From where the confidence came he didn't know, because inside he was nervous about how he looked, how he sounded, whether or not he was eating too fast and eager, but he looked in Carmen's eyes and said, "Does that mean you think I'm handsome?"

She smiled but didn't answer, a smile that said, "You're such a smartass."

"Carmen's playing the part of Anita. Do you remember that role? Bernardo's girlfriend?"

"How come I've never seen you before?" he asked her.

"Actually," said Bollen, "she lives in Ashland. We're cheating a bit by importing her, but I just couldn't see a white girl playing the part of Anita. As you probably know, we take theater pretty seriously around here, what with the Shakespeare Festival."

"Last year, they did a production of *Bus Stop* that won a national high school competition. It's a play by Tennessee Williams."

"William Inge," Joey corrected.

"Are you sure, Joey?" He looked at Bollen, who nodded. "Oh, yeah, that's right. William Inge."

"*¿Eres Mexicana?*" he asked Carmen.

"*Puertoriqueña. Y tú?*"

"*Soy Chicano,*" he said.

"*¡Ay, Chicano!*" she said. "*No me gusta esta palabra.*"

"Do you sing and dance?" Bollen asked.

"I just don't have time for this," he said. "Sorry, man, but I'm not interested."

"Look," Bollen said. "Let me just give you the script, okay?" He handed him the book. "If you like the part, come by Wednesday at about three, to the theater, and we'll read you through it, have you sing a little. Prepare a song if you can, otherwise we'll have you sing something. Then we'll show you some dance steps."

He handed the script back. "Not interested."

But he wouldn't take it. "Just read it," he said, "tomorrow you can return it."

"*No quiero ser el único latino,*" Carmen said.

* * *

And he did read it that evening, sitting on Amy's bed as she smoked cigarettes and ran lines with him. "You'd be great in this play," she said.

"Can you open a window?"

"I'd be so proud of you."

"But those drama kids are weird. They're white kids who hang out in the cafeteria, acting all goofy. What would my friends think if I were a dramie?"

"I think they would be proud of you, too."

"What if I audition and don't get the part?"

"Oh, you'll get it," she said.

"Oh, shit. Check this out," he said, reading the script. He leaned in closer so she could read it too.

"What?" she said, resting her head on his shoulder. She smelled of cigarette smoke.

"Looks like I have to kiss Anita a couple of times."

"Let me see," she said, reading. "She better not be pretty," she said.

"Oh, I'm sure she's not," he said.

"You better not enjoy it."

"I'm going to hate it," he said, thumbing through the script. "Oh, my god!"

"What?"

"It says here that we have to use tongues."

She hit him. "You liar."

"Hey, does anyone remember seeing that movie *West Side Story?*" Joey asked the KA boys one evening as they drank beer in Johnny's backyard, the music coming from the shack Johnny shared with Clemente, who sat on the ice chest, drinking his beer.

Me preguntaste porque quiero morir
¿No es obvio?

"I remember watching that," said Clemente, rubbing his chin, eyes glittering with sadness. "That was cool, man. Made me want to be in a gang."

"They ought to do a movie out of us," said Johnny.

"That'd be cool," said Kurt. Over the silhouette of a house rooftop shone a constellation of stars in the dark sky, Orion, and Joey could make out the arms pulling the bow's string.

"So you guys think *West Side Story* was cool?" Joey asked.

"*West Side Story* was a bunch of faggots," said Gilbert. "Guys dancing around with their tight *puto* jeans."

All the others laughed, and he and George high-fived.

"Yeah, that was kind of stupid," Johnny said.

"I liked the knife fights," Joey said.

"Yeah," Walter said. "That was bad."

He went on and on about it, until he was certain they all thought it was the coolest movie ever. He told them it was probably the first time Latinos were portrayed positively, with no bullshit, even though they were Puerto Ricans and not Chicanos.

Clemente stood up, opened the ice chest, and grabbed another cold can. "The first time I seen that movie on TV, I remember saying, 'Daaamn. They look like me.'"

"Clemente's right," Joey said. "Wouldn't it have pissed you off if they got white guys to play the Puerto Ricans?"

They all agreed it would have pissed them off.

"They need Latinos in that play," Joey said.

"Play?" someone asked.

"I mean, they need Latinos in the movies."

"Hell, yeah," they agreed.

One night as he lay in bed, the script on his chest, he stared at the ceiling, and someone knocked on his bedroom door.

"Get out here," Rachel said. "I need to talk with you."

She walked away, and he followed her to the living room, where she sat at her piano and opened the top. She started with a few warm-up chords. The curtains were open, the porch light coming in, the streetlights yellow outside, a distant dog barking, that same dog that always barked every night, a husky voice, big. She turned around. She was radiant and in a good mood. "I'm going to play," she said, "and I want you to start in when you feel it."

"What are you talking about?" he said.

"We're going to prepare a song for your audition."

She played a few bars of songs he recognized. "The crooner songs show off your voice the best," she said, "so let's try one." Suddenly she started playing "Just in Time."

"How do you know I sing these songs? How do you know about the audition?"

"I hear you," she said, hitting a few happy notes, "and your girl-friend called." She played a light tune. She tried to imitate Amy's voice, but all she did was exaggerate the high pitch: " 'Did Joey tell you about *West Side Story?*' " She played a few more bars and stopped. "Just sing," she said, playing the intro again.

So he joined in.

"You left me on the edge of the city . . ."

"No, no, Joey. You're not alone. Listen to the notes. Pay atten-tion. Your voice is fine. Wonderful even. I love listening to you. You're a natural, but talent doesn't mean anything if you don't learn your craft."

She started the song again. "You'll hear when it's time to come in. On what key."

When he sang faster than the music, she told him to slow down, to listen to the beat and to think of his voice as part of it, like an instrument, not in opposition or separate from the music. They did the song several times until he got it right and belted it out so loud the windows seemed to rattle:

". . . so very very cruel to meeeeeee . . ."

She slammed on the keys, and he thought she was mad, but she turned around and said, "Very good. Let's try a duet. Do you know 'Can I Touch You'?"

"I don't think so," he said.

"Sure you do," she said, thumbing through a songbook. "It's got to be on one of those albums you collected." She started to play and sing.

"You can come closer
You can touch me.
Can I touch you?
You can kiss me.
I can really really kiss you?
Yes, you can kiss me."

"I know that song," he said, excited.

And she taught him Mexican songs, too, Trio Los Panchos, Javier Solís, and her favorite, Pedro Infante.

* * *

233

After that night they spent many nights together at the piano, and he was happy. He came home early and waited in the living room for her to come with an armful of piano books, sometimes around eight o'clock, but sometimes not until past ten, when she got home from school. She had moved her stuff into the family room and made an office for herself, a stack of books piled on a small table, a desk pushed into the corner, a table lamp, under the glare of which she read and wrote. William, of course, figured out she was going to school, but he said nothing to her about it. Sometimes when she studied late at night, she fell asleep in her office, occasionally on the same night that William fell asleep on the cot in his garage. On one such night, Joey wandered into their cool, dark bedroom, and he lay on the king-sized bed, the satiny comforter cool on his skin, the smell of perfume and aftershave, and he fell asleep.

"Okay, let's take it from the top," she'd say when she came out, ready to play piano. They started each evening with "Let's Call the Whole Thing Off."

Sometimes as they sang, they winked at each other, and sometimes on high notes Joey put his arm around her. Sometimes her fingers froze, and she'd look up at her singing son and say, "I think you're a little off," and he'd say, "Yeah? Well, you're plain nuts," and she'd start back up in the song where she had left off.

One night as they sang "Two Sleepy People," they noticed that Billy was sitting on the arm of the couch watching them, and he must have been there for quite a while because he wasn't looking surprised, just like he was enjoying the show. So every night he joined them, but he didn't sing. He clapped along and applauded when the songs were finished.

They only sang when William was at work, and although they never mentioned it, they all knew why they quit at a certain time each night, right before he came home, and they went off to their separate rooms.

When William walked into the house one night early from work, they all froze. He stood in the doorway, framed by darkness. He looked around. "What the hell's going on here?" he said.

"They're singing," said Billy.

"Is this some sort of family meeting?"

"They're just singing," said Billy.

"Horseshit. I want to know what the hell's going on." His gaze jerked back and forth.

"What are you talking about, Dad?" Billy asked.

Rachel and Joey stared in amazement.

"Don't think you could fuck with me," he said.

"Oh, you're so tough," she said, and she started playing again, as if he wasn't there, and the music seemed to make him angrier, but then she started singing, her sweet voice high and smooth, and Joey joined in.

William walked to his bedroom.

They kept singing song after song, some of which Billy joined in, although he couldn't carry a tune very well.

William came in the room and stood next to them and said, "I'm sorry. I guess I'm acting a little . . . Well, sorry."

They went on and he watched, and before long they were all singing. William snapped his fingers and at one point tried to hit a high note, but it was squeaky and off-key, and they all laughed and encouraged him to keep going and he did, pretending to try falsetto and causing Billy to hold his hands over his ears, and they laughed some more. This was the way it was supposed to be, a family that sings together, a family that laughs, like the Brady Bunch, a Chicano Brady Bunch. *La Bola Molina.*

* * *

One night Rachel and Joey stayed up and discussed music until his head felt heavy and he couldn't pay attention anymore. Suddenly she hit the keys of the piano. "I have a plan," she said.

"What do you mean?"

"I'm going to become a Spanish teacher."

"You think Medford needs Spanish teachers?"

"Who said anything about Medford?" she said.

"Or Ashland, for that matter," Joey said.

William came in. "Don't stop on account of me," he said, in a good mood, and he went to the kitchen.

"I'll tell you later," she whispered.

She turned around and started playing some dark, classical tune, little laughing imps. He knew where she was: that quiet place inside of herself to where she withdrew so often. He knew the blank look in her eyes, had seen it while she walked across the house or sat in a chair or played piano as if her fingers were not connected to the rest of her. He knew she would be there for the rest of the night. Joey touched her shoulder, and like an instinct, or perhaps in a motion of her playing, she shrugged his hand away. Her fingers moved smoothly over the keyboard, long skinny fingers the color of porcelain, the notes snapping and popping a song of sadness and beauty.

He spotted Carmen and Mr. Bollen sitting in the front row. Some boys sat in a circle next to the orchestra pit, giggling and slapping each other like girls, and a group of girls sat in the aisles, talking and studying their lines. He walked down the steps toward the stage. One of the boys saw Joey. "Oh, my God!"

Everyone turned toward the Chicano, and with the exception of Carmen, they were all white. They stared at him with his gangbanger baggy pants and crisp white T-shirt. He didn't belong. He felt like Yank in *The Hairy Ape.*

"Joey," said Bollen, standing up. "Come on down. How are you?"

"I'm okay," he said.

Carmen remained seated and said, "Hey."

"Hey," he said.

Bollen walked up a few stairs to meet him, touched his shoulder, and led him down toward the stage. "Cast, cast," he said. "This is Joey Molina. He's going to be trying out for Bernardo."

They stared. One of them whispered, "That's the guy that fought Randy Abbot."

"I'm glad you made it, Joey," Bollen said.

"Yeah, thanks," he said, trying to sound cool, but he was so nervous he pictured himself putting his palms on his cheeks and yelling, "*Eek!*"

One of the girls sitting in the middle of the theater was tall, dorky, skinny Leah, from his English class. When their eyes caught, she smiled and waved, her braces shining. Joey nodded his head at her.

"You know one of the girls?" Bollen asked.

"Leah's in my class," he said.

"Perfect. She's a Shark."

He led him to the stage. "What do you want to do first? A few dance steps? A song? Or would you like to do lines?"

"Where are we going to do it at?" He swallowed.

"Onstage," he said.

"Are all these people going to be here?"

"Well, Joey, if you play the part, there'll be a lot more people than this."

"Well, obviously, but . . ."

"It's part of the package."

Bollen noticed a rolled-up piece of paper in Joey's back pocket, "Is that the song you're going to sing?"

"Uh, yeah, I guess."

"Great." He grabbed it. "You can start off with a song. Allison, where's the pianist?"

A chubby blond girl dressed in black, including black-framed glasses, walked over with a clipboard, a pencil tucked in her ear.

"Joey, this is Allison. She's the stage manager."

"Hi," she said, beaming. "You look perfect," she said. "Exactly how I picture Bernardo."

"Uh, thanks."

"Could you please go get the pianist?" Bollen asked her. "She's in the back room, finding songs."

"Finding songs in the back room?"

"Yes, in the back room finding songs. She keeps them in boxes." He turned to Joey. "Old songs and show songs, like 'Gary, Indiana.'"

"You think she has 'Let's Call the Whole Thing Off'?"

"Inevitably."

"How about *'Cielito Lindo'*?"

"Who knows?"

Joey pictured the pianist in a dusty room bent over boxes of sheet music, pulling them out in piles, paper sailing around the room, the songs different colors of pages, red for love songs, blue for sad songs, and yellow for songs of despair. White was fear.

"This is pretty special, Joey, that we're doing this play," said Bollen. "Not very many high schools have ever done it before. But I got connections in New York with the company that owns it. It's going to be an awesome production."

"That's great," he said, thinking of blue *"Cielito Lindo"* in a box.

"Would you like to meet the cast?"

"Maybe later. Do you think she has 'You're Mean to Me?'"

"Hi, Joey." It was Leah. She looked so tall standing next to another girl. "We're Shark girls. We just want you to know, you *really* look the part."

"You think so?"

"Oh, yeah," said the other girl, giggling.

"But you know, there's a problem," Joey said, and where this confidence came from he didn't know, because he really was nervous. Yet he leaned into Leah like he was going to tell her a secret, the smell of her strawberry shampoo so familiar to him. The other girl leaned in, and they both listened attentively. Even Bollen listened, although he pretended like he wasn't paying attention.

"What?" the girls said, almost in unison. "What's the problem?"

"It says in the script . . ." And he took the book from the short girl and thumbed through it until he found the first description of Bernardo. "It says here that Bernardo is . . . *handsome.*" He slammed the book shut and handed it back.

"Oh," said the girl, both she and Leah laughing, looking at each other and then at Joey. "You *really* fit the part."

"You think so?"

Carmen shook her head and rolled her eyes.

It was a long walk around the orchestra pit, and he practically had to step over the circle of boys. When one of the boys, the one in the red shirt, put his palm on his chest and scowled, his braces sparkled. "Oh, God," he said.

Joey walked up the steps to the stage. The pianist entered, carrying the music, which she set on her piano, and she sat. The dramies started to take seats. "Good song," she said, thumbing through the white pages. "Any specific place you'd like to start?"

"No, I guess not," he said.

Then Mr. Bollen clapped. "Okay, people. Let's please be quiet."

If everyone hadn't been watching before, they were now. The guys who had been sitting in the circle whispered to each other and giggled and looked at Joey as if they wanted and expected him to fail.

Sweat dripped down his back. He looked toward the exit, at those shining red letters, E.X.I.T.

The pianist played, and when it was time for him to come in, she nodded her head and closed her eyes.

He cleared his throat, but nothing came out.

She stopped. "Am I off-key?"

"Huh?" he said.

The boys giggled and whispered.

"Is everything okay?"

"Fine." He felt the saliva slide down his throat.

The pianist mouthed, Ready? and she started again.

He closed his eyes and pictured himself in a movie musical. Just a role.

Joey Molina?

Why are you kneeling on the stage?

I want grass.

When the music reached the point where he was supposed to sing, he held out his arms and opened his mouth—but he looked in the audience and saw that Leah's face looked very serious, her fingers on her chin as if analyzing him, and he suddenly saw Sherry in the audience, legs crossed, and body bent forward to get a better look—so he stopped.

The boy in the red shirt stood up and yelled, "Next!" and they all laughed.

Mr. Bollen said, "That's enough, Burt."

The pianist stood up, walked over to him, and leaned over and whispered in his ear, "Pretend like we're alone." And then she walked back to the piano and sat.

The music started again. He belted it out.

"Hey you cats!
Gather around!
I got a story to tell.
About a boy who liked to dance
so much he could never settle down . . ."

As he walked to the edge of the stage, he held the word *down* for a few wavering notes, and then he sang, "He would dance on a stone." He pointed to Leah and winked, and she and her friend giggled.

He grabbed a chair, put one leg on it, and crooned.

Had he had a coat, he would have held it over his shoulder by a finger.

Then, at the end of the song, he ran across the stage and slid to a stop, went to his knees, held out his arms, and held the closing note until it echoed through the building.

"That little boy
is meeeeeeeeeeeeeeee. . . ."

The kids rose up and applauded and yelled.

Mr. Bollen had a big smile on his face. "Wow," he said. "You got quite a voice on you, Molina!"

The rest of the audition went great. He picked up the dance steps with little problem and even added some variations. When he was supposed to spin around, he twirled on one toe and spun around twice instead of once, landing with almost perfect balance. Clearly, he needed some direction, but it came naturally to him. He could kick high, too.

The choreographer told him that she was going to try and teach him something very difficult. "Don't get frustrated," she said. "Don't be so hard on yourself if you don't get it the first time. Basically, I'm just seeing how you take direction." She explained he was to dance across the stage, jumping up on one leg—here was the tough part—spinning in the air, and then landing on the other foot. He was to do this all across the stage. She showed him, and her svelte dancer's body made it seem so effortless, and when she got to the other side of the stage, she asked him to try it.

He did it the first time.

She nodded her head and looked down at Bollen, sitting in the front row. "I could work with this guy," she said.

Finally, he was asked to act.

The first scene, with Carmen, was when Bernardo and Anita tease each other. That was easy for both of them.

The next scene they read was the dance at the gym with his favorite Bernardo line, which he delivers to Riff, the leader of the Jets, the white street gang. "I understand the rules, native boy," he said.

It was magic. This is what he was meant to do, and if he had been diverted away from it before, he knew now that he would never drift away again. He was an actor. And a singer. An entertainer.

After the scene, the boy in the red shirt put his hand on Joey's shoulder and said, "I don't want to be a Jet anymore. I'm a Shark now." And they all laughed.

"Joey, we'd like you to be Bernardo," Bollen said, and the cast clapped and cheered.

Carmen smiled and said, "Way to go, Nardo!"

"Cool," Joey said.

Rachel, seated at the table, looked angry, but he thought it was just the mood she was in.

"Hi, Mom," he said, standing right in front of her. He had this urge to put his arms around her and kiss her, but instead he tapped a one-two-three beat on the table and sat opposite her. "So. Guess what?"

Her hands went into red fists. "Joey, how could you?"

"What?" he said.

"You . . ."

"What did I do?"

"What the hell is this garbage?"

Then he noticed on the table in front of her were two *Playboy* magazines that he had hidden under his mattress.

"Oh," he said.

She stood up. "What is wrong with you, Joey? Look at this." She opened a page to a big-breasted blond woman naked on a leather armchair. "Her legs are wide open like an animal."

"I'm sorry," he said.

"Do you think women are animals??"

"No," he said.

"Do you want to be like your father?"

"No," he said.

"I don't ever want to see this garbage in my house again. Is that clear?"

"I'm sorry," he said.

"Women are not animals," she said.

"No, they're not."

"You're just like your father."

"I'm not!"

"Get the hell out of here. I don't want to see you again."

He went to his room, shut the door, and lay in bed. After a while the piano started, "Moonlight Sonata." She messed up in the exact spot, her hands so angry that the random notes rose around him like a jail. Then she started on another piece, which was slow and sad and beautiful. On one hand, it had a New Age triangle of repetitive notes, which varied every third time to a higher note and then went back over and over until it was so familiar it might have been his own rhythm, and the other hand played bass, like the voice of loneliness.

He rose from his bed and opened the bedroom window and climbed out. Droopy was excited to see him, running circles around him and yelping, but he ignored him, and when he reached the fence, he pushed him away with his foot and then climbed over.

She was wearing the same short dress she had worn to school that day because she had barely gotten off work at the doughnut shop. She kissed him at the door, and when he looked at her legs and said, "Wow," she spun around like a model and said, "Like it?"

"It's nice," he said.

She screamed when he told her he was Bernardo, and to celebrate, her mom called the kids together and they all smoked a joint. Then the two of them went into her bedroom. She sat on the bed with her legs open, showing her tight underwear under her short dress, while he stood pacing, reading his lines, trying to pretend not to be looking at her sitting there. Finally, he walked over and closed her legs. "What did you do that for?" she asked.

"Women are not animals," he said.

She smiled and slowly opened them again. He threw down the script and jumped on the bed and crawled on top of her and kissed her.

"I love you, Joey," she said, scratching his chest.

"Me too."

He began kissing her neck.

"Joey?"

"Yeah?"

"You love me, don't you?"

"Sure, I do."

"I'm not an animal," she said.

"No, baby, you're not an animal."

"I'm Joey's girl."

"Yes."

"Joey's girl!"

"Yes . . .

"Yes . . .

He went to pee and Billy was in the bathroom with the door open, combing his hair and making faces in the mirror. Joey stepped inside, closed the door, and pulled down his sweats.

"Hey, fat boy," Billy said.

"Fat boy, my ass, look at this bod." He wasn't wearing a shirt, so he flexed his chest muscles so that the pecs moved up and down. The muscles in his stomach twitched. "I guess your prediction was wrong," he said.

"What prediction?" Billy asked, exposing his teeth and examining them in the mirror.

"That picture you drew. Remember? 'Joey Molina, twenty-six years old, eating empanadas.'"

"I don't know what you're talking about. What picture?"

"A long time ago," he said. "Pigs are scattering to get away from me."

"Oh, yeah. I still got that."

"You were wrong, *ese.* Check out this bod. Not an ounce of fat. When I'm twenty-six, I'll be looking good."

"You still got ten years to mess up your life. We'll talk then, fat boy."

"Know what else? I'm Bernardo in *West Side Story.*" He waited for a reaction, but all Billy did was pick at his teeth. "I got the part, man."

"So, does that mean you're going to run around in tights? Like Tinkerbell?"

"I'm going to be Nardo. Leader of the Sharks."

Billy washed his face, stood up, and looked at himself in the mirror. "Stay away from Dad today."

"Why?"

"You know the Kennedy heads in the bedroom?" He cupped his hands and let water fill up, and he drank and slightly winced, as if he had gulped a shot of vodka. "Mom broke them last night. John and Jackie."

From the master bedroom, they heard the toilet flush and then the basin water run.

"Let's hope that she's close to leaving that asshole."

"What about the family?" Joey asked.

"What family?" Billy said, looking in his brother's eyes, and then he punched him on the arm. "So you're going to be in a play?"

"*West Side Story,*" he said.

"You're going to be a famous actor someday?"

"Maybe. Right now I'm going to make me some breakfast."

He would never forget what happened that morning in the kitchen. Years later he would remember it in vivid detail, and although he might have added some of the details, the colors, the smells, he didn't change or exaggerate the truth of the matter. The truth would always be the same: the hatred in his father's eyes, the clenched fists, LOVE, HATE, the violence. He may not have remembered exactly what he was wearing that morning, but he pictured himself in sweat pants and no shirt, and maybe he didn't remember exactly what day it was, Tuesday, Wednesday, Thursday, but he was certain that it was midweek, and he knew that it was the day after he had gotten the part of Bernardo, the morning after he had snuck out and slept over at Amy's house. He remembered, too, that it was a beautiful day, cloudless, smokeless, as if there had never been a lumber factory in Medford.

But of course the strongest, most disturbing details of that morning were his father's clenched teeth, eyes red with anger, kicking repeatedly, unleashing a rage that could have only belonged to multiple generations of Molinas.

Now, a few minutes before it would happen, Joey was in the kitchen by himself. He was happy and excited to make breakfast. Happy to be an actor again. He wanted to celebrate by eating eggs with cheese, fried bologna, refried beans, and toast covered with yellow margarine. He fantasized that he was a restaurant owner and imagined the words on the menu that would describe such a fantastic breakfast, *The Joey Molina "Good Morning" Special! Scrambled eggs smothered with melted cheese, tasty bologna fried to Chinese-hat perfection, and a pile of toast with your choice of fruity jellies and marmalades.*

He could hardly wait.

Droopy scratched at the kitchen door and barked, but Joey didn't know that would turn out to be an important detail, ominous, prophetic, the sound. No, it was just a bark.

"Are you hungry, little fellow?" he yelled through the door.

Droopy barked and whined.

"One doggy special coming up!"

Crunchy meaty chunks generously stacked in a bowl.

The back door had a window on the top half of it, and occasionally Droopy's paws reached up. "Oh, how cute!" Joey said. "Such tiny pawskies!"

He grabbed the bag of dry food and opened the door, the sun cool and fresh, and some birds were singing and maybe it was spring because he remembered things blooming, yellow sunflowers, golden poppies. "A beautiful day," he said as he pushed Droopy back with his foot so he wouldn't run into the house.

"Good morning, little fella!"

The dog jumped on Joey.

"Ow! No! Down!" He raised his hands as if he would hit the dog. "See?" he said, shaking his finger at him. "Here I am trying to be all nice to you, and all you can do is think about yourself. Just for that, I'm not going to feed you." He held the cool bag close to his chest and could smell the dried beef flavor (or was it chicken? pork? He wasn't sure, just that it smelled like dry meat).

"Nope!" he said to Droopy. "This delicious food is mine now. You're just going to have to starve today, you worthless mutt."

The dog tilted his head and stared.

"Yes, sir, you're about the most worthless dog there is. How did you get so worthless? You don't deserve food. No, sir." Then his voice got high-pitched. "No, sir. No, sir! Him a piece of shit."

He leaned over the dog.

"My baby want to starve?"

Droopy got so excited that he yelped and cried and barked.

"All right, all right, that's a pretty convincing argument," he said. "Even dummies got to eat."

He poured his bowl full of food, but the dog sniffed at it and then looked up at Joey.

Inside, Joey pulled out a carton of eggs and a package of bologna. On the edge of a bowl, he cracked an egg, opened it, and let the slimy innards fall into the ceramic cradle. Then he cracked another and another. He mixed the eggs with a fork, his wrist moving so fast that the eggs became spinning, blurry yellow, and he sang like an Italian chef,

"Mama mia
pizzaria
flavor of Italy!"

He sprinkled salt and pepper. He put a pan on the stove. Reached for a loaf of bread. He had to uncover the toaster, because the counter was a mess, smeared with food stains and cluttered with used paper towels and dirty dishes and a can opener, which shone in the sun like a medieval torture tool. "Mama mia!" he yelled. "I'm afiring the dishwasher!"

He should have left the kitchen.

He should have gone to school without breakfast, but he stayed, because in his mind he could smell the fried bologna and cheesy eggs.

He put the bread in the toaster and lowered it.

He turned around and walked across the kitchen to the sink below the window, took a clean coffee cup from the dish rack, and filled it with tap water while he looked out.

Across, through the neighbor's kitchen window, he could see the teenage girl running around as if trying to get ready in a hurry, while her mother leaned against a counter, smoking a cigarette and shaking her head.

Joey drank the water.

The neighbor boy, Ronny, entered their own kitchen carrying a cereal bowl with a big spoon sticking from it. Their windows were opposite each other. Holding a big empty bowl, Ronny Morris looked like Oliver Twist about to ask for more. He put the bowl in the sink and looked up, and for a few seconds they stared at each other as if they were each other's reflection. Then Joey smiled. Joey liked Ronny. Ronny liked Joey. Ronny waved. Joey lifted his cup as for a toast and took another drink. Ronny looked around and found a glass, which he filled with tap water, lifted, and drank.

Suddenly Ronny's eyes grew wide; he waved good-bye and left.

Droopy barked and scratched.

Joey turned his neck and saw his dad come in, his eyes red and squinting. He hadn't shaved yet either, and Joey always thought that made him look mean, like a gangster. "You better shut that dog up," he said as he walked over to a cupboard and pulled it open.

"Droopy, shut up," Joey yelled, and he was relieved that the dog actually shut up.

"Working the day shift this week?" Joey asked.

"No shit, Sam Spade." The coffee can he grabbed from the shelf was empty, so he threw it into the sink. The next one he pulled out was unopened under the plastic lid. "Shit," he said. He set it on the counter and impatiently pawed through the silverware drawer, the forks and spoons clanking with intensity. "Where the hell is the can opener?" he said.

Joey lifted it from the counter, glad it was there, and he handed it to his father. He wanted out of there, decided that he wouldn't have eggs and bologna, but he had to wait for his toast. The eggs in the bowl he could hide in the pile of dirty dishes, but if he left the toast, his father would get him for wasting food.

Droopy scratched on the door and whined.

The father ran the water over the metal coffee filter of the percolator and then shook it dry and stuck it in the pot.

Joey looked inside the toaster slots at the bread, hoping to see the edges had begun to brown (Come on, bread! he thought), hoping to hear the "pop" when they shot up, ready to eat.

The father breathed through his nose, like puffing, as he measured spoons of coffee grounds and dumped them into the filter. "Fucking bitch."

The toaster's heating wires glowed orange, but the bread was still white.

At last, the toast popped up.

Joey held the hot slices in his palm and tried to leave, but he saw the margarine stick and feared that if he left it out, the father would notice, so he placed the toast on the rim of a glass and took a knife caked with dried mustard, wiped off as much as he could with a used paper towel, and stuck it into the stick of margarine.

Droopy barked repeatedly.

"You better shut that dog up," he said.

"Droopy, shut up," Joey yelled, but he barked some more and then scratched on the door. His black and white paws reached up to the window.

"No, Droopy!" he yelled, but he barked more, so as quickly as he could, he went out the back door. Droopy whined and tried to jump on him. On his knees, he firmly held the dog's head in his hands and looked into his eyes. "Please, be quiet. Now. Shut up."

The dog squirmed out of Joey's grasp, and he barked.

"Shut up."

But he kept barking and more and more loudly. Joey stood there dumbly, not knowing what to do. "Please," he said.

That's when the father came from the house. "Shut the fuck up," he yelled.

Droopy started barking at him, not the same way that he barked at Joey, but as if the father were an intruder, his body stiffening and his tail pointing straight up.

"Little fucker," William yelled. He came toward the dog, his teeth clenched, his eyes raging. He cocked his foot back and let out a kick so hard that Joey heard the thump of the steel-toed work boots against Droopy's body. The dog collapsed, as if his legs gave out, and the father came closer, because he wasn't finished. He kicked, over and over, the face, the ribs, the head. Over and over.

Joey sat in the back with the dog, whose head bled into a yellow towel. Joey bawled like a baby. For a second he saw an image of himself in the car, as if he were one of his homeboys standing on the curb as the car passed, saw his head and shoulders framed by the window like one of his father's busts. He looked like a little wimp. He felt the instinct to wipe his tears and act like a man. He was a gang leader who saw death all the time, not a little snotty-nosed kid who knew nothing of pain. He looked down at Droopy.

One of his eyes was bleeding.

Joey kept crying.

As they waited for the doctor who was working on the dog, Joey and Rachel sat on hard orange chairs in the lobby.

She took in a big breath and closed her eyes. "He's not a good human being," she said.

"I'm sorry," Joey said.

He started crying again. He saw himself again. "*Boo-hoo,*" crying like a stupid, worthless baby. He was worthless to the core. Hadn't he just stood there in shock while his father beat his dog? "I'm sorry."

"About what?" she asked.

"I'm sorry for being so much like him."

"Oh, Joey, you're nothing like him."

"I got the part," he said. "I'm Bernardo."

"Oh, that's wonderful. I knew you would. Look, Joey, Friday morning at five o'clock, be ready."

"For what?"

"I'm taking you somewhere, so be ready."

"Where?"

"There's something you should know."

"You mean the *plan?*" he asked.

"The plan," she said.

The doctor came out, smiled serenely, and said, "He's going to be all right." He was a tall thin white man with perfect teeth and a fatherly look. "What happened?" the doctor asked.

And Joey, like he was six years old, started crying again.

The doctor held his shoulder and squeezed. "It's okay, son," he said. "Let it all out."

He was certain he looked ridiculous with this white doctor on one side and his blond-haired mother on the other side, comforting him, a black-haired Indian boy dressed like a Chicano gangbanger.

He hit it off with the effeminate guy, whose name was Burt Blunk and who played the part of Action, a Jet, and could sing and dance so well he might have gotten the lead if he looked any different. He had severe acne, and his jaw was bigger than the rest of his face, his forehead pushed back, and he was nearly walleyed. Onstage he lost his effeminate quality and looked pretty tough, and the "Officer Krupke" song, which he led, was the best number in the play, Joey told him.

But he insisted that Joey's was better. The script calls for the

"America" song to be sung by the Shark girls, but Bollen liked the movie version better, where it's sung by Anita and Bernardo, a kind of a war of the sexes, so that's how they did it.

"Your song is better," Joey said.

"No, yours is," Burt said.

"Okay, you're right, mine is."

"No, I see your point. Mine's the best."

And they'd giggle until they attracted too much attention.

One time, as they were sitting in the audience, Joey told Burt that he wouldn't mind being with Carmen in real life. She was on-stage with the girl who played Maria, a short white girl with her hair dyed black. Carmen's voice carried through the theater, the Puerto Rican accent slight and authentic and very sexy, Joey thought.

"But she's got a boyfriend," he told Burt. "And I have Amy." Then he asked Burt which girl he would want to be with.

"Are you serious?" he said.

"Yeah, which one would you want to be with the most?"

He slapped Joey on the shoulder.

"What was that for?" he asked.

"Are you completely clueless, Molina?"

"What do you mean?"

"For someone who has a lot of street smarts, you don't know much." He smiled a Cheshire cat grin, as if Joey should be able to read something from it.

"You don't like girls?"

"Bingo."

"Oh, you're, uh . . ."

"That's right."

"Oh, well, I like girls."

"Duh," he said. Onstage, Bollen was talking with the girl who

255

played Maria, while Anita, sitting at the sewing machine, dreamily took a look around the theater, at the ceiling, the walls, then at Joey, and their eyes caught. He smiled. She stuck out her tongue at him and turned away.

"She likes you," Burt said.

"You know, this is the first time I've met a person like you, you know, with your sexual preference."

"Oh, you've met plenty of us. You just didn't know it."

"Well, that may be."

Mr. Bollen was laughing, and then he hugged Maria and walked off the stage for them to try the scene again. "Mr. Bollen," said Burt.

"Him too?"

"Yup."

"Wow. I guess I *am* naive."

"Joey, wake up," she said. He looked up at her, crossing her arms, impatient. "I told you be ready by five."

"I'm ready," he said, trying to gain his full mind. "I had a dream."

She put her hands on her hips and sighed. "What about?"

"I don't remember."

"Get up. Let's go."

Rachel held a cup of coffee as she drove through the dark town, a ceramic cup with no lid, practically filled to the top. Joey was amazed that she hadn't spilled any.

She took a sip.

"Where are we going?" he asked, looking out his window.

"*Pa' viejo,*" she said.

"Old age?" he asked.

A paperboy, walking alone in the darkness, threw a paper—a white bat in flight—to the porch of a white house. As the car passed under a streetlight, Joey's full face flashed in the reflection of the glass, but when it passed, he saw the sleepy houses and yards.

They drove out of town and through rural streets lined with pear orchards, past the old labor camps and then onto a road winding up a foothill. She parked on a plateau of Rosy Ann Hill. He was wide awake now, enough to wonder what she was going to tell him, what the plan was.

"Look at the town," was the first thing she said. Below, a basin of lights shone among patches of blacker black, the trees. "It doesn't look so bad from up here."

"So tell me the plan," he said.

"Look," she said.

Slowly, yet with a speed that surprised him, that he thought only possible on TV or in the movies, the town below began to turn rose colored, slowly, gently. As the sun broke over Rosy Ann Hill, light spread across the town like slowly spilled wine, and it rushed up the opposite mountains. "Wow," Joey said. "That's pretty cool."

"Isn't it?"

When he looked at his mom, he noticed that she wasn't looking at the sunrise, she wasn't looking down the hill, but at Joey, as if he were the thing of beauty.

"What?" he said.

"You got a good heart, Joey."

"Oh?"

"Don't forget that."

He looked back down the hill, could see the main avenue crossing the town like a scar. "Thanks." He thought of Amy and suddenly felt guilty. He wasn't a good man, he wasn't loyal to her since he had noticed Carmen, thought of her in "that way." He felt a sudden urge to call Amy and say that he loved her, and he resolved that from now on he would stay away from Carmen as much as possible. He wasn't a good person.

Rachel started the car and said, "Let's go get some breakfast."

"Really?" Joey asked. "At a restaurant?"

"How about Newberry's?"

After ordering, she told him the plan. She would be getting her degree in less than a year. Then she'd go back to California and teach high school. If she liked it, she'd do it forever; if she didn't, she'd take night classes toward a master's degree and get into administration, but meanwhile she would have her teaching job, and would not need anyone else's income. She didn't want to be in Oregon. She hated it, hated how no matter how long she lived there, if she ever talked to people who lived in the town, eventually they would say something racist, something about Mexicans or about how Californians were ruining their state with all the immigration. "Don't Californicate Oregon," they would say.

She recalled when the neighbor lady brought over an eighth-grade English grammar book she had found in her attic. She told Rachel that it was hers at one time, but that maybe Rachel could use it more. "It could help you with your English," she said.

This, the woman who had been living next door to her for years, with whom she had had conversations, a woman who had probably never read a book since high school. Rachel reluctantly took the book from her, her face turning red with anger, and she said, "This particular approach to language has been pedagogically discredited."

"Yeah," said the lady, "I like them too."

She wanted out of Oregon, but mostly, she wanted to be away

from William. She would have left him years earlier, when it occurred to her in a clarity unprecedented by experience that he wasn't a good man—she would have left him then and gone back to Fresno—but she had no money and would have had to move in with her mother. William, she knew, wouldn't be quick to send her money, even if the court did order it after a year of fighting with a lawyer she couldn't afford. William had an income too significant to not take advantage of, an income that she too had worked toward. With his salary, she didn't have to work and could go to school full-time. Let him pay for it.

The breakfast arrived, hot and salty-smelling, and Joey immediately put ketchup on his hash browns and began to put jelly on his toast. He looked happy.

Rachel looked at her breakfast as if it were just a fact.

"But that's not the only reason I stayed with him. I would have left the bastard a long time ago. Do you remember that night we went to that company dinner? I would have left the next day."

"What happened that night?" Joey asked, putting down the knife.

"We had just gotten to Medford, remember?"

"Yes!" he said, impatient to hear the story. "Tell me. I've been waiting for years."

"He rented a tuxedo and bought me a new dress. At first, it was such a beautiful night, so I thought. I was stupid and arrogant. Everyone thought I was beautiful, or at least they told me as much, and I liked it. Too vain to notice all the attention your father got from some of the wives. I mean, I noticed, but I didn't notice until later how he really felt about it. He could have slept with any of them; they treated him like he was some exotic creature, some noble savage in a tuxedo for the first time. They asked him if it was true that he had a tattoo on his chest. He smiled. They asked him about the tattoos on his fingers, LOVE and HATE.

"Men flirted with me, but carefully, as if they didn't want to offend your father. One man told me that he knew better than to mess with the wife of a macho Latin man. I felt like slapping him. Is that what he thinks of me, the wife of a macho? That's when it hit me. Your father was the best minority token they could have asked for, handsome, young, with a wife not bad to look at. In fact, those *norteamericanos* were surprised to find out that I was Mexican, surprised to hear my accent, like they didn't know Mexicans could be light skinned. They thought I was an American, a blond white woman, until I spoke and they heard my accent. Then they guessed I was from Spain. 'I'm Mexican,' I must have said a million times that night. You can imagine the image they had of your father with a blond wife, because to them, success for a man is a pretty blond woman on his arm. And they call Latino men macho.

"There was this sixteen-year-old girl bored with the party. I saw her sneaking drinks of her mother's champagne, so she was probably a little tipsy, the daughter of one of the executives. When she saw how much her mother was fawning over your father, she must have thought she could get her mother back for something, to hurt her mother.

"Who knows what she thought, but she kept looking at your father, and whenever he said something at the table, she said, 'Gaw, Mr. Molina! Really?'

"At first I just thought it was cute that she had a crush on your father, but later I saw how disgusting it was. Your stupid father ate it up. He felt like a king.

"And then I caught them.

"At first they were just exchanging glances and smiles, but then they were mouthing words to each other. Finally, there it was, right under the table, her hand on your father's knees and he had his hand in her dress, on her bare thigh, his fingers slightly massaging. He's drunk by now, of course, but that's no excuse. I was going to leave him, Joey, I was going to leave him, but you know why I didn't?"

"Why?"

"Because of you."

When she came home angry and William disappeared for the weekend, she knew things would never be the same between them, but she had to have a plan. She got a job right away after that, but the pay was so little it would have taken her twenty years to save anything that would help. In Medford, there were few opportunities for women to earn money. The idea of leaving him with such a large income, a single man, in a town where he could find a wife to take her place in no time, was too bothersome. Over the next few years she lived out the days of her life as anyone else would live theirs, and at times, as happens to most people, she lost sight of the plan and lived the days as if they were not connected to anything else but the moment. And like everyone else, there were moments of happiness, a new song she learned on the piano, a sunset as she drove home, an unexpected etymology. She liked seeing Joey in the corner of his bedroom reading yet another book he had bought at the secondhand store.

Then William would do something stupid, something that showed his worthlessness, and she would count accounts to see how far she was from going away. For a few years, things seemed okay, and she had thought little of the plan. She knew she didn't love William, but she found herself tolerating living in the same house. She didn't have sex with him, except for a few times when her desire was too great to resist, and she used her husband for sex (a detail Joey didn't want to hear).

"Let's just leave him, Mom. We don't need him."

She explained that to leave William, Joey would either have had to go with her to Fresno or stay with his father, and either way he would be swallowed by forces darker and stronger than himself. In Fresno, she'd be poor. The so-called wealth of her family when she was a teenager wasn't even as much as an illusion anymore. After her father died, all her mother had was that house in Pinedale, and her siblings were successful bums who moved off to other states with their white spouses and never sent money. The neighborhood she grew up in had become even more dilapidated in recent years. Pinedale was gang territory, said to be one of the toughest barrios in the city. In front of little houses that lined the streets, *cholos* barbequed and drank beer, and gunshots consistently rang out in the night air like the town clock. On New Year's Eve, so many guns went off at midnight that every year at least one person was killed. If Joey went to live there with his baggy pants and his illusion of being Chicano, he'd be swallowed by the streets. Either he'd become a gang member—a real gang member, Rachel emphasized, not a pretend gang member—or he'd be killed. The alternative, staying alone with his father while Rachel went to Fresno, would be even worse.

After a few months alone with him, he would become him. Billy she didn't worry about. He hated his father and would find a way out of the house. Most likely he wouldn't want to go back to Fresno, but would stay in Oregon with his girlfriend, Charley. Her dad loved Billy and treated him like a son. "He'll be an excellent husband," Rachel said.

But Joey, too weak, too easily led astray, would be overtaken. "I couldn't let that happen to you."

"Why?"

"There's something about you that worries me," she said.

"What?"

She smiled. "I'm not telling."

He looked down at his breakfast, untouched, cold. The waitress came by, and Rachel asked for the check. She nibbled on her toast and ate a forkful of scrambled eggs. Joey gobbled down his food in a few minutes and then ate her cold bacon.

"So here's the thing," she said to her son as they walked back to her car. She got in, he got in, but before starting the engine, she turned toward him. Looked him in the eyes. "You're just not ready to hear everything."

"What's that supposed to mean?"

"In time, okay? But here's the thing: do me this favor. Stay away from your father. Avoid him as much as possible. I'm not kidding, Joey. You just have to hold out for a little longer, and we'll be away from him for good. Keep your distance. Promise?"

"Why?"

"So you don't become him."

Each night he left the theater without saying good-bye to anyone because they all had their own cars or rode together, and he didn't want anyone to offer him a ride. He didn't want to be close to them outside of the theater, just in case he saw some of his friends, who wouldn't understand why he would want to hang out with dramies. In the theater, they could be friends, but outside was different, and the actors seemed to understand this. Whenever Burt Blunk saw him in the schoolyard hanging out with his tough friends, he didn't even look his way, let alone try to talk with him, but during rehearsals they giggled and slapped each other and made funny voices and faces and did impressions of famous people.

Regardless of the reason that he walked alone every night, he began to enjoy it. The time to think, to feel the peacefulness of his days, became for him an important ritual, something he had never had before, because usually whenever he was alone he began to think too much, to worry about something, and needed to be around someone so he wouldn't have to struggle with his thoughts, as if the very presence of another being somehow assured him that he was all right. But not now. He was so happy with his life that he wished he could share it with himself, to go back in time to when he was twelve, afraid to leave Fresno. He imagined that twelve-year-old Joey was walking with him on this cool, moonlit night. He told him, "See, everything turned out fine. The future was fine."

The twelve-year-old Joey nodded his head, said, Yeah, he sure was enjoying this play a lot more than he would have enjoyed playing the king, but still he felt a little sad about missing it, and he missed Sherry Garcia.

Joey pictured her black eyes and mischievous smile as she bent back his wrists and challenged him to show how tough he was, and he felt a slight sense of loss. "Yeah, she was cool," he said, wondering how she would react to see him now, a *cholo,* a tough guy, but still an actor. "You should try to call her," the twelve-year-old suggested, but Joey said no, that he would wait, that he would see her again some-day. He was no longer the skinny weak kid he used to be. "I'm not that weak!" said the twelve-year-old. "No offense," said the teenager. Now he was chasing the future. And he reminded twelve-year-old Joey how wonderful Amy was, "the point being, little Joey, the future didn't turn out as bad as you thought."

Then they felt the presence of Joey "Fat Boy" Molina at twenty-six, and turned to see him walking beside them eating empanadas, shaking his head as if the other selves were fools. On his flabby arm was a tattoo that said FAT BOY.

"What do you want?" Joey said.

"You don't know shit about the future," he said.

"I know it's going to be fine," and little Joey nodded his head in emphatic agreement.

"So you think," said older Joey. "But the future is something to fear. Fear it, Ophelia! Fear it!"

In unison, the younger Joeys said, "Shut up, fat boy."

"You'll see."

The neighborhood gave way to a dark, unlit road lined with houses so dilapidated it was hard to believe people still lived in them, yet he knew Randy Abbot lived in one of them with his mother.

On his side of the street lay a field of pine trees and tall weeds, where people had dumped piles of junk, branches, grass, dirt, a hollowed-out car, washing machines. Through the tree trunks, he could see the lights of a busy street at the other end.

Suddenly he heard an engine and muffled rock music. A pair of headlights appeared at the end of the street, getting bigger and brighter as they came toward him, his shadow rising in the trees like a rubber giant. Before he could make out what kind of car it was, it slowed to a crawl, the lights so bright he had to cover his eyes. It slowed down even more and rolled toward him, a red four-wheel-drive pickup. Perry Doyle. He could barely make out the shapes in the cab, three of them, but he recognized Randy Abbot sitting shotgun. It slowly passed, the dash lights glowing like a candle on the golden faces of the boys, clear as a Dutch painting.

The truck stopped, and Randy Abbot got out.

Joey pivoted on the heels of his black work boots and ran into the field. He swerved between the trunks of trees as the weeds and rocks crackled underfoot. He could hear Randy's heavy footfalls behind him. Light from the other end of the field filtered through the trunks and branches like lasers shooting on and off, but he could barely see where he was stepping and his foot sunk into a pile of branches, and he tripped to his knees. He pulled himself out and went around the pile and ran, but he came across Joey at twenty-six, running beside him. "You're going too fast," said Fat Boy, out of breath.

He heard Abbot running behind him, and through the trunks of the trees, he saw the red four-wheel-drive truck speed down the street, headed around the block to head him off at the main road. He jumped over a discarded sink, his legs extended in the air midstride, but his foot landed on a log, and he lost his balance, fell backward, and slid across weeds and rocks, scraping his elbows and feeling something sharp poke his back.

He stood up and ran through the trees, the pain on his elbows sharp like cuts. At last he reached the sidewalk. Down the street, the truck had just turned the corner and pulled into the traffic coming toward him. In the opposite direction, across the street, about a block away, was his safety.

A gas station. The blue-and-red sign perched on a sky-high pole, so it could be seen from the freeway, which roared beyond a cluster of giant eucalyptus trees. The lights colored the street and the sidewalk and the tops of the trees. If he ran across, perhaps he could reach it before they could, so he was about to do that when a car pulled over and stopped right in front of him.

The blue-and-red sign reflected on the windshield, but through it he could make out a shape, and then, as it leaned over the passenger's seat, a face. A smile. It was Leah. She rolled down the window.

"Hi, Joey. Want a ride?"

When she got to his house, she turned off the engine. He hadn't said much the entire ride because he was busy looking back to make sure they weren't being followed, and his elbows hurt. Now he looked at her. With a finger, she flicked the keys hanging from the ignition, making little ringing sounds. "What are you going to do the rest of the night?" she asked without looking at him.

"I don't know," he said. He touched his elbow and felt the moisture and the sting. "What about you?"

"Work on McNally's paper. Although I don't know why I put so much effort into them. I'll get a B no matter what."

"Yeah." The neighbor's porch light flashed on. "I take it you're going to college," he said.

"Of course," she said. "You too?"

"My mom said she'd kill me if I didn't."

"Hey, you want to go get something to drink?" she asked. "A milkshake or something?"

He would have liked to, but he didn't have any money, so he said, "It's getting kind of late."

"Yeah," she said.

He laughed.

"What?" she said.

"I just thought of something funny."

"What?" she said.

"I pictured Burt in a real gang fight. Slapping his opponent."

She nodded. "Oh," she said.

"Did you know he's gay?" he said.

"Of course."

"He says Bollen is too."

"Yeah, that's true. Haven't you ever been in a play before?" she asked.

"No, this is the first."

"Really? Amazing. Anyway, a lot of theater people are gay." She tucked her hair behind an ear and smiled at him, her braces glittering. When she turned away, she put her hands on the steering wheel. Suddenly she started to make engine noises, her lips puttering like a race car, changing gears, first, second, third, the car going faster and faster and the engine screaming louder and louder, and then she turned the steering wheel and made high-pitched skid sounds. *Errrrrrrrrrrrrrrrr.*

"Watch it!" he yelled. "We're headed right toward that fruit stand!"

"Oh, crap," she said, and she made crashing sounds.

"Look at those cantaloupes roll down the street," he said.

"And watermelons down the sidewalk," she said.

"And bananas."

"Rolling bananas?" she asked.

"Bananas shooting through the sky like spears."

"Tomatoes splattering on innocent bystanders," she said.

"Oh, my God!" he yelled, pointing out the windshield. "A lady pushing a baby stroller!"

She turned the wheel, and together they made the skidding sounds. *Errrrrrrrrrrrrrrrrrr!*

"Did I miss her?" she asked.

"Yeah," he said, looking back. "But you ran over that Boy Scout troop."

"Never liked the little fascists anyway," she said.

Suddenly, they were silent.

She looked at him. "It shouldn't take too long. One milkshake. Come on, I'm buying."

"All right. Sure."

"Great." She started up the car and turned it around and headed out of the court. She drove downtown to Main Street, and everything was closed except for the doughnut shop, plate-glass windows all around, bright with lights, and a few timeless cars parked out front, shining factory red and blue paint jobs under the lights. She pulled into the lot.

"My girlfriend works here," Joey said. Amy stood at the counter, handing a cup of coffee to some bald man.

"You have a girlfriend?" she asked.

269

"That's her," he said.

Amy was joking with the bald man, and she took a rag and pretended to want to hit him with it. He was a middle-aged man with glasses. Amy punched some figures into the cash register, a silver box.

"Amy's your girlfriend?" Leah asked.

"I keep forgetting how small this town is. Everyone knows everyone."

"That's for sure. See that man she's talking to? Know who he is?"

He shook his head.

"He works with my mother. He's a doctor."

"Your mother a nurse?"

"No, she's a doctor, too."

"Oh. And your father? Is he a nurse?"

"It's just my mom and me."

"No siblings?"

"A brother away at college."

The bald doctor took the change from Amy, but he didn't go to a table. He stood there and joked around with her more. Inside there were a few occupied tables, and in the corner he saw Billy and his girlfriend, Charley, sitting at a booth, slurping sodas through straws. "Great, my brother's here. Can we go somewhere else? I mean, my brother would ignore me, but Amy'd expect me to talk with her. You and I wouldn't get a chance to really talk."

"Would she get jealous?"

"Probably."

"Well, a girl like me is definitely nothing for a girl like her to get jealous about."

They stopped at a fast-food place next to the freeway and went inside and ordered shakes, him chocolate, her cherry, and they sat in silence sipping through the straws but not saying anything, yet it wasn't awkward; in fact, it was comfortable, until he thought about the possibility of being seen by one of his friends with such a dorky girl. He looked at the entrance and out the windows. He forgot about his scraped elbow, so when he put it on the table, it stung so bad he winced.

"What happened?" she asked.

"I fell."

She lifted his arm, and then she blew on the elbow. "You should clean that up."

"Whatever you say, doc."

She smiled, her braces showing. She was such a dork, Joey thought. "You know what I used to think about you?" he said. "I mean, before I knew you."

"What?" She sat erect, looking interested.

"I don't know if I should tell you."

"No, it's too late, you have to now."

"Well, I thought you were kind of . . ."

"What?" she laughed.

"Never mind."

She slapped his hand. "No, what? Geeky, right? You thought I was a geek. Didn't you?"

"No, that's what I think of you *now.*"

"Hey!"

"No, seriously, I thought you were interesting."

"Interesting?"

"So what did you think of me?" he asked.

"I didn't think of you," she said, sipping through her straw.

Out the window, the freeway buzzed with cars going other places, back down to California or up farther into the Northwest, to places he still hadn't seen.

* * *

She drove him home, and when she stopped in front of his house she kept the engine running. "I was thinking," she said.

"What's that?"

"What are you doing Saturday night?"

"My friends are having a barbecue. Why?"

"I'm having a party, and I wanted to invite you."

"Oh. Too bad."

"See you," she said.

He stood on the curb until she drove off. Then he walked to the house and heard the piano. He sat on the porch and listened. Suddenly the garage door opened, and there stood his dad. Off in the distance a dog barked and a train was passing.

"Hey," William said.

Joey said hey.

William sat next to him.

A distant train whined.

The piano sang.

"She's good," William said.

"Yeah," Joey said, as if he didn't care what the man had to say, and he stood up to go into the house.

"Joey?" said William.

The boy turned around. "What?"

"I'm sorry about the dog. I messed up. I messed up bad."

One morning, the father stood before the son, who was looking in the refrigerator for something to make for breakfast.

"Let's go, boy," he said.

"Go where?" Joey said.

"Newberry's. I need to get some stuff."

Joey, excited, pictured eating breakfast at the food counter, and he was ready to get on his shoes and go, but he wondered what his mom would think. Was this the kind of thing she warned him about when she warned him to stay away from his father? Certainly she didn't mean this, she couldn't mean Newberry's. The other day as he had been walking to his bedroom, he had felt an arm pull him back and throw him into a corner, his mom's blue eyes piercing into him.

"Be careful," she said. "I think he senses something. He's going to be very nice to you. But remember, it's only a mask."

And sure enough the father had been nice to him. He had come home one day with a box, handed it to Joey, and said, "Open it." Joey, who loved gifts, couldn't help but show his happiness. He sat at the table and tore open the box, pulling a ceramic statue, with the comedy and tragedy masks, the actors, the symbol of the thespian. "This is cool! Did you make this?" he asked.

"No, I bought it," William said, "I thought of you."

Those masks were Joey's symbol, his life, and it was something he didn't have to hide from his friends because coincidentally, the comedy and tragedy actors' masks were also symbols of the barrio, of the gang life. Many Chicanos had tattoos of the masks on their arms, or they wore T-shirts with that image or had it airbrushed on the hoods of their low riders. In the barrio it meant "Have fun now, cry later."

The future will be only sadness, crying, death, so you might as well have fun while you're young.

Now William wanted his son to go with him to Newberry's, rarely ever went by himself, and he knew it was something Joey enjoyed, too.

"Come on, let's go," said William. "I'll buy you breakfast."

"Really?' Joey said.

"Scrambled eggs await thee, my lord!" said the father, like a Shakespearean actor. "Go get thee dressed."

Excited, Joey went to his room and put on his shoes, and then he went to the bathroom, where he would have wet his hair down, but his mother, walking down the hallway, said good morning. "Good morning," he said, feeling guilty. He went back to the living room, where his father waited for him, keys in his hand, at the front door. "I'm not going, Dad."

"What do you mean?"

"I got work to do," he said. "Besides, I'm looking forward to making breakfast. Toast and eggs and stuff."

"I'll buy you breakfast," he said. "We'll go to McDonald's if you want."

Joey definitely liked Egg McMuffins, and he was tempted. "No, I better not."

"I've never known you to give up McDonald's," the father said. He looked at his son, scrutinized him, until Joey couldn't stand his gaze and went back to the kitchen to prepare his food. The father stood in the doorway.

"Is everything okay?" he asked.

Joey looked over at his father and, seeing his face, he looked away. He opened the refrigerator. "Everything's fine, Dad."

William left the house, and Joey leaned against the refrigerator and listened for his father's car. When he heard it start, he opened the refrigerator and pulled out a carton of eggs. Suddenly the door opened. His father walked into the kitchen, shadow first.

"Joey, there's something I should tell you."

"What is it?"

"I guess I should have told you, but, you know, sometimes life gets in the way." He took two steps closer to his son, his face broken, soft. He scratched his head. "I just pictured it."

"Pictured what?"

"Don't ever stick a fork in the toaster, all right? Don't ever do that."

Joey chuckled.

"I'm not joking, son. You could get shocked, and it could kill you."

"Dad, I'm sixteen years old."

"You think the toaster gives a shit how old you are? You think it's going to ask for your ID? It doesn't care who you are. It'll shock you."

"I'll be careful."

"The wires in the toaster have electrical currents."

"I'll remember that.'

"It doesn't care if you're dumb or smart."

"I'll remember."

"Dummy like you could get killed."

"Okay, Father, message received," he said, as if his father were an idiot. "You can go to the store now."

"Don't talk to me like that, boy. I'll kick your ass."

"Yeah, whatever," he said, back toward his father, pulling a cold egg from the carton. He held it gently in his palm, but then he grasped it in a fist, but not hard enough to crack it. He pictured throwing it in his father's face. "Asshole," he mumbled under his breath. His father, walking out, said, "Dumb little shit."

He got to kill a boy. He moved around him, the knife in his fist like Clemente had taught him, taking jabs, and then he moved in fast and shanked him in the heart. The boy's face showed surprise, wide eyes, open mouth, and then he looked at the wound in his stomach. He fell and died. Joey turned around, and the Sharks cheered him as he held up his victorious knife, but before he could say anything, he felt the stab in his back and he collapsed to his knees.

He didn't want to overact, so in his death he simply let out a little "Ugh" and fell forward, sprawled on the floor. Mr. Bollen stopped them. "Joey, you're being killed by Tony, the guy you hate. The chicken."

"Yeah. So?" he said, standing up and dusting off his pants.

"You look like you're lying down to take a nap."

The cast laughed.

"Well, what do you want?" he asked, feeling resentment but not wanting to show it.

"I want you to *die* die."

"Die die?"

"Make some noise. Do some acting."

The cast laughed again, and Joey was getting pissed. They started again, and out of rebellion he decided to overdo it. He yelled out when the knife went into him, loudly, a scream really, and as he went down he grabbed one of the Sharks and almost pulled him down with him. He wanted Bollen to see how wrong he was, but as the other cast members reacted to his acting, he felt it. Like he was dying.

"Excellent," Bollen said. "Let's do it again."

At the barbecue, he told them about some of the stupid shit the actors did. "They don't understand gangs at all," he said. They were standing against the backyard fence, each of them with a beer. "Hey, you know what?" said Clemente, who was a little drunk. "It's a good thing you're there, *ese,* representing the people. *En serio.*"

Amy grabbed Joey's arm and led him to a reclining lawn chair. They sat, her between his legs, and he held her in his arms. The music was playing some oldies, Mary Wells, and everyone was spread out across the yard. Kurt and George were playing horseshoes. Walter stood over the barbecue, flipping the chicken and steak. It smelled good, until Amy lit up a cigarette and the smoke went right up Joey's nose. "I'm a little pissed off at you," she said.

"What for?"

"I mean, I understand you have to rehearse. But I don't see you much anymore."

He kissed her on the neck, stood up, and told her he'd be back when she was done with her cigarette. "I'll put it out, Joey, if that's what you want," she said, like she was irritated with him.

"That's okay, baby," he said, leaning over and kissing her on the lips. "I have to take a piss."

He went into the little shack and found Johnny and Gilbert smoking out. Johnny pulled a baggie from a drawer and filled the pipe with more pot and handed it to Joey, who took the first hit and handed it to Gilbert. After it went around once, George and Kurt walked in and wanted some too, so he had to fill it up again. Amy came in and then Clemente, and they ended up smoking more, until Walter showed up at the door, holding a chicken leg in his fist with one big bite missing, and said, "Food's ready."

"Shit yeah," they said, and filed out the door. Amy grabbed him by the arm and said, "Let's get out of here."

"Let's eat," he said.

"Joey, is there someone else?"

"Of course not."

Every night after rehearsal, Leah gave him a ride home. One time they pretended they were aliens from another planet driving through town to study humans. The McDonald's, they guessed, was where humans went to worship, the golden arches being some sort of religious symbol and Ronald McDonald one of their gods. When she pulled up to a red light, Joey rolled down the window and said to some old lady in the car next to them, "Take us to your leader." Leah burst out laughing and socked him hard on the arm. Sometimes she parked in front of his house and they talked, and one night when he knew only his mom was home, he invited Leah into the house. Rachel and Leah talked about composers, and they laughed about a bunch of other things, and after she left, Rachel said, "She's great, Joey. I really like that girl."

One time he went to her house, which was like a mansion. The furniture was so white he was afraid to touch it. In all his life, other than the movies, he had never seen the inside of such a rich house. He stood in the middle of the living room, looking up at the high beamed ceiling, at the wooden staircase, the glass doors that led to a formal dining room. What he liked best were the wooden floors, so shiny you could see the reflection of the furniture and yourself walking across the room. "Wow!" he said.

"What?" she said.

"You guys are rich," he said.

"Oh, yeah, right," she said.

"Wood floors are so cool," he said, remembering the audition in fifth grade, the shiny floors of the gymnasium, Sherry Garcia mooing like a cow.

Her mom was very professional-looking in a business skirt and blazer, sitting at a big oak desk doing paperwork. She said hello and then went back to work. Leah and he went up the stairs to Leah's bedroom. He lay on her big white bed while she picked some music to play. On one of her walls she had a glossy poster with a big-eyed cow looking right at him, and the caption underneath read, "What's Moo?" He asked her why she had gotten it.

"I think he's cute. I like those eyes. They're so big."

"Fat eyes," he said.

"Yeah, that's it," she said. "Fat eyes." And she looked at him. "Like you," she said. "You've got the biggest eyes I've ever seen. If you were a girl, you'd be so beautiful."

"Is that supposed to be a compliment?"

"Sorry."

He told her that he used to want a cow and to name it Herman, and she said that when she was a kid she wanted a pig and would have named it Hanover. A slow song came on, and she said, "Okay, we need the proper lighting for this." Her light had a dimmer, and she lowered it and then turned on a table lamp with a red shade. She sat on the bed next to him, and eventually she lay down and they stared at the rose-colored ceiling and talked about when they were kids and what they wanted to do with their lives. He admitted he wanted to be an actor, and she said she wanted to get a Ph.D. in literature and teach at a university.

"Your mom doesn't mind that you have me in your bedroom?" he said.

"She trusts me," she said. "It's not like we're going to do anything." She turned her head and looked at him.

"No, of course not," he said, looking into her eyes. She didn't turn away.

"That would be weird," she said.

A week before the opening, the school newspaper sent a reporter to watch a rehearsal and to write about the play. The picture that came out in the school newspaper was of Riff and Bernardo in the knife fight. All Joey's friends thought it was cool, and Amy cut it out of the paper and hung it on the wall of her bedroom. It would stay there until the near future, when her family would flee up north to Eugene, where they would sell beads at the Saturday market.

Opening night. Joey was backstage.

The house lights went down, and everything became quiet.

The orchestra started, and the audience applauded.

Bollen had told Joey that if you work hard enough on a play, if you're dedicated, then no matter how bad it might seem the week before opening, it all comes together in the last days, and he was right. Everything went off. People cheered the dance numbers and songs. The dance at the gym got a standing ovation. Bernardo challenged Tony, flirted with Anita, negotiated with the Jets, killed Riff, got killed, and then waited backstage for the play to finish.

When he walked out into the lights for the curtain call and saw the sea of people applauding, it was the best feeling in his life. In the back row, his friends stood up and yelled, "Joey! Joey Molina!" Even Clemente was there. And so was Amy, smiling broadly. Closer to the front were the Molinas, his mom and dad, Billy and his girlfriend, Charley, a chubby blond in cowboy boots. He bowed and took his place in line. Maria and Tony, the leads in the show, came out to a standing ovation. Then the curtain shut and the cast was excited, hugging each other, telling each other how wonderful they were. Leah came up and gave Joey a big hug. "You going to get pizza with the rest of us?" she asked. "I can give you a ride."

His friends wanted to party with him afterward, so he told her maybe he'd show up later.

"Oh, come on, Molina. It'll be fun," said Burt. "I'll let you sit next to me," he said, winking suggestively.

"Will you let me hold your hand under the table?" Joey winked back.

"Maybe," he said.

"Well?" said Leah. "Are you going?"

"I can't," he said.

After a while they were allowed to go into the lobby to seek out their loved ones. When he walked out, he could see his family in the lobby, pressed against the wall as if nervous to be around so many people. He walked toward them, but a group of people he didn't know surrounded him and extended hands and told him how great he was. Through the crowd he saw Karla Horton, red hair and green eyes shining. "You stole the show, Joey Molina," she said to him through a filter of other bodies.

"Karla, right?" he said.

"Yeah," she said, disappearing. "Nice."

Carmen grabbed him. "Come here, Joey." She led him to a man and woman. "These are my parents," she said. They smiled and extended their hands for a shake and said in Spanish that it was nice to meet him and that they enjoyed the show. Carmen's boyfriend was there too, a young Latino, handsome like a teenage heartthrob, and Joey noticed that she introduced him by his name, not by the title "my boyfriend." They shook hands.

Across the heads he saw that his family looked out of place, fidgeting, staring at the ceiling, reading posters from past plays, so he said good-bye to her family and made his way across the lobby, but he kept getting stopped by people who wanted to talk to him and to tell him he was good. The bright faces and eyes circled around him and smiled at him and through some shoulders he saw the shadow of Sherry Garcia facing him with her arms crossed and looking proud, but the blur of limbs and light blocked her out and he said thanks and thank you and walked through the crowd, and suddenly Burt Blunt's face, glowing with joy, appeared in front of him.

"Joey, come here," he said.

He led him through the crowd, people turning to look at him, and near the bathrooms, standing next to a garbage can, stood a man he knew, but only after he turned away did he see the image of Joey at twenty-six eating an empanada and shaking his head in pity.

"This is my mom and my brother," Burt said. They smiled and shook his hand. "Isn't Joey the coolest?" said Burt, standing right beside him as if proud.

Finally, he made it to the Molinas. They faced him.

"There he is," William said, holding out his arms as if presenting him to the family. "The actor."

"Hi," he said.

"Joey, you were wonderful," Rachel said, holding her purse in front of her with both hands.

"Thanks."

"Yeah, that was pretty good, man," said Billy, lightly punching him on the arm. "Seriously. I'm surprised how good it was."

"Yeah," William said. He reached out for a handshake. "I'm proud of you."

"Thanks."

"We all are," Rachel said.

They stood silent for a while, and then Charley said, in her southern accent, "You were really good."

"Thanks," he said.

They were silent again.

"We have a cake at home. When you get home we'll celebrate a little," Rachel said.

"Really? A cake?" he said. "That's great."

"Joey, you're good at this," said Rachel.

* * *

After his family left, after the lights went out in the lobby, he went to the dressing room and packed his stuff in his backpack, makeup, books, and he sat before the lit-up makeup mirrors. He smiled at himself, liked himself, nodded his head in approval. Outside, his friends stood in the darkness under a tree, like soldiers waiting for the dawn.

He walked into the darkness. They surrounded him, Johnny, Walter, Gilbert, George, Kurt, and Clemente. They gave him hand-shakes and said that it was baaad, and to celebrate they were going to get him fucked up.

Clemente bought a bunch of beer and some tequila, they said. And *yesca.*

"Orale," Joey said, in his best Chicano drawl.

Amy was leaning against a tree, smoking a cigarette, looking at him as if she were angry. "I better go talk with my *jaina,"* he said. He walked over to her and held her in his arms. She put her head on his shoulder. "Joey."

"What?"

She kissed his chin. She smelled like stale cigarette smoke.

"Didn't you like it?" he asked.

"You were great," she said, "but I'm sure everyone and his brother has been telling you that."

"Everyone and who?"

"His brother. It's an expression."

"Everyone and his brother. Sounds interesting."

"Joey Molina."

"What?"

"You didn't tell me she was so pretty."

"Who?"

"Your girlfriend."

"You mean Bernardo's girlfriend?"

"Do you enjoy kissing her?"

"Only you," he said, kissing her, wincing at the ashtray taste.

"You're such a liar."

"Come on," he said, "let's go party."

Back in Johnny's backyard they drank beer and smoked a bunch of pot and they kept giving him shots of tequila and making toasts. He got so drunk that he forgot that his family was waiting for him with a cake, and it wasn't until past midnight when he remembered.

He told Amy they had to go, and they walked the five or six blocks to his house, mostly stumbling, zigzagging through a small field of pine trees, and the light breaking through the trunks hurt his eyes. It smelled of garbage and pine needles. "I am so buzzed," Amy kept repeating. "Like a bee buzz buzz."

"You're not buzzed," he said. "You're drunk." And they stumbled on and Joey was dizzy and she grabbed his arm and stopped against an abandoned washing machine, barely white anymore, with the lid pulled off and the belly filled with mud and leaves, and she vomited into it. Joey, although drunk, smiled at the irony.

When they got to the house, Billy's truck was gone. They walked up to the porch and could hear the piano play an angry tune. "Shit," he said, "I got to sit down."

"What's the matter?" Amy slurred.

He leaned over his knees and held his stomach.

And then it came—he barfed all over the grass. "Oh, shit," he said swaying. He looked at Amy but could barely see her, she was blurry. "Fuck," he said, "I'm drunk."

He hadn't noticed that the piano had stopped and that Rachel was standing in the doorway. He turned around, and she was framed by light. He protected his eyes from the glare. "God damn you, Joey.

You're drunk!" William came out of the house too. "Boy, I oughtta kick your ass." His parents' silhouettes stood in the door frame.

"I'm sorry," he said. "We was just celebrating."

"Oh," said Amy, sitting down on the porch. "Oh, my," she moaned, swaying like she might get sick.

Rachel shook her head in disgust.

"You deserve a beating, boy," said William.

"We were celebrating the play," he said.

"If this is what happens when something good happens to you, I'd rather see you fail," Rachel said.

The next day he woke up in his bed. A plastic trash basket from the bathroom was next to it, smelling like tequila-flavored barf. He felt a tremendous thirst, so he went to the kitchen for some ice water. That was the most drunk he had ever been, this morning the worst he had ever felt.

The cake was wrapped in plastic, sitting on the table. It had once said "Congratulations, Joey," but all that was left was "Con" on the top and below that "Joe."

Droopy barked and scratched on the kitchen door. Joey felt dizzy again, nauseated. He bent over the kitchen garbage can. The smell of the rotting food rose to his nostrils and made him feel worse. He let it all out. "*Ahhhhhhhhhhhhhhhh!*"

When the phone rang, it sounded so loud that it scared him.

He picked it up.

"Joey?" she said.

"Hey, Amy," he said. "Shit, my head."

"Joey," she mumbled.

"What's the matter?"

She was crying.

"Amy, what's wrong?"

"Do you remember how I got home last night?" she asked.

"No, I was pretty out of it."

"Well, I was too, but I remember. I'm sure."

"What do you remember?"

"Everything," she said. "All of it."

Two things kept him from Amy and his friends: Rachel and the run of the play. Every night that he wasn't performing, he was at brush-up rehearsals, and every night, thankfully, the performances went as well as the first night. Joey even felt himself getting better as the nights went on. Each show sold out, so the school was considering extending it for another weekend, and Joey hoped that they would. It kept him away from his friends, but one night William and Rachel got together and spoke to Joey. Rachel said that she didn't trust him anymore, so instead of an eleven o'clock curfew, he had to be home before it got dark. "You're kidding," he said.

"Oh, no, I'm not," she said.

He spent his evenings and nights alone in his bedroom with his books. When his parents went to bed, he went out into the living room to watch *Movies Till Dawn,* but Billy no longer came home some nights, so unless the movie was a musical or a Marlon Brando movie, he went back to his bedroom and read more plays. He read everything he could find at secondhand stores and the library by Eugene O'Neill, even a collection of one-acts he had written when he was still an un-known writer, published for the first time by a university press. He read Arthur Miller and a lot of French theater, from Molière to Beckett, and like many actors before him, he felt the strong need to be in *Waiting for Godot*. He began to write his own plays, dialogues really, and he read them aloud to himself, doing the distinct voices of the characters. Rachel wouldn't even let him go to the cast party on closing night because she didn't want to see him come home drunk. He told her that the theater people were unlikely to have booze at the party, but she knew he was lying and told him how disgusted she was to see him plastered, how disgusting Amy was. His friends began to think that he was avoiding them, that he was becoming a dramie. Out of embarrassment, Joey didn't want to tell them that he was on restriction, "docked," as his mom put it ("Joey, you're docked!"), so he made up lies and wrote them in his *Book of Lies*.

After the performances, the cast did things together, went for pizza, for ice cream, or hung out at someone's house, and sometimes he would go to these places with Leah, if she brought him home early enough so that his mom wouldn't notice.

On closing night, all of *West Side Story* was having a cast party, but Joey couldn't go. All that night Joey, Burt Blunk, and Leah tried to think of ways to convince Rachel to let him go to the cast party. Burt said, "Tell her that it's required. You won't graduate if you don't go."

"She won't buy it," Joey said.

"Okay, that you need to go because you have a rare theater disease and the only cure is cast-party punch."

"No, I got it!" Leah said. "Joey's not really an actor at all, but a spy acting like an actor. He's a government agent following Burt Blunk—a known Communist—who is selling secrets to the Chinese."

Burt grabbed Joey's shoulders and pulled him back and forth. "I just know you gotta be there!" he said, pretending to cry.

"Oh, I'm going to miss you so much," Joey said, also pretending to cry.

"Boo-hoo," said Burt.

"Group hug," said Leah, and they all embraced and pretended to tearfully say good-bye.

He liked how theater people hugged so freely.

But Rachel wouldn't let him go to the cast party no matter how much he pleaded. Instead, he paced his bedroom like a prisoner.

His friends wanted to hang out with him that night too, and when he told them he had plans after the play, they thought he was going to the cast party. "You're not becoming a dramie, are you?" asked Gilbert.

"No, man," he told them. "I wouldn't go to that party."

Now Rachel was at the piano and the father was in the garage, and Billy and Charley went to hang out at the doughnut shop where Amy worked, so while the cast party was going on across town, he sat on his bed, legs crossed, and read *Death of a Salesman*, the play Bollen was doing next. Bollen wanted him to audition for Biff. When he finished reading, he realized his legs burned from being in that position for too long. He could barely bend them to walk across the room to get them working again, but he paced the floor with energy and emotion, perhaps enhanced by the piano music, dark and seemingly formless, like voices coming from all directions. He liked *Death* more than the first time he had read it, when he was in the eighth grade and he had bought an Arthur Miller collection at the secondhand store. He was almost grateful that he had stayed home, grateful for the discipline, because had he gone to the party, he probably would have gotten drunk. His mom was forcing structure on him, and he wondered if that were part of her plan. It was warm inside his bedroom.

He set the book on the bed and opened his door and walked

down the hallway, sharp piano notes snapping off the walls. Dim, almost dark, Rachel's figure appeared in the light, her pale fingers moving over the piano keys. He watched for a while to see if it might be safe to try an escape into the backyard. He walked silently past her, and her eyes were closed, her cheeks white. He walked into the dark kitchen. Dirty dishes piled up in the sink, soaking in moonlight.

In the backyard, Droopy jumped on him for affection and followed him. The dog had to wear a big plastic cone on his head to keep him from scratching his eye, which the father had injured in the beating. Joey reached the side of the house; the window of the garage was full of light. He peeked in and saw his dad sitting on a swivel chair, opposite his latest head, which was a Jesus with a mean look on his face. The father, resting his chin on his clenched hands, stared at mean Jesus.

Joey walked back and forth, quickly, as if expending energy. "Okay, Droopy, here's the thing: I can do Willie Loman. Biff is a great role. I could play him, the son, but Willy, the father, I hear his voice, Droopy. So clear."

Droopy followed him, the big contraption on his head causing his neck to sway with each step.

"I'm the father, not the son," he said.

Piano notes thumped from inside the walls of the house like children trapped in a box.

Then suddenly he heard singing voices.

"I'm gonna put a bullet in his head
and party with the vato *when he's dead!"*

Droopy growled.

He thought at first that these singing voices were in his head, but through the slits of the fence he saw movement.

"Where the fuck is Chuck?" said a voice.

"Fuck Chuck," said the other.

"*Chupa* Chuck," said the first.

Then both voices sang.

"I'm gonna put a bullet in his head!"

Joey held his position against the wall, as if petrified. What he should have done, he would think later on that night when he recalled all that happened, was pick up a rock just in case he needed to defend himself. But he did nothing but freeze and hope the voices would pass. He would later say to himself, "Stupid, Joey, you worthless son of a bitch. You just stood there."

Even after a pair of hands appeared on the top of the fence and the tip of a head emerged like Kilroy, he stood still. A pair of eyes scanned the yard. "Fuck, someone's back there," said the voice.

"No way," said the other.

"Fuck you, I ain't lying."

"Maybe it's Joey."

"Joey Molina!"

Then one voice sang in the tune of "Louie, Louie."

"Joey, Joey, oh, baby, you gonna die."

Then both voices.

"Joey, Joey, oh, baby, you gonna die."

His father might have heard the laughter and singing, so he rushed toward the fence.

"Who is it?" he said.

Then from above him he heard, "What's happening, homes?" Gilbert's eyes were looking down on him, gleaming, black sparkles, and he smiled. Then Joey saw an eyeball blinking through the slat of the boards. He looked up at Gilbert. "Is that George?"

Gilbert looked down to the other side of the fence and sang, "Play that funky music, white boy."

"Shh," Joey said. "My dad's in the garage."

Gilbert climbed over the fence and jumped into the backyard, his feet thumping hard on the earth, and Droopy came over and growled at him. "It's okay," Joey said, patting him on the back.

Droopy calmed down with Joey's caress.

"Shit, what the hell's up with that dog?" Gilbert said. "You got a dog from outer space and shit."

George jumped over the fence, thump. Droopy started barking, and Joey told him to shut up, but even after he let him go, the dog wouldn't take his eyes off George, like he hated him.

"What the fuck is that?" said George, looking at the dog.

"What are you guys doing here?" Joey asked.

"What are *you* doing here?" Gilbert asked. "I thought you'd be with your dramie friends."

"You a dramie now, ain't you?" asked George.

"I told you I wasn't going to the cast party."

"We was just wondering."

"You guys got any weed?" Joey asked.

"Check this out," said George. He pulled out a metal pot pipe and lifted it to his mouth. "One-hit shit," he said. He flicked his lighter, which made Droopy flinch, and the flame lit up George's eyes and red face. He sucked in, his cheeks caving in, sucked the smoke deeper and deeper into his lungs, pounded his chest to stop himself from coughing and then held it in. He handed it to Gilbert, who said, "No, give it to the actor."

George handed it to Joey.

As George let the smoke come from his lungs, he handed Joey the lighter.

Gilbert sang, "Play that funky music, white boy."

"Shhh," Joey said. "My dad's in the garage." He indicated the light in the window. They could see his shadow slide across the wall.

"What's he doing in there?" Gilbert asked.

Joey took the pipe to his lips, lit the flame, and pulled in some smoke, which was harsh and smelled like skunk, and then he coughed it out and kept coughing so hard that he had to kneel down, and Droopy looked worried. After a while, he recovered, and everything was weird, blurry, slow. "Fuck," he said. "What is this shit?"

"Special imported," said George.

Gilbert took another hit. George looked down at Droopy. "Come on, dog," George said to him, like he wanted to fight, slapping the air. Droopy barked. Joey held him. "It's okay," he said.

"That's a funny-looking dog, man," George said.

Gilbert peered through the garage window like a Peeping Tom, and he seemed fascinated, his mouth hanging open, his eyes wide with wonder. "Check this out, George. This old man is tripping."

George, excited to see, took a big step toward the window, almost stepping on Droopy, who barked and took a snap at George's ankle. "Fucking dog," he said, as if he would kick him, and Droopy barked twice.

"Shh," Joey said, bending over the dog. Now Gilbert and George were both peeking into the window, laughing. "What a trip," said George.

Joey calmed Droopy and went to the window.

"He's getting stoned," Gilbert said. "Joey, you never told us your dad gets high."

"That's because he doesn't," Joey said, but when he peeked

through the window, he couldn't believe it. The father had a pipe and was trying to light it, and he was taking tokes from it. "No way," he said to himself. This couldn't be real. Everything did seem surreal. Joey was stoned.

The father put the pipe on a counter and walked to the middle of the garage, hands on his hips, wearing nothing but white short pants so small they looked like underwear. His tattoo spider slithered all over his chest and his back and up his arms. Suddenly he raised his arms to the ceiling, his eyes closed, as if soaking up the power of God.

"You got a weird-ass father," Gilbert said.

Joey decided he wouldn't try out for *Death*. The last time Bollen had mentioned it, Joey was going to try out, so as far as he knew, he could expect to see Joey auditioning for the part of Biff. When the drama teacher found out that he wasn't going to, he was angry. "Of course you're going to try out," he said.

He told Joey that the play would be judged by representatives from the Shakespeare Festival in Ashland, and three high school actors statewide would get to participate in one of the festival's productions. In addition, the high school actors would be provided with a trip to Edinburgh, Scotland, for the theater festival. "Joey," he said, "the whole town's full of plays and theater people."

How interesting, Joey thought, an entire town of dramies, young and old, walking around in costumes, acting weird and flamboyant, a place where he could act like himself and not have to worry about what people might think. But what were the chances of winning anyway? he thought. "I'm sorry, man, this drama shit ain't for me," he said.

"It *ain't?*" Bollen said.

"That's right," Joey said, nodding his head once, playing with his chin *cholo*-style. "It's a bunch of shit."

"Come here," Bollen said, and he led Joey to the back row of the theater and told him to sit down. He sat next to Joey and leaned over. "I'm going to tell you something, Joey."

"You're in love with me?" Joey said.

"To hell with you, Joey Molina." He pointed his finger. "What makes you different from all the other talented actors I see—and there's a lot of them, believe me—what makes you different, is you *have* to act."

"What do you mean, I have to?"

"You won't be able to live without it, Joey. And I don't mean acting a persona in everyday life, like the way you act with your friends. I mean you *have* to act. You'll have no peace without it."

"Fuck this shit," Joey said, standing up. He walked out of the theater, into the cold day, but down the hall he saw Randy Abbot and Perry Doyle hanging around their lockers, looking around as if trying to find something to do. He went back into the theater. The kids turned around to watch him. Bollen turned around.

"What?" he said.

"I'd like to read for Willy," Joey said.

Bollen hung the cast list on the window of the theater office, so one morning Amy and Joey went and read it. There it was, Joey Molina as Willy. "I got it," he said to Amy.

"That's great," she said, but she looked like she didn't mean it, like she was sad about it. She had been distant ever since the night they came to his house drunk, but when pressed about it, she wouldn't talk, so he assumed she was embarrassed about having been so drunk and that she knew Rachel had no respect for her now. Amy never came over anymore, and the few times he went over to her house all she wanted to do was lie in bed holding him, no sex, until she fell asleep. It seemed that Billy and Charley spent more time with her than Joey spent with her, because they were always at the dough-nut shop where Amy worked. Sometimes when Billy came home he would tell Joey, "Man, why don't you call your girlfriend? She misses you."

"You're happy about it, aren't you?" he asked Amy. "That I got the part? It's a great part."

"I'm happy," she said, with unhappy eyes.

"I could win a trip to Scotland. I'd be flying on a plane."

"Great."

"Oh, honey," he said, holding her in his arms. She stiffened in his embrace.

Later, as they were hanging out in front of the school with the gang, Amy told them he was going to be in another play.

"*¿En serio?*" said Gilbert, like he knew it all along.

"I hope at least this time you're playing a Chicano," said Johnny.

"He's going to be Willy Loman," Amy said, as if the name were disgusting.

"Guillermo Lomán?" Johnny asked.

"It's a good play," he said.

"You're going to play a white guy?" Gilbert asked.

"That's cool," said Walter. "You're a good actor, man. I wouldn't mind being in a play someday."

"Yeah, a play about some dumb-fuck nigger," said Gilbert.

"Fuck you, beaner," said Walter.

"Why do you like doing that shit for anyway?" asked Gilbert.

"It's fun, I guess."

"It's not real, man, like playing house," Gilbert said.

A few of them laughed.

"Fuck that," said Johnny. "Joey was bad as Bernardo."

"That's right," said Walter. "You keep acting, Joey. Do it for us."

The stage manager for *Death of a Salesman* was Leah.

Not only did he see her every night at rehearsal, but every night she gave him a ride home, and they rarely went straight home. Sometimes they went to her house and watched her big-screen TV or they went to get something to drink, and at times he took her home and she'd come inside and she and Rachel would talk for hours. Rachel looked so radiant and happy, and a few times she played show tunes on the piano while Leah and Joey sang. Ever since the night Joey came home drunk, things seemed to be relaxed between his parents, as if now that they had a common person by whom they could be disgusted, they started to like each other. He was happy to have what seemed like a normal family that he could share with Leah. When he walked Leah to the car, they would talk some more, about the play, their families, school, and sometimes they would read their English papers to each other and comment on them, but she still got Bs.

"Your papers are always better than mine," Joey said. "He's a misogynist, remember? He hates women."

"That's right," she said.

One night William took them all out to dinner, Rachel, Joey and Leah. They went to a 1950s-style café that specialized in burgers and fountain drinks. They sat in a booth next to the window, and William looked on the menu for beer and said he couldn't find any.

"Good," Rachel said. "No beer tonight."

"All right, no beer," he said.

Joey and Leah shared a menu, alone behind the large plastic-covered pages, and she kept pointing at things and said, "What about the Big Bopper Burger?" and Joey would point at something and say,

"What about the Rock Around the Clock Club Sandwich?" so close together he could smell her hair. After they ordered, they talked about the plays. Joey said that even though Willy was white, he understood him, and felt what he felt, and Leah asked what white had to do with anything. Joey said probably nothing, that when good white writers write about white people they write deep characters, but when they sometimes write about Mexicans, it's almost embarrassing, and it's a good thing Arthur Miller had no Chicano characters.

"Okay, so what are you saying, that *West Side Story* was an embarrassing portrayal of Puerto Ricans?" she asked.

No, he admitted, he thought the script portrayed Latinos fairly, but Mr. Bollen and the cast had understood little about Latinos and gangs and that was why in one scene when the Sharks come onstage, Bollen actually wanted them to yell things like *"Andale! Arriba! Arriba!"* but Joey refused because he said it was a stereotype that Bollen probably got from Speedy Gonzales cartoons. William spoke a bit about his gang days, and Rachel said everyone thought she was crazy for falling for a pot-smoking hoodlum.

"Pot-smoking?" Joey asked.

When their food arrived, the father insisted that they say grace, and after they did everyone crossed themselves except for Leah. William asked her wasn't she Catholic, and she said she wasn't raised to be religious.

"She's going to burn in hell," Joey said, and she nudged his side with her elbow, and he pretended that it hurt, so she pretended to be sorry and rubbed him where it hurt.

"Is that some kind of religious thing?" William said, pointing to her T-shirt. He leaned over the table to get a better look at the image stretched across her chest. She rarely wore a bra, and her nipples slightly pushed through the fabric.

"It's a bear," she said. "A teddy bear."

"A bear, huh?"

After dinner they all ate ice cream desserts and Leah couldn't finish hers so Joey ate hers too, and Leah asked how he could eat so much and be so skinny. When Rachel got up to go to the ladies' room, she asked Leah if she wanted to go too, and they came back ten minutes later giggling like girls.

Joey couldn't remember a night he had enjoyed more with his parents.

Before she got into her car, Leah stepped close to him and said, "Give me a hug." She felt good. He watched her car drive away.

One day he went out to the front of the school during lunch to hang out with the gang, and he saw Amy leaning against Johnny's car with George. They were talking like old friends, and George was saying stuff that made her laugh. At one point she hit him on the arm and he laughed and put up his arms as if he were defending himself. Then they both looked at Joey, and their smiles left. George drifted over to where Kurt was playing hacky sack by himself, and he joined the game.

"Hey," Joey said, leaning against the car next to Amy.

"Hey," she said, watching the game of hacky sack. George kicked the sack so high in the air that he jumped up and hit it with his head as it was coming down. Amy laughed. "I got to go," Joey said, and started to walk away when she yelled, as if scolding him, "Joey!"

He turned around. "What?"

She came over to him, held him in her arms, held her face to his chest. "Don't go." He kissed her on the forehead, which smelled of stale smoke.

George looked over at them.

299

* * *

On weekends he and Amy spent time together at her house getting high with her mom or getting drunk in Johnny's backyard, but the smell of her cigarettes and her bulldog face like she was always angry started to get to him. Many things about her started to irritate him. Perhaps that was responsible for what happened next.

It happened backstage. Bollen was starting and stopping a scene between Biff and Linda, fine-tuning it, so Leah and Joey were walking around backstage, which was full of old props and set pieces from previous plays, couches, soda fountain counters, telephones. They were improvising, playing with these toys. He picked up an old phone and said into it, "Hello, Mama! War's over! I'm coming home. And I'm bringing my new wife. Her name's Edie. Edie Amin."

She picked up a dinosaur head from an old production of Thornton Wilder's *The Skin of Our Teeth,* and she put it on her head and pretended to be primping herself in a mirror. "I've been feeling so old lately," she said. "Do you think I'm getting old?"

"Prehistoric," he said.

He sat on a barber's chair and said, "A little off the top, Sam."

She came up behind him and acted like a gay hairdresser. "Oh, I'll make you look so good."

He stood up, walked to the black walls, and said, "Dear, I think our honeymoon house is fine, but we really should paint the walls."

"You don't like black, honey?" she said.

"I've never even tried black honey," he said.

She giggled. Then she indicated the walls. "But the color's so avante-garde," she said.

"Too depressing," he said. "And this, after all, is our first home as man and wife."

"You mean woman and husband." She gently touched the walls with an open palm, and then she looked at him with affection. "You really think it's too depressing?"

"I do."

They faced each other, their faces so close that they could smell each other's breath. She was a few inches taller than him. "We don't want to be depressed," she said.

"No, we don't want that," he said, looking into her eyes. They moved in closer. Their chests pressed against each other.

"What do we want?" she asked.

And that was it.

They were kissing.

Her mouth was wet and sweet like bubble gum. She tightly held his face with her palms, and he ran his hands through her hair. It was only when they heard Bollen call for her, "Leah!" that they stopped. They held each other and looked into each other's eyes, both of them breathing hard. "That was weird," she said.

"Yeah," he said. "It sure was."

She looked down, as if embarrassed, and then up at him again, smiling, and then they heard, "Leah!" She laughed nervously and ran off. "I'm coming," she said.

After rehearsal that night they walked to the parking lot, not saying anything, but both of them knew the truth of it: they liked each other. They weren't uncomfortable after what had happened, because it felt right. He put his finger in her belt loop at the back of her waist. "You know what I want right now?" she said.

"What?"

"An ice cream."

"Well, then let's go. Er, except I don't have any money."

"I'm buying." She looked up at the sky. "Look," she said. "The moon."

"What about it?" he said.

"Just the moon," she said, bumping him with her hips. As they walked, he pulled her closer, by the belt loop, so that their hips bumped with each step.

"Just the moon," he said, looking up. "Ain't nothing but the moon."

"How corny," she said. "Ain't nothing but the moon. I mean, really!"

One night after rehearsal they went to her house. Her mother wasn't home, and they went to her bedroom to listen to music. Joey sat on the edge of her bed and watched her pick out some music. When she turned around, he was so moved by her looks that he swallowed. She stood up, so tall, and she saw the look on his face. "What?" she said.

He stepped closer.

She turned out the light, the only glare coming in from her window, which shone a blue hue on their faces, as if they were underwater. They stood facing each other; without saying a word, she stepped closer. Joey reached out to her and began to take off her T-shirt, slowly, and then he pulled it over her head. Leah rarely wore a bra. He looked at her small breasts. She slowly pulled off his T-shirt, over his head, and she looked at his chest.

Then, as if on cue, they took off their pants and underwear and stood naked in the blue light, facing each other. They walked toward the bed.

After the first time that night they said nothing, just held each other for a long time, but after the second time they talked and laughed and listened to music. Joey got up naked to change the music, and Leah gave out catcalls and said "What a bod!" and then she would get up to pick the next song, but all Joey could do was look at her and say, "You're incredible."

She got in bed and snuggled next to him, warm, naked. "You think so?" she asked.

"How come I never noticed before?"

They kissed, and then they made love a third time.

Afterward he said, "You know, it just occurred to me. You're not a virgin."

"Neither are you," she said.

Every night after rehearsing *Death* they spent with each other, and most nights they parked and made out in some dark park, or they went to her house and read to each other or listened to music, and if her mom wasn't home they made love. They took bubble baths together. They made omelets in their underwear and ate off the same plate. They were grateful to *Death*, because they knew that without it, they would have never lived this way with each other. And they didn't want the play to end. "That *Death* would last forever!" they would say to each other. One day it occurred to Leah to ask if Joey had broken up with Amy, something she assumed he had done, but she began to get suspicious because he favored going places together where no one would see them. He said "of course" he had, but one night she found out that he was a liar.

They walked from the theater to the dark empty parking lot, when suddenly a low rider blasting music pulled in front of them. He removed his hand from Leah's belt. Johnny was driving. In the passenger seat was Kurt. Amy was in the backseat. "Let's go," said Johnny. "Thought we'd give you a ride today."

He looked at Leah, apologized with his eyes.

He opened the door and got in the backseat. "Hey, baby," Amy said, and she kissed him on the lips, her arms around his neck, as she looked at Leah. "See you," she said.

Then Johnny drove off.

"Wait. Stop," Joey said.

"Why?" Amy said.

"Leah has my script. Stop. I need it." He jumped out the car and ran to Leah, who was getting into her car. He wouldn't let her shut the door. "What? What do you want?" she said, trying to get the door shut. She pushed him away.

"Come on, Leah."

"Leave me alone, Joey. Go with your girlfriend."

"Leah, stop!"

"Why? Why should I stop?"

"I think I love you," he said.

Leah slammed the door shut. He knocked on her window.

"Yeah? Great way to show it, Joey. I mean, that was great."

"I'm going to break up with her tonight. Right now. I promise."

"What?" She rolled it partway down, but she didn't face him. "It's a little late for that."

"Tell me you feel the same way as I do," he said.

"Oh, no shit!" she said. "Duh!" she said. She hit her steering wheel. "What the fuck do you think, Joey Molina?"

"Give me an hour. I'll call you in an hour."

"How could you be with us both at the same time?" she said.

"Leah, I haven't so much as kissed her since we've been together. I've only seen her at school. I promise."

"Not once?"

"Not one kiss, nothing. I'm with you. I want to be with you. Please, give me an hour."

She looked at him. "Okay," she said, and she started her car. "An hour," she said.

"Promise," he said.

"See you," she said, and she drove off. He stood there watching her little box-shaped car turn out of the lot and putter down the street. Johnny honked his horn. He went back to the car, climbed in the backseat, and plopped down. "Where's your script?" Amy asked.

"I forgot," he said. "I already know my part."

As Johnny drove toward Amy's house, she cuddled up to Joey. In the backseat the music was extra loud because that's where the speakers were, the bass from "Lowrider" pounding on the seats so that they all moved with the beat.

"Did you miss me?" she whispered.

"I don't know," he said, looking out the window. They were on the freeway, passing rooftops and billboards.

"You don't know?" she said, and she hit him playfully.

"You guys want to smoke out?" said Johnny, holding a joint.

"No, I better not," he said. "I got to get home."

"What?" He couldn't hear Joey over the music.

He yelled, "No. I have to go home."

"Can you roll down the windows, please?" He didn't want to get high. He wanted to be with Leah. He thought of how she stood taller than him, how when she smiled her braces showed on her upper teeth. She was so cute. So dorky and cute. He smiled. He thought about her in her little car, how she was so tall she almost touched the ceiling.

Amy kissed him on the cheek. "So what do you mean, you don't miss me?"

"I'm so busy these days, I hardly have time to think of anything."

They were silent.

"So how was your day?" she asked, putting her hand in his shirt and touching his flat stomach.

"All right," he said.

Johnny took them to Amy's, and they got out and thanked him for the ride. "You guys sure you don't want to hang out? We're going to the lake."

"No, thanks," he said. "You could go if you want," he told Amy.

"I'm staying with my man," she said.

They drove off, the bass bumping all the way down the street.

"Joey, is something wrong?"

"Yeah, I think so."

They walked over to her carport and leaned against the car. Amy sat up on the hood.

"What is it?"

"I don't know. It's just that something's not working for me."

"What do you mean? The part? Billy Loman?"

"I don't know. I guess I'm just too busy. There's too many things going on in my life. I can't handle this."

"Handle what?"

He looked away, at the street, lined with shabby apartments and duplexes.

"Us."

"Come here," she said, jumping off the car. She grabbed his hand and led him inside.

Her seven-year-old brother was smoking a joint and watching TV, the screen light glowing blue on the walls and on his face. He slowly looked up at them. "Hey," he said. The kid was so stoned his head seemed too heavy for his neck. They went inside her bedroom, and she closed the door.

She sat on the bed, and he sat opposite her on a chair against the wall. She crossed her legs and said, sternly, "What is it?" Above her shoulder hung the picture from the school paper, Joey crouched, with a knife, his teeth showing, his eyes full of hatred.

"He should be studying or something."

"What are you talking about?" she said, as if irritated.

"Your brother. Doesn't this get old?"

Now Amy looked so short and lumpy.

"You are such a stereotype, Joey."

"What do you mean?"

"So what are you saying, that a normal family is going to be any different, any better for my brother? Maybe he'll become a lawyer. I suppose next thing you'll tell me is that I need a father."

"I don't know, Amy. I'm sorry. It's just right now I don't think I could be a very good boyfriend."

She lit a cigarette, took a drag, blew the smoke up to the ceiling, and then said, "Why?"

"My life. There's too many things going on."

"It's Leah, isn't it?"

"Leah?" he said, as if the idea were preposterous. "She's a friend."

"I see the way she looks at you," she said.

"Leah? No way."

She held her cigarette, quite sophisticated-looking, her elbow bent. "I love you. Do you understand that? I love you. We belong to-gether." She took a drag and then let out the smoke. "I don't want to break up."

"I think it would be best."

She put her cigarette in an ashtray on the nightstand, and then she lay on her bed. He felt terrible, so he sat on the bed and rubbed her shoulders. He leaned over her, put his lips near her ear. "It's okay," he said.

"No, it isn't," she said. "I don't know what to do now."

"You'll find someone else. You're so . . . pretty."

"No, no," she said. "That's not it." She sat up. "Joey, remember that night we got drunk and your father took me home?"

"Look, Amy, let's just give the breakup a try. At least until the play's over."

"Joey!" she yelled. "Listen to me." She grasped both his arms, dug her nails into them. "He raped me."

"Who?"

"Your father."

He shook off her hold. "You're crazy. My father wouldn't do something like that."

"Damn it, Joey, he forced me," she said, grabbing his shoulders.

He stood up. "He can be an asshole, but he's no rapist."

Then she cried and spoke fast like a child. "I tried to keep quiet because I love you so much and I wanted things to work out with you because we belong together, I'm sure of it, I know we do. Even my mom thinks so. So I kept it to myself, but now, now I don't know what to do." She looked like she was in a lot of pain, her face smeared with tears, her eyes red. "I can't forget it."

"No, no," he kept saying, walking back and forth. "He's not like that."

She stood up and grabbed his hands and guided him, as if he were the afflicted one. "Oh, Joey." On the bed, in her arms, feeling fingers in his hair, caresses on his back, he believed her story.

"I'm not an animal," she whispered.

She disengaged and grabbed a cigarette from the nightstand.

He came to her, ran his palm over her sweaty forehead, and kissed her wet eyes. "I'm sorry. I'm so sorry. You must hate him."

He remembered the deer dying in the road, and he remembered being surrounded by the blackness of night, his father with a shovel, standing in the glare of the headlights, arrogant, impatient, his shadow like a stick man stretching as far as the light reached, the shadow of his head and shoulders cast on the top of the pine trees.

Go somewhere with your character.
Be Willy Loman.

Allow the salesman to feel, but you feel nothing outside of him.

Give up your spirit for Willy's spirit. Let him enter you each night. In real life say only what you need to, but in the process you will neglect not only those feelings that leave you with pain, but also those that should never leave you.

Once, while sixteen-year-old Joey lay in bed in the dark at night, six-year-old Joey tried to say something to him. Rachel's piano was playing a dark song, low and slow like crawling black widows—and he wouldn't listen to himself as a boy. Joey at six years old visited him at night or in his dreams, and he said, "I have to tell you something," but sixteen-year-old Joey ignored him or told him to get lost, and twenty-six-year-old Fat Boy Joey would show up in the corner of a dark room, and he'd say to the six-year-old, "Yeah, get lost."

"This is something you're really going to have to hear," the child whined.

The present Joey thought only of his lines, only of Willy, only of that time Biff came to the hotel and saw . . . that was painful enough, but it wasn't his pain, not for long anyway, because every night of rehearsals, he was able to let it out in such a way that it burdened him less, he was able to give it to whomever was watching. Like Leah, who sat in the audience with her clipboard during rehearsals and who sometimes had to get up and go to the bathroom to cry. She didn't know why Joey didn't call her that night, so she wouldn't talk to him outside of rehearsal, and inside of rehearsal she said only what she had to as stage manager. He didn't have the will to explain things to her. His life was falling apart, and playing the part of Willy Loman was to where he retreated. It tore him apart to see his mom and dad get along so well. He focused on Willy's past, Willy's regrets, and whenever they did the scene where Willy breaks down and cries in front of his wife, Joey broke down and cried.

Mr. Bollen said he was going to win the contest.

Whatever six-year-old Joey had to tell him was lost forever. Little Joey went away.

Leah only asked once why he hadn't called her, and he said nothing to her, just stood there blankly looking at her. "What scene are we doing today?" he asked her.

She looked at the clipboard, read the rehearsal notes, and said, "We're working act three, Molina. Be ready."

All his other friends he simply avoided, before school, after. During lunch he didn't eat, he didn't want to, he just went to the library and sat by a window that overlooked the freeway, the I-5 with its traffic of cars and diesel truck's going to California or heading up north, to whatever was up there, perhaps snowcapped mountains with running rivers. Medford was not a place but a passage, somewhere people had to go through to get to where they really wanted to be. Sometimes he felt as if he were destined to be there forever.

At home he barely spoke. Billy was always with Charley or at the doughnut shop where Amy worked. Rachel always seemed to be at school, and when William wasn't working, he spent his hours in the garage molding clay.

So on opening night he didn't expect that anyone would come to see him, either family or friends or Amy. It was a house full of strangers. Right before the play, he gave up his spirit.

After the play, Bollen came to the dressing room and hugged him. Then he said, "You better get out to the lobby, Joey."

Maybe, Joey thought, somebody came to see him after all, but as he stepped into the lobby it was just a crowd of strangers, voices murmuring. But then someone saw him and said, "It's him." The crowd parted as he stepped closer, and they all faced him. Suddenly they applauded. They crowded around him. Someone's arm handed him flowers, he felt hands on his back, his shoulders, his arms. A girl he recognized from class asked him to sign her program.

"When you're famous," she said, "I can say that I knew you."

After the crowd left and the actors were packing their clothes in their lockers or sitting in front of lighted mirrors wiping off their stage makeup, he found Leah onstage rolling up an extension cord in her hand and arm. She wore a long black skirt and a black top. He walked up the stage, and she turned around, nodded, and said professionally, "Good job, Molina."

He faced her. She looked away, wrapped the cord more along the length of her forearm. "What do you want?" she said.

"I'm sorry," he said.

* * *

She gave him a ride home, and on the way he told her what Amy had said.

"Maybe she's lying," Leah said. "Maybe it's her way of hanging on to you. Apparently it's working."

He told her he believed her, and even if it were a way to keep him, it didn't work. He had woken up the next morning, and Amy was getting ready for school, sitting in a chair, bent over, tying her shoes. "Good morning, baby," she had said.

He told Amy that it didn't change anything. It was still over. He didn't want to be with her. "I'm in love with Leah."

Leah gave him rides again, at first straight home, but after a while they started parking next to the park and talking, sometimes they held each other. They didn't kiss or make love, but each night they were getting closer and closer to each other, and for the first time in his life, Joey had someone to talk to about what he carried in his heart.

Then one night while in the car and in each other's arms, mixing each other's smells, the warmth of their breaths, got them sexually aroused, and they made love slowly and gently as if for the first time. Twenty-six-year-old Joey, Fat Boy, appeared in the darkness of the backseat and said, masturbating, "Fuck her, Joey. Slip her the salami."

One afternoon she picked him up before the play, and when he got in the car, she screamed and hugged him, waving the newspaper in his face. "You're the coolest," she said. The first time he read it, he actually cried, tears and all. He read it over and over again and analyzed each word and phrase to try and find the hidden meanings. The review was excellent, and almost the entire article was about him. It said that Joey Molina was sure "to make Medford famous." He may very well become, the article said, "a local point of pride."

She parked at the school, while he read over and over, but before she got out of the car, she told Joey that she had something to tell him. "It's important," she said.

He looked up, and he felt better than he had in a while, and he figured it was because of her and the review. He kissed her and said they could talk afterward. She said that would be best, because she didn't want him to think about what she was going to tell him while he was onstage. She was hinting to him the enormity of her announcement, but Joey, thinking of the review, didn't catch on.

After the show, he went to the lobby, and as usual, people surrounded him, congratulated him, said he was great, and then out of the crowd came the girl with red hair and green eyes, face to face with him, a smile. "Hi," she said. "You were terrific."

"Karla Horton," he said. "You really think so?"

"Medford pride," she said, "although I like your hair much better when it's black." She touched his hair, ran some fingers through it. It was painted gray.

"Well, I could change it back in ten minutes, but you have to promise to wait for me."

"What are you proposing?" she asked.

"You have a car?" he asked.

"Of course," she said.

"Let's go for a drive," he said.

She said she had come to the play with her father. She could drive home with him and get her car and pick him up in fifteen minutes in front of the school, and then she left. Then it hit him: he was finally going to be with Karla Horton. He remembered what his brother had said to him years ago when he first saw her. "Don't wish you could be with her, make it happen." He had, after all these years, finally made it happen, and it was so easy, and he felt a sense of power he had never felt before. He couldn't believe his destiny, and he started to get sexually aroused just at the thought of being alone with her. He made his way through the lobby and went backstage to the dressing rooms, where he stripped and got into the shower, singing, happy, strong, erect, until he remembered Leah.

He washed the gray out of his hair and got dressed, and then he asked Burt Blunk if he would do him a favor and tell Leah that something came up, an emergency, and that they could talk tomorrow. "What kind of emergency?" Burt coyly asked, as if he could see in Joey's eyes that he was up to no good. "Oh, you're so bad!" he said, as if he were proud of Joey.

Joey quickly got dressed and snuck out of the theater, but when he got in front of the school, he realized that Karla had picked a bad place for them to meet, because it was the only road that went by the school, so all the people who had been in the theater had to drive by, their headlights sliding across his body and face. Some people waved or yelled something encouraging out their windows. After a while, the cars stopped and it was dark, and he waited. He paced back and forth, up and down the stairs of the school entrance, remembering her, holding her image in his mind as if it were a glossy *Playboy* he had hidden under his mattress. Finally, he thought, finally!

Women are not animals.

Leah was probably by now backstage putting things away. As stage manager, she was always among the last to leave.

He felt like a fool. Karla wasn't going to come. More than twenty minutes must have passed. He sat on the steps. Then a car pulled up, and his heart raced.

It was Leah.

She rolled down the passenger window.

"What are you doing, Joey?" she asked him.

"What am I doing? Didn't Burt tell you?"

"Not much," she said.

"Something came up," he said.

"That's what he told me. What came up?"

"What came up?" he repeated. "What came up is a family thing. I'll explain later."

"Do you want a ride?"

He looked around. No Karla Horton. "Uh, well, maybe."

"Come on, silly. Get in."

The moment before he stood up from the cement step, he felt a shadow come up behind him, and he smelled her perfume. "Joey," she said, stepping into the light, so beautiful, so radiant, Karla Horton. He stood, faced her. "I'm parked in the back," she said. "Are you ready?" She wore a tight black skirt with a slit up her golden thigh.

He turned around to look at Leah, framed in dim light in the window of her car.

"Something came up, huh?" she said.

"Come on, I'm parked back here," Karla said.

"You're such a jerk, Joey Molina," said Leah, speeding off. "Asshole!"

Karla's smell, her perfume, so sexy, her eyes, so green, so sexy. She wore a blue sweater, the top button undone, revealing the hint of a lacy blue bra. Her neck was soft, golden. "What's up with her?" she asked, watching Leah's car speed off.

"She's jealous," he said.

"Well, she's not much to cry over," said Karla. "You could do a lot better than *that.*"

"You think so?" he asked.

"Let's go," she said.

They got into her tiny shiny sports car and sped around corners and through tree-lined streets and the blurring lights of downtown, with the windows open, the wind blowing her red hair all around, her red lips sparkling. He had to remind himself that this was true, that he was finally with the one he wanted, *really* wanted, had always wanted. This was success. This was what he was made for.

Joey Molina, your life has arrived!

She drove out of town through apple trees and turned onto a dirt road and went past the shacks where the KA boys had gotten into their only gang fight. Suddenly, he wondered if he was being set up. Maybe she was going to take him to meet the white boys. She parked on the riverbank, between some pine trees, and she put on the radio to a top-forty station.

He looked outside, into the black tree trunks, looking for shadows. Fear overtook him, and he jerked when he felt a hand on his shoulder.

"So, tell me about yourself," she said, turned toward him, as if ready to hear a good story, her legs on the car seat.

The sweater she wore seemed to have an extra button undone, and now he could see her cleavage, smooth, perfectly curved. He felt himself getting erect. Part of him wanted to say that he had better get back—what if Randy and Perry appeared at his window, pulled him from the car, and beat him with branches and left him by the river? He turned around to make sure his door was locked.

By now Leah must have been at home, in her bedroom, probably throwing things that reminded her of him against the wall. He pictured the poster on her bedroom wall of the cow saying *What's moo?* and he smiled.

"So, tell me your story," said Karla.

He wanted Leah. He was in love with her, but he didn't listen to that stupid part of himself, because twenty-six-year-old Joey, sitting in the backseat and goggling Karla's breasts, peeking in the triangle of her skirt, said, "Boy, if you give up this opportunity, you'll never forgive yourself. Never ever."

Joey looked at her.

"Come on, Joey, tell me about yourself. Is it true you were a gang leader in L.A.?"

"Is that what you heard about me?" he asked.

"I heard a lot of things about you. I'm not sure which is true. Funny, we've never really talked."

He leaned in and kissed her.

She tasted like cool spring water.

They kissed and kissed and kissed . . .

She pulled away from him and said, with confidence in her green eyes, "You're a very sexy man, Joey, but . . ."

He scooted closer, and with a sense of power, he unbuttoned her sweater.

He uncovered her blue bra, a nipple rising out of one cup, so perfect, and then he unhooked the bra straps from her shoulders and helped the blue lace slide down her breasts. One of her breasts had three large freckles.

"Oh, God, this is great," said twenty-six-year-old Joey from the backseat. "You'll never forget this, boy. Never."

Joey reached for Karla, kissed her on the wet lips, then down the neck, and then he put his nose between her breasts, perfume and warmth.

But that's all she would let him do. When he tried, she wouldn't let him put his hand in her skirt.

"What kind of girl do you think I am?" she said, buttoning

up her blouse. "Let's just talk. Were you really a gang leader?" she asked.

"I guess you could say that," Joey said. He kissed her again and tried to undo her sweater buttons again, but she stopped him this time and leaned back in her seat. "We're going a little too fast," she said.

"We're young," he said, "that's how we do things."

"Does that line work with other girls?"

"It's not a line."

"And I'm not some airhead girl who can be talked into doing things I don't want to do. I'm pretty smart, Joey. Let's just talk, okay? I'm not saying I wouldn't enjoy being with you, but let's not be led by our desires, okay? Not just yet."

They spent the rest of the evening talking, she asking him questions and he answering like a child angry at his parents, his arms crossed, hoping she would feel guilty and they could make out again.

Finally she said, "Whatever," shook her head, started the car, and drove him home without a word. Since he was acting angry at her, trying to make her feel guilty for not letting him have her, he didn't speak either, so the entire ride was quiet other than his occasional exaggerated sighs. When they got a few blocks from his house, he realized that he had little time to change his attitude if he wanted to see her again. So he told her in a soft voice about the time he and Billy were walking around Medford, their first day in town, and suddenly a pickup truck drove by and someone yelled, "Go back to Mexico!"

"Can you believe that?" he asked.

In front of his house, before getting out of the car, he asked her, "When can I see you again?"

She said, "We'll see."

"Give me your number," he said.

"I'll call you," she said. "Give me yours."

"I can't call you?" he asked.

"My father doesn't really like me to get phone calls."

"He's pretty strict?" Joey asked.

"Yeah, real strict."

She found a piece of paper in her glove compartment and wrote his number with lipstick.

"Call me," he said.

"Sure thing," she said.

Her tiny sports car shot out of the court and around the corner.

As he walked toward his house, he heard a crash coming from inside. Then he noticed that the window in the living room was busted, glass sprinkled all over the porch, and he heard his father yell, "I'll kill you!"

He ran up the path to the front door.

Inside, Billy and William were facing each other, hatred in their eyes, and Rachel stood near the piano. She looked at Joey and then back at the two angry men. "I'm the one that should kill you," Billy said.

"Come and try it, you shit!"

Billy called him a disgusting pervert and picked up bags he had packed and walked toward the door. William threw a chair at him, missing, and Billy watched it roll impotently on the floor. "You're pathetic," he said, and he walked out.

"See you, bro," he said. He took off in his truck, skidding as he turned out of the court.

"She's lying," William said. "The little bitch is lying."

"When the police come and take you away, I'll laugh at you." She went into the hallway and came out again with a white suitcase.

"This isn't the first time he's done this," she said to Joey, placing the case next to another white one she had packed.

"Shut up!" he told her.

"Your father has a history," she said.

"You better shut up." He stepped in closer.

"What are you going to do, hit me?"

"Just shut up."

"I caught him groping a girl."

"You're full of shit," the father said, enraged. He left the house, slamming the door hard enough to rattle what windows were left.

She hunched over a suitcase on the floor, trying to fit more clothes inside and pushing them down. Then she tried to close the lid. She looked up at Joey. She looked back at her suitcase and pushed down.

"Are you leaving?" he asked.

"Oh, yeah," she said, as if the answer should be obvious. "Go pack your bags, if you're coming."

"I can't leave the play," he said.

"It's up to you." She got the case to close, and she stood up. "I'll be gone before he gets back."

"Where is he?"

"Who knows. Raping another little girl, maybe."

He stood still, watching her pack her bags and boxes, his face blank. He felt nothing. Tomorrow night's performance he would feel something.

She walked up to him.

"You know about this, right? About Amy?"

"Yeah."

"Then why are you being such a jerk?"

"What are you talking about?"

"You act as if *I'm* hurting *you*. Look at your face, as if I hurt you. God damn you! How dare you? Your father raped your girlfriend. He raped her. You should hate him."

"I do. I do."

"He's the one that hurt you. Not me. The look of him, the sound of his voice, the stupid heads he has all over the house should make you tremble with hatred. If you don't leave right now, Joey, you *are* him."

"The play."

"That's no excuse for living with him. Quit playing victim and wake up. How can you even think of living with him, Joey? After what you know happened, how can you live with him?"

"Just until the play's over."

"Amy's dignity is more important than the play, than any play. Do you see what's happening? You're becoming your father. You're being swallowed up. Just like I was, for a while, and look what it did to me. Do you remember the story of how I met your father?"

"Of course. He was on the bike, and your brothers ran after him."

"Do you remember the part where he swerves through the brothers and then when he reaches the other side, he looks back at me as he balances his bike without putting his feet to the ground?"

"Yeah, that's my favorite part."

"Well, there's a part of that story I've never told you. I saw something that day. I swear to God, Joey, I saw his future that day. He was unique. I don't remember what I thought I was seeing at the time. At the time I just probably thought it was because he was so damn handsome. I fell in love with him, and I thought about what it was I saw that day he balanced his bike. I thought he was a great man. With a future so great it made me tremble. For many years I believed that he was a great man. I could help him to that greatness, stupid me. What a stupid girl I was.

"Well, one day, when we were still in Fresno, I woke up next to him. No special day. I just woke up, and I knew he would never be great. And after we moved here to Oregon, I realized he's not even a good person.

"But I know how connected we are to our past, not just as individuals, but as people, as *familia*. I never regretted marrying your father, because of you guys. You were all meant to be.

"Joey, I came to believe that the greatness that I saw in your dad's soul that day as he balanced his bike belonged to someone else. Joey, I thought it was you. This boy could be great, I thought."

"Thought? As in past tense?"

"I *thought* you were something. Reading all those books, talking to yourself behind your closed door. I heard you have dialogues with yourself, about things you read, or you'd make characters and different voices, all night long. And I heard you sing.

"Then one day I saw that you're already like him. You were already being overtaken. I wrote your sister about it, how you came home drunk after perhaps the most important and successful night of your life. Do you know that your father got so drunk on our wedding night that I spent all night holding his head over a toilet bowl and wiping vomit from his mouth?

"Well, your sister knew the story. Not only do we talk on the phone, but we've been writing back and forth. She knew about my wedding night. She wrote back reminding me of it, how similar it was, 'As if Joey, all these years, is the shadow of that night, a shadow of him leaning over the toilet bowl, a shadow that spread across the wall of your little apartment and slid into the earth to stay alive, and it keeps repeating itself, sliding on the walls of today.'

"Your sister writes beautifully. I always knew that she did, but never did I realize it. Not like it hit me that day. I picked up her letters over the years and went through them a fourth and fifth time, because I always read her letters more than once in the first sitting. And I thought, My God, she's brilliant.

"Anyway, I'm going to be near your sister."

"She's the great one now? I'm not worth staying around anymore?"

"Oh, shut up, Joey. I gave up on looking for greatness. I'm going to teach. Get your bags and come with me. You have hope. I'm not saying you don't have potential. I don't know if you'll ever be able to handle success, but you have hope to be a decent human being. Get your bags. Get away from that man. Leave with me tonight."

"I can't leave the play. I can't let them down."

"Okay. It's your choice."

William didn't come home that night, nor did Billy, so after Rachel left, Joey was alone in the house, talking to the other Joeys, the six-year-old, the twenty-six-year-old, and looking in the mirror and talking to himself, the teenager, so it was like there were four Joeys. The Joey in the mirror looked most like him at the present time, of course, but he trusted him the least. At least he knew where he stood with Fat Boy, but with his reflection in the mirror he wasn't sure. The darkness around his head and shoulders brought out an evil gleam in his eye, a slight smirk, as if he were someone else, maybe one of his father's heads. What was he doing on the other side of the mirror, how was *he* dealing with Leah, his father, and Amy?

"What's the right thing to do?" he said to the arrogant reflection.

"Fuck 'em," Fat Boy answered, sitting on the side of the tub, eating empanadas. "Literally and figuratively. Get what you can for numero uno." He pointed to himself.

"Just so you know," Joey said to Fat Boy, "I'm never going to be like you."

"You *are* me," said Fat Boy.

He sat on the toilet and faced the six-year-old, the skinny boy pressed against the wall as if scared, hanging on to the towel rack.

"Joey," he said. "What should we do?"

"What do you mean?" the boy asked.

"I don't know what to do."

"Get the redhead in bed," said Fat Boy. "Did you see them tits?"

"You don't exist," Joey said, standing up and approaching the mirror.

"Karla's so fine I'd eat the corn out of her shit," said Fat Boy.

The reflection looked back, smirked, with that evil gleam in his eyes. Joey stepped away. "Do I go with what I think is right, or what I feel is right?" he asked the six-year-old, who shrugged his shoulders. "My mind or my heart?"

"Seriously," said Joey to his child version. "What would you do?"

"Okay," the boy said. "I'm going to tell you something. I like Leah."

"I like Leah, too," he said to the boy. "My heart says to go with her, but my mind tells me that I have a responsibility to Amy. Maybe the right thing would be to marry her."

"Pork the redhead!"

"Maybe you shouldn't listen to your heart or your mind, but to God," said the boy.

"Spare me," said Fat Boy. He pointed at the boy, "This kid is a phony. He's not a very realistic six-year-old. No six-year-old talks like that."

"Would you shut up?"

"Sounds like a bad TV after-school special."

Joey got on his knees, faced the six-year-old, reached out as if he could grab those tiny shoulders, but of course there was no matter to grab, so his hands fell awkwardly at his sides.

Fat Boy chuckled. "That boy's gone forever."

He felt foolish, pictured himself alone in the bathroom, on his knees, talking to someone not even there. "Do you trust my choice?" he asked, closing his eyes, opening them, and seeing the boy.

"Whatever I choose to do, do you trust me?"

"Don't trust him," said Fat Boy. "He's a fuckup, believe me, I know. I'm the only one here who knows what's going to happen. I'm the only one from the future. I've lived the most years of your—of *our* miserable life. Within twenty-four hours, you're going to fuck up real bad. It's your destiny."

Joey shook his head, walked out of the bathroom, alone in the house. All the curtains were open, light blasting the place. He stood still and felt a cold wind swish by him, as if a spirit flew past, perhaps a ghost from the house, someone who had died there, he didn't know, or maybe someone from his past, some Molina from another generation. To get rid of the spirits, he walked from room to room, singing a song he knew.

"Out in the sea was a stone
My girl sat down to tell it her pains."

He walked into the mouth of the narrow kitchen and stepped toward the back door, sunlight blasting through the frame of the window. He opened the door. Light and Droopy shot inside. "Come on in," Joey said, watching the dog run around the rooms, so excited he leaked and whined and barked. Joey laughed freely, slid down the door, and sat on the floor, Droopy rushing him and darting back and forth between Joey and the kitchen, his nails clicking on the linoleum, like a cartoon dog running in place before he gets going.

Eventually the dog calmed down and lay next to Joey.

"Get up, boy! You're free."

Droopy squealed.

He slowly followed Joey from room to room as the teenager sang.

"In the dense fog
I have lost the road.
Let me spend the night
in the cabin with you."

Between songs he talked to his dog, who always listened, head tilted, tongue out. "You know what you need?" Joey said to the dog. "Some bologna."

He walked to the refrigerator singing a commercial bologna song, but there was an open package of weenies, so he pulled those out instead. As he fed the dog from his fingers, he knew that he didn't *want* to marry Amy, but it was the right thing to do.

But what if there was nothing wrong with wanting to be with Leah? They could be a couple, but then he thought of what his father did to Amy. How could he think of hurting her more? She was willing to keep it to herself for the sake of their relationship, and the more guilty he felt, the more he was sure that he should marry Amy. Her mom felt it, that they would get married. Maybe that was his destiny. He tried to imagine a conversation with his mom, to ask her about it, and he pictured her figure hunched over the piano. He closed the curtains to let it get darker inside the house. He imagined her sitting at the piano playing "Moonlight Sonata," and messing up, but her figure was vague, ghostlike, fading in and out of the air.

Then he sat at his mother's piano, closed his eyes, caressed his fingers against the cold keys. He pictured a dark room with a piano, a woman playing, light coming from her fingers. He wanted to play "Moonlight Sonata," but of course he had no skill as a pianist, so instead he sang, making up words for "Moonlight Sonata."

> *"I love you*
> *Yes, I do*
> *Where are you?*
> *where are you?*
> *Damn it! Damn it! Fuck!"* (where the song messed up)

And then he heard it.

A voice.

Who knew from where it came?

Joey, if you stay with your father, you'll never know the right thing to do.

And he wouldn't spend the rest of his life trying to figure it out, either—that is, the "right thing." He'd just live the days, doing what he wanted to do at the moment, and he'd end up like Fat Boy at twenty-six. That was not what he wanted, because what he really wanted was life with the hope of becoming a better person, someone his family could love, someone Rachel and Leah could love. What else was there? And perhaps if he tried to do the right thing, the right path would be revealed at each step of his life. The right choices would more often than not lead him to where he needed to be in life, where he should be in life. And he had a vague idea where he needed to be, and he knew it involved acting. Damn, Joey, he said to himself, that's pretty good. What you're thinking is pretty good. Maybe you're not a complete dummy.

But he was smart enough, he hoped, not to trust an epiphany. No matter how strong some great realization may feel at the time, it may sound stupid later on. This whole "be a better person" stuff could later on seem childish, naive, and on some level, a selfish wish.

If he ever wanted to figure it out, he still needed instruction from his mother, his sister, sources other than his father.

He'd return to California.

Droopy lay down on one of Joey's feet.

"You're coming with me, fella."

Pinedale was a rough barrio. He'd either have to join a gang or stay away from them. He would have to change costumes, to put away his baggy pants and crisp white T-shirts, and wear a different costume, maybe like a college boy, polo shirts, tan slacks, a book bag hanging from his shoulder. He'd go to Fresno State, major in theater arts. He was going to be an actor.

He got some green plastic trash bags and stuffed his books and his clothes into them. He called Amy, and they met at the park, and he held her and said he was sorry for what happened to her and that he was leaving his father's house. He'd find some place to stay until the play was over, and then he would go back to Fresno with his mom. Amy said that he could stay with her, and he kissed her and said he'd think about it, and she said, "What's there to think about?"

He couldn't wait to tell his mom that he wouldn't live with the man.

He couldn't wait to tell her that he was coming to Fresno to be with her and Vero, and they could be a family again. She was probably still on the road to California, somewhere on I-5, but he wanted so much to call her, to tell her of his decision, as if to tell her that, yes, he understood.

And there was hope for him.

To celebrate his decision, he made a sandwich piled high with lunch meat, bologna, thick slices of Spam, and a slab of Velveeta cheese. He spread the mayo on the slices of white bread, put on sliced pickles and tomatoes, and then put the two pieces together and was about to take a great big happy bite.

But he heard a loud knock on the front door.

Voices.

Droopy barked viciously at the doorframe.

He put down his sandwich. He peeked out the curtain and saw Gilbert and George waiting on the porch. He walked out of the house. Closed the door behind him.

¡Q-vo!" said Gilbert.

"What's happening?" said George.

"*¿Qué pasa?*" Joey said. He noticed that on the far end of the porch was a stranger, a Chicano in a tank top, muscular, tattoos on his arms, and a shaved head. He had a scar on his neck. He stood firm and his legs apart, like a bulldog.

"This is my cousin," said Gilbert. "We call him Pelón."

Pelón took two firm steps toward Joey and said, *"Q-vo."* He extended his thick arm for the Chicano shake.

"Joey," he said, doing the shake, feeling the guy's strength.

"He's from Fresno, too," Gilbert said to Pelón.

Pelón squinted his eye as he looked at Joey. "What part?"

"Uh, north side."

"North side?" he said. "Where north side?"

Gilbert and George were closing in on Joey, interested in the conversation.

"Pinedale," Joey said. "In fact, I'm going to be moving back."

"*¿De veras?*" asked Pelón. "Shit," he said, extending his hand for another Chicano shake. "You *vatos* are crazy over there. I'm from the Flats."

"Hey, man, let's smoke out," George said. "Pelón brought some good shit from Fresno."

Joey didn't want to smoke out, but it was still several hours before he had to be at school for the play, and pot wore off pretty quickly, so he suggested that they walk the few blocks to the park and smoke out there. He told him that he had to lock up, so he went inside and took some big bites of his sandwich until it was half gone, and then he put Droopy out in the back and gave him the rest of the sandwich.

Droopy gobbled it up.

Ronny Morris, the boy from next door, sat on his porch, looking at Joey and his friends without trying to be noticed looking. "What you looking at, white boy?" Gilbert said to the boy.

"*Cálmate,*" Joey told Gilbert. "That little *vato*'s all right. How's it going?" he said to Ronny.

"Hi, Joey," Ronny said.

The boy watched Joey and the *cholos* walk away, until they were nothing more than moving dots at the end of the street.

The *cholos* walked like warriors through the streets of Medford, and Joey began to feel good. People watched them walk, kids got out of their way, some cars slowed down.

Pelón asked, "You going back to Pinedale, huh? Damn, everyone over there is F-14. That what you claim?"

"Well, over here in Gringolandia, it's kind of different," Joey said.

"You better claim 14. They'll smash you."

"I'm from over there," he said. "It's my barrio."

"I hope so."

* * *

He liked angel dust right away. He knew that people could do some crazy shit when they smoked it, that dust made some mild people violent, and there was no pain when you're high. Not only did it make him feel powerful, but he liked the name of it, and kept saying it over and over as they smoked it, "angel dust angel dust," and he pictured sparkling powder sprinkled over his head by the glowing hands of angels, but of course dust was dust. PCP. He wouldn't remember much from that night. He remembered the boys watching him with knowing smiles as he took his first hit, the strange smell, the taste, the rush. He could hardly wait for it to go around again for another hit. He remembered the park as a series of light and shadow, lights from homes across the street, shadows from the trees, light from the full moon, from the streetlamps. He saw the lines of darkness that made the shadows of the telephone poles, he saw cars passing by on the I-5, which was as high as the trees, like a celestial highway.

He remembered the four of them playing tackle and wrestling, their godlike shadows cast on the tall brick fence that separated the park from people's backyards. Their laughter rose through the trees, to the sky, echoing throughout the park, like thunder, lightning. He remembered sitting on the cool grass and the taste of vodka—someone had a bottle, which went around—each drink making him feel stronger than before, more energetic, omnipotent. He had to get up to expend energy. He stood up and shook his arms, and then he started punching the air, dancing like a boxer, punching the air.

George stood up and said, "Let's have a slap fight."

They got some pretty good hits to each other, and they laughed and kept fighting, and Joey liked it because he felt no pain. Gilbert and Pelón joined them in a battle royal, all of them hitting each other. Pelón slapped the hardest, but it didn't hurt, he could just feel the impact, and Joey felt good when he got more than a few good hits to Pelón's head and face. He fought better than he thought he could. When Pelón punched him, Joey punched back, and they started laughing, and they high-fived each other while they wiped their bloody lips with the other hand. Then Gilbert grabbed Joey and pulled him close and they started walking and the others followed, toward the light of a supermarket. "Joey's my homie, *ese*. We'll always be friends."

"That's right," Joey said, patting Gilbert's shoulder. *"Por vida."*

"Shit, me too," said George, appearing on the other side of Joey, putting his arm around him. "I met this *vato* when he first moved here man, fresh from Califas."

And Joey believed it, these boys were his friends. They would always be his friends, and if he saw a glimpse of the future, he might see himself coming back to Medford for a visit, Gilbert introducing him to his wife and *chavalitos*.

Pelón caught up with the boys and they all walked toward the lights.

"Gotta have your homies," Pelón said. "You never do them wrong."

They reached a strip mall, a grocery store shining at the center like a modern cathedral, people walking in and out, cars swimming around the lot. They made faces at kids in their mother's grocery carts or in the backseats of cars. They whistled at pretty girls, threatened boys their age.

In the back of a grocery store, through the window, through a well-lit colorful aisle of food boxes, cereals, crackers, cookies, Joey saw a clock. He saw that the play would be starting in less than half an hour. "Fuck," he yelled, and the guys looked at him and then tried to see what he was looking at.

"Got the munchies?" one of them asked.

"I got to go," he said.

He walked through the parking lot, lifting his arms to protect himself from the beams of light that shot at him, his friends tiny figures in the background, their arms gesturing to Joey. A car skidded and honked and some man with sparkling eyeglasses yelled out his window, "Get out of the way."

He entered a dark, narrow street lined with small homes and tall trees, muttering to himself, "I got to get home." He walked toward a stone church, a black cross on top set against the starry sky.

Suddenly he heard the rumbling of an engine coming from behind, and the headlights shone over his shoulders and stretched his shadow like spilled blood across the asphalt. He turned and saw the boys, in chiaroscuro, standing in front of the truck, carrying clubs like night watchmen.

Joey ran.

He ran all the way to the stone walls of the church, and he stopped and wondered why he had run in that direction.

The boys surrounded him.

But he felt big, not just because his shadow in the headlights stretched to the top of the church, but because of the drug. "Come on, fuckers," he said to the three silhouettes. He saw a green bottle, picked it up, and smashed it against the stone wall, and the green glass glittered as it slowly fell to the ground. On the cement floor against the wall of the church, tiny shards of green light sparkled.

He waved the bottle at the boys. "Why don't you come over here and get me, pretty boys."

"I think we'll do that," one of the boys said.

Joey rushed into the silhouettes and swung the broken bottle. He felt it going into flesh, sliding across an arm, a face, and he felt good. Knees and fists and feet pounded him from all sides, but all he felt was the impact. Angel dust had made him strong, superhuman, and perhaps a bit evil. He saw the church turning upside down, and he realized that he was falling. They were kicking him, and his green bottle was gone. He grabbed an ankle and bit with all his might and that person screamed and fell to the ground. He pictured his teeth bloody, and he heartily laughed and grabbed another ankle of another boy and bit into the salty denim, into flesh and bone.

"Fucker's crazy," someone said as they all backed up.

"That's right," he said. "I'm crazy Joey!"

He looked up at the moon above the black cross and howled, "*Oooooooooooowwwwww!*" He felt evil, and it felt good. They backed up, but Joey jumped on one of the boys, both of them falling to the sidewalk, and he pulled the boy's ears and slammed his head repeatedly against the sidewalk while he howled at the moon, "*Oooooooooooooow!*" He brought his thumbs up to poke out the boy's eyeballs, and he would have done it, but he felt a greater force pulling him by the arms. They dropped him, and ran off. They got in the truck and sped away. Joey chased after them, in the middle of the street. "Come on back! I'm not done with you," he shouted, the moon shining full, directly above him, his shadow a giant on the concrete field.

Suddenly "Moonlight Sonata" played in his head.

"Where are you? Where are you?" he yelled, in key. "Damn it! Damn it!"

The truck disappeared around the corner.

He stood in the middle of the street.

He howled at the moon, beat his wet chest with his fists.

This feeling was too good to waste. He wanted to fight. He could beat anyone. He wasn't afraid of anything, not Pinedale, not the white boys, no one, not even his father. He was like a god.

He walked toward his own home to tell his father once and for all what he thought of him, maybe even rough him up a bit for what he had done to Amy.

When he reached his street, he saw his house sadly sitting at the end of the court. He walked like a man determined to settle a score. No light came from inside the house, no sounds, no voices.

The curtains hung blackly in the windows, where the glass reflected lights from the street and the moon. Through the neighbor's window, a curtain moved and a head appeared, but Joey didn't notice this, and would only find out months later when Ronny Morris spoke of it in court, where his father would be tried for the rape of Amy and the attempted murder of Joey.

He opened the door into the dark house. He stepped into the doorframe. The pieces of furniture within the darkness, blacker patches around the room, seemed to face him, waiting to ambush him. He walked in, shut the door, and stood in the tomb of darkness. Then he flicked on the light.

Such a familiar place.

He looked at the couch, sagging from use.

He pictured Billy and himself sitting there, watching TV, and his mom at the piano. The two boys looked up at him, standing before the door. Billy said, "Be careful, Dad'll be home soon."

"Fucking let him come" he yelled.

"Act, Joey," said Rachel.

He had to act. He didn't want to sing or eat or pretend to talk with different versions of himself; rather he wanted to hit something with all his strength. He wanted to hit and hit until his knuckles bled. He rushed the TV and punched it twice, breaking the glass. He stood up straight and kicked it a couple of times. He turned around; the couch was empty. The boys gone. He yelled and picked up the bust on the top of the TV and raised it and was about to throw it through the window, but no. It was César Chávez. Even drugs wouldn't make him forget that. He gently set it down.

But an idea came to him, an evil, wicked idea. He smiled.

He ran out of the house, leaving the door open.

Ronny Morris, in the window next door, watched Joey walk to the garage, try the door, and discover it was locked. Joey backed up and ran with his shoulder into the door, but he fell back on his butt. He laughed at the door, at the challenge, and he walked back to the edge of the front porch and screamed as he ran shoulder first into the door.

It gave to the weight of his body, and he flew inside, sliding on the concrete floor. He got up and felt for the cord hanging from the ceiling, the light, and he pulled it. A hanging bare bulb lit up the garage, the middle, so that the walls stayed in a circle of shadow.

A thousand heads filled the shelves lining the walls. He walked over to his father's workbench and clicked on the lamp, and the room lit up more, revealed the faces on the shelves. One shelf was of political figures, caricatures of Nixon, McGovern, and corrupt politicians with big teeth, licking their lips with greed.

He looked at all the walls, at his mother, an entire shelf of her likenesses, and his sister, and his brother, and there was a shelf of Joeys. Then he saw something he hadn't noticed before, a new head, Amy.

He ran to the shelf and pulled her head off and threw it on the concrete floor. Then he took one of his own heads from the shelf. It felt good when he released it, heard it shatter, and saw the pieces mix in on the floor with Amy's pieces. Then one by one and then two by two and then as much as he could sweep off the shelves at once, he let them shatter on the floor. He felt great, euphoric, so from the corner of the room, he picked up his father's shovel, and he danced around the garage knocking heads from the shelves. Spiders crawled out over faces and into noses and across eyes.

The neighbor boy, Ronny, looking through the window, only saw a shadow on the garage wall, a figure holding some big stick, or it could have been a flute, a trumpet, the way the shadow seemed to be dancing around the hanging lightbulb, like a native dancing under the full moon.